THE CRITICS HAIL

BY THE RIVERS OF BABYLON

BOOKS BY NELSON DeMILLE

By the Rivers of Babylon
Cathedral
The Charm School
The General's Daughter
The Gold Coast
The Lion's Game
Mayday (with Thomas Block)
Night Fall
Plum Island
Spencerville
The Talbot Odyssey
Up Country
Wild Fire
Word of Honor

Nelson DeMille

By the
Rivers of Babylon

WARNER BOOKS

NEW YORK   BOSTON

Art direction by Diane Luger
Cover design by George Cornell
Cover photo of palm trees by Peter Langer
Cover photo of fire by Sa'ad Mohammed/epa/Corbis

Warner Books
Hachette Book Group USA
1271 Avenue of the Americas
New York, NY 10020

Printed in the United States of America
ISBN-13: 978-0-7394-7788-5

This book is dedicated to Bernard Geis, who took a chance;
my wife, Ellen, who took a bigger chance;
and my parents, who had no choice.

I wish to thank Captain Thomas Block for his invaluable technical assistance and Bernard Geis and his staff at Bernard Geis Associates, particularly Judith Shafran and Jessie Crawford, for their superb editorial guidance.

Our struggle has barely begun. The worst is yet to come. And it is right for Europe and America to be warned now that there will be no peace. . . . The prospect of triggering a third world war doesn't bother us. The world has been using us and has forgotten us. It is time they realized we exist. Whatever the price, we will continue the struggle. Without our consent, the other Arabs can do nothing. And we will never agree to a peaceful settlement. We are the joker in the pack.

—Dr. George Habash,
Leader, The Popular Front
for the Liberation of
Palestine (PFLP)

We Jews just refuse to disappear. No matter how strong, brutal, and ruthless the forces against us may be—here we are. Millions of bodies broken, buried alive, burned to death, but never has anyone been able to succeed in breaking the spirit of the Jewish people.

—Golda Meir
Brussels, February 19,1976
The Brussels II Conference
on the Plight of Soviet Jewry

By the
Rivers of Babylon

FRANCE: ST. NAZAIRE

Nuri Salameh, apprentice electrician, patted the oversized pockets of his white coveralls again. He stood, slightly bowed, in the middle of the huge Aérospatiale plant, unsure of his next step. Around him, other immigrant French-speaking Algerians seemed to move with an unreal balletlike slowness as they marked time in anticipation of the bell that would signal the end of their work shift.

The late afternoon sun streamed in dusty, moted shafts through the six-story-high windows and suffused the badly heated plant with a warm golden glow that contrasted with Salameh's breath fog.

Outside the plant, the airport lights were coming on. A flight of metallic blue Mirages floated over the airfield in a V-formation. Buses began lining up to take the Aérospatiale workers to their homes in St. Nazaire.

Inside the plant, additional rows of fluorescent lights flickered on, momentarily startling the Algerian. Salameh looked around quickly. At least one other countryman avoided

3

his darting eyes. Salameh knew that his fate was no longer in his own hands nor, he suspected, in the hands of Allah.

With the Arab's ancient character flaw, he soared on the wings of hope and rose from the depths of despair to the most dangerous peaks of overconfidence. He began walking briskly across the concrete floor.

In front of him, the huge Concorde sat on metal scaffolding. Forming jigs, to guide the assemblers, arched over, under and around the fuselage and wings. Much of the aircraft's skin was missing and workers were crawling over the long body, like ants crawling over the half-eaten carcass of a giant dragonfly.

Salameh climbed the stairs to the top platform of the scaffolding and crawled onto the forming jig that ran along the base of the twelve-meter-high tail. On one of the unpainted aluminum tail plates was stenciled the production number, 4X-LPN.

Salameh looked at his watch. Ten minutes until the end of the shift. He had to do it now, before the night riveters closed the tail section. He grabbed a clipboard hanging from the jig and scanned it quickly. He looked back down over his shoulder. Below, an Algerian looked up as he swept metal filings from the floor, then turned away.

Salameh felt the sweat form on his face, then turn cold in the concrete and steel chill of the factory. He wiped his forehead with his sleeve, then lowered himself between two stringers into the rear of the partially skinned aluminum fuselage. The tail section was a maze of laser-welded struts and curved braces. His feet rested on the supporting cross members directly over the number eleven trim tank. He crouched down and crab-walked from strut to strut toward the half-finished pressure bulkhead.

Salameh peered over the bulkhead and looked down the length of the cavernous fuselage. Six men walked over the temporary plywood floors, laying bats of insulation between the passenger cabin and the baggage compartment in the belly of the craft. They alternately lifted the plywood, laid the bats, then placed the plywood back between the struts and beams. Salameh noticed that, along with the insulation, the men were laying sections of honeycombed porcelain and nylon armor. Overhead, fluorescent work lights were strung along the top of the cabin. There was a light strung into the tail also, but Salameh did not turn it on. He crouched for a few minutes in the darkness of the tail section behind the half-finished bulkhead.

• • •

At length, Nuri Salameh cleared his throat and called into the cabin, "Inspector Lavalle."

A tall Frenchman turned from the emergency door which he had been examining and walked toward the chest-high wall. He smiled in recognition at the Algerian. "Salameh. Why are you hiding like a rat in the darkness?"

The Algerian forced an answering smile. He waved the clipboard at the structures inspector. "It is ready to be closed up, no?"

Henri Lavalle leaned over the bulkhead. He shined his high-intensity light into the tapering tail section and made a cursory inspection. He took the clipboard from the Arab with his other hand, and flipped the pages quickly. You could not trust these Algerians to read the schedules of inspection correctly. Inspector Lavalle checked each page again. Each inspector had made his mark. The electrical, hydraulic, and fuel-tank inspection marks were in order. He rechecked his own structures inspection marks. "Yes. All the inspections have been accomplished," he answered.

"And my electrical?" asked Salameh.

"Yes. Yes. You did fine. It is complete. It can be closed up." He handed the clipboard back to the Algerian, bade him good night, and turned away.

"Thank you, Inspector." Salameh hooked the clipboard onto his belt, turned, and made his way carefully, in a crouch, over the beam work. He looked surreptitiously over his shoulder as he moved. Inspector Lavalle was gone. Salameh could hear the insulators packing their tools, climbing out of the fuselage and down the scaffolding. Someone shut most of the work lights off in the cabin and the tail section grew darker.

Nuri Salameh turned on his flashlight and pointed it up into the hollow tail. He climbed slowly up the strutwork until he could almost touch the point where the two sides of the tail met. From one of his bulging side pockets, he removed a black electrical box, no larger than a packet of cigarettes. The box had a metal parts number plate on it that identified it as S.F.N.E.A. #CD-3265-21, which it was not.

From his top pocket he took a tube of epoxy and squeezed the glue onto an aluminum plate, then pressed the box firmly against the side of the plane and held it for a few seconds. He then pulled a telescoping antenna from the black box and rotated it until it was clear of the metal sides of the tail.

He shifted his position quietly and braced his back against a strut and his feet against a crossbar. It was not warm in the confining tail, but sweat formed on his face.

With an electrical knife, he stripped a section of insulation from a green wire with black hatch marks that led to the tail navigation light. He pulled a length of matching wire from his pocket. On the end of the wire was attached a small, bare metal cylinder the size of a Gauloise cigarette. The other end was bare copper wire. He spliced the copper end onto the navigation light wire and taped the splice carefully.

Salameh began slowly climbing down the framework. As he descended, he ran the green wire along a bundle of multicolored wires until he reached the bottom of the fin where it joined with the fuselage. He let the wire drop through the cross struts beneath his feet.

Salameh stretched face down on the cold aluminum cross struts and reached down until he could touch the number eleven fuel trim tank below. Through the few missing plates on the bottom of the fuselage, he could see the tops of men's heads as they passed beneath the great plane. Sweat streamed from his face and he imagined that it must be dripping onto the men, but no one looked up.

From another pocket Salameh took a mass of white puttylike substance weighing about half a kilo. He molded the substance carefully over the tip of the number eleven trim tank. He found the dangling green wire and ran his fingers down to the end of it until he felt the small metal cylinder that was attached. He pushed the cylinder into the soft putty and pressed the putty firmly around the cylinder. The shift bell rang loudly, startling him.

Salameh rose quickly and wiped the clammy sweat from his face and neck. His whole body shook as he clawed his way through the confining struts toward the open section of the tail. He heaved himself out of the dark tail onto the jig, then jumped onto the platform of the scaffolding. The whole operation, lasting an eternity, had taken less than four minutes.

Salameh was still shaking as the two riveters from the second shift stepped onto the platform. They regarded him curiously as he tried to regain his composure.

One of the riveters was a Frenchman, the other an Algerian.

The Algerian spoke to him in French. "This is ready?" He held out his hand.

Salameh was momentarily confused until he saw that both men's eyes were fixed on the clipboard that still hung from his belt. He quickly unhooked it and handed it over. "Yes. Yes. Ready. Electrical. Structures. Hydraulic. All inspected. It can be closed up."

The two men nodded as they checked the schedules of inspection. They then set about preparing the aluminum plates, rivets, and rivet guns. Salameh stood watching for a moment until his knees stopped trembling, then climbed unsteadily down the ladder and punched his time card.

Nuri Salameh boarded one of the waiting buses and sat silently among the workers, watching them drink wine from bottles, as the bus made its way back to St. Nazaire.

Salameh got off the bus in the center of town and walked through the winding, cobbled streets to his roach-infested flat above a *boucherie*. He greeted his wife and four children in Arabic, then announced that dinner should be delayed until he returned from an important errand.

He took his bicycle from the dark, narrow stair landing and walked it into the alley, then pedaled onto the s⁁reet. He rode down to the waterfront where the Loire met the Bay of Biscay. His cold breath streamed from his mouth as he panted from his exertions. The tires needed air and he cursed as the bicycle bounced against the uneven cobbles.

The traffic thinned out in the darkening streets as he pedaled past the active waterfront area to the deserted area that held the great concrete U-boat pens built by the Germans during World War II. The bombproof pens rose up from the black water, grey, ugly, and blast-scarred. Tall loading booms towered over the docks on the waterfront and caught the last of the sunlight from the bay.

Nuri Salameh wheeled his bicycle to the rusted stairs that descended to the pens and pushed it into a clump of wild bay laurel shrubs. He carefully descended the creaking stairs.

At the water's edge, he made his way over the top of the moss- and barnacle-covered retaining wall and approached one of the covered pens. The smells of diesel oil and sea water filled his nostrils as he stood and read the faded, flaking sign painted on the mossy concrete. There was the usual *Achtung!*, then some other words in German, then the number 8. Salameh approached slowly, and entered the submarine pen through a rusty iron door.

Inside, he could hear the sound of water gently lapping against the walls. The only illumination came through the open entrance from the lights across the river. Salameh felt his way along the length of the catwalk toward the open end of the tunnellike pen. He was shivering in the damp, stagnant air. Several times he suppressed a cough.

Suddenly, a light from a flashlight struck him in the eyes, and he covered his face. "Rish?" he whispered. "Rish?"

Ahmed Rish shut off the light and spoke softly in Arabic. "It is done, Salameh?" It was more a statement than a question.

Nuri Salameh could sense the presence of other men on the narrow catwalk. "Yes."

"Yes," answered Ahmed Rish. "Yes." There was a malignant satisfaction in his voice.

Salameh thought back to those dark Algerian eyes that had followed him all day. The Algerian riveter with the Frenchman—and the others—had looked at him with thinly veiled complicity.

"The inspections were completed? The tail is to be closed tonight?" Rish's voice had the tone of a man who knew the answers.

"Yes."

"You placed the radio on the highest point inside the tail—close to the outer skin?"

"Right on the outer skin, Ahmed."

"Good. The antenna?"

"It is extended."

"The splice? The radio will receive a constant trickle charge from the aircraft's batteries?"

Salameh had rehearsed this in his mind many times. "The splice was from the tail navigation light. The splice wire is not conspicuous even on close inspection. I even matched the wire color. Green. No one will ever see the radio, but if that should happen, I placed an Aérospatiale parts number plate on it. Only an electrical engineer would not be fooled by it. Any other maintenance people would either not see it, or if they did, they would think it belonged."

Rish seemed to nod in the darkness. "Excellent. Excellent." He did not speak for a moment, but Nuri Salameh could hear

Rish's breathing and smell the man's damp breath. Rish spoke again. "The electrical detonator was properly fixed to the other end?"

"Of course."

"The *plastique?*" He used the universal French word for the explosive.

Salameh recited what he had been taught. "I molded it over the tip of the fuel tank. The tank at that point is slightly rounded. The *plastique* was approximately ten centimeters thick from the tip of the tank to the detonator, which was placed in the exact rear center of the charge. The result was a natural shape-charge which will blow inward and penetrate the tank." Salameh licked his cold lips. He had no sympathy for these people or their cause and he knew he had committed a great sin. From the start, he had no wish to get involved with this thing. But every Arab was a guerilla, according to Rish. From Casablanca, in Morocco, across five thousand kilometers of burning desert to Bagdad, they were all guerillas, all brothers. Over one hundred million of them. Nuri Salameh didn't believe a word of it, but having his parents and sisters still in Algiers helped to persuade him to carry out this deed. "I was proud to do my part," said Salameh, to fill the silence, but he knew it would do no good. He suddenly realized that his fate had been sealed the moment he had been approached by these men.

Rish seemed not to have heard. He had other things on his mind. "The *plastique*. Would you say it blended in well with the shape of the tank? Perhaps we should have had you spray it with aluminum paint," he said absently.

Salameh was eager to pass on good news, to placate, to dispel the demons of doubt. "No one goes back there. It is sealed off from the pressurized cabin by the pressure bulkhead. All hydraulics and electrical are serviced from small access panels on the outside. Only a failure of some component would make it necessary to remove the riveted plates. That side of the fuel tank should never be seen by human eyes again." He could definitely hear the impatient breathing of at least three other men in the shadow behind Rish. It had become completely dark at the end of the tunnel. Occasionally, a ship's klaxon would sound on the river or bay, the muted dissonance rolling across the water and into the cold submarine pen.

Rish murmured something.

Salameh waited for the worst. Why meet in a dark place

when a comfortable bistro or apartment would have done as well? In his heart he knew the answer, but he sought desperately to reverse his preordained destiny. "I have applied for the transfer to Toulouse, as you wished. It will be approved. I would be honored to do the same thing on the other one there," he said hopefully.

Rish made a noise that sounded like a laugh and it sent a chill down Salameh's spine. The charade would not last long now. "No, my friend," said the voice in the darkness. "That is already attended to. Your joker is in the deck and the other will be safely in the deck shortly."

Salameh recognized the metaphor. That was what these people called themselves and their operations—the jokers in the deck. The game was played among civilized nations until the joker turned up—in an airport massacre, a hijacking, a letter bomb. Then, the game of the diplomats and ministers became confused and frantic. No one knew the rules when that joker landed on the green baize table. People screamed at each other. Guns and knives were produced from under the table. The polite game turned ominous.

Salameh swallowed a dry lump. "But surely—" He heard a noise. Rish had clapped his hands.

Quickly and expertly, Salameh was pinioned to the slimy wall of the sub pen by many hands. He felt the cold steel slice across his throat, but he could not scream because of the hand across his mouth. He felt a second and third knife probing for his heart, but in their nervousness, the assassins only succeeded in puncturing his lungs. Salameh felt the warm blood flow over his cold, clammy skin and heard the gurglings from his lungs and throat. He felt another knife come down on the back of his neck and try to sever his vertebrae, but it slid off the bone. Salameh struggled mechanically, without conviction. In his pain, he knew that his killers were trying to do the thing quickly but in their agitation were making a bad job of it. He thought of his wife and children waiting for their dinner. Then a blade found his heart, and he heaved free of his tormentors in a final spasmodic death throe.

Rish spoke softly as the shadows knelt down over Salameh. They took his wallet and watch, turned his pockets inside out, and removed his good work boots. They slid him over the side of the catwalk and held him suspended by his ankles above the black, stagnant water that lapped rhythmically against the sides of the pen. The water rats, which had chirped incessantly during the short struggle, became still, waiting. They stared with beady red eyes that seemed to burn with an inner fire of their own. Salameh's face, running with rivulets of blood, touched the cold, black water, and the murderers released him. He disappeared with a barely discernible splash. The sound of the water rats diving from the catwalks into the rank, polluted waters filled the long gallery.

The masked workers made a final sweep with their pneumatic spray guns. The guns shut down with a hiss. The Concorde gleamed enamel white in the cavernous paint room. There was a stillness in the room where there had been sound and movement a short time before. Infrared heat lamps began to glow eerily. The paint fog hung in the unearthly atmosphere around the aircraft which glowed red with reflected light. Air evacuators pulled the fog from the great room.

The evacuators turned themselves off and the infrared lamps dimmed and blackened. Suddenly, the dark room filled with the blue-white light of hundreds of fluorescents.

Later, white coveralled men filed in quietly as one might enter a holy place. They stood and stared up at the long, graceful bird for a few seconds. It seemed as though the craft were standing long-legged and proud, looking down its beak at them with the classical birdlike haughtiness and indifference of the sacred Ibis of the Nile.

The men carried stencils and spray guns. They rolled in 200-liter drums of a light blue paint. Scaffolding was rolled up and long stencils for the striping were unfurled.

They worked with an economy of words. The foreman, from time to time, checked the designer's sketches.

An artist placed his stencils over the tail section where the production number still showed a faint outline under the new white enamel. The production number would now become the permanent international registration number. He stenciled on the 4X, the international designation for the nation that owned and would fly the aircraft. He then stenciled LPN, the individual registration of the craft.

Above him, on a higher scaffold, two artists peeled off the black vinyl stencil attached to the tail. What remained against the field of white was a light blue six-pointed Star of David, under which were the words, EL AL.

BOOK ONE

ISRAEL
THE PLAIN OF SHARON

*They have healed also the hurt of . . . my
people . . . saying, Peace, peace; when
there is no peace.*
        Jeremiah 6:14–16

*. . . they have seduced my people saying,
Peace; and there was no peace: . . . .*
        Ezekiel 13:10–11

1

In the Samarian hills, overlooking the Plain of Sharon, four men stood quietly in the predawn darkness. Below them, spread out on the plain, they could see the straight lights of Lod International Airport almost nine kilometers in the distance. Beyond Lod were the hazy lights of Tel Aviv and Herzlya, and beyond that, the Mediterranean Sea reflected the light of the setting moon.

They stood on a spot that, until the Six Day War, had been Jordanian territory. In 1967, it had been a strategic spot, situated as it was almost half a kilometer above the Plain of Sharon on a bulge in the 1948 truce line that poked into Israel. There had been no Jordanian position closer to Lod Airport in 1967. From this spot, Jordanian artillery and mortars had fired a few rounds at the airport before Israeli warplanes had silenced them. The Arab Legion had abandoned the position, as they had abandoned everything on the West Bank of the Jordan. Now this forward position had no apparent military significance. It was deep inside Israeli territory. Gone were the bunkers that had

15

faced each other across no man's land and gone were the miles of barbed wire that had separated them. More importantly, gone too were the Israeli border patrols.

But in 1967 the Arab Legion had left behind some of its ordnance and some of its personnel. The ordnance was three 120mm mortars with rounds, and the personnel were these four Palestinians, once members of the Palestinian Auxiliary Corps attached to the Arab Legion. They were young men then, left behind and told to wait for orders. It was an old stratagem, leaving stay-behinds and equipment. Every modern army in retreat had done it in the hopes that those agents-in-place would serve some useful function if and when the retreating army took the offensive again.

The four Palestinians were natives of the nearby Israeli-occupied village of Budris, and they had gone about their normal, peaceful lives for the last dozen years. In truth, they had forgotten about the mortars and the rounds until a message had reminded them of their pledge taken so long ago. The message had come out of the darkness like the recurrence of a long-forgotten nightmare. They feigned surprise that such a message should come on the very eve of the Peace Conference, but actually they knew that it would come precisely for that reason. The men who controlled their lives from so great a distance did not want this peace. And there was no way to avoid the order to action. They were trapped in the shadowy army as surely as if they were in uniform standing in a parade line.

The men knelt among the stand of Jerusalem pines and dug into the soft, dusty soil with their hands. They came upon a large plastic bag. Inside the bag were a dozen 120mm mortar rounds packed in cardboard canisters. They pushed some sand and pine needles over the bag again and sat back against the trees. The birds began to sing as the sky lightened.

One of the Palestinians, Sabah Khabbani, got up and walked to the crest of the hill and looked down across the plain. With a little luck—and an easterly wind sent by Allah—they should be able to reach the airport. They should be able to send those six high-explosive and six phosphorus rounds crashing into the main terminal and the aircraft parking ramp.

As if in answer to this thought, Khabbani's *kheffiyah* suddenly billowed around his face as a hot blast of wind struck his back. The Jerusalem pines swayed and released their resinous scent. The *Hamseen* had arrived.

• • •

The curtains billowed around the louvered shutters of the third-floor apartment in Herzlya. One of them slammed shut with a loud crack. Air Force Brigadier Teddy Laskov sat up in his bed as his hand reached into his night table. He saw the swinging shutters in the dim light from the window and settled back, his hand still on his .45 automatic. The hot wind filled the small room.

The sheets next to him moved and a head looked out from under them. "Is anything wrong?"

Laskov cleared his throat. "The *Sharav* is blowing." He used the Hebrew word. "Spring is here. Peace is coming. What could be wrong?" He took his hand away from the pistol and fumbled for his cigarettes in the drawer. He lit one.

The sheets next to Laskov stirred again. Miriam Bernstein, the Deputy Minister of Transportation, watched the glowing tip of Laskov's cigarette as it moved in short, agitated patterns. "Are you all right?"

"I'm fine." He steadied his hand. He looked down at her. He could make out the curves of her body under the sheets, but her face was half-buried in the pillow. He turned on the night light and threw back the sheets.

"Teddy." She sounded mildly annoyed.

Laskov smiled. "I wanted to see you."

"You've seen enough." She grabbed for the sheets, but he kicked them away. "It's cold," she said petulantly and curled into a tight ball.

"It's warm. Can't you feel it?"

She made an exasperated sound and stretched her arms and legs sensuously.

Laskov looked at her tanned naked body. His hand ran up her leg, over her thick pubic hair, and came to rest over one of her breasts. "What are you smiling at?"

She rubbed her eyes. "I thought it was a dream. But it wasn't."

"The Conference?" His tone revealed an impatience with this subject.

"Yes." She placed her hand over his, breathed in the sweet-smelling air, and closed her eyes. "The miracle has happened. We've started a new decade, and now the Israelis and the Arabs are going to sit down together and make peace."

"*Talk* peace."

"Don't be skeptical. It's a bad start."

"Better to start skeptical. Then you won't be disappointed with the outcome."

"Give it a chance."

He looked down at her. "Of course."

She smiled at him. "I have to get up. She yawned and stretched again. "I have a breakfast date."

He removed his hand. "With whom?" he asked, against his better judgment.

"An Arab. Jealous?"

"No. Just security conscious."

She laughed. "Abdel Majid Jabari. My father figure. Know him?"

Laskov nodded. Jabari was one of the two Israeli-Arab Knesset members who were delegates to the peace mission. "Where?"

"Michel's in Lod. I'll be late. May I get dressed, General?" She smiled.

Only her mouth smiled, Laskov noticed. Her dark eyes remained expressionless. That full, rich mouth had become quite accomplished at showing the full range of human emotion, while the eyes only stared. The eyes were remarkable because they conveyed absolutely nothing. They were only for seeing things. They were not a window into her soul. The things she must have seen with those eyes, Laskov thought, she wished no one to know.

He reached out and stroked her long, thick black hair. She was exceptionally pretty, there was no doubt about that, but those eyes . . . He saw her lips turn up at his stroking. "Don't you ever *smile?*"

She knew what he meant. She put her face in the pillow and mumbled. "Maybe when I get back from New York. Maybe then."

Laskov stopped stroking her hair. Did she mean if the peace mission was a success? Or did she mean if she got good news of her husband, Yosef, an Air Force officer, missing over Syria for three years? He had been in Laskov's command. Laskov had seen him go down on the radar. He was fairly certain Yosef was dead. Laskov had a feel for these things after so many years as a combat pilot. He decided to confront her. He wanted to know where he stood before she went to New York. It might be months before he saw her again. "Miriam..."

There was a loud knock on the front door. Laskov swung his feet over the side of the bed and stood. He was a solid bearlike man with a face more Slavic than Semitic. Thick, heavy eyebrows met on the bridge of his nose.

"Teddy. Take your gun."

Laskov laughed. "Palestinian terrorists hardly ever knock."

"Well, at least put your pants on. It might be someone for me, you know. Official."

Laskov pulled on a pair of cotton khaki trousers. He took a step toward the door, then decided that bravado was foolish. He took the American Army Colt .45 automatic out of the night table and shoved it into his waistband. "I wish you wouldn't tell your staff where you spend the night."

The knock came again, louder this time. He walked barefoot across the oriental rug of the living room and stood to the side of the door. "Who is it?" As he looked back across the living room, he noticed that he hadn't closed the bedroom door. Miriam lay naked on the bed in a direct line with the front door.

Abdel Majid Jabari stood in the darkened alcove of Michel's in Lod. The café, owned by a Christian Arab, sat on the corner near the Church of St. George. Jabari looked at his watch. The café should have opened already, but there was no sign of life inside. He huddled into the shadow.

Jabari was a dark, hawk-nosed man of the pure, classical Saudi-peninsula type. He wore an ill-fitting dark business suit and the traditional black and white checked headdress, the *kheffiyah*, secured with a crown of black cords.

Throughout the last thirty years, Jabari rarely went out alone during the hours of darkness. Ever since the time he had decided to make a personal and private peace with the Jews in the newly formed state of Israel. Since that day, his name had been on every Palestinian death list. His election to the Israeli Knesset two years before had put his name at the top of those lists. They'd come close once. Part of his left hand was missing, the result of a letter bomb.

A motorized Israeli security patrol went by and eyed him suspiciously but did not stop. He looked at his watch again. He had arrived early for his appointment with Miriam Bernstein.

He couldn't think of another person, man or woman, who could bring him to such a deserted rendezvous. He loved her, but he believed his love was strictly platonic. This was an unusual Western notion, but he felt comfortable with it. She filled a need in him that had existed since his wife, children, and all his blood relatives had fled to the West Bank in 1948. When the West Bank had come into Israeli hands in 1967, he could think of nothing for days but the coming reunion. He had followed in the wake of the Israeli army. When he got to the refugee camp where he knew his family was, he found his sister dead and everyone else fled into Jordan. His sons were reported to be with the Palestinian guerilla army. Only a female cousin remained, wounded, lying in an Israeli mobile hospital. Jabari had marveled at the hate that must have filled these people, his countrymen, as his cousin lay dying, refusing medical aid from the Israelis.

Jabari had never known such despair before or since. That day in June 1967 was far worse than the original parting in 1948. But he had rallied and traveled a long road since then. Now he was going to discuss the coming peace over breakfast with a fellow delegate to the UN Conference in New York.

Shadows moved in the street around him and he knew that he should have been more careful. He'd come too far to have it end here. But in his excitement and anticipation of seeing Miriam Bernstein and going to New York, he had become lax in his security. He had been too embarrassed to tell her to meet him after sunrise. He couldn't fault her for not understanding. She simply didn't know the kind of terror he had lived with for thirty years.

The *Hamseen* blew across the square picking up litter, rustling it across the pavement. This wind didn't blow in gusts but in one long, continuous stream, as though someone had left the door open on a blast furnace. It whistled through the town, each obstruction acting as a reed in a woodwind instrument, making sounds of different pitch, intensity, and timbre. As always it made one feel uneasy.

Three men came out of the shadow of a building across the road and walked toward him. In the predawn light, Jabari could see the outlines of long rifles tucked casually under their arms. If they were the security patrol, he would ask them to stay with him awhile. If they weren't . . . He fingered the small nickel-plated

Beretta in his pocket. He knew he could get the one in front, anyway.

Sabah Khabbani helped the other three Palestinians roll a heavy stone across the ground. Lizards scurried from the place where the stone had stood. Revealed under the stone was a hole a little more than 120mm wide. Khabbani pulled a ball of oiled rags out of the opening, reached his arm into the hole, and felt around. A centipede walked across his wrist. He pulled his arm out. "It's in good condition. No rust." He wiped the packing grease from his fingers onto his baggy pants. He stared at the small, innocuous-looking hole.

It was an old guerilla trick, originated with the Viet Cong and passed on to other armies of the night. A mortar tube is placed in a large hole. The tube is held by several men and mortar rounds are dropped into the tube. One by one the rounds begin to hit downrange. Eventually, one round strikes its target: an airfield, a fort, a truck park. The firing stops. Now the mortar is registered for elevation, deflection, and range. Rocks and earth are quickly packed around the mortar with care to insure that the aim is not changed. The muzzle of the tube is hidden with a stone. The gunners flee before the overwhelming fire-power of the conventional army is brought to bear on their position. The next time they wish to fire—a day, a week, or a decade later—they must only uncover the preaimed muzzle. There is no need to carry the cumbersome paraphernalia of the big mortar. The heavy baseplate, bridge, and standard, weighing altogether over 100 kilograms, are not needed. The delicate boresight is not needed, nor are the plotting boards, compass, aiming stakes, maps, or firing tables. The mortar tube is already registered on its target, lying buried, waiting only for rounds to be dropped into its muzzle.

Khabbani's gunners would fire four rounds each, then cover the muzzles with the stones. By the time the high angle rounds began hitting, one by one, the gunners would be far away.

Khabbani took a rag soaked in alcohol solvent, reached into the long tube, and swabbed the sides. He worried about these buried tubes. Were they really well aimed in 1967? Had the ground shifted since then? Were the rounds safe? Had trees grown up into the trajectory of the rounds?

His rag showed dead insects, dirt, a little moisture, and just a trace of rust. He would find out shortly if it was safe to fire.

"Richardson." The voice was muffled, but Laskov was sure of it. He unbolted the door.

Miriam Bernstein got out of bed naked and leaned against the doorjamb in the pose of a Parisian lady of the night against a lamppost. She smiled and tried on a sexy come-hither look. Laskov was not amused. He opened the door slowly. Tom Richardson, the U.S. air attaché, stepped in at the moment Laskov heard the bedroom door close behind him. He looked at Richardson's face. Had he seen her? He couldn't decide. No one registered much emotion at that hour. "Is this business or social?"

Richardson spread his arms out. "I'm in full uniform and the sun isn't even up."

Laskov regarded the younger officer. He was a tall, sandy-haired man who was chosen for the attaché job more for his ability to charm than for his ability to fly. A diplomat in uniform. "That doesn't answer my question."

"Why do you have that hardware stuck in your pants? Even in D.C. we don't answer the door like that."

"You should. Well, have a seat. Coffee?"

"Right."

Laskov moved toward the small kitchenette. "Turkish, Italian, American, or Israeli?"

"American."

"I've only got Israeli and it's instant."

Richardson sat in a club chair. "Are we going to have one of those days?"

"Don't we always?"

"Get in the spirit of things, Laskov. There's going to be peace."

"Maybe." He put a kettle on the single gas jet. He could hear the shower running on the other side of the wall.

Richardson looked at the closed bedroom door. "Am I disturbing something? Were you making a separate peace with a local Arab boy's sister?" He laughed, then said seriously, "Can we speak freely?"

Laskov came out of the kitchen. "Yes. Let's get this business out of the way. I have a full day ahead of me."

"Me too." Richardson lit a cigarette. "We have to know what kind of air cover you have planned for the Concordes."

Laskov walked over to the window and threw open the

shutters. Below his apartment ran the Haifa–Tel Aviv Highway. Lights shone from private villas near the Mediterranean. Herzlya was known as the air attaché ghetto. It was also Israel's Hollywood and Israel's Riviera. Herzlya was the place where El Al and Air Force personnel lived if they could afford it. Laskov detested the place because of its privileged atmosphere, but an accident of social grouping had put most of the important people he had to deal with in Herzlya.

The smell of the western sea breezes, which usually carried into the apartment, was replaced by the dry east wind carrying scents of orange and almond blossoms from the Samarian hills. Across the highway, the first shaft of sunlight revealed two men standing in the alcove of a shop. They moved further into the shadow. Laskov turned from the window and walked to a high-backed swivel chair. He sat down.

"Unless you came with a chauffeur and a footman, I think someone is watching this apartment."

Richardson shrugged. "That's their job, whoever they are. We have ours." He leaned forward. "I'll need a full report on today's operation."

Laskov sat back in his chair. His dogfighter chair. At get-togethers his friends would regale each other with the old fights. The Spitfires. The Corsairs. The Messerschmitts. Laskov looked at the ceiling. He was flying his mission over Warsaw again. Captain Teddy Laskov of the Red Air Force. Things were simpler then. Or so they seemed.

Shot down for the third time, in the last days of the war, Laskov had returned to his village of Zaslavl, outside Minsk, on convalescent leave. He found the remainder of his family, barely half of whom had survived the Nazis, murdered in what the Commissars called a civil disturbance. Laskov called it a pogrom. Russia would never change, he decided. A Jew was as much a Jew in unholy Russia as in Holy Russia.

Captain Laskov, highly decorated officer of the Red Air Force, had returned to his squadron in Germany. Ten minutes after arriving, he had climbed into a fighter, bombed and strafed an encampment of his own army outside of Berlin, and flown on to an airfield occupied by the American Second Armored Division on the west bank of the Elbe.

From the American internment camp, he had made his way, finally, to Jerusalem, but not before seeing what had become of West European Jewry.

In Jerusalem, he had joined the underground Haganah Air

Force, which consisted of a few scrapped British warplanes and a few American civilian light aircraft hidden in palm groves. A far cry from the Red Air Force, but when Laskov saw his first Spitfire with the Star of David on it, his eyes misted.

Since that day in 1946, he had fought in the War of Independence of 1948, the Suez War of 1956, the Six Day War of 1967, and the 1973 Yom Kippur War. But the war dates meant nothing to him. He had seen more action between those wars than during them. He'd flown 5,136 sorties, been hit five times and shot down twice. He carried scars from shattered plexiglas, burning aviation fuel, flak, and missile shrapnel. He walked slightly bent as a result of having had to eject out of a burning Phantom in 1973. He was getting old and he was tired. He rarely flew combat missions anymore, and he hoped, and almost believed, that after the Conference there would be none that would have to be flown again. Ever.

The kettle whistled and Laskov stared at it. Richardson got up and shut it off. "Well?"

Laskov shrugged. "We have to be careful who we give that kind of information to."

Richardson walked quickly up to Laskov. He was white and almost trembling. "What? What the hell do you mean? Look, I've got reports to make. I've got to coordinate our carrier fleet in the Med. Since when have you kept anything from us? If you're insinuating that there's a leak..."

Laskov wasn't prepared for Richardson's outburst. They had always bantered prior to getting to the point. It was part of the game. The reaction to what Laskov thought was a joke was inappropriate. He decided that Richardson was tense, as everyone else would probably be today. "Take it easy, Colonel." He stared hard at the young man.

The mention of his rank seemed to snap him out of it. Richardson smiled and sat down. "Sorry, General."

"All right." Laskov got up and picked up the telephone with a scrambler attached to it. He dialed The Citadel, Israeli Air Force Headquarters. "Patch me into the E-2D," he said.

Richardson waited. The E-2D Hawkeye was the newest of Grumman's flying radar craft. The sophisticated electronic systems on board could detect, track, and classify potential belligerents or friendlies on land, sea, and air at distances and with an accuracy never before possible. Its collected information was fed into a computer bank and transmitted via data link back to Strike Force Control, Civilian Air Traffic Control, and Search and Rescue units. It also had electronic deception capabilities. Israel had three of them and one was airborne at all times. Richardson watched as Laskov listened.

Laskov replaced the phone.

"They see anything?" Richardson asked.

"Foxbats. Four of them. Probably Egyptian. Just maneuvers, I suspect. Also a Mandrake recon in the stratosphere. Probably Russian."

Richardson nodded.

They discussed the technical data as Laskov made two cups of passable coffee. The water stopped running in the bathroom.

Richardson blew steam off the cup. "You using your 14's for escort?"

"Of course." The Grumman F-14 Tomcat was the best fighter craft in the world. But so was the Mig-25 Foxbat. It depended on who was flying each craft. It was that close. Laskov had a squadron of twelve Tomcats that had cost Israel eighteen million dollars apiece. They were sitting, at that moment, on the military end of Lod Airport.

"You going up, too?"

"Of course."

"Why don't you leave that to the younger men?"

"Why don't you go fuck yourself?"

Richardson laughed. "You have a good command of American idiom."

"Thank you."

"How far are you going with them?"

"Until we run out to the edge of our range." He walked to the window and looked into the dawn. "With no bombs or air-to-ground stuff, and on a day like this, we should be able to do a thousand klicks out and then back again. That should take them out of the range of the Land of Islam, in case anyone has any crazy ideas today."

"Not out of range of Libya, Tunisia, Morocco, and Algeria. Look, you can land at our base in Sicily if you want to stay with them that far. Or, we can get a bunch of KAGD's to refuel you in flight, if you want."

Laskov looked away from Richardson and smiled. The Americans were all right except when they were getting panicky about trying to keep the peace at any cost. "They're not going all the way over the Med. The Concordes are going to file a last-minute flight-plan change that will take them up the boot of Italy. We've gotten them special clearance to fly supersonic over Italy and France. We'll break with them east of Sicily. I'll give you the coordinates and your carrier 14's can pick them up if you want. But I don't think that will be necessary. Don't forget, they can go Mach 2.2 at 19,000 meters. Nothing but the Bat can match that, and they'll be out of range of any of their bases—Arab or Russian—by the time we leave them."

Richardson stretched. "You expecting any trouble? Our intelligence tells us it looks O.K."

"We always expect trouble here. But frankly, no. We're just being cautious. There will be a lot of important people on those Concordes. And everything is at stake. *Everything*. All it takes is one crazy to fuck things up."

Richardson nodded. "How's ground security?"

"That's the Security Chief's problem. I'm just a pilot, not a guerilla fighter. If those two goofy-looking birds get airborne, I'll escort them to hell and back without a scratch on them. I don't know from the ground."

Richardson laughed. "Right. Me, neither. By the way, what are you packing besides your .45?"

"The usual ironmongery of death and destruction. Two Sidewinders and two Sparrows, plus six Phoenix."

Richardson considered. The Sidewinder missiles were good at five to eight kilometers; the Sparrows, at sixteen to fifty-six kilometers; and the Phoenix, at fifty-six to a hundred and sixty. The Hughes-manufactured Phoenix was critical to get the Foxbat before it came into dogfight range with its greater maneuverability. "Take a tip, Laskov. There's nothing up there at 19,000 and Mach 2.2 but Foxbats. Leave your 20mm cannon rounds home. There are 950 of them and they weigh. The Sidewinder will get anything that gets in close. We did it on a computer once. It's O.K."

Laskov ran his hand through his hair. "Maybe. Maybe I'll keep them in case I feel like knocking down a Mandrake."

Richardson smiled. "You'd hit an unarmed reconnaissance plane in international air space?" He spoke softly, as though there were someone close by who shouldn't hear. "What's your tactical frequency and call sign today?"

"We'll be on VHF channel 31. That's 134.725 megahertz. My alternate frequency is a last-minute security decision. I'll get it to you later. Today my name will be Angel Gabriel plus my tail number—32. The other eleven Cats will also be Gabriel plus their tail numbers. I'll send you the particulars later."

"And the Concordes?"

"The company call sign for aircraft number 4X-LPN is El Al 01. For 4X-LPO, it's El Al 02. That's what we'll call them on the Air Traffic Control and El Al frequencies. On my tactical frequency, they have code names, of course."

"What are they?"

Laskov smiled. "Some idiot clerk at The Citadel probably spends all day on these things. Anyway, the pilot of 01 is a very religious young man, so 01 is the Kosher Clipper. The pilot of 02 is a former American, so in honor of that great American airline slogan, 02 is the Wings of Emmanuel."

"That's awful." Miriam Bernstein walked into the living room, dressed in a smartly tailored lemon-yellow dress and carrying an overnight bag.

Richardson stood up. He recognized the beautiful, much talked about Deputy Minister of Transportation, but was enough of a diplomat not to mention it.

She walked toward Richardson. "It's all right, Colonel, I'm not a working girl. I have a high clearance. The General has not been indiscreet." Her English was slow and precise, the result of seldom used formal classroom English.

Richardson nodded.

Laskov could tell that Richardson was somewhat unsettled by Miriam. It amused him. He wondered if he should make an introduction, but Miriam was already at the door. She turned and addressed Laskov. "I saw the men in the street. I've called a taxi. Jabari is waiting. I must rush. See you at the final briefing." She looked past Laskov. "Good day, Colonel."

Richardson decided not to let them think he was totally in the dark. "*Shalom*. Good luck in New York."

Miriam Bernstein smiled and left.

Richardson looked at his coffee cup. "I'm not going to drink any more of this swill. I'll take you to breakfast and drop you at The Citadel on my way to my embassy."

Laskov nodded. He walked into the bedroom. He slipped on a khaki cotton shirt that might have been civilian except for two small olive branches that designated his rank. He pulled the automatic from his waistband. He buttoned his shirt with one hand and held the .45 with the other as he walked to the window. Below, the two men, whoever they were, looked quickly down at

their shoes. Miriam got into a waiting taxi and sped off. Laskov
threw the .45 on the bed.

He felt uneasy. It was the wind. Something to do with an
imbalance of negative ions in the air, they said. The ill wind went
by many names—the *Foehn* of Central Europe, the *Mistral* of
Southern France, the *Santa Ana* of California. Here it was
called *Hamseen* or *Sharav*. There were people, like himself, who
were weather-sensitive and suffered physically and phychologi-
cally from the effect. It wouldn't matter at 19,000 meters, but it
mattered here. It was a mixed blessing, this first hot wind of
spring. He looked into the sky. At least it was turning out to be a
perfect day for flying.

2

Abdel Majid Jabari sat staring at a cup of black Turkish coffee laced with arak. "I don't mind telling you I was badly frightened. I came very close to shooting a security man."

Miriam Bernstein nodded. Everyone was jumpy. It was a time of celebration, but also a time of apprehension. "My fault. I should have realized."

Jabari put up his hand. "Never mind. We see Palestinian terrorists everywhere, but in fact, there are not many left these days."

"How many does it take? You especially should be careful. They really *do* want you." She looked at him. "It must be difficult. A stranger in a strange land."

Jabari was still high-strung from his dawn encounter. "I'm no stranger here. I was born here," he said pointedly. "You weren't," he added, then regretted the remark. He smiled in a conciliatory manner and spoke in Arabic. "'If you mingle your affairs with theirs, then they are your brothers.'"

Miriam thought of another Arabic saying. "'I came to the

29

place of my birth and cried, "The friends of my youth, where are they?" And Echo answered. "Where are they?"'" She paused. "That applies to both of us, I suppose. This is no more your land now, Abdel, then it was mine when I landed on these shores. Displaced persons displacing other wretched persons. It's all so damned . . . cruel."

Jabari could see that she was on the verge of slipping into one of her darker moods. "Politics and geography aside, Miriam, there are many cultural similarities between the Arabs and the Jews. I think they have all finally realized that." He poured a glass of arak and raised it. "In Hebrew, you—we—say *shalom alekhem*, peace unto you. And in Arabic, we say *salaam aleckum*, which is as close as we've gotten to it up to now."

Miriam Bernstein poured herself a glass of arak. "*Alekhem shalom*, and unto you, peace." She drank and there was a burning in her stomach.

As they sat at breakfast they spoke about what might happen in New York. She felt good talking to Jabari. She was apprehensive about sitting face to face with Arabs across a conference table at the UN—the long-heralded confrontation—and Jabari was a good transition for her. She knew he had been far from the mainstream of Arab thought for thirty years, and his loyalties were with Israel; but if there were such a thing as a racial psyche, then perhaps Abdel Jabari reflected it.

Jabari watched her closely as she spoke in that husky voice that sometimes sounded weary and often sounded sensuous. Over the years, a bit at a time, he had come to know her story as she had come to know his. They had both known what it was to be the flotsam and jetsam of a world in upheaval. Now they both sat at the top of their society and they were both in a position to change the currents of history for better or worse.

Miriam Bernstein was a fairly typical product of the European holocaust. She had been found by the advancing Red Army in a concentration camp, whose purpose was as obscure as its name, although the words *Medizinische Experimente* stuck out in her mind. She remembered that she had once had parents and other family—a baby sister—and that she was Jewish. Beyond that, she knew little. She spoke a little German, probably learned from the camp guards, and a little Polish, probably learned from the other children in the camp. She also knew a few words of Hungarian, which had led her to believe that this was her nationality. But mostly she had been a silent child, and she neither knew nor cared if she was a German, Polish, or Hungarian Jew. All she knew for certain, or cared about, was that she was a Jew.

The Red Army had taken her and the other children to what must have been a labor camp, because the older children worked at repairing roads. Many of them died that winter. In the spring, they all worked in the fields. She had wound up in a hospital, then was released into the custody of an elderly Jewish couple.

One day, some people came from the Jewish Agency. She and the old couple, along with many others, traveled across war-ravaged Europe for weeks in crowded railroad cars that gave her nightmares. They boarded a boat and went to sea. At Haifa, the boat was turned away by the British. The boat attempted to unload the people further up the coast at night. A fierce battle broke out on the beach between the Jews, who were trying to secure the beachhead, and the Arabs, who didn't want the boat to unload. Eventually, British soldiers broke up the fight and the boat sailed away. She never knew where it went because she had been one of the people who had been landed on the beach before the fight. The old couple, whose name she could not remember, disappeared—dead on the beach or still on the boat.

Another Jewish couple picked her up from the beach and told the British soldiers that her name was Miriam Bernstein and that she was their child. She had strayed from their house and gotten caught in the fighting. Yes, she was born in Palestine. She remembered that the young couple were very poor liars, but the British soldiers just looked at her and walked away.

The Bernsteins had taken her to a new kibbutz outside Tel Aviv. When the British left Palestine, the Arabs raided the settlement. Her new father went to defend the kibbutz and never returned. As the years passed, she discovered that her older stepbrother, Yosef, was also an adopted refugee. She found nothing unusual about that because she imagined that most children in the world—or in her world—came from the camps and rubble of Europe. Yosef Bernstein had seen what she had seen, and more. Like her, he knew neither his real parents nor his real name, his nationality nor his age. They became young lovers and eventually married. During the Yom Kippur War, their only son, Eliahu, was killed in action.

Miriam Bernstein had taken an early interest in private peace groups and had cultivated the good will of the local Arab communities. Her kibbutz, like most, was hawkish, and she felt increasingly isolated from her friends and neighbors. Only Yosef had understood, but it was not easy for him, a fighter pilot, to have a dovish wife.

After the 1973 War her party appointed her to a vacant seat in the Knesset in recognition of her popularity with the Israeli Arabs and with the women's peace movement.

She quickly came to the attention of Prime Minister Meir and the two became personal friends. When Mrs. Meir resigned in 1974, it was understood that Miriam Bernstein was her voice in the Knesset. With Mrs. Meir's backing, she rose quickly to a deputy minister's post. Long after the grand old woman no longer sat in the wings of the Knesset, Miriam Bernstein held on to her seat and her post through one government crisis after another. On the surface, it appeared—and she believed—that she survived every Cabinet shuffle because she was exceedingly good at whatever she did. Her enemies said that she survived at least in part because of her striking good looks. In fact, she survived in the high-mortality world of parliamentary politics because she was an instinctive survivor. She was not consciously aware of this side of her character, and if she were ever confronted with a synopsis of her political machinations or a list of the people she had politically eliminated, she would not have recognized that it was Miriam Bernstein who had done those things.

Whenever she thought back on Mrs. Meir's help and support, it was always the small things that stood out, such as the times the Prime Minister took her back to her apartment after an all-night Cabinet session and made her coffee. Then there was the time the Cabinet requested that she adopt a Hebrew name in keeping with government policy for office holders. Mrs. Meir—formerly Mrs. Meyerson—understood her reluctance to sever the only thread she had with the past and supported her resistance to the change.

There were people who thought that Miriam Bernstein was being groomed to fill Mrs. Meir's old job someday, but Miriam Bernstein denied any such ambitions. Still, it had been said that Mrs. Meir was appointed Prime Minister *because* she didn't want the job. The Israelis liked to put people in power who didn't want power. It was safer.

Now she held a job that she coveted more than Prime Minister: Peace Delegate. It was a job that hadn't existed a few months before, but she always knew it would exist someday.

There was much to do in New York, and there was personal business to attend to there, also. Yosef had been missing for three years now. She wondered if she could find out something about his fate from the Arabs when she got to New York.

Jabari noticed a small disturbance outside and instinctively put his hand in his pocket.

Miriam Bernstein seemed not to notice. She was caught up in what she was saying. "The people have elected a government ready to exchange concessions for solid guarantees, Abdel. We have shown the world that we will not go under. Sadat was one of the first modern Arab leaders to understand that. When he came to Jerusalem he was following in the footsteps of countless others who have come to Jerusalem since the beginning of recorded time to find peace, and yet he shattered a precedent of thirty years' standing." She leaned forward. "We have fought well and have won the respect of many nations. The enemy is no longer at the gate. The long siege is ended. The people are in a mood to talk."

Jabari nodded. "I hope so." He looked over her shoulder at the crowd gathered in the street as she continued to talk. He felt her hand over his. "And you, Abdel? If they founded a new Palestine, would you go?"

Jabari stared straight ahead for a long moment. "I am an elected member of the Knesset. I don't think I would be welcome in any new Palestine." He held up his mangled hand. "But even so, I might take that chance. Who knows—I might be reunited with my family there."

Miriam Bernstein was sorry she had asked the question. "Well, we will all have decisions to make in the future. What's important now is that we are going to New York to discuss a lasting peace."

Jabari nodded. "Yes. And we must strike now while the mood is in the air. I have this fear that something will happen to break the spell. An incident. A misunderstanding." He leaned forward. "All the stars—social, historical, economic, military, and political—are aligned for peace in the Holy Land as they have not been in millennia. And it's spring. So it can't hurt to talk. Right?" He stood. "But I wish we were in New York already and the Conference were under way." He looked into the street. "I think our planes are coming in. Let's have a look."

People from the café were hurrying into the street.

Approaching Lod Airport from the north were two Concordes. As the first aircraft began its descent, the crowd could see the blue Star of David against the white tail. There was some scattered applause from the mixed Arab and Jewish crowd.

Miriam Bernstein shielded her eyes as the Concorde dropped lower and approached from out of the sun. Beyond the airfield, the Samarian hills rose up off the plain. She noticed that new almond blossoms had come out during the night and the hills were smudged with pink and white clouds. The rocky foothills were softly green and carpeted with brilliant red anemones, cream-colored lupins, and yellow daisies. The yearly miracle of rebirth had returned, and along with the wildflowers brought into bloom by the *Hamseen*, peace was breaking out in the Holy Land.

Or so it seemed.

Tom Richardson and Teddy Laskov left the café in Herzlya and got into Richardson's yellow Corvette. They hit the heavy Friday traffic of Tel Aviv and the car slowed to a crawl. At a traffic light a block from The Citadel, Laskov opened the door. "I'll walk from here, Tom. Thanks."

Richardson looked over. "O.K. I'll try to see you before you scramble."

Laskov put one foot out of the door, then felt Richardson's hand on his shoulder. He looked back at Richardson.

Richardson regarded him for a long second. "Listen, don't get trigger-happy up there. We don't want any incidents."

Laskov stared back with cold, dark eyes. His brows came together. He spoke loudly, above the noise of Tel Aviv's traffic. "Neither do we, Tom. But the best we've got are going to be on board those birds. If anything that looks military gets on my radar screen, and if it's in missile range, so help me, I'll knock it out of the goddamn sky. I'm not putting up with any fly-bys, reconnaissance, or harassment horseshit from *anyone*. Not today." Laskov slid his big bulk out of the low-slung car and moved as if he were heading for a barroom brawl.

The light was green, and Richardson edged ahead. He wiped the sweat from his upper lip. At King Saul Boulevard, he made a right turn. Laskov, big and burly, was still in his mind's eye. He could actually see the great burden on the man's broad shoulders. There wasn't a top military commander in the world who didn't wonder if he was going to be the fool to start World

War III. The old warrior, Laskov, liked to bellow, but Richardson knew that if and when a quick, tactical decision had to be made, Laskov would make the right one.

Richardson turned onto Hayarkon Street and stopped in front of the American Embassy. He finger-combed his damp hair in the rear view mirror. The day had gotten off to a bad start.

Through the car's sun roof, he could see two white Concordes overhead. The bright sunlight gave them an ethereal glow. One was in a holding pattern, heading out to sea. The other was heading in the opposite direction as it began its final descent to Lod. For a split second, the aircraft seemed to cross paths and their delta wings formed the Star of David.

Sabah Khabbani chewed slowly on a piece of pita bread as he stood looking through his field glasses at Lod Airport. He shifted the glasses. Below, on the Plain of Sharon, the plowed earth was a rich chocolate. Between the cultivated fields, the Rose of Sharon and the lilies of the valley flowered as they had done since long before Solomon. A distinctive grey area marked Ramla Military Prison where so many of his brothers were wasting away their lives. To the south, the rocky Judean hills, brown a few days before, had turned red and white, yellow and blue, as wildflowers blossomed. Around him, the Jerusalem pines, part of the reforestation program, swayed as the *Hamseen* came over the crest. The old Palestine of his boyhood had been beautiful in a wild way. He had to admit the Jews had improved on it. Still . . .

Khabbani removed his strapless old watch from his pocket and looked at it. In less than one hour, the VIP lounge should be full. Any time between then and takeoff was all right, according to his instructions. Khabbani considered. The terminal was actually a little beyond the maximum effective range of his mortars, but if the *Hamseen* held, he could reach it. If he did not reach the terminal, the rounds would fall short and land in the parking ramp where the Concordes would be. It didn't matter. It was only necessary to cause an incident and have the flight canceled. Khabbani wasn't sure he liked this thing he was doing. He shrugged.

One of his men gave a low call. Khabbani looked to where the man was pointing. Two Concordes, traveling in trail, were heading for Lod from the north. Khabbani studied them in his field glasses. Such beautiful aircraft. He had read that they each held 113,000 kilograms of fuel. A quarter-million kilograms together. That would make an explosion that they would feel in Jerusalem.

3

The city of Lod, the ancient Lydda, baked in the early spring heat wave. The first *Hamseen* of the year was unusually early. The scorching, dry, Sirocco-like desert wind from the east blew across the city with increasing strength. The *Hamseen* would last a few days, then the weather would become balmy. According to Arab tradition, there were fifty such dog days a year—the Arabic word *Hamseen* meaning fifty. The only *Hamseen* that was welcome was the first, for with it, the wildflowers of the Judean and Samarian hills and fields opened and the air was thick with sweet scents.

At Lod International Airport, the tarmac shimmered. On the ramps, where the air liners were parked, an unusually large contingent of Israeli soldiers stood with their weapons slung. In the passenger terminal, security men in nondescript clothing and wearing sunglasses stood with newspapers held in front of them.

Throughout the day, *sherut* taxis and private cars, carrying well-dressed men and women, pulled up to the doors of the main terminal. The occupants were quickly ushered inside the terminal and into the VIP lounge or the El Al Security office on the top floor.

At the far end of the field stood a cluster of military huts. Commandos in camouflage fatigues stood in various degrees of alertness. Behind the huts, a squadron of twelve American-made F-14 Tomcats stood on the concrete hardstands. Mechanics and armorers worked on the fighters and spoke to pilots and flight officers.

The road coming down from Jerusalem wound through Lod and the ancient Moslem quarter of Ramla on the way to Lod International Airport. Since morning, the inhabitants of Lod and Ramla had noticed the unusually heavy civilian and military traffic. In the past, such activity had been a prelude to yet another crisis. This time it was different.

In Lod, the Greek Orthodox Church of St. George was filled with Christian Arabs and other native Christians of indeterminate Crusader and Byzantine ancestry. No special service was being conducted, but people had come, drawn out of a sense of wanting to be in a special place with others—of wanting to participate in some small way in events that were to touch their lives.

In the city's synagogues, men sat in small groups hours before the sundown service and spoke in quiet voices. In the market square, near St. George's, Jewish women shopped for the Sabbath meal among the pitched stalls. There seemed to be a touch of lightheartedness in the bargaining and purchasing, more so than on a usual Friday afternoon, and people tarried in the market place much longer than was necessary to complete their business.

In Ramla, the square in front of the Great Mosque, Jami-el-Kebir, was crowded long before the Muezzin called the faithful to prayer.

The Arab market was as crowded, but noisier than the one in Lod. The Arabs, lingerers by nature, seemed more so as the market and streets filled with every manner of conveyance, from Land Rovers and Buicks to Arabian stallions and camels.

In Ramla Military Prison, Palestinian terrorists were able to hope that at least some of them might soon be free men.

The mood of Lod and Ramla was like that of the rest of Israel and the rest of the Middle East. Here in this part of the world, virtually every powerful, historical force had met at one time or another and had used the terrain as a battleground. Trying to live in peace in this area, said one proverb, was like trying to sleep in the middle of a crossroad. Thousands of armies, millions of men, had marched over this small spot on the map known as the Holy Land. But more than just armies had met in those seemingly desolate hills and deserts. Ideologies and faiths had met, clashed, and left a legacy of blood. Nearly every culture in the East and West was represented by ruins, standing like gravestones over the countryside, or buried like corpses beneath it. It was difficult to dig in modern Israel without uncovering the ruins—and, mingled with the ruins, the bones.

Ramla and Lod typified the agonizing history of the ancient land; the divisiveness and the unity of modern Israel. They reflected the mood of the complex, multireligious state. Hope without celebration. Despair without weeping.

El Al's Security Chief, Jacob Hausner, dropped the ornate French telephone receiver back into its cradle. He turned to his young assistant, Matti Yadin. "When are these bastards going to stop bothering me?"

"Which bastards, Chief?" asked Yadin.

Hausner brushed a speck from the top of his satinwood Louis XV desk. He had decorated his office out of his own funds, and he liked to keep it neat. He walked over to the big picture window that overlooked the aircraft parking ramp and opened the heavy velvet drapes. Fabric-fading sunlight poured in. "All of them." He waved his arm to indicate the world at large. "That was The Citadel. They're a little concerned."

"I don't blame them."

Hausner regarded Yadin coolly for a second.

Yadin smiled, then looked at his boss with an expression of sympathy. It was a tough job at the best of times. For the past few weeks it had been hell for everyone in Security. He studied Hausner's profile as the man stared out the window, lost in thought.

Jacob Hausner was a child of the Fifth *Aliya*, the fifth wave of immigration to Palestine. This *Aliya* had been made up mostly of German Jews who had left their old homeland to return to their more ancient one after Hitler came to power in 1933. They were a lucky or, perhaps, farsighted group. They had all escaped the holocaust in Europe while it was still possible to do so. They were also an affluent, well-educated group, and they had brought with them much-needed capital and skills. Many of them had settled around the older German colony in the seaport of Haifa, and they prospered. Hausner's early years were typical of the rich German Jews in Haifa during the prewar period.

When World War II broke out, Hausner, just seventeen, had joined MI-6, British Secret Intelligence Service. Being trained by the British in that occupation, he approached it in much the same fashion as his teachers—with the attitude of a dilettante. But also like so many British spies with this attitude, he was exceedingly good at his job. If he considered it only as a necessary wartime hobby, so much the better. He was a rich young man who looked and acted like anything but a spy, which was the idea.

Outside of Haifa, he easily passed as a German. The job called for a lot of party going and social climbing among the German colonies in Cairo and Istanbul, and Hausner was good at it. His mind grasped the most intricate details of that strange and shady business of leading two lives, and he loved it almost as much as he loved Chopin, Mozart, and *Sachertorten*.

Hausner had joined a private British flying club in a fit of boredom before the war and had become one of the few licensed civilian pilots in Palestine. Between intelligence assignments, he pestered the British to let him log hours in Spitfires and Hurricanes so that he could keep his skills sharp.

After the war, he went to Europe and bought scrapped warplanes for the illegal Haganah Air Force. He had bought the first British Spitfire that General Laskov had flown in, but neither man was aware of the fact.

After the 1948 war, it was natural that Hausner, with a background of intelligence work and flying skill, should become one of El Al's first security men.

Compared to most Jews who came of age during that period, his life had been one of relative ease. He now lived in Herzlya in a small villa on the Mediterranean. He kept a series of mistresses and more casual acquaintances there but still faithfully visited his family in Haifa on the religious days.

In appearance, he reminded most people of a European aristocrat. He had a thin, aquiline nose, high cheekbones, and thick white hair.

Hausner looked at Yadin. "I hope they let me go on this flight."

Yadin shook his head and smiled. "Who would they crucify if the planes blew up, Chief?"

"We don't use the words *blow up* in the same sentence as the word *plane*, Matti." He smiled. He could afford to smile. Everything was going well. He had a perfect record and he saw no reason why Concordes 01 and 02 should spoil that record.

Matti Yadin got up and stretched. "Do we hear any rumblings from our intelligence services?"

Hausner kept staring out the window. "No. Our Palestinian friends are very quiet—whatever is left of them."

"Too quiet?"

Hausner shrugged. He was a man who refused to make guesses based on no information. No news simply meant no news. He had faith in his country's intelligence services. They had rarely failed him. If an insect hit any part of the web of Israeli Intelligence, the web quivered and the spider, at the center, felt it. Anything outside the web was too far removed to worry about.

Hausner drew the drapes and turned away from the window. He straightened his tie and jacket in a wall mirror, then walked across the office and opened the door into the adjoining conference room.

Yadin followed him and moved off toward the far wall, where he found a seat.

The conference room, which was crowded and noisy, became quiet. Everyone turned toward Hausner.

Around the large circular table sat some of the most powerful people in Israel. There was Chaim Mazar, head of Shin Beth, Israel's Internal Security Service; Brigadier General Itzhak Talman, the Air Force Chief of Operations; General Benjamin Dobkin, representing the Army's Chiefs of Staff; Miriam Bernstein, Deputy Minister of Transportation; and Isaac Burg, head of Mivtzan Elohim, "The Wrath of God," the anti-terrorist group.

There were also five members of the Knesset present besides Bernstein. Along the walls, junior aides sat in chairs and a secretary was preparing to take notes at a small desk. Hausner came toward the table.

The group was an *ad hoc* committee put together to ensure the safety of the Concorde flight. One of their jobs was to question Hausner, and they meant to do it.

Hausner noticed that he was the only one present who was wearing a suit, as usual. He looked at Miriam Bernstein directly. Those eyes again. Nothing. Why, then, did he feel that she was always judging him? And then there was her sexuality. Hausner did not wish to admit to himself that she did not so much *use* it as that it was simply there. A fact. A sensual woman. He looked away from her. Strictly speaking, the Minister of Transportation was his boss. Perhaps, he thought, that produced the tension. He remained standing and cleared his throat. "I agreed to be at this meeting so that we wouldn't have any more doubts about my ability to get an airplane off the ground." He held up his hand to stifle a half-dozen incipient protests. "Okay. Forget it."

The sparsely decorated room was illuminated by a large picture window with the same view as from Hausner's office. He walked to the window. At the far end of the parking ramps, away from the other planes, the two long, sleek Concordes, each with a Star of David on its tail, stood gleaming in the bright sunlight. Around the aircraft stood Hausner's security guards, armed with Uzi submachine guns and sniper rifles. The army had sent over a ten-man squad of infantry, too, which did nothing to improve Hausner's mood.

Everyone was conscious of the quiet. Hausner pointed dramatically. "There they are. Pride of the fleet. They cost a mere eighty million dollars each, with the spare tire and radio. We charge all passengers first-class fare, plus a twenty-percent surcharge, and yet we haven't made a *shekel* from them, as you know." He looked at Bernstein, who was one of his severest critics in the Knesset. "And you know one of the reasons El Al hasn't made a profit? Because *I* demand the tightest security that is humanly possible. And good security has a high price." Hausner moved a few feet down the length of the bright window. Squinting eyes followed him. "Some of you," he began slowly, "were worried about profit a few short months ago, and you were willing to let security become lax because of it. Now, the same people," he looked at Miriam Bernstein, "are concerned that I have not done enough." Hausner walked back toward an empty seat and sat down. "O.K. Let's get this over with." He looked around the table. He spoke in a fast staccato voice. "We've had those birds on the line for thirteen months. Since the time that we got them, they have never left the sight of my security people. We've had the bulkheads and baggage holds armored while they were being built at the factories in St. Nazaire and Toulouse. All maintenance is done only by El Al mechanics here at Lod. Today, I personally checked the fuel going into the craft. It was pure Jet A kerosene, I assure you. When we first got the Concordes, I demanded and got an auxiliary power unit installed in the front wheel well. The rest of the world's Concordes have to be started by an external ground power unit. By installing the APU, I can dispense with two trucks going up to my birds at foreign airports—the preconditioned air truck and the ground power unit truck. We can start our own engines anywhere, any time, after which the birds are self-supportive. We took the extra weight penalty of the nine-hundred kilogram APU, as we've always taken the extra weight penalty in the name of security. You can't make money that way, of course, but I won't have it any other way. And neither will you."

Hausner looked around, waiting for a comment, but there was none. He continued. "We also go through the extra expense and bother of performing most services only here at Lod. For instance, no water bowser gets near my birds except here at Lod. If you fly El Al, you're pissing Jordan water in Tokyo. The toilet service is only done here, also. Furthermore, after every flight, the cleaning service, supervised by my personnel, goes over each plane very thoroughly, in case anyone decided to leave a package for us. We probe the seats, examine the toilets, and even open the barf bags. Another point—the galley service is done at Lod and nowhere else. As for the food on these Concordes, I checked it myself as it was being stowed in the galleys. You have my assurance that everything is kosher. In fact, the company rabbi ate the meal and all he got was indigestion." Hausner leaned back and lit a cigarette. He spoke more slowly. "Actually, in one very important respect, this flight is more secure than any other. On this flight we don't have to worry about the passengers."

Hausner nodded toward Matti Yadin. "My assistant has volunteered to head the security team on Concorde 01. I have volunteered to do the same on 02. However, the Prime Minister has not yet informed me if I am to go with the mission." He looked slowly around the table. "Are there any other questions regarding El Al security? No? Good."

There was a long silence. Hausner decided that since it was his conference room, he was supposed to be chairman. He turned to Chaim Mazar of Shin Beth. "Would you like to make a report?"

Mazar got up slowly. He was a tall, thin man with the eyes of someone who had been in Internal Intelligence for a long time. His manner was abrupt—some thought rude. He began without preamble. "The big worry, of course, is some maniac with a small, shoulder-fired, heat-seeking missile standing on a roof somewhere between here and the coast. I can assure you that there is no one standing on any roof between here and the coast. Nor will there be anyone standing around anywhere in the flight path at takeoff. I have asked the Defense Minister to call short air-raid drills in the flight path. There will be helicopters over the whole area. There has been no sign of guerilla activity of any sort inside of Israel. I am confident there will be no problems. Thank you." He sat down.

Hausner smiled. Short and to the point. Good man. He turned to Isaac Burg, the head of Mivtzan Elohim.

Burg remained seated but leaned slightly forward. He was a short, gentlemanly looking, white-haired man with a twinkle in his blue eyes. He affected fussy habits and mannerisms that were very disarming. In reality, he had no such habits. He was much younger than he looked, and he was capable of killing in cold blood while he searched his pockets for a nasal spray. No one would have believed that he was the man who had nearly completed the job of wiping out the multitude of Palestinian guerilla organizations around the world. His men had been brutal in hunting down the last of the disorganized groups, but the result had been an almost complete end to terrorist attacks at home and abroad. Burg smiled. "We ran into a Palestinian guerilla just the other day in Paris. He was an important member of Black September. One of the last. We questioned him with much vigor. He assures us that there are no plans that he is aware of to disrupt the peace mission. The guerillas are so dispersed and untrusting these days that we can't be sure they speak even to each other. But one of my men, who is a ranking member of one of the Palestinian intelligence services, informs me that there is nothing planned."

Burg fumbled for his pipe and finally located it. He stared at the pipe for a long second, then looked up. "Anyway, as far as we know, the Arab governments now want this Conference to succeed as much as we do. They've let us know through various sources that they are keeping a close watch on known and suspected guerillas in their nations. In case they are a little lax, we are doing the same thing." He stuffed an aromatic blend into his pipe bowl. "John McClure of the CIA, who is attached to us, informs me that his agency has not picked up any rumblings from Arab groups around the world. Mr. McClure, incidentally, is beginning his home leave tomorrow and will be flying with the peace mission as a courtesy." Isaac Burg smiled pleasantly as he lit his pipe. The sweet smoke billowed over the table. He looked at General Dobkin. "How about the Arab hinterlands?"

Benjamin Dobkin rose and looked around the room. He was a solidly built man with a thick neck and close-clinging, curly black hair. Like most Israeli generals, he wore plain combat fatigues with the sleeves rolled up. His massive arms and hands were what most people noticed first. He was an amateur archeologist, and the strenuous digs into the ancient tells had added a lot of bulk to his already massive frame. When he had commanded an infantry brigade, every man in the brigade became a willing or unwilling archeologist. Not a drainage trench, a latrine, a foxhole, or anti-tank ditch was dug without the soil being sifted at the first possible opportunity. Benjamin Dobkin was also a religious man, and he took no pains to hide his deep faith. Officer Evaluation Reports on Dobkin always included words like "solid," "steady," and "self-possessed."

He clasped his massive hands behind him and began. "The problem is—has always been—that guerillas can get away with the most outrageous antics in the hinterlands of underdeveloped countries. Israeli Army Operations cleaned out many of these Fatahlands. The Arab governments themselves partially finished the job." He looked around. "But unlike some of my friends here, the Army cannot and will not exclude the possibility of some sort of aggression by Palestinians or other Arabs originating out of these rural Arab areas where there are still pockets of guerillas. The Army has only limited access, but we do send many Army Intelligence people there, where, with luck, they pass as Arabs. We spy out the land." He hesitated. "As we've always done. As we did three thousand years ago. 'And Moses sent them up to spy out the land of Canaan, and said unto them, "Get you up this way southward, and go up into the mountain: and see the land, what it is, and the people that dwelleth therein, whether they be strong or weak, few or many."'"

Ya'akov Sapir, a left-wing Knesset member who was anything but religious, interjected. "And these army spies of

Moses, if I remember correctly, reported that this land was a land flowing with milk and honey. I don't think anyone has trusted an army reconnaissance report since then."

There were a few tentative laughs around the table and from the chairs along the wall.

General Dobkin regarded Ya'akov Sapir for a long moment. "And as a member of the Knesset Postal Committee, I think you might be interested to know that the Corinthians' replies to Paul's letters are still sitting in the Jerusalem Post Office."

This brought more laughter.

Hausner looked annoyed. "Can we dispense with these learned Biblical barbs, please? General? Would you continue, please?"

Dobkin nodded. "Yes. All in all, it looks good. My counterparts in the Arab countries have sent word that they are moving to neutralize the remaining guerilla pockets where they can be located."

Chaim Mazar leaned forward. "What kind of operation *could* they mount against this peace mission if they weren't neutralized, General?"

"Sea and air. We are still concerned about sea and air. The Navy Department has assured me, however, that the flight path of the Concordes over the Mediterranean is being thoroughly patrolled not only by their craft and the American Sixth Fleet but also by the navies of Greece, Turkey, and Italy, who are staging a NATO exercise along the flight path. In addition, a sea-to-air missile, of the type that would be needed to bring down an aircraft flying at the height and speed of the Concordes is much too sophisticated to be either owned or operated by terrorists. And even if they did own one and managed to launch it at sea, the Air Force escort would have ample time to identify it, track it, and shoot it down. Isn't that correct, General?" He looked at Itzhak Talman, Air Force Chief of Operations. Everyone turned toward Talman.

Itzhak Talman rose. He walked toward the picture window and looked into the distance. He was a tall, handsome man with a clipped British military mustache and the look of a dashing ex-RAF pilot. He spoke a mixture of bad Hebrew and worse Yiddish with an upper-class British accent. Like the British officers whom he emulated, he had a cool, detached, and imperturbable manner. But like a lot of those old officers of the Empire, Talman was play-acting. Actually, he had a highly nervous, emotional nature, but he kept it very well hidden.

Talman turned back and faced the table. He spoke in a dispassionate voice. "My very best fighter officer, Teddy Laskov, is personally leading a squadron of hand-picked pilots, who are in turn flying the best fighter craft in the world. They are, at this moment, supervising the arming and maintenance of those twelve craft at the far end of this airfield. Teddy Laskov assures me that he can spot, track, intercept, and shoot down anything in the sky, including Foxbats, SAM's, and Satan himself, if he gets on the radar." He looked around the room over the heads of the men and women assembled there. "Air Force Intelligence informs me that not only have the guerillas never had the capability to make an aerial attack, but they have none now. But *if* anyone were to mount an attack against those Concordes, they would have to put up, into the air, what would amount to the most powerful air fleet in the Mediterranean." Talman stroked his mustache. "Teddy Laskov is the best we've got. As soon as those birds break over the coast, they are my responsibility, and I accept that responsibility with no hesitation." He walked back to his seat.

Teddy Laskov, who had been in the corridor listening, opened the door quietly. Several heads turned toward the object of Talman's praise. Laskov smiled self-consciously and waved his hand to indicate that no one was to pay him any attention. He stood against the wall.

Miriam Bernstein had been trying to catch Hausner's eye. Hausner studiously ignored her. He looked around the table and toward the seats along the wall, but no one appeared to have anything further to add. "All right, then—"

Miriam Bernstein rose. "Mr. Hausner."

"Yes?"

"I'd like to add something here."

"Oh."

"Thank you." She offered Hausner a smile which he seemed not to notice. She looked down and shuffled through some papers in front of her, then looked up. "I've been listening very carefully to what has been said here, and while I'm impressed with the precautions that have been taken, I am frankly worried about the spirit they were taken in and especially the language used to describe these precautions. Gentlemen, we are going to this *veida*, this Conference, to make a *Brit Shalom*, a Covenant of Peace."

Miriam Bernstein paused and looked around the table, meeting the eyes of each man in turn. "Talking of shooting things from the sky, of questioning suspected Arabs in friendly countries with much vigor, of sending Army spies into Arab lands—these are justifiable under some circumstances, but at this moment in our history, I would take the risk of keeping a very low, nonaggressive profile. We don't want to go into the United Nations like a bunch of cowboys with our six-shooters blazing. We want to go there looking as if we came to talk peace."

She drew her lips together as she thought of the words she would use to speak reason without appearing to speak surrender. She had been associated with the peace wing of her party for many years and felt obligated to give this warning as they stood on the threshold of seeing peace become a reality. She had not lived in a place that was at peace for one day in her entire life. She extended her hands, palms up, in a conciliatory gesture. "I'm not trying to create a problem where none exists. I'm just saying that all military and intelligence operations should come to an almost complete halt during the weeks ahead. This is an act of faith on our part. Somebody has to holster his gun first. Even if you should see Satan himself on your radar screen, General Talman, don't shoot him out of the sky with one of your missiles. Just explain to him that you are going on a peace mission and that you will not be goaded into an aggressive act. He will see that you mean to have your peace, and that—and Providence— will send him away." She looked around the room and her eyes fixed on Teddy Laskov for a split second.

He looked back and found something in those eyes that few people had ever seen, but he wasn't quite sure what to call it.

She looked up over the heads of the people around her. Outside, past the airfield, were the rocky hills where Khabbani and his men were arguing about when to fire. The heat of the *Hamseen* permeated the small room.

Miriam Bernstein looked around the room again. "There are those among us who do not want to give up at the peace table what they bought in blood. I understand this. I do. And I know all the rebuttals to the peace-at-any-cost philosophy. We all do. I even believe many of them. I'm just asking you all to think about what I've said over the next few days. Thank you." She sat down and busied herself with the papers in front of her.

No one made a reply. The room was very still.

General Talman rose and walked over to Teddy Laskov. He took him by the arm and they both walked out into the corridor. Eventually, people began speaking in quiet voices to those sitting near them. Then the meeting broke into small groups as final plans were coordinated.

Jacob Hausner tuned out the low voices around him and regarded Miriam Bernstein for a long time. There was a subtle undercurrent between them. He felt it. Unresolved, it would surface at the most unexpected moment. He remembered suddenly and vividly the time she had refused an invitation to spend the weekend at his villa. He bristled now at the thought of it. Then he sat back and looked at the ceiling. To hell with her. He had other things besides Miriam Bernstein to occupy his thoughts.

There had been a lot of practice over the years for this moment. The Palestinians had always considered El Al a military objective, and the attacks had begun almost the same day El Al had in 1948. But it was the more spectacular terrorist operations of the 1960s and 1970s that had grabbed the headlines.

The last incident had been the attempted hijacking of an El Al 747 out of Heathrow Airport. Ahmed Rish had been the mastermind of that plot. Hausner's face grimaced at the name. Rish. One of the last—and probably the best—of a bad lot. They'd had him in Ramla Military Prison once, too, after he had been arrested at Lod Airport on an unknown mission. In 1968, before Israel adopted a policy of refusing to negotiate with terrorists, they had exchanged him, along with fifteen other terrorists, for the Israeli passengers on the El Al flight that had been hijacked in the attempt to capture General Sharon. Hausner had thought it was a mistake then, and later events had proved him correct.

He wished that Ahmed Rish had turned up dead in one of the Mivtzan Elohim raids over the years. Rish's specialty was airplanes, and the thought of Rish on the loose, an unrepentant and deeply committed terrorist, disturbed him. Hausner had been one of his principal interrogators at Ramla. Rish was one of the few terrorists who had made him lose his temper. Hausner remembered striking him. In his report, he concluded that Rish was a very dangerous man who ought to be locked up forever. But he had been released.

Rish had turned up in a lot of places since then, each one of them too close to an El Al plane. There were rumors that Rish had been one of the terrorists who had escaped the Entebbe raid. Probably true, thought Hausner.

When Isaac Burg had mentioned a guerilla caught in France, Hausner's memory had been jogged. Rish had been spotted in France over a year ago, after the Heathrow operation. Why France? Hausner recalled that something about that had bothered him at the time. What was it? France. Rish. Rish's *modus operandi*. That was it. There was something about Rish's *modus operandi* that had struck him at the time. Rish wasn't a gun-toting, half-crazed hijacker. He didn't take many personal risks. Rish operated in a very remote, circumspect manner.

Why France? Why not the big Arab communities in Germany? The only Arab group of any size in France was the Algerians. Rish was an Iraqi, though he was fighting for the Palestinian cause. To the rest of the world, Arabs were all the same. But to each other they were not. Also, to the French police, who were used to Algerians, an Iraqi would stick out.

Yes, Rish was an insect who had touched the net of Israeli Intelligence not so long ago, and it had quivered. They had spotted him not in Paris but in the countryside. Strange. Once in Brittany and once in the South by the Spanish border. Why? Suddenly, the thought struck Hausner that there was a weak link in this whole security chain somewhere, and he didn't know what or where it was. A chill ran down his spine.

There was a psychological profile of Rish on file, plus a standard identikit. He'd get them out. And he'd place a call to the French SDECE. Hausner looked around. Everyone was still conversing in small groups. He rose. "If no one needs me any longer, I'll get back to my job."

No one answered.

"Madame Deputy Minister?"

"Don't let us keep you," said Miriam Bernstein.

"I won't." He looked around the room. "Please feel free to use my conference room as long as you wish. Excuse me." He turned and walked to the door, then looked back. *"Shalom,"* he said sincerely.

4

Captain David Becker, pilot of El Al Concorde 02, sat in the Operations Room next to his First Officer, Moses Hess. Across the long table from Hess sat the flight engineer, Peter Kahn, an American Jew, like Becker.

On the walls were maps, charts, and bulletins. One wall was a large window that faced out onto the airplane parking ramp. The two Concordes sat beyond the partially shaded ramp in the harsh sunlight.

On the other side of a glass partition in the Operations Room was the Dispatcher's Office with its teletypes and weather maps.

On the far end of the long table, in the Operations Room, sat the flight crew of El Al Concorde 01. There was Asher Avidar, the pilot, a hot-headed Sabra whom Becker considered much too young and impulsive to fly anything but the military fighters that he had formerly flown. Next to Avidar was Zevi Hirsch, the First Officer, who Becker thought would have been the pilot except for his age, and Leo Sharett, the flight engineer, who also counterbalanced Avidar's brashness.

51

Avidar was speaking to his crew, and Becker strained to hear and understand the rapid Hebrew. This was a very carefully planned flight, and Becker wanted none of Avidar's lone-eagle antics. He had to follow Avidar on the long trip, and fuel was a critical factor at Mach 2.2.

Becker checked the most recent weather maps for the flight while he listened to Avidar briefing his crew.

Becker was an exceptionally tall man, and for that reason he had been denied fighter training in the American Air Force when he entered service at the start of the Korean War. In ROTC, they had failed to point this height limit out to him, and he found himself ferrying troops on C-54 transports. Eventually, he partially satisfied his lust for combat by joining the Strategic Air Command. He waited patiently through the 1950s for his chance to vaporize the city in Russia that was assigned to him, though he knew he would not see the destruction. The city was Minsk, or, more precisely, the airport to the northwest of the city. His bomb would have also incinerated Teddy Laskov's hometown of Zaslavl, which was a coincidence that neither man had become aware of during their chance conversations.

Eventually, with age, his aggressive tendencies waned, and with the coming of the Intercontinental Ballistic Missiles, he found himself in cargo planes again. Then came Vietnam and he was put back into a B-52. He vaporized lots of people there, but he had long since lost the appetite for it. During the 1967 War, he volunteered for the re-supply flights to Israel. His enlistment ran out on his last flight to Lod, at the same time that his twenty-year marriage did, so he stayed and married the Israeli Air Force girl who always gave him a hard time about the shipment manifests.

The Israeli Air Force did not have nor need anything like the huge long-range bombers he knew so well, and there were only a few C-130 military transports in the Hel Avir, the Air Corps. But he really didn't want to go back into the military, anyway. He just wanted to fly. Eventually, he landed a job flying El Al DC-4 cargo planes.

In the U.S. Air Force, he had logged thousands of hours of heavy jet flying. He had also been checked out on the American FB-111 supersonic bomber and thus was one of the few men in Israel who knew how to fly big planes at supersonic speeds. When El Al bought the Concordes, Becker went to Toulouse for training. Now he was going to fly the single most important flight in his career, and he meant to make certain that it went well.

Becker glanced into the Dispatch Room as the door from the corridor swung open. He could see Generals Talman and Laskov enter. They spoke with the personnel for a few minutes, then came through the connecting door.

Everyone in the Operations Room, all reserve officers in the Hel Avir, stood.

Talman and Laskov smiled and motioned for everyone to be seated. Talman spoke. "Good afternoon. Well, we have just come from a security meeting and I want to tell you all that everything looks fine. But for added security, we are going to advance your takeoff time to three-thirty. In addition, you are not flying over the Med to Madrid, but instead you will go up the Italian boot and head for Orly to refuel. We have permission to fly supersonic over Italy and France. Everything, including new flight plans, maps, and weather charts, is taken care of. No one will deplane at Orly. Same procedure as the Madrid plan." He looked at each man. "Gentlemen," he paused, looking for the right words as he stroked his clipped mustache, then said only, "have a good flight. *Shalom*." He turned and walked back to the Dispatch Room.

Teddy Laskov sat on the table. "All right. We have a minute for a last bit of coordinating. I'll monitor you on Air Traffic Control and on the company frequency the whole time I'm with you. But if we want to speak to each other, we must do so on my tactical frequency, channel 31. That is your 134.725. If, for some reason, I believe that the frequency is no longer secure—of if you do—say the words, 'My number three fuel tank indicator has become inop,' and we will all meet on the alternate tactical which will be channel 27, your 129.475. Clear? All right. I'll stay with you until you get to 19,000 meters and Mach 2.2. Maybe I'll hang around if my fuel is good. You'll be all right after that. Are there any questions?"

Avidar stood up. "Let me lay it on the line, General. Who's got tactical control of this flight? I mean, I'm the flight leader of these two Concordes and you're in charge of your people and you outrank me in the Hel Avir—but this is a civilian flight. Let's say we're attacked. Let's say I want to take evasive action, but you want us to hold a steady course so you know where we are. Who's the boss?"

Laskov regarded Avidar for a long time. Whatever else people thought of the young pilot, at least he didn't waste time beating around the bush. Also, he had no qualms about verbalizing the unthinkable. Laskov nodded. "All right. Fair question, Asher. Let me repeat what you've already been told. We foresee no trouble. But if... if we are attacked, you will follow the rules for heavy bomber missions. Since Israel has no heavy bombers, let me acquaint you with those rules. They are simple. The first rule is you hold course until you get instructions from the fighter escort leader—me—to take individual evasive action or for everyone to change course, speed, or altitude. For rule number two, see rule number one. Does that answer your question?"

"No." He sat down and looked away.

Laskov tried a conciliatory tone. "Look, Asher, flying escort is always a pain in the ass for everyone. We don't have these long-range escort situations in Israel, so it's new to you—but in a war I was in a thousand years ago, it was proved time and again that the sheep have to stay with the flock and listen to the sheep dogs, or else the wolves get them. No matter how many sheep in the flock seem to be getting picked off by the wolves, I assure you, it is worse trying to go it alone. Now, the analogy is not exact, but you get the message." He tried a fatherly look, but Avidar was having no part of it. Laskov shrugged and turned toward Becker. "David? Anything on your mind?"

"No, General. I think that wraps it up, except for the call signs on the tactical frequencies.

Laskov stood up. "Right. I am the Angel Gabriel plus my tail number, which is 32. My squadron is Gabriel with their tail numbers. You, David, are the Wings of Emmanuel. Asher, you are the Kosher Clipper. Well, anyway, it will be Emmanuel and Clipper on the air." Laskov looked at his watch. It was just two P.M. "One more thing. In addition to the regular peace mission delegates who appear on your passenger manifest, you might get a few extra VIP's. There will be an American on board, too. John McClure. Some sort of embassy man going home on leave. Tell your Chief Stewards to expect an addendum to the manifest."

Becker flipped through his clipboard and found the manifest. "There's another compatriot of mine coming, too, General. Tom Richardson, the air attaché. You must know him. He has some business in New York."

Laskov paused. That must have been a last minute development. Laskov knew it meant something, but he didn't know what. Maybe just a friendly gesture. He nodded. "He's sort of a professional acquaintance—a friend when he's not trying to tell us our business. If he doesn't like the kosher food, kick his ass out over Rome. Avidar, if he's on your flight, don't try to argue politics or religion with him. He has neither."

Becker smiled. "He asked to be on my ship. I'll take good care of him."

"Do that," said Laskov, absently. He walked toward the connecting door to the Dispatch Room where he could see Talman talking to the Chief Dispatcher. He turned around and faced the men who had all stood up again. "David. You said he *picked* your ship?"

Yes, sir." Becker handed Laskov the manifest.

Laskov looked at it. Next to Richardson's name, which was penned in at the bottom, were the numbers "02." He knew the combined manifest showed neither plane nor seat selection at this point. Plane selection was a state security matter and would be decided at the last moment. Seat selection was to be left to the individual delegates so that they could group into committees and get some work accomplished on the flight. Laskov wondered why Richardson requested a specific plane since he didn't know if any friends or acquaintances would be on that plane. Why not wait until he saw how the delegation broke up? Both planes would only be a little over half full. Maybe he wanted to fly with Becker. He looked up. "Did he know you were flying 02?"

"I think so. I guess he figured he could sit in the jump seat and chat on the way over. He doesn't speak Hebrew that well."

"I guess so. All right, men. Have a good flight. See you at about 5,000 meters. *Shalom.*"

The VIP lounge, down the corridor from both the Operations Room and Hausner's office, was crowded with about a hundred people. The drapes had been drawn to help the air conditioners, but the lounge was still warm. The darkness, however, gave an illusion of coolness. Every minute or so, someone would part the drapes a bit and look at the two Concordes, standing by themselves and ringed by soldiers.

Yaakov Leiber, the Chief Steward on Becker's aircraft, walked into the VIP lounge. Little Yaakov Leiber, as almost everyone called him, was very nervous. He wished someone else were briefing the passengers on this flight. He was used to giving his little speech in the VIP lounge, but this group was different. He recognized many of the faces and names.

In addition to the twenty Peace Delegates, there was an unusually large support group of aides, research assistants, secretaries, interpreters, and security people. The lounge was quite smoky, Leiber noticed, and the bar was, as usual, empty.

Yaakov Leiber cleared his throat. "Ladies and gentlemen. Ladies and gentlemen." He raised his hands.

The room became quiet in stages. Heads turned. They noticed the small man in the oversized white uniform, who wore bifocals so thick that his eyes looked like oysters.

Leiber put his back to the bar. "Good afternoon. I am Yaakov Leiber, Chief Steward on El Al Concorde 02."

"I'm glad he's not our pilot," observed a man in the back. A few people laughed.

Leiber smiled. "Actually, I used to be a pilot, but once I forgot to bring a telephone book to sit on and I crashed into a hangar."

There was laughter and even some applause.

Leiber stepped closer to the crowd. "I just want to acquaint you with some things." He spoke about seat selection and the new boarding time for several minutes. "Are there any questions?"

The mission's Orthodox Rabbi, Chaim Levin, stood up. "You understand, young man, that today is Friday—and you are confirming for me that we are going all the way to New York and will still land before the Sabbath begins. Is that correct?"

Leiber held back a smile. It was a peculiarity of El Al flights that there was hardly ever a rabbi on board, even during the week. Some rabbis wouldn't fly on the national carrier because the El Al crews had all broken the Sabbath at one time or another. They flew on foreign carriers because it didn't matter to them if those crews broke the Jewish Sabbath or their own Sabbath. The two rabbis on the peace mission, one Orthodox and one Conservative, had decided to make an exception and fly El Al for the appearance of national unity. "Yes, sir," said Leiber. "Sundown in New York is at 6:08. But we'll be going a little faster than the sun, so we'll land at about two P.M. New York time."

Rabbi Levin looked at Leiber for a long time.

"In other words, Rabbi, we'll land one and a half hours before the time we started," said Leiber. "You see—"

"All right, I understand. I've flown before, you know." He regarded Leiber, the Sabbath-breaker, with a stare he usually reserved for pork-eating Jews. "If we land one second after sundown, you'll hear from me."

There were some laughs, and Leiber smiled, too. "Yes, sir." He looked around. "The meal is pot roast and potato kugel. There will be several movies available if anyone is interested. My wife, Marcia, who is much prettier than I am, will be one of your stewardesses on 01." Like many couples who flew often, it was the Leibers' policy never to fly together. They had children. He hoped no one would infer anything from this arrangement. "Are there any questions? Then, thank you for flying El Al—although I don't see how you could have done otherwise." He held up both hands. *"Shalom."*

Captain David Becker completed his line check of Concorde 02. He stood in the shadow cast by the drooping nose cone. A squad of infantry stood around the aircraft and glanced at him from time to time. An El Al security man, Nathan Brin, approached. "How's it going, Captain?"

"Good."

"We're satisfied. You?"

Becker looked at the plane and nodded.

"See you upstairs." He walked off.

"Right." Becker stared up at the craft. This white bird of peace looked like anything but a dove. It was a sea bird of some sort, Becker decided. A stork. A gull, maybe. It sat up high on long legs because of the high-pitch angles you had to use with a delta wing. If it weren't for the long legs, it would drag its ass on the ground when it took off or landed. God made sea birds with long legs for that reason. The technicians at British Aircraft Corporation and Aérospatiale had come to the same design conclusion. So had the Russians when they built their supersonic airliner, the TU-144. Brilliant. It was good to see that God was right, thought Becker.

Then there was the nose cone. The beak. It stayed down during takeoffs and landings, like a bird's, for better visibility. It was raised during flight for aerodynamic streamlining. The British, French, Russians, and God—not necessarily in that order—had independently found the same solutions for the problems of flight. Aircraft had started off as rigid structures and their performance was, therefore, confined to rigid parameters. Birds were flexible. Man started making aircraft flexible with movable ailerons and rudders. Then came the retractable landing gear. Then the swing-wing jets. Now there were noses that dropped.

Becker looked down the length of the plane. It was not really a big aircraft. The fuselage was fifty-two meters long and the delta span was only twenty-seven meters. Gross weight with passengers and fuel was 181,000 kilograms, about half as heavy as a 747.

One of the last refuges of the old English system of weights and measures was to be found in the cockpit of an airplane. All the world's pilots had been trained in both the English language and the English system of measurement. It was a world standard, and it was not easy or necessarily desirable to do away with it altogether. Most instruments were dual marked and pilots shifted easily from one system to the other in their conversations. Next to the Mach air speed indicator in the Concorde was the quaint knot indicator. To Becker, it was a fixed point in a rapidly changing world. He pictured an old square-rigger bravely trying to make five knots against a headwind.

Becker began a final walk-around. He stood under the portside delta and looked up. No, it wasn't built to move a couple of hundred tourist-class passengers around. It was built to move seventy VIP types faster than sound to their peace missions, oil deals, and foreign lovers. An elitist aircraft. Maximum speed was Mach 2.2—about 2,300 kilometers per hour, depending on air temperature. The speed of a high-velocity rifle bullet. And at that speed, flying was an aeronautical limbo where many of the standard rules of flight were suddenly changed.

There were a lot of peculiar demands at supersonic speeds. There was the big drag factor at the speed of sound. The delta wings helped there, but deltas had poor handling characteristics. They yawed and rolled and the plane became difficult to fly. Delta wings had to approach at high angles of attack, and if you got on the back of a thrust curve, air speed management was very difficult.

If you lost an engine in a regular commercial jet, nobody got too upset. Lose one at supersonic, and you could easily lose control of the aircraft. Then the plane would flip-flop and disintegrate.

The skin temperature could get up to 127 degrees Celsius at Mach 2. If you got above that, the plane wouldn't immediately become unglued, but you would weaken the structure and you might pay for it on another flight.

At Mach 2.2, you have to think fast. If you wanted to level at 19,000 meters, for instance, you had to start doing it at 17,000. If you corrected too fast, you'd have the passengers hanging from the baggage racks.

Then there was the thing that had bothered Becker from the first day he had taken the Concorde up to 19,000 meters. It was the problem of sudden cabin decompression of the type that can happen if you are hit by a missile, or if there is a small explosion on board, or if somone shatters a window with a bullet. In a conventional commercial aircraft, flying at relatively low altitudes, about 9,000 meters, cabin decompression was not a critical problem. The crew and passengers put on overhead oxygen masks and breathed until the aircraft descended into thicker air. But at 19,000 meters, you needed a pressure suit to make breathing possible, even with an oxygen mask. Lacking pressure suits, you had only a few seconds of usable consciousness to get down to where you could breathe with a mask. There was no way to do that at 19,000 meters. You put the mask on, but you blacked out anyway. The on-board computer sensed the problem and brought the plane down nicely, but by the time you got down to where you could breathe with the mask, you woke up with brain damage.

Becker had a recurring nightmare: a brain-damaged crew coming out of their blackout—sucking on the oxygen masks, if they still had the wits to grasp that simple necessity—trying to figure out what all those funny lights and dials in front of them were, while their eyes rolled and saliva drooled from their mouths. And all the while, the computerized Concorde held steady, waiting for a human hand to guide it. Neanderthals in Apollo. And in the back, seventy idiot passengers, in different states of mental debility, making faces and grunting. In his nightmare, the Concorde always landed and there were people on the observation deck waving. Won't they be surprised when their friends and lovers come down the stairway? Becker closed his eyes. He knew it wasn't possible to bring it home from those altitudes after more than thirty seconds' loss of oxygen. It was only an irrational nightmare. Yet he kept feeding a simple command to the conditioned-response part of his brain: *If nothing in the cockpit looks familiar anymore, touch nothing.* The fuel would eventually run out.

Becker wiped the sweat from his face and looked out across the field. Fifty meters away, Avidar was looking up at Concorde 01. He wondered if Avidar had nightmares like that. No, not Avidar.

5

Miriam Bernstein sat in the VIP lounge, drinking coffee with Abdel Jabari. Jabari saw the other Arab delegate, Ibrahim Ali Arif, come in, and he excused himself to speak with him.

Bernstein saw Jacob Hausner sitting alone at the bar. She stood up, hesitated, then walked toward him, but he didn't turn. "Hello."

He glanced over his shoulder. "Oh. Hello."

"Look, I'm sorry if I made some people uncomfortable before."

He stirred his drink. "No problem."

"Good." She stood silent for a moment. "So. Are you coming with us?"

"Yes. I just heard from the PM. I'll be on 02."

She didn't know why that should be good news, but she felt a sudden surge of something like well-being before she could sublimate it. "I'll be on 02 also."

There was silence.

She forced a smile and spoke again. "Do you want to change planes—or do you want me to?"

61

Why did he feel so strongly that the remark was made to provoke him? Hausner had a gut feeling that she was repressing some strong emotion and that it had to do with him. He looked at her. There was absolutely nothing in that face to reinforce his feeling, but it persisted. "I don't think that's necessary."

She looked into the mirror. Her eyes drifted between her own expression and Hausner's as if to make sure no one's mask had slipped. Her expression was all right, but she could see the tension in her body. She realized that she was almost standing on tiptoes. He always had that effect on her. She relaxed and smiled neutrally. "Nice of you to come. Can they spare you here?"

Hausner drained off his drink. "They had their choice of keeping me here for a crucifixion or letting me go and hoping I'd go down with the ship if something happened."

She nodded. "So you chose to go down with the ship."

"They chose. I think they'd like to see me go down and the ship stay up. But you can't have it both ways. Buy you a drink?"

"I don't drink, but—"

"Nobody in this goddamn country drinks. When I was in the RAF, nobody flew unless they were blind." He pushed his glass toward the bartender. "Well, see you on board."

She looked at him. "Right." She turned and walked off.

Matti Yadin came up to the bar when he saw Miriam Bernstein move away. "That bitch giving you a hard time again, boss?"

Hausner thought a moment. "I'm not sure."

Teddy Laskov walked into the VIP lounge, looking for Tom Richardson. He had some things to ask him. He was also supposed to give Richardson the alternate tactical frequency that he and Talman had just selected. He considered calling it into the American air attaché office, then thought better of it. For a reason that he couldn't fully explain, even to himself, he decided to keep the information from Richardson. If the Americans really needed it when he got airborne, they could get it from Talman at The Citadel.

Laskov saw Hausner and Miriam speaking at the bar. He saw her turn and walk off. If he didn't know that they detested each other, he'd have to say that she looked hurt by something Hausner had said. He was surprised at the jealousy he suddenly

the occupied West Bank. He didn't trust telephones, but he had little choice and less time.

Jacob Hausner stuck his head into his outer office. "Did the French SDECE call back yet?"

His secretary looked up. "No, sir."

"Damn it." He looked past her toward the window. The buses were almost filled. "I have to go. I'll probably fly back with one of the Concordes tomorrow. If anything important comes in while I'm in the air, call The Citadel and they'll put it out to the Concorde over the scrambler. I'll be on 02."

"Have a good trip. *Shalom.*"

"That's what this whole goddamned thing is all about. *Shalom.*" He walked quickly down the corridor.

Matti Yadin looked out the window of the bus that was going to Concorde 01. He saw Hausner hurrying by below him. "Boss!"

Hausner turned and looked up.

Yadin leaned out. "If you don't want to ride with—you know—I'll switch with you."

Hausner shook his head. "No. That's all right. It's a short flight. Besides, it's bad luck to change flight plans." Hausner hesitated. He was still worried about something, but he didn't know exactly what. He'd developed a bad feeling about this flight, all of a sudden, and he could see in Yadin's eyes the same uneasiness. "Remember Ahmed Rish?"

"How could I forget him?" said Yadin.

"How, indeed? Just think about him and radio me if anything clicks. See you in New York."

Yadin forced a smile. *"Shalom."*

Hausner reached up and grasped Yadin's hand, something he had never done before.

Chaim Mazar stood in the control tower of Lod Airport with a pair of field glasses to his eyes and looked out at the buses approaching the Concordes. A glint of light from the roof of an apartment house in Lod caught his eye and he swung the glasses toward it. He grabbed for his field radio as he kept his glasses trained on the building. He spoke rapidly into the mouthpiece. "Chopper Control, this is Tower. I saw a flash of light in quadrant thirty-six. Pink stucco apartment house. The roof. Get somebody up there."

Mazar watched as a Huey helicopter descended on the roof of the house within seconds. Four of his men jumped out with Uzi sub-machine guns before the helicopter landed. A few seconds later, a voice sounding out of breath came over his squawk box. "Tower, this is Huey seven-six."

"Roger, seven-six. Go ahead."

"No problem, Tower. Young lady with a sun reflector." There was a pause. The voice sounded amused. "Sunbathing in the nude, over."

Mazar wiped the beads of sweat from his forehead and sipped from a glass of water. "Roger. There's supposed to be an air-raid drill in progress. Get her something to wear and place her under arrest. Keep her in the chopper until you can turn her over to the police."

There was a long pause. "Roger, Tower."

"Tower, out. Mazar slumped back into his chair next to the air traffic controllers. He turned to one of them. "That was a little rough, but it's been a long day."

Sabah Khabbani lay at the crest of the hill and looked hard through his field glasses. The day was bright and clear, but nine kilometers was a long distance. It appeared as though the Concordes were loading. This was as good a time as any. He raised his hand. He waited until a helicopter passed over.

Behind him, in the pines, the three men knelt a few meters from each other. They each held a mortar round poised above the small hole in the ground. Next to each man were three additional rounds. They would each alternate two high explosive rounds with two white phosphorus rounds. The twelve rounds should blanket the entire area between the terminal and the Concordes. If one piece of incendiary matter punctured a fuel tank—and there was no reason why that shouldn't happen—no one would survive.

They watched Khabbani closely. His arm dropped. With shaking hands, each of the men let his round slip out of his fingers. They could hear the rounds slide down the long tubes. They covered their ears and opened their mouths to equalize the pressure of the impending blast.

Brigadier General Itzhak Talman stood in the Operations Room of The Citadel and looked at the radar and visual displays from the E-2D Hawkeye. He could see Laskov's twelve F-14's as they maintained a holding pattern off the coast. Indicated on other display consoles were scheduled airline traffic, a few private planes, and ships at sea. A computer flashed several messages on various cathode ray tubes and printed readout tapes. Talman turned up the volume on one of the radios and heard Laskov speaking to his squadron. So far, so good. He poured a cup of coffee and took a seat. All he could do now was wait.

Captain Ephraim Dinitz waited until he heard the dull thud of the rounds striking the firing pins at the bottom of the tubes. That should satisfy the military court if there should be a question later concerning intent. He and his men ran out from the trees and rocks. Dinitz shouted in Arabic. "I arrest you under military law! Place your hands on your heads!"

The three Palestinian gunners stared alternately between the silent mortars and the closing Israeli soldiers. Slowly they rose to their feet and placed their hands over their heads.

Khabbani looked back over his shoulder and watched the whole scene unfold thirty yards behind him. His heart sank and a lump came to his throat. He saw himself in Ramla Prison staring vacantly through the barbed wire for the rest of his life. He would never touch his wife or children again except through that barbed wire. He got up and leaped from the crest of the hill. A soldier shouted. Khabbani ran stumbling over the rocks, the wildflowers going by in a blur beneath his feet. Another shout. The staccato report of an automatic weapon. He saw the bullets hit around him and it was several seconds before he realized he was no longer running but lying on the ground, bleeding quickly to death.

Chaim Mazar picked up his field radio. From the tower he could see the hills where it had all happened. He nodded. "All right, Dinitz. Interrogate them immediately and call me back." He sat back in his chair. He realized that those miserable Palestinian peasants knew less than he did about who was behind that pathetic attempt. Those mortars had been spotted ten years before and left there to see who would come around and use them. The detonators had been removed from the rounds, of course. He'd had the spot watched more closely than usual for the last week. In addition, someone had tipped off one of his agents earlier in the day.

It was such a clumsy and foolhardy attempt that Mazar couldn't believe it was meant to succeed. All he could think of was the English expression, red herring, or the Hebrew words, sacrificial lamb. That's what those unfortunate Palestinians were. Everyone was supposed to relax their guard now that the great terrorist attempt had been foiled. But Mazar didn't see it that way. If this *was* a red herring, then that could only mean that there must still be an undiscovered plot to sabotage this peace mission. But for the life of him, he couldn't imagine what it could be. He shrugged.

The Air Traffic Controller looked up from his radio. "Concordes are ready to roll, sir."

Mazar nodded. "Then give them clearance and get them the hell out of here."

The flight crew of El Al Concorde 01 completed their checklist. The Concorde rolled out to the edge of the 4,000-meter runway. The radio crackled. "Cleared for takeoff, El Al 01 and 02. Two-minute intervals. Have a good flight."

"Roger." Avidar pushed the throttles forward and the big bird screamed down the runway.

David Becker sat in the left-hand seat and watched through the windshield as 01 lifted gently from the earth. He turned to Moses Hess. "Count off two minutes for me, will you, Moses?"

Hess nodded and looked at his watch.

Behind them, on the port side of the flight deck, Peter Kahn sat in front of the flight engineer's long control console. The lights and gauge needles were all steady. He turned to Becker and said in English, "All systems still go."

Becker smiled at the English idiom. "Right."

"One minute."

In the cabin, the passengers and flight attendants spoke in low voices. The manifest showed ten delegates and twenty-five support personnel. There were also two stewards and two stewardesses, plus the Chief Steward, Leiber. They sat in a group, immediately behind the flight deck. Scattered among the passengers were six security men with Jacob Hausner in charge. Tom Richardson had found a seat next to John McClure and was carrying on a one-sided conversation with the taciturn man. General Dobkin was reviewing the notes he would present to the Pentagon brass. Isaac Burg sat by himself, reading a newspaper and sucking on his unlit pipe. Rabbi Levin had picked a religious argument with one of the delegates. The total manifest, with crew and flight attendants, numbered fifty-five. The extra baggage allowance had placed the Concorde very near its maximum takeoff weight, especially considering the existing air temperature.

Miriam Bernstein sat behind Abdel Jabari, who was sitting with Ibrahim Arif, the other Arab delegate on board 02. A nervous young Security man, Moshe Kaplan, stared at the two black and white checked *kheffiyahs* from across the aisle.

The cabin was small and the seats were two-and-two across, with barely enough room for a man 180 centimeters tall to stand. But the French had designed the interior with their typical flair for such things, and the appearance was one of luxury. The lack of space didn't matter much because the Concorde was seldom airborne for more than three and a half hours at a time.

A final touch to the decor was provided by a large wall-mounted Machmeter which let the passengers see the aircraft's speed. The red neon lights read MACH 0.00.

In the cockpit, Hess looked up from his watch. "Let's go."

Becker released the brakes and pushed the throttles forward. The aircraft began to move. It gathered speed as it rolled down the long, shimmering runway.

"Sixty knots," Hess announced.

"Everything's good," called Kahn, as he ran his eyes across his panel.

Becker called for the afterburners.

The flight engineer moved his poised fingers to ignite the two outboard afterburners, then the inboard pair. "Afterburners— all four," he called. Simultaneously, there was the sound and sensation of a two-phased thud that made the procedural words unnecessary.

"One hundred knots," said Hess.

The runway was already half-gone and the undulating waves of heat that rose from the blacktop made the remaining length look even shorter than it was. Pools of mirage water formed and evaporated with increasing speed. Becker blinked his eyes. *Concentrate on the instruments. Forget the visual.* But he kept staring out of the windshield. The heat waves mesmerized him. They also distorted and foreshortened the end of the runway. It looked as though they had run out of blacktop. He felt beads of sweat form on his forehead and hoped Hess wouldn't notice. He pulled his eyes away from the sunlit windshield and stared down at the console. The air-speed needles were moving rapidly now. His left hand squeezed more tightly on the wheel as he nudged the column slightly rearward. Involuntarily, the muscles in his buttocks tightened and he rose imperceptibly from his seat. *Up, up, damn you!*

"V-one," said Hess. His monotone masked the significance of his words as the air speed rose through 165 knots. They were now committed to fly, even if a blinking light or flickering gauge indicated otherwise. "V-R," he said.

Becker began tugging more earnestly on the control column. The nose tire of the aircraft lifted off the hot blacktop. The Concorde's wings canted themselves skyward, biting into the air flow at a greater angle. They were eating up runway at the rate of 75 meters a second, and for a brief moment Becker felt his nerve slip away. All the old demons of doubt that had haunted him since flight school began chattering in his brain. *Why should it fly? There's something wrong, Becker, and no one has the balls to speak up. Why is the gauge over there flickering? Who built this plane, anyway? Why do you think you can fly it? Becker! Abort! Abort! You're going to die, Becker! Abort!* He felt his neck muscles tighten and his hands and knees were shaking.

"V-two," said Hess with what Becker thought was just a hint of anxiety in his voice.

Becker felt the wheel loosen in his hand as the main wheels rose from the runway. He looked down at the console. Two hundred twenty knots on the air-speed gauge. The rates of climb were moving rapidly and the altimeter was winding even faster. Becker held the airplane by the palm and fingers of one hand. He smiled and cleared his throat. "Gear up." The sound of his own voice, steady and even, seemed to chase the perverse imps from the cockpit. But he heard their familiar parting promise. *We'll kill you next time, Becker.* He waited out a sequence of lights, then said, almost too loudly, "Climb power." He lowered his voice. "After-takeoff check." He banked the aircraft slightly to follow in the flight path of his sister ship. "And when you get a chance, Peter, ring the cabin for some coffee." He settled back and his muscles loosened. There would be a landing and takeoff at Orly and then again in New York. He would be back at Lod within twenty-four hours. Then he would resign, effective immediately. He knew it had been coming for a long time. He felt it every time his sphincter tightened on takeoff and landing, every time his loins went loose when he hit an insignificant air pocket, every time he had to wipe the sweat from his palms when he flew through a line of thunderstorms. But it was all right. It had happened to better pilots than himself. The trick was to look it in the eye and say, "I quit."

"Quit what?" asked Hess.

Becker swung his head and stared at him. "What?"

"Quit what? What do you quit?" Hess was going over his checklist as he spoke.

"Quit . . . drinking coffee. Coffee. I forgot. I don't want any."

Hess looked up from his checklist and stared at him. His eyes met Becker's and they both knew. "Right." He called out to Kahn. "Only two coffees, Peter."

Becker wiped his palms and face openly. It was all right now. Hess had a right to know. He lit a cigarette and inhaled deeply.

6

Concorde 02 began its steep, graceful climb. The long landing gear assemblies had already risen into the belly of the craft. Hess pulled another hydraulic lever, retracting the flaps and activating the droop-nose to its streamlined position. The flight deck became very still, with only the murmur of electronic noises in the background. Becker banked the craft 30 degrees and put it on a due west heading over Tel Aviv. The dual altimeter indicated 6,000 feet and 1,800 meters and air speed was 300 knots. He lit another cigarette. So far, so good.

Becker rolled the Concorde out of its turn and sat back in his seat. His eyes took in all the instruments. The Concorde was an electronically controlled aircraft, somewhat like a space capsule. When the wheel or rudder pedals were moved, for instance, an electrical signal was sent to the hydraulic control activators. It was this, rather than cables or rods, that moved the exterior control surfaces. The computer would feed artificial stability and resistance back into the controls for the pilot to sense. Without this pressure to fly against, there would be nothing for the pilot to feel as he moved his controls. Pilots weren't used to that, and so the men at Aérospatiale and British Aircraft Corporation told the computer to put artificial resistance into the control movement. It was all psychological, reflected Becker, and all very strange and becoming stranger with each new technological breakthrough. Long before he felt the fear, he had felt this alienation in the cockpit. Yes, it was time to let the next generation take the controls.

They were over the beach outside of Tel Aviv. Becker took a pair of field glasses out of his flight kit and scanned the ground. Normally, the beach would be covered with thousands of bikinis, but the air-raid drill had sent everyone indoors. Becker saw his home in Herzlya, as he always did. He saw the empty chaise longue in his yard and wondered if his wife knew that he was part of the reason that everyone had to interrupt their first spring sunbathing. Ahead of him stretched the dark blue Mediterranean and a cloudless azure sky. Becker eased back on the wheel a bit more and gave it more throttle. The aircraft picked up speed and altitude.

Ahead, he could see 01. The Concorde might be an ungainly looking bird on the ground, but in flight it was the technocrats' contribution to pure aesthetics. It was a beautiful aircraft to fly, also, but Becker always had the uneasy feeling that the computers would fail him someday. Not really fail so much as betray. Those marvelous computers that could do a thousand things simultaneously; things that three human crewmen could not do, no matter how hard they worked. Those computers would lure him up to 60,000 feet—19,000 meters—and Mach 2.2 one day, and then quit. A message would flash on the cathode tube: *Fly It Yourself, Stupid.* Becker forced a smile. Two more takeoffs and three more landings.

He hit the transmit button on his console and spoke into his headset microphone. "Air Traffic Control, this is El Al Concorde 02. Over."

"Go ahead, 02."

"Roger. Company aircraft in sight. I'm at 380 knots, indicated. Accelerating to point-eight-zero, Mach."

"Roger. Level off at 5,000 meters."

"Roger." He pushed the selector switch to the company frequency. "El Al 01, 02 here. I have you dead ahead. I'm about eight kilometers back. I'll close to about five and get a little below you. Don't stop short."

Avidar acknowledged. They spoke for a while and coordinated speeds.

Becker got to 5,000 meters and closed in on Avidar. He spoke to Air Traffic Control. "El Al 01 and 02 in formation. Holding at 5,000 and now at point-eight-six, Mach. Waiting for unrestricted clearance to 19,000."

"Roger. Stand by. There's an Air Iran 747 at flight level six-zero-zero. Maintain 5,000 meters.

Avidar called Becker on the company frequency. "El Al 02, this is 01. See if you can raise our sheep dog. I don't see him."

Becker switched to 134.725. "Gabriel 32, this is Emmanuel."

Teddy Laskov had been monitoring the El Al and ATC frequencies and switched to channel 31 to meet Becker. "Emmanuel, this is Gabriel 32. I hear you fine. I can see you and Clipper at my eleven o'clock low position. Leave one radio on this frequency."

"Roger, Gabriel. When we get unrestricted clearance from ATC, we're climbing to 19,000 and accelerating to Mach 2.0 on a heading of 280 degrees."

"Roger. I'll be with you. So far, so good."

"So far. I'm going back to company frequency. The copilot will monitor you."

"Roger—break—Hawkeye, this is Gabriel 32. How are your blips?"

The E-2D Hawkeye was almost five kilometers directly above the Concordes and F-14's. It had been simultaneously monitoring all three frequencies. The Air Control officer on board picked up his radiophone. "I have you all spotted and plotted, Gabriel. Do you see a craft approaching from a bearing of 183 degrees? About 180 kilometers distance from you? Not a scheduled airliner."

Laskov spoke into the intercom to his flight officer behind him. "See anything, Dan?"

Daniel Lavon looked down at the combined television and cathode ray tube. "Possible. Something's at the southwest edge of our radar. A little over 160 kilometers and approaching our intended flight path at right angles."

The E-2D Hawkeye, with a crew of five and a cabin full of the latest electronic equipment, was in a better position to detect and classify aircraft than the F-14's. The flight technician on the Hawkeye spoke to Laskov. "We're trying to contact this craft, but we can't raise him."

Laskov acknowledged.

The E-2D command information controller got on the phone. "Gabriel, the unidentified craft is moving at approximately 960 kilometers per. He is on a course and speed that will bring him across your intended flight path, but at 1,800 meters below you and Emmanuel and Clipper at your present altitude."

"Roger, Hawkeye. Contact the son-of-a-bitch and tell him to change course and speed, or both."

"Roger, Gabriel. We're trying."

Laskov considered. In about a minute, the unidentified craft would be within the 160 kilometer range of his Phoenix. If this craft had a pair of Russian Acrid missiles, it couldn't engage the Concordes until it was within 130 kilometers. This 30-kilometer difference in range between the Russian Acrid and the American Phoenix was all the difference in the world. It was the reason why the F-14 was king of the sky. It had a longer reach. It was like two knights, one with an eight-foot lance and one with a ten-foot lance. In a few more minutes, though, Laskov would no longer have the advantage. "Hawkeye, I'm going to engage this target before he gets within 130 kilometers, unless you can identify him or he identifies himself."

General Talman rose from his chair in the Operations Room of The Citadel. He grabbed a radiophone and cut in quickly. "Gabriel, this is Operation Control. Look—you're the man on the spot. You have to make the decision, but for God's sake, consider all the angles." He paused. "I'm behind you, whatever happens. Out." Talman didn't want to tie up the radio net with a political discourse. It had all been argued long before this. He stood and watched the converging radar blips on his screen as he stroked his mustache.

What Laskov had wanted from Talman was an unequivocal order to fire at will. But he knew better.

"Gabriel, this is Hawkeye. Listen. He is not—repeat, not—military because we do not pick up any sophisticated radar emissions from him."

"Then what the hell goes 960 kilometers per hour?"

"Probably a civilian jet, Gabriel. Wait one. I have something coming in on the radio."

Laskov shouted into his microphone. "I don't give a good goddamn if it *is* a civilian jet. A civilian jet can be fitted to fire an air-to-air missile, too. Get me an I.D. on this guy, or he goes!"

There was no reply.

Danny Lavon spoke into the intercom. "General, this is a lot of bullshit. I'll take the responsibility. You can say I panicked and pushed a button. I've got him locked in now on—"

Laskov broke squelch on the intercom and cut him off with an electronic whine. When he released the squelch button, Lavon had stopped speaking. "Listen, son. You just follow orders. No more of that."

The Air Control officer came back on the air. "Gabriel, this is Hawkeye. Listen, we just spoke to Air Traffic Control in Cyprus. Our unidentified is a civilian Lear jet, Model 23, with a French registration. He filed a flight plan from Cairo to Cyprus to Istanbul to Athens. Six on board. Businessmen. French passports. We have their frequency and call sign. Trying to raise them now."

Laskov wasn't satisfied. "Trying to? Bullshit. They are within 130 kilometers and you have their frequency and you have the best radios made. What's the problem, Hawkeye?"

"It might be theirs, Gabriel."

"Roger." Laskov let out a long breath. He looked out of his plexiglas windshield. The two Concordes floated below him like paper airplanes. "Clipper and Emmanuel, this is Gabriel. Are you monitoring all of this?"

Becker and Avidar responded affirmatively.

"All right. Tell ATC you want to change to a due north heading and you want permission to climb unrestricted to 19,000, *now*."

Becker and Avidar acknowledged. Avidar called Air Traffic Control and he received word that there was a TWA 747 and a Lufthansa 707 above them and that they would have to wait five minutes for their unrestricted climbs.

Laskov didn't think he wanted to wait even five seconds. He spoke to Lavon on the intercom. He didn't speak to the rest of the squadron on the radio because he didn't want Talman or anyone else to hear. "Arm the Phoenix, Daniel. Prepare to engage the target." He thought of Miriam Bernstein. *Even if you should see Satan himself on your radar screen ... don't shoot him out of the sky with one of your missiles.* And Richardson. *Listen, don't get trigger-happy up there. We don't want any incidents.* Then, he thought of what lousy jobs he had had all his adult life. "Hawkeye, this guy has about sixty seconds to live unless he speaks to us."

It was the Hawkeye pilot who responded this time. "Roger,

Gabriel. We can't raise him. I'm sorry. I can't do anything else. I
understand your position. Do what you think is best."

"Thanks."

Talman broke into the net. "I'm with you, Gabriel." Talman
was beginning to think there was something wrong. If the Lear's
radios were bad, he would probably have headed back and
landed at Alexandria. If they weren't bad, why wasn't he
answering? He'd heard the Hawkeye call on Lear's frequency.
Hawkeye had spoken to the Lear in French, then English, the
international language of flight, and finally, even Arabic.
Talman spoke into the radio. "It stinks, Gabriel."

"Right." Laskov spoke into the intercom. "Where is he?"

Lavon glanced at his radar. "About sixty-five kilometers—
and climbing."

It was already too late for the Phoenix. "Arm the Sparrow
and . . . engage the target."

"Right, General." Lavon moved an electrical switch and then
slid back a small plate on the armament console. Under the
panel was a red button. He put his finger on it.

"Gabriel, this is Emmanuel." Becker's voice sounded
strained.

Laskov held up his hand to stop Lavon and acknowledged
Becker.

"The Lear is calling us on company frequency."

"Roger." Laskov quickly turned up the radio on the El Al
frequency. Lavon called the rest of the squadron and instructed
them to monitor also.

"El Al Concorde 01 and 02. This is Lear number five-four.
Can you hear me?"

Laskov felt a cold chill run down his spine. The accent was
unmistakably Arabic.

Becker and Avidar acknowledged.

The Lear spoke again. The voice was slow and precise.
"Listen very carefully. We have important information for you."

Becker and Avidar again acknowledged. There was an
apprehensive tone in their voices.

Laskov realized that the Lear was stalling for time. He spoke
to Lavon. "When I raise my hand, fire."

Talman stood motionless in the center of the Operations
Room. He stared in disbelief at the radio speakers. He
whispered to himself, "What the hell . . . ?"

The Lear came back on the air. The voice spoke very quickly

now. "In the tail of each Concorde is a radio-controlled bomb. *Radio-controlled*," he stressed. "Have no doubts about that. It was placed in 01 at St. Nazaire and in 02 at Toulouse. It is attached to the number eleven fuel tank. I know you have an escort of twelve F-14's. If I see the smoke trail of their missiles coming at me, or if I see the flash of their cannon, I will push the buttons on my radio detonator and blow you both up. Do you understand that? Are the F-14's monitoring? Do *you* understand that?"

Laskov refused to acknowledge. He sat and stared.

Avidar, his voice shaking with rage, shouted into the radio. "Bastard!"

Becker spoke evenly into his radio. "Roger." He pushed the PA button and spoke calmly. "Would Mr. Hausner, General Dobkin, and Mr. Burg come up to the flight deck, please?"

Laskov hung his head on his chest. He simply couldn't believe it. All that planning and all that security . . . He removed a pair of field glasses from an old leather case by his feet. He placed them in his lap and stared down at them. The glasses were the only thing besides his uniform that he had taken out of Russia. He raised them and looked out into the blue sky. He could see the green and white Lear 23 approaching now, trailing a long, thin line of exhaust from its two turbojet engines. He was close. In fact he was too close for the minimum 16-kilometer range of the Sparrow and too far for the maximum 8-kilometer range of the Sidewinder. The Lear turned 90 degrees and flew alongside Concorde 02. Laskov could see that a plexiglas observation bubble had been cut into the rear of the cabin roof. There appeared to be someone looking out of the bubble, and Laskov knew the man probably had field glasses trained on *him*. He lowered his glasses.

The Lear, either by luck or by design, stayed inside the 8-kilometer dead space between the Sparrow and the Sidewinder. That dead area had bothered a lot of Western military people, but it wasn't considered critical under most circumstances. In a conventional fight, Laskov would have just pulled up or held back until he could use the appropriate missile. But he was afraid to make any sudden maneuvers because he knew the Lear's observer was watching his squadron out of the rear bubble. He held his flight on a steady course. He spoke softly to Lavon. "Arm the Sidewinder, in case he gets in closer." But he knew it was no good. The Lear was holding too close to the Concordes even to consider missiles now.

The Lear made a small correction in course and positioned itself about 150 meters under Concorde 02 and just forward of 02's nose cone. From where Laskov was positioned, above the Concordes, he could barely see the Lear.

Talman sat slumped in his chair. The personnel in the Operations Room were completely still. Talman saw the blips of the Lear and 02 merge, and he knew Laskov was powerless to do anything with his missiles. The whole damned thing had happened so fast. He looked at the digital chronometer on the wall. From the time Laskov had seen the Lear on his radar to now had been less than ten minutes. Somehow, he had always known it would happen. All it took was one or two madmen. With modern technology, anything was possible. A single insignificant nobody could alter the destiny of nations. An atomic bomb planted in a city. A biological agent in a water supply. A bomb on a Concorde. How could you guard against something as preposterous as that?

Hausner, Dobkin, and Burg stood on the flight deck as Becker explained what had happened. Tom Richardson and John McClure had come into the cockpit, uninvited. They had seen the Lear approach and they knew something was wrong.

McClure slouched against the flight engineer's console, chewing on a wooden match. He was an extremely tall, thin man, who reminded some people of the unbearded Lincoln. A Midwestern twang completed the image. "Should've taken Pan Am home," was all he said when Becker had announced that they were being hijacked.

Burg turned to Becker. "Do you want me to get the Foreign Minister up here?"

Becker shook his head. "I don't need any politicians to give me advice. We will make the decisions right here. Just stand by." From time to time, Becker could see the nose of the Lear poke out from under his long nose cone. It reminded him of what an infantryman had told him once in Vietnam, of how the VC liked to get very close during a firefight so the Americans couldn't use their heavy weapons without killing their own men. He knew Laskov was in a bind. They were *all* in a bind.

Hausner seemed far away, almost disinterested. Then an odd

smile came to his face. He remembered now what it was he couldn't remember before. Rish had been seen in those small villages of France. The names of the villages had meant nothing to him then. Israel had had no Concordes at the time. Now he realized that those obscure French villages were near St. Nazaire and Toulouse. He remembered his words at the security meeting. *We've had those birds on the line for thirteen months. Since the time that we got them, they have never left the sight of my security people.* That was the weak link. *Since the time we got them....* St. Nazaire. Toulouse. What an idiot he had been.

Becker looked over his shoulder and addressed Hausner. "Could it be possible? A bomb, I mean?"

Hausner nodded. "Sorry."

Becker began to say something, then turned away.

The radio crackled, again, and Matti Yadin's voice came over the speaker. He knew Hausner would be in the cockpit, too "You were right, boss."

Hausner didn't respond.

Becker called Laskov on the tactical frequency. "What do we do, Gabriel?"

"Stand by." Laskov could see the nose of the Lear poke out from the nose of Concorde 02. He looked at the cannon button on his control wheel. In his mind's eye, he fired and sent sixty 20mm cannon rounds a second streaking over the Concorde's windshield and into the cockpit of the Lear. But he didn't have any 20mm cannon rounds, and even if he did, he wondered if he would risk it. There was a chance before, but not now. He thought of Richardson and Bernstein and felt betrayed. Betrayed by well-intentioned people, but betrayed nonetheless. He pushed the cannon button. The combat camera rolled and made a movie for the men at The Citadel. Laskov pounded on the console in front of him.

The voice from the Lear came back on the Concordes' radios. "I assume your escort is monitoring El Al frequencies. Listen closely, fighter pilots. I have an observer looking back at you. If I see the flash of your cannon, I will push the button and blow up the Concordes. I do not mind dying. Now, listen to me—you must break off and return to base. You can do nothing here. If you do not turn away in sixty seconds, I will blow up the lead Concorde to make you understand that I am very serious."

Avidar called Laskov on the tactical frequency. "All right, sheep dog. What now?"

Laskov considered opening his throttles, ducking under the Concorde and ramming the Lear. They might not expect to see a quarter-million kilograms of airplane screaming down on them. They might panic. But even if he hit them, the mid-air explosion would certainly damage Concorde 02.

Avidar's voice came back on the radio. "What do we *do*, Gabriel?"

The Lear came over the El Al frequency. "Concordes. I think you are talking to your escort. It will do no good. They have fifteen seconds to turn back."

Laskov wondered if the Lear would blow up the Concordes as soon as his F-14's moved off. Or did the Lear—whoever the hell he was—want hostages? He switched to the El Al frequency and spoke to the Lear for the first time. "Learn this is the fighter escort. We are not—repeat, not—leaving. We are all returning to Lod. You must follow and land with us. If you do not comply, I am going to—" suddenly, the term "engage you" was not appropriate. "I will kill you," he said softly.

The voice from Lear laughed back at him. "Your time is up. Go away or these deaths will be on *your* head."

Hausner knew who was speaking to them. He put his hand on Becker's shoulder. "I know that man. Tell Laskov his name is Ahmed Rish. He will do whatever he says he will do. Tell Laskov to go away."

Richardson nodded. "They can't mean to harm us or they would already have detonated the bombs. This is a hijacking, pure and simple. Ask them what they want." He paused. "And tell Teddy Laskov that I'm sorry about the 20mm."

Becker turned to Dobkin and Burg. They nodded. He passed Hausner's and Richardson's messages to Laskov, then called the Lear. "Who are you people and what do you propose?"

Rish's voice came back loud and clear. "It doesn't matter who we are. Our purpose is to escort you somewhere and to hold you as hostages until it suits our purposes to let you go. No one will be harmed if you do exactly as we say. However, if your escort doesn't leave in one second, I am blowing up the lead aircraft."

Danny Lavon spoke on the intercom. "If he has a bomb on board, there is nothing we can do here anymore, General. Maybe we can pull off and engage him from 160 kilometers out."

Laskov called Talman. "Control, I'm coming home."

Talman spoke quietly into the radio. "My fault, Gabriel."

Laskov knew it wasn't anyone's fault, but there would be a lot of people saying that in the coming days.

The Lear came over the radio again. It was the same voice, Laskov noticed—Rish—but this time it had lost some of its composure. Rish was screaming to him to turn back. Laskov ignored the voice for a few seconds and took stock of the situation. He wondered how the Lear could have filed a flight plan that would bring him so close in time and space to the Concordes. Especially since the Concordes' takeoff time had been moved up half an hour. He also had the distinct impression that the Lear was able to hear him on his tactical frequency. He spoke the words, "My number three fuel tank indicator has become inop," and the F-14's, plus the E-2D, Talman and the Concordes switched to the alternate tactical frequency. Laskov called Clipper and Emmanuel on the new frequency. He spoke quickly. "Listen. That son-of-a-bitch was monitoring the primary tactical frequency. I don't know how he got it and he may have this one, too. but I'm going to talk to you, anyway. We're not abandoning you. The E-2D will keep you spotted. We'll hang back a few hundred kilometers. Call me on this frequency and let me know what's happening. If the time comes when you decide to risk it, we'll charge in and let loose with Phoenix at 160 kilometers distance. There's a good chance they won't spot the vapor trail if they're not looking for it. Do you understand?"

Everyone acknowledged in turn.

Ahmed Rish screamed into his radio over the El Al frequency. "I know you are talking! Enough of this nonsense. Enough! Five seconds." He put his finger on a radio detonator button labeled 01. "One, two, three—"

Laskov spoke on the El Al frequency. "Good luck." He gave the order and the flight of F-14's banked steeply to the right. They completed a 180-degree turn and were out of sight in seconds.

Becker couldn't see them go, but suddenly he felt very alone.

7

Avidar didn't like the way the situation was being handled. He had been slowly increasing his speed and he estimated that he was at least ten kilometers ahead of the Lear and Concorde 02. How much range could a radio detonator have? Certainly not more than ten or twelve kilometers. He looked at his altimeter. He was slightly over the 5,000 meters assigned to them by Air Traffic Control.

Air Traffic Control had seen the Lear blip merge into the El Al 02 blip and had seen the flight of F-14's pull away, but had not monitored any of the conversation on the El Al frequency. Still, the controller knew something was wrong. He called the Concordes. "If everything is all right with you, you can proceed unrestricted to 19,000 meters. Sorry about the delay."

Rish, who was apparently also monitoring ATC, told them to acknowledge.

Avidar and Becker acknowledged. Avidar looked at his speed indicator. He was flying at an air speed of 1,000 kilometers per hour. If he gave it full throttle and kicked in his afterburners, he could be at Mach 1 and at least three more kilometers away in less than fifteen seconds.

Rish's voice came back on the radio. "Very good. Very sensible. Now, you will leave your navigation lights on and follow me. I am going to proceed on a magnetic heading of 160 degrees, at 300 knots indicated air speed. El Al 02 will follow directly behind me. El Al 01 will fall in behind 02. We are going to descend to 150 meters. Do you understand?"

Becker and Avidar acknowledged.

The Lear began its bank to the left and Becker prepared to follow.

Asher Avidar hit the afterburner switches. He then began pushing forward on the throttles as fast as the engines could take the fuel. He aimed for the center of a cumulus cloud to his front. The four huge Rolls Royce Olympus engines generated 70,000 kilograms of thrust and the Concorde streaked off.

Zevi Hirsch screamed at Avidar. "What the hell—"

Leo Sharett turned from the flight panel. "Asher, *don't*—"

Matti Yadin, who was still on the flight deck, grabbed Avidar's arm, but Avidar pushed him away. Yadin pulled his Smith & Wesson .22 and put it to Avidar's head. Avidar quickly brushed it away as though it were an annoying insect.

In Concorde 02, Moses Hess grabbed Becker's arm and pointed out the windshield. Becker watched as Avidar's aircraft disappeared inside the cloud.

In the passenger cabin of 02, everyone knew by now that something was wrong. Yaakov Leiber leaned over an empty seat and watched the plane carrying his wife disappear off the starboard side. Then he saw it reappear again out of the cloud.

One of the six Arabs in the Lear shouted to Ahmed Rish. Rish watched as the Concorde streaked 'off. He grabbed the radio detonator from the seat. There were two red buttons. Without looking, he put his finger on the one marked 02 and began to press, then realized his mistake. He slid his finger onto the button marked 01.

Concorde 01 sailed upward. The number eleven fuel tank automatically began to fill with kerosene as the computer determined that the center of gravity should be more aft for the speed and angle at which the aircraft was moving. In the passenger cabin, the large digital Machmeter read MACH 0.97 and the seat belt lights came on. The passengers looked concerned when the G forces pushed them into their seats as the aircraft banked. The Machmeter read MACH 0.98, then MACH 0.99.

Ahmed Rish pressed the button. A radio signal, keyed only to the receiver on El Al 01, flashed across the sky.

The radio detonator barely received the signal at eleven kilometers. The receiver transformed the weak signal into an impulse that closed the switch and allowed the current from the tail navigation lights to flow down the wire into the detonator embedded in the plastic explosive.

The Machmeter read MACH 1.00 and the Concorde broke through the sound barrier. The tail tank, with 4,000 liters of fuel in it, exploded and blew out the pressure bulkhead. A tongue of flame shot into the passenger cabin as the Machmeter flashed MACH 1.10. The oxygen masks dropped from their overhead compartments as the cabin lost pressure.

Asher Avidar knew he had lost his gamble even before he heard the explosion. The controls suddenly went loose in his hands and the lights on the flight console began blinking on one by one. The door between the cabin and the cockpit blew open and the crew could hear screams behind them. Hirsch turned around and looked down the length of the aircraft. He saw daylight. All he could say was, "Oh, God!" Behind him, Matti Yadin lay on the floor, bleeding from where the door had hit him in the face. Avidar turned to Zevi Hirsch. He screamed above the sounds of rushing air. "It's better this way! You can't give in to these bastards!" Hirsch stared at him.

Becker watched as his sister ship fought to maintain control. With a cool detachment, he realized from the billowing orange flames that the bomb *was* on the number eleven trim tank—a place that was inaccessible from the cabin. He assumed that the bomb itself was a small device—the bigger danger was the exploding fuel. He spoke softly to Peter Kahn. "Override the computer and pump number eleven dry." He turned to Hess. "Get on the PA and tell the passengers to move toward the front of the cabin." He wondered if the pressure bulkhead would contain the blast. He hoped he wouldn't have to find out.

Becker stared out of the windshield, mesmerized by the sight. Hausner, Dobkin, Burg, Richardson, and McClure crowded behind the flight seats riveted to the same scene.

El Al 01 began its incredibly beautiful dance of death. The delta wing aircraft yawed and rolled like a graceful glider. Becker knew what Avidar was going through as he pulled and pushed at levers, throttles, switches, and buttons. But it was a losing battle.

Concorde 02 closed in on its dying sister. Becker called for field glasses and watched. A small propeller dropped out of the belly of the fiery bird and Becker knew that at least the computer was still functioning. Like the damaged brain of a big animal, it realized that it was in danger, but unlike the brain of a human, it didn't comprehend that the wound was mortal, and it continued to struggle to stay alive. The computer had sensed the electrical and hydraulic failures, so the propeller—really a windmill—was released to turn an electric generator and hydraulic pump. The French had called this feature *très pratique*, but the British called it desperate. Becker knew that, in this case, the new power source would only make the problem worse. Broken electrical wires would come alive and hydraulic fluid would squirt from open pipes. Damaged nerve endings and severed arteries. But the mechanical heart still beat and the mechanical brain still functioned. Becker was sickened by the picture in his field glasses. He put the glasses down and rubbed his eyes and temples.

In the dying Concorde, Avidar and Hirsch were reacting out of pure instinct—responding to each new crisis—because there was nothing else to do in the pilots' seats of a doomed aircraft. Leo Sharett sat calmly in front of his flight engineer's console, performing his job of systems management long after there were any systems left to manage. His instrument lights began to blink off one by one. The Concorde began to tumble tail over nose, like a silver leaf in a gentle wind. Then, mercifully, it disintegrated in a flash.

Becker could hear the anguished cries coming from the cabin behind him. Above all the voices, he could hear little Yaakov Leiber screaming for his wife.

Becker could see some debris floating toward them, and he made a violent maneuver to avoid it. The five men standing on the flight deck fell to the floor. In the cabin, passengers were thrown from their seats. Peter Kahn belatedly put the seat belt sign on and spoke into the PA microphone. "Everyone stay seated. Everything is going to be all right." He quickly explained the situation.

Everyone got up from the floor of the flight deck. Hausner looked at Dobkin and Burg. They turned away from him.

The Lear jet came back on the radio. It was Rish's voice

again. It sounded high-pitched and near hysteria. "They forced me to do that!" he screamed. "Now, you listen to me! You will follow me and do exactly as I say, or you will share their fate!"

Hausner grabbed the microphone from the console. "Rish, you bastard! This is Jacob Hausner. You goddamned murderer. When we get down, I'm going to kill you, you son-of-a-bitch!" He began a long string of peculiarly Middle Eastern invectives in Arabic.

Rish's voice came back over the speaker after Hausner finished. Rish was clearly fighting for self-control. He spoke slowly. "Mr. Hausner, when we get down, the first thing I am going to do is kill *you*."

Hausner began another tirade in Arabic, but Becker grabbed the microphone from him. He switched to the alternate tactical frequency to call Laskov, but all he could hear was a high-pitched, whining sound.

Rish's voice came over the company frequency, barely audible above the radio interference. "You are no longer able to communicate with your escort or with me. Just follow." The high-pitched whine became louder.

Becker turned down the volume on all the radios. "He jammed us. Probably has a broad band transmitter on board." He looked around the flight deck. "I think he holds all the cards." He looked at Burg, who was the senior man present.

Burg nodded. He looked very pale. Everyone did. The image of El Al Concorde 01 hurtling nose over tail had made them literally sick. Burg nodded again. "Let me go and speak to the Foreign Minister and the passengers. They should all know what is happening." His voice was choked. "Excuse me." He walked out of the cockpit.

Tom Richardson cleared his throat. "Maybe we should just let the pilots fly now."

Dobkin nodded. "Yes. We must speak to each of the passengers and tell them what we expect of them when we land. We must start organizing a psychological defense against the pressures of being held hostage. That is very important."

"Yes," said Hausner. "Good thinking. I imagine it's going to be a long captivity. At least for you."

Richardson spoke up. "Don't worry about that, Mr. Hausner. That son-of-a-bitch was just trying to scare you."

McClure spoke for the first time since he'd announced his preference for Pan Am. "Don't be an ass, Richardson. That man just murdered fifty people. If he said he was going to kill Hausner, he'll kill him."

"Thanks," said Hausner.

"Got to tell it like it is," said McClure. He produced another wooden match from his inexhaustible supply and put it between his lips.

The Concorde followed the Lear southward. Hausner stayed on the flight deck while the others went back intø the passenger cabin. He couldn't face anyone just then. He felt totally responsible, although in fact it was Talman's word of caution and Laskov's minute of indecision that had put the situation beyond saving. It was Laskov's mellowing with age, his sharp military instincts blunted by the promise of peace. It was the anxious voices from the Hawkeye assuring Laskov that the Lear was only a group of businessmen. It was bad French security at the assembly plants. And it was everything else that had happened over the past several thousand years, all coming together under those cloudless skies, thousands of feet above the Mediterranean. But Hausner dismissed these thoughts. He was wishing that he had switched planes with Matti Yadin.

8

General Talman sat in his chair in the middle of the Operations Room at The Citadel. He avoided the eyes of his staff and the technicians around him. They had all seen Concorde 01 disintegrate on the radar screen.

Talman could still see the Lear and Concorde 02. They were approaching the Sinai coast. As long as the E-2D picture remained clear, he could track them. But, eventually, he knew the Lear would force the Concorde to fly at treetop level, and they might be lost in the ground clutter over the land.

Teddy Laskov's flight officer, Danny Lavon, watching on his radar, came to the same conclusion. "They're losing altitude fast, General. We're not going to be able to see them over the Sinai."

Laskov didn't answer.

Talman picked up a scrambler phone and called out every squadron he had. He ordered them to violate Egyptian air space

89

and fly a course that might enable them to spot the Concorde on their radar. One of Talman's aides placed a call to Cairo. The Egyptians would cooperate, but it would be a while before the call could be routed through.

David Becker followed the Lear as it dropped to within a hundred meters of the water. The Sinai coast came up very quickly and they shot over it. Becker lowered the nose cone for better visibility. The desert streaked by below in a blur and the big Concorde bumped wildly in the updrafts. Becker didn't know what Rish had in mind, but he had no doubt that the man was insane. The Lear was relatively easy to maneuver through this low-level turbulence, but it was all Becker could do to keep the huge Concorde straight and level. His indicated air speed was only 250 knots, and he knew that if he went much slower he would stall. Yet the Lear seemed oblivious to his problems. It alternately gained and lost speed as he followed it. The small craft made slight corrections in heading and altitude that were difficult for Becker to follow. He concluded that the Lear's pilot wasn't much of a flyer. Becker had already extended the initial flaps for an extra margin, and he was constantly adjusting the power. Kahn pumped fuel into the number ten midsection tank in an attempt to help keep the aircraft in the proper balance.

Becker's mouth was dry and his heart thumped as he grasped the controls. On his right was the Suez Canal, below him the Mitla Pass. To his front, the ground was rising quickly. His sea level altimeter read 330 meters or 1,100 feet, but he could see that he was still no more than the same 100 meters above the ground that he had been when he crossed the coast. In the distance, he could make out the hazy brown peaks of the southern Sinai range that he knew were 800 meters high. He wondered if the pilot of the Lear understood that they should begin climbing now if they didn't want to meet those mountains.

Hess looked at Becker. "Dave, this guy is going to kill us."

Becker turned up the radio volume, but all he could hear was the jamming device. "Son-of-a-bitch!" He screamed into his headset. "Rish! Lear! We can't hold this altitude! You are the dumbest son-of-a-bitch who ever sat in a cockpit!" The jamming continued and he turned down the volume. "Bastard!"

Peter Kahn called out from the flight engineer's station. "Captain, we're burning 585 kilograms of fuel a minute."

"How much flight time do we have left?"

"Less than two and a half hours."

Becker looked at his watch. It was a little after four. If Rish was planning another Entebbe, they would never make it. "Well, if I knew where the bastard was leading us, I'd know if we should be scared shitless or not." Becker cursed his bad luck. Two more takeoffs and three more landings. Now, it looked like only one more landing and no more takeoffs.

The Lear banked sharply to the left and Becker followed, but his turn was not as steep as the Lear's and he wound up to the right of it when he came out of the turn. He quickly corrected and got behind it again. He asked Kahn to pass him the field glasses. He looked at the Lear, which was now about a thousand meters to the front of him. He could see the plexiglas observation bubble clearly. Someone was staring back at him with field glasses. "Sons-of-bitches." He put down the glasses. He waited for the imps in his head to start laughing at him. But they were not there. He breathed deeply. He felt strangely calm, more assured than he had felt in a very long time. Was this the way it was when you knew it was all over?

Hausner, who had been sitting quietly in the jump seat, looked up. "What are the chances of our people tracking us on radar?"

Hess looked over his shoulder. "At this altitude, over land, just about zero. The E-2D has a computer thing of some kind that can sort out images from the ground clutter, but we've been over Egypt for some time and I don't think he would follow."

"How about the Egyptians?"

Hess shook his head. "They have those Barlock ground radar units from the Russians that can see low-flying craft, but we're behind Henry Kissinger's line now. The Egyptian radar is pointed east toward the Israeli lines. We've probably been spotted visually from the ground, but by the time the Egyptians figure out what the hell is going on we'll be over the Red Sea if we hold this course. They can't help us, anyway, even if they wanted to. Right?"

"I was thinking of Laskov's offer to send a missile out," said Hausner. "Would we go for that if he still has us on his radar?"

Becker spoke as he held the plane steady. "*If* he has us on his radar, and *if* we're still airborne after dusk, I might consider it. This time of day, it's not too hard to see a missile's vapor trail. Electronic detonator signals go faster than missiles." Becker worked the rudder pedals as the Concorde's tail yawed left and right. "But we're damn close to the Lear. On a radar screen we look very, very close. It would have to be one hell of a shot to hit him instead of us."

Hausner stood up. "I'm going to take a look at that pressure bulkhead."

"Go ahead," said Becker. "But I've already thought of that. There's no way to get back there from here—as you know. But you're welcome to climb out on the tail if you'd like." Becker regretted the remark immediately, but his nerves were becoming more frayed with each minute of flight.

Hausner walked out of the cockpit. He began the long walk down the aisle. No one spoke to him. Little Yaakov Leiber stared at him through tear-filled eyes. The men who had been at the security meeting turned away from him.

Miriam Bernstein touched his arm as he went by, but he ignored it. He tapped two of his men on the shoulder as he walked by, and they got up and followed him.

Hausner entered the rear galley and walked through it into the small baggage compartment where the crew and flight attendants kept their luggage. There were also passengers' jackets and coats on hangers along the wall. He flung aside the clothing and stared at the pressure bulkhead.

Talman listened as each of his ten squadrons over the Sinai reported in to the Operations Room. No visual sighting. No radar sightings. Laskov reported last. "I'm coming into Eilat to refuel. I want fuelers waiting for us on the strip. When I get up again, I'm not coming back down until I find them. I want you to get American tankers on station to refuel us in mid-air next time. I'm going to fly over every inch of this area until I find them. The pilots and flight officers will take turns sleeping and flying."

Talman shook his head. "Wait one, Gabriel." He looked at his illuminated situation map. With every minute that passed, the extent of the air space in which the Concorde could conceivably be increased geometrically. He looked at the concentric circles on his map that encompassed the last spot where they were sighted, over the coast. They had been flying for a half an hour since they were last seen, at a speed of about 500 kilometers per hour. They could have headed off in any direction after that. The radius of the last concentric circle was 250 kilometers, if he assumed that last speed. He punched the information into a computer and read the digital display. The air space to be searched was already 196,350 square kilometers, without taking into account altitudes from 150 meters up to 8 kilometers. Every minute of flight time would increase the number of square kilometers and cubic kilometers. He pushed his radio button. "Gabriel, they could be heading for Lod, for all we know. Come home. We'll know where they are soon enough. We've violated enough foreign air space for one day. So far, the Egyptians have been very patient. But now they want us out. They promised to send aircraft up to look. Don't push, Gabriel. That's what the hijackers want and that's what we're trying to avoid. Come back to the barn, old man." He paused. "That's an order."

Laskov gave a crisp acknowledgment.

Talman sighed and called in the rest of his squadrons. What he didn't say over the unsecured air waves was that American satellites were already trying to spot the Concorde. Also, American Lockheed SR-71 reconnaissance craft, successors to the U-2, were already in the troposphere, flying at Mach 3, photographing the entire Sinai Peninsula. The satellite and SR-71 information would take days to be interpreted. It was a long shot, but it was better than doing nothing. Talman suspected, also, that Russian satellites and Mandrakes were doing the same thing. He wondered if the Russians would give Tel Aviv a call if they had any luck. His last ace in the hole was electronic eavesdropping. The powerful electronic ears of both the American National Security Agency and Israeli Intelligence might eventually vector in on the sound of the broad bank jamming device. In almost every country of the world, men and women, paid agents, sat in the upper levels of their houses and took shifts listening and recording every radio transmission that was broadcast in their vicinity. Eventually, one of these people might pick up the sound of the airborne broad band transmitter that they were instructed to listen for. But Talman knew that the Lear, so close to the Concorde, would be transmitting a very weak signal. The chances of picking it up were small, though not impossible.

Talman was satisfied that he had done everything that could be done, for the moment. He picked up the telephone and called the Prime Minister. He gave a situation report, then turned in his resignation. He hung up before he received a reply. He got up from his chair, walked over to his Deputy Chief of Operations, General Hur, and spoke to him for a moment. Then he took his hat and walked out of the Operations Room. Everyone watched quietly as the door shut behind him.

The Concorde climbed in slow stages over the mountains of the Sinai. Becker could see that the Lear wanted to keep within 150 meters of the ground, but the sudden rises and falls in the land made for a sickening roller coaster ride. Several of the passengers were already ill.

Mount Sinai rose up in front of them and the Lear skipped over the top with barely fifty meters to spare. Becker pushed forward on the throttles and cleared the peak. His ground altimeter bounced wildly between fifty and a hundred meters as the huge delta wings were buffeted by updrafts. He'd had enough. He pushed the throttles forward again and began to climb over the Lear. The Lear suddenly accelerated and rose up directly in front of him. Becker chopped back on the throttles and the Concorde shuddered as it approached a stall. He quickly moved the throttles forward once more until he got well above stall speed, then held it steady.

"That was too close," commented Hess. His voice was a little shaky. "I guess he means for us to follow, no matter how hard we have to work at it. He must know what a terrific pilot you are, Dave."

Becker wiped the cold sweat from his forehead. The Lear descended to its previous altitude and reduced its speed again, and again Becker fell in behind him. He felt like an obedient child following a truant officer to some undisclosed place of punishment, and the feeling was humiliating. He knew that Rish was prepared to cause a mid-air collision if things didn't go exactly his way. Becker's hands shook from rage more than from fear.

Hausner's men were stripping away the plastic laminate from the steel bulkhead with their commando knives. Hausner watched as the steel wall was revealed, piece by piece. There was no possible way to get through it. "Any good ideas?"

One of his men, Nathan Brin, steadied himself on the bouncing floor and looked up. "How about a desperate idea?"

"Let's hear it."

The young man rose and spoke quickly. "We can take the powder from our rounds and a container from the galley and make a shapecharge, put an electric wire to it, and blow a hole in the bulkhead. With a few coat hangers and a flashlight we can snag the wire that leads to the bomb and pull it off."

Hausner turned to the other man, Moshe Kaplan. "Kaplan, is this the kind of man I'm hiring these days?"

Brin turned red. "What's wrong with that idea?" he demanded.

"It's dangerous. And what makes you think there is a wire instead of a battery?"

Brin thought. "There must be an aircraft power source to the radio receiver and to the detonator. *Something* detonated the bomb on 01 and it wasn't a battery planted over a year ago."

Hausner nodded. "All right, if it is a wire, then it must be connected to something with a constant and stable voltage. Something like the tail navigation light." He thought a moment, then rushed out of the baggage room and back up the aisle toward the flight deck.

Becker turned around as he heard Hausner enter the cockpit. "Any luck?"

"Listen, the power source for this radio and detonator might be the tail navigation light. Turn it off."

Becker considered. He remembered that Rish had made a point of telling them to leave their navigation lights on. All aircraft always flew with them on, anyway. Why emphasize it? "There are other power sources back there. All the hydraulics in the tail are also electrically activated and monitored, including my tail bumper wheel and the rudder. I can certainly shut off the tail navigation light and I can even cut off the power to my tail bumper wheel, but I can't shut off the rudder. I need it to fly."

Kahn spoke up from the flight engineer console. "I thought of all that, too. There's a good chance that the power source *is* the tail navigation light. But any radio-controlled bomb would have a battery back-up, and the battery would get a steady trickle charge from one of those sources in the tail. Even if it's been in place for years, the radio battery is fully charged every time we start our engines. But I may be wrong. I can shut off the tail navigation light and bumper wheel assembly, and we can fly away from here. Maybe we'll be blown up. Maybe we won't. Anybody want to try it?"

Nobody did.

Hausner sat in the jump seat and lit a cigarette. The momentary elation was gone. "Maybe we could lift a section of the cabin floor and then we could also lift the armor mesh and insulation and stamp through the aluminum roof of the baggage compartment. In the baggage compartment it might be easier to get through the bulkhead into the tail."

Becker shook his head again. He didn't like people making holes in his plane and burrowing around in it. "You know the baggage compartment is pressurized. The bulkhead down there is just as thick as the one in the cabin. Even if you could get through—I don't want any holes. No going through floors. I can't risk it. Too many wires."

Hausner stood up and forced a smile. "Then I don't suppose you'd like the idea of using cartridge powder to blow a hole in the pressure bulkhead?"

Becker laughed in spite of the situation. "Sorry." He knew that Hausner was a man who would rather die than face life after what had happened here, unless he could personally save the situation. He also knew that Hausner was a man under sentence of death, anyway. He couldn't trust his judgment any longer. "Mr. Hausner, thank you for what you're trying to do. But as Captain of this aircraft I have to veto any ideas that would endanger this craft or the people on it. As long as we're airborne, I'm in command. Not you, not Burg, not the Foreign Minister. Me." He glanced over his shoulder. "Look, Jacob, I know what you're going through, but just take it easy. We have about two hours of flying time left. Let's see what happens."

Hausner nodded. "All right." He left the flight deck.

9

The Concorde passed over the tip of the Sinai Peninsula and headed toward the Red Sea, following the Lear as it banked sharply left and headed toward Saudi Arabia. Becker was curious about where they were going, but their destination seemed less and less important.

With its nose dropped and its tail and flaps down, the Concorde looked more than ever like a big, forlorn seabird that wanted to land on the water below, but, for some reason, could not. Becker looked at the whitecaps on the Red Sea until he was mesmerized by them.

"Coast coming up, Dave."

The Saudi Arabian shoreline slid by quickly. The ground was flat as far as he could see. He breathed a sigh of relief. "It won't be so bad now."

Hess glanced over at him. "That's one way of looking at it. Want me to take the wheel for a while?"

Becker looked at him. He wondered if Hess could fly a formation with the Concorde under these conditions. He decided to be blunt. "Can you fly it?"

"I can fly the crate it came in."

Becker smiled and let go of the controls. He fished in his pocket for a cigarette. He almost felt good. If ever a pilot had reason to lose his nerve, the flight over the Sinai was it. No matter what happened now, he was comforted by the thought that this, his last flight, had been his best.

The Lear picked up speed quickly and was doing about 800 kilometers per hour. Hess fought to keep the Concorde at 150 meters above the ground.

Ahead, Becker could see a few Bedouins on camels, staring at them. The sinking sun cast the huge delta shadow in front of the aircraft, over the Bedouins. The camels spooked and bolted clumsily as it passed. He drew on his cigarette. Now, over the flatlands, the flight looked safe enough, but Becker knew that, with the increased speed and the 150-meter altitude, any small dip in the nose would send them screaming into the ground before there was a chance to correct.

Peter Kahn looked up from his instruments. "One hour and fifty minutes fuel remaining, skipper."

Dobkin came onto the flight deck. He put this hand on Becker's shoulder. "How is it going?"

"All right. Any thoughts?"

Dobkin nodded. "We had a little meeting back there."

"And?"

"Well . . . we have concluded that they are very clever fellows. First of all, they didn't go into a long political harangue, like these chaps usually do, so we don't even know who they are, except that they're probably Palestinians. If Hausner hadn't recognized Rish's voice, we wouldn't even know that. This all makes it very hard for our intelligence people to begin work on this."

"Not good," said Becker.

"Not good at all," agreed Dobkin. "They further changed their *modus operandi* by jamming our radios. That can only mean that we're going to a secret destination. This time, there won't be a thousand newsmen at an international airport when we land. There will be no Entebbe rescue, either, because no one will know where we are. We're going to be held incommunicado."

Becker had come to similar conclusions. He had suspected he'd be putting the Concorde down in the desert, and now he was sure of it. He hoped, at least, it would be a hard-packed airstrip like Dawson's Field.

Dobkin seemed to be reading his thoughts. "Can you put it down anywhere?"

"Anywhere but a swine yard. No problem. Don't worry about it."

"I'll try not to."

Hausner took a seat next to Miriam Bernstein. They spoke quietly for a while. They both shared a sense of guilt that they were trying to relieve by speaking to each other. A steward, Daniel Jacoby, had taken charge of the flight attendants and was giving instructions to serve a meal and drinks, whether anyone wanted them or not. Hausner ordered a double Scotch. He stirred his drink. "I can't believe I could have overlooked that."

Miriam Bernstein took a sip from his drink. "They would have found another way to do it."

"Whatever way they found, I would have been responsible."

"I keep thinking about Teddy... General Laskov. He fell into the same trap we all did. I know he would have reacted differently if I hadn't..."

"I can't believe those sons-of-bitches really pulled this off."

"Jacob... I heard someone saying that this Rish knows you. He threatened—"

"I should have shot the son-of-a-bitch when I had him."

"Did he say, on the radio, that he was going—"

"Don't listen to rumors. There will be a lot of those in the days ahead."

She put her hand on his arm. "Remember when you asked me... if I would come out to your place..."

Hausner laughed. "Don't start saying things you'll be sorry for when we're back in Tel Aviv. I might hold you to it."

She smiled. "I never really understood you. I've always admired you... but you frighten people."

"I don't want any deathbed confessions. We are not quite ready for that yet."

"All right."

They spoke about other things. Dinner came, but neither of them could eat.

Abdel Majid Jabari spoke to Ibrahim Ali Arif, the other Arab delegate on board. He spoke in a rapid, soft, susurrant Arabic. "This is a tragedy beyond measure."

Arif ate rapidly as he spoke. "I feel very awkward at this

moment. I feel like Daniel in the lions' den."

Jabari watched as the portly man stuffed food into his mouth. "Don't always think of your own discomfort, my friend. This tragedy transcends that." He lit a cigarette. "I feel worse for the Jews who staked their reputations and careers on Arab goodwill."

"I still feel personally uncomfortable. And I don't believe in blood guilt. Uncomfortable, yes—guilty, no. Guilt is a Jewish emotion." He looked at Jabari's untouched tray. "Do you mind?" He placed it over his own tray.

Jabari sipped his arak. "Anyway, the lions' den is out *there*," he pointed in the direction of the Lear. "These are our countrymen in here. You must be able to look them in the eye—without discomfort. Have no doubts that we will share their fate."

Arif laughed between bites. "We should be so lucky, my friend. Even if *they* are eventually released, you know very well that *we* are marked for special attention. This is the lions' den and that is the lions' den. We are men who have no country, no people, no haven. We are doomed men. I think I could eat another meal. Steward!"

The Lear turned northward and the Concorde followed. They left Saudi Arabia and flew into Iraq. The sun was low on the horizon and there were long purple shadows over the land. Becker began to become more worried. "Flight time?"

"Half an hour," answered Kahn.

One of the things that had always fascinated Becker about the Middle East was the absence of any real dusk. One minute it was light, and the next it was dark. Landing on something other than an airfield in the daylight was bad; landing at night could be a disaster. "What's going to run out first, Peter?"

Kahn knew what he meant. He already had a chart book open. "Sun sets officially at 6:16 around here. End-of-evening nautical twilight is five minutes later. It is now 6:01. We have twenty minutes of usable light and twenty-nine minutes of fuel. Approximately."

Becker could see the moon above the darkening horizon in front of him. A few stars showed in the dark edge of night. To the north, out his left windshield, Polaris was rising. Below, the shadows became longer and changed from purple to black. The desert was incredibly beautiful, thought Becker.

Hess called out to him. "Look."

Becker looked out the front windshield. In the distance, the ground sloped downward and he could make out a strip of lush green land. A river wound its way through clusters of date palms. Beyond the river, which was almost below him now, he could see another large meandering river. The Tigris and Euphrates. Beyond the Tigris, the mountains of Iran rose up over a thousand meters. His altimeter showed that the land had dropped from 180 meters above sea level to nearly sea level. They were indicating nearly 300 meters above the ground now and the Lear made no move to descend to its previous 150 meters.

"This has to be the end of the line," said Hess.

Becker looked down at the land between the rivers. Mesopotamia. The Fertile Crescent. Cradle of civilization. After the expanse of stark brown desert, it was a relief to see it. He wondered if they might fly north to Baghdad. Subconsciously, he was looking for the vapor trail of Laskov's missile. He put out his cigarette and turned to Hess. "I'll take it from here."

The Lear began a wide left-hand circle and Becker followed. The Lear started to lose altitude and Becker knew they weren't going on to Baghdad.

Hess hit the seat-belt and smoking-light signals. He took the PA microphone. "We are making a landing approach. Please remain seated. No smoking."

"Tell them, thank you for flying El Al," said Becker.

"Not funny," said Kahn.

"Fuel?" said Becker.

"Technically empty," said Kahn.

"Never mind the technical." After all the computers and electronics there was still that other thing that fliers called by many names.

Kahn hesitated. "Maybe 2,000 kilograms."

Becker nodded. That was less than five minutes' flight time under good conditions. He could make a perfect landing in five minutes if they began soon. In a bad landing or an aborted landing that necessitated a turn-around, he wouldn't make it. He waited to hear the awful sound of silence as the engines flamed out one by one.

The Lear pulled out of the turn at a 90-degree angle to his circle and began heading due north on a straight descending flight path.

In the distance, Becker could see a straight road running north and south. "I think that's our landing field. He rolled out of his turn and fell in behind the Lear.

Hess extended the landing gear and put down the initial approach flaps. "I've seen better."

The sun was almost gone and the road was barely visible. On both sides of the road, Becker could make out low scrub bushes and uneven terrain. They began their final approach.

Dobkin and Hausner burst into the cabin. Dobkin shouted something to him.

Becker was angry. "Go back to your seats! I'm trying to land this damned thing."

They made no move to leave. "We've taken a vote," said Hausner.

"This is not the Knesset. Be quiet!"

Below, four pair of headlights came on, strung out on either side of the road and partially illuminating it. Someone was waving a high-powered light at what Becker assumed to be the intended threshold of the approach. The Lear flew over the threshold and Becker could see its flaps go down. Becker shook his head to clear the fatigue. He scanned his instruments. They were blurry. He looked up, out the windshield. The lights below bothered his eyes. He knew he could become quickly disoriented in this kind of situation. Pilots had been known to try to land upside down on the Milky Way when they were fatigued, and transferred their eyes from their instruments to visual contact. They could mistake the stars for landing beacons and rivers for runways. He rubbed his eyes.

Hausner stepped behind Becker. "The vote was unanimous. Otherwise we wouldn't consider it."

Becker eased off on the throttle and called to Hess for full flaps. He held the wheel in one hand and the throttles in the other. He tried to line the nose up between the headlights. He kept his eyes on the Lear's navigation lights. "What vote? What the hell are you talking about? I'm making a final approach on the most fucked-up runway I've ever landed at. What do you want?"

Hausner spoke quickly. "The bomb is no good on the ground. Becker! The most it will do is mangle the tail."

"Go on." Becker could see the Lear touch down and bounce. The Concorde passed over the threshold and Becker pulled off more power. The big aircraft began to settle to earth.

"We've voted to fight on the ground," said Hausner. "My men have some weapons. Can you put us down somewhere else?" Hausner was almost shouting.

Becker could feel the cushion of air forming below the big delta wings. He shouted back. "Why didn't you ask me two minutes ago? Trucks and men flashed by on both sides under the delta wings. The road was bad and the aircraft bounced dangerously. About two kilometers ahead, at the point where his rollout should end, was another group of vehicles with their headlights on.

To his left front was a high, gently rising hill that he knew must overlook the Euphrates. Hausner screamed something at him. Becker made a quick decision before he had time to think about it rationally. He pushed the throttles forward and the huge aircraft rose again. He pushed heavily against the control wheel and rudder pedals. The Concorde yawed to the left toward the Lear.

The Lear had taxied off the left side of the road and rested among the groups of vehicles that Becker had seen at the end of his intended rollout. Ahmed Rish watched from where he was standing on the wing of his Lear. At first, he thought that the Concorde had bounced badly and was skidding off the road. Then he noticed the position of the rudder and flaps. He dove into the Lear, shut off the jamming device, and screamed into the radio. "STOP! STOP!" He reached for the radio detonator, as the Concorde came hurtling directly at him, only a few meters from the ground.

The Concorde was doing 180 knots and its landing gear barely cleared the earth. The delta wing provided more of a cushion of air than a conventional straight wing could. Becker aimed at the rising terrain to his left. The low-volume squeal on the radio stopped, and he could hear Rish's voice screaming at him. In fact, he saw the Lear less than fifty meters in front of him, directly in his path. For a wild moment, Becker considered ramming the Lear, but he realized that killing Rish wouldn't save them and hitting the Lear might kill them all at that speed. He had to clear Rish's aircraft.

There was no possibility of using the throttle or afterburners now. If he did, the Concorde would rise, and when the tail went, they would all die. Or if the afterburners used the last of the fuel and the engines flamed out, they would die. He had to keep the aircraft down, but not so low that they would hit the Lear or any other ground obstruction. Becker held his breath as the Concorde shot over the Lear. The landing gear missed the Lear and the Concorde sailed on. Now the ruins of a wall rose up in front of him. He took a chance and pulled back gradually on the wheel. The nose lifted slightly. As he streaked over the wall, he felt the rear bumper wheel hit it. The Concorde shuddered. Becker pulled back on the wheel again, and the nose came up to meet the rising hill. He would have liked to vault over the river, but he knew he had about two seconds before Rish pushed the button.

The Lear bounced wildly against its tie-downs as the Concorde shot over. Swirling debris pummeled the small aircraft and the men and vehicles around it. A huge dust cloud rose up and blinded everyone on the ground. Rish fumbled for the radio detonator, found it, and felt for the buttons.

Becker snapped back the throttles. Rish was still screaming on the radio. The main landing gear touched the side of the hill as the Concorde's nose flared upward. Becker reversed the thrust of the engines. The rear bumper wheel hit and bounced. The nose fell and the nose landing gear hit the ground. The aircraft bounced violently, throwing the men standing behind Becker to the floor. The computerized wheel-braking system alternately applied and released pressure on the wheel brakes. Most of the tires blew out. Then the tail exploded.

Becker shut down all four engines. Hess pulled the fire-extinguishing lever. Kahn shut down all the systems. The Concorde rolled wildly up the incline, sucking debris into its engines with a sickening sound. The engines spooled down, and the only sound left was that of the remaining tires bumping over the rocky slope.

Becker felt the rudder pedals go slack even before he heard the explosion. He knew there were still fuel fumes in the number eleven tank, and he tried to imagine how bad the damage might be. He wondered if the bulkhead had held. A secondary explosion of a full fuel tank would completely destroy the aircraft. Without the tail and rudder, the aircraft was completely uncontrollable, even on the ground.

Suddenly, the front landing gear collapsed and everyone on the flight deck pitched forward violently. The nose plowed a deep furrow into the ground as the aircraft continued its rollout. Debris turned up by the nose cone began striking the windshield, causing spider-web cracks. Becker instinctively hit a hydraulic switch and the outer protective visor began rising into place over the windshield. He crouched down in his seat and looked up and out of the downward-sloped cockpit. A ruined structure loomed up a hundred yards ahead. Becker braced for the crash. Something flew up and punctured the windshield before the outer visor was fully raised in place. The glass slivers flew into the cockpit and slashed Becker's hand and face. He shouted, "Hold on!" The Concorde slowed, then came to a quiet halt some meters from the structure.

Becker looked up. "Everyone all right?" He looked to his right. Moses Hess lay slumped over the control column, blood pouring from his head. There was a huge hole in the windshield directly in front of him.

Becker shouted behind him. "If you're going to make a fight of it, get the hell out of the airplane!"

Peter Kahn got up and shouted into the cabin. "Evacuate! Flight attendants! Emergency evacuation!"

Yaakov Leiber had unfastened his seat belt even before the aircraft came to a halt. He ran to the forward port door, rotated the handle, and threw the door open. The opening door activated the pressure bottles and inflated the emergency chute tucked under the doorsill. Hausner's six men were the first ones out. The other two stewards were leading the passengers down the aisle toward the chute. The stewardesses opened the two emergency doors next to the seats over the wings. They led the passengers out onto the wings and down to the leading edge of the big deltas. People began jumping off the wings and sliding down the chutes.

Hausner picked himself up from the flight deck and half-ran, half-crawled to the starboard door on the flight deck. He opened it and jumped down before the chute inflated. He was barely on the ground before he started shouting orders to his men. "Down the slope! Move! The bastards will be coming up from the road! Over there! Get out a hundred meters!"

Dobkin followed Hausner out the door. He made a quick appraisal of their situation. They were on high ground, which was good. The area around the aircraft was flat and the ground fell away on all sides. To the east it sloped gently down to the road. To the west it fell off sharply down to the river. He could not see the north and south extremities in the dark. As for weapons, they only had perhaps a half-dozen .22 pistols, one Uzi submachine gun, and one rifle. He knew the Arabs had a lot more than that. He looked up at the tail assembly. It was badly mangled, but that didn't matter any longer. The rear pressure bulkhead must have been blown in because there was baggage strewn in the wake of the Concorde. Toilet kits, shoes, and pieces of clothing lay in the deep furrow like seeds waiting to be covered for the spring planting. The last of the sun died away, and the sky was filled with cold white stars. Dobkin suddenly felt a chill and realized that the *Hamseen* was blowing here. It would be a long, cold night. He wondered if any of them would see the sun rise.

Isaac Burg stood on the tilted delta wing as the other passengers jumped off. He turned and climbed up the fuselage and made his way toward the mangled tail. He braced himself against a twisted longeron and stared down toward the road about half a kilometer away. He could see truck lights bouncing across the uneven slope and the shadows of men as they ran in front of the slow-moving vehicles. He drew his pistol, an American Army Colt .45, and waited.

Jabari and Arif slid down the chute and ran clear of the aircraft, Jabari helping the big Arif as he stumbled. They fell and crawled behind a small rise in the ground. After several seconds, Jabari looked over the top of the hillock. "I don't think it will explode."

Arif panted heavily. He wiped his face. "I can't believe I voted to fight."

Jabari leaned back against the earth. "You said yourself you were doomed anyway. As doomed as Jacob Hausner. Did you hear what was being said before? Hausner slapped Rish when he was in Ramla."

"Bad luck for Hausner. But at least he will die for a reason. I never slapped anyone except my wife, but Rish will cut my throat with as much glee as he cuts Hausner's."

Jabari lit a cigarette. "You are a very self-centered man, Ibrahim."

"When it comes to *my* throat, yes."

Jabari stood up. "Come. Let's see where and in what manner they propose to fight. Perhaps we can help."

Arif remained seated. "I'll sit here. You go ahead." He removed his checkered headdress. "Do I look Jewish now?"

Jabari laughed in spite of himself. "How is your Hebrew?"

"Better than half the members of the Knesset."

"Well, Ibrahim, if the time comes, it's worth a try."

"Avraham . . . Aronson."

Tom Richardson stood at the river side of the slope and looked down at the Euphrates. John McClure walked up behind him and put his foot on a low mound. Richardson could see a revolver in the hand resting across his knee. Richardson rubbed his cold hands together. "This was a bad move."

McClure spit out his match and found another one. "Maybe."

"Look, I don't feel obligated to hang around. There doesn't seem to be anyone on the river bank. Let's go. We could be in Baghdad by this time tomorrow."

McClure looked at him. "How do you know where we are?"

Richardson remained motionless.

"I asked you a question, Colonel."

Richardson forced himself to look into McClure's eyes and hold contact. He said nothing.

McClure let the silence drag out for a few seconds, then raised his revolver. He spun the chambers and noticed Richardson flinch. He spoke softly. "I think I'll stick around."

Richardson eyed the big pistol. "Well, I'm going," he said in a calm voice.

McClure could see several flashlights moving along the river bank. Three football fields away. That was the only way he would ever estimate distance. Three hundred yards. About 270 of those ridiculous meters. "They've already gotten around us." He pointed.

Richardson didn't bother to look. "Could be civilians."

"Could be." McClure raised the revolver, a big Ruger .357 Magnum, with both hands and fired two shots at the lights. The shots were answered by a burst of automatic weapon fire. Both men ducked as green tracer rounds streaked up at them. McClure reloaded. "Settle back and relax. We might be here a long time."

• • •

Nathan Brin rested the M-14 on a rock. He turned on the battery-powered starlight scope and looked across the landscape. The scope gave everything an eerie green color. He twirled the knobs until the image was clear. He saw that they were among the ruins of a city. It all looked very lunar to Brin. All except the twenty or so Arabs walking nonchalantly up the slope from the direction of the road. A few hundred meters behind them, the trucks had stopped at the beginning of the slope. The Arabs were about 200 meters away now. He placed the cross hairs over the heart of the man in front. The man was Ahmed Rish, but Brin didn't recognize him. He squeezed the trigger slightly, then remembered his training and swung the rifle to the last man in the file. He squeezed back harder on the trigger. The silencer-flash suppressor spit, and the only sound was the operating rod working back and forth. The man dropped silently. The file, oblivious of the dead man lying behind them, continued up the slope.

Brin swung the rifle to the man who was now the last in line. He pulled the trigger again. Again, the only sound was the metallic slamming of the bolt and operating rod. The man fell. Brin smiled. He was enjoying himself, despite all his upbringing to the contrary. He swung the rifle and fired again. The third man fell but apparently let out a sound. Suddenly, the Arabs scattered among the rocks. Brin straightened up and moved behind the rock. He lit a cigarette. He'd done it. For better or worse, they were committed to the fight. He rather enjoyed the prospect. He heard a noise behind him and swung the rifle around. Hausner was staring at him. Brin smiled. "All right?"

Hausner nodded. "All right."

Becker stared out into the dark night. "Where the hell are we?"

Peter Kahn had noted the coordinates on the Inertial Navigation System readout before the impact. He was reading an air chart by the lights of the emergency power system. "Good question."

Becker unstrapped his seat belt and pulled himself out of his seat. He took Hess's head in his hands. His skull had been crushed by a large brick that lay now in his lap. There was no sign of life. He let the head fall gently and wiped his bloody hands on his white shirt. He turned to Kahn. "He's dead, Peter."

Kahn nodded.

Becker wiped his sweating face. "Well, get back to work. Where the hell are we?"

Kahn looked down at the chart again and made a mark along a protractor. He looked up. "Babylon. We are by the rivers of Babylon."

Becker placed his hand on Kahn's shoulder and leaned over the map. He nodded. "'Yea,'" he said, "'yea, we wept when we remembered Zion.'"

BOOK TWO

BABYLON
THE WATCHTOWERS

By the rivers of Babylon, there we sat down,
  yea, we wept, when we remembered Zion.
  We hanged our harps upon the willows in the midst thereof.
For there they that carried us away captive required of us a song;
  and they that wasted us required of us mirth, saying,
  Sing us one of the songs of Zion.
How shall we sing the Lord's song in a strange land?

If I forget thee, O Jerusalem,
  let my right hand forget her cunning.
If I do not remember thee,
  let my tongue cleave to the roof of my mouth;
  if I prefer not Jerusalem above my chief joy.
                    Psalms 137:1–6

And Babylon, the glory of kingdoms,
the beauty of the Chaldees' excellency,
  shall be as when God overthrew Sodom and Gomorrah.
It shall never be inhabited,
  neither shall it be dwelt in from generation to generation:
  neither shall the Arabian pitch tent there;
  neither shall the shepherds make their fold there.
But wild beasts of the desert shall lie there;
  and their houses shall be full of doleful creatures;
  and owls shall dwell there,
  and satyrs shall dance there.
And the wild beasts of the islands shall cry in their desolate houses,
  and dragons in their pleasant palaces:
  and her time is near to come,
  and her days shall not be prolonged.
                    Isaiah 13:19–25

10

There was a stillness on the hilltop, broken only by the ticking sounds made by the cooling of the four Rolls-Royce Olympus engines. The great white aircraft, with its front landing gear collapsed and its nose in the dirt, resembled some sort of proud creature brought to its knees. For a moment time seemed to falter, then a nightbird chirped tentatively, and all the other nocturnal creatures resumed their sounds.

Jacob Hausner knew that everything—their lives, their futures, and perhaps the future of their nation—depended on what happened in the next few minutes. A determined assault by the Palestinians right then would carry the hill, and that would be the end of all their brave talk of defense. He looked around. In the weak light he could see people moving aimlessly around the Concorde. Some, he suspected, were still in shock from the crash. Now that the time had come, no one knew what to do. The actors were willing, but they lacked a script. Hausner decided to write one on the spot, but he wished he had Dobkin and Burg nearby to coauthor it with him.

Hausner took the M-14 from Brin and looked down the slope through the telescopic lens. The three Arabs lay among the rocks where they had fallen. Hausner could see at least two AK-47 automatic rifles on the ground. If he could get those, it would put more substance behind their bluff.

He turned to Brin. "I'm going down there to retrieve those weapons. Keep me covered." He handed him the M-14 and drew his Smith & Wesson .22.

One of Hausner's other security men, Moshe Kaplan, saw him start down the hill and caught up with him. "Deserting already?"

Hausner whispered. "If you're coming along, keep low and keep quiet." He noticed that Kaplan's .22 had a silencer on it.

They made their way in short rushes from rock to rock. One man would cover and the other would move. Hausner noticed that what he took to be rocks were actually huge pieces of dried clay and earth that had apparently broken off and fallen from the face of the hill. His movements caused other hardened slabs to break loose and slide downward. It would be difficult for an enemy to attack upward if they had to duck bullets as they moved through shifting clay and sand.

From the crest of the hill, Brin watched through the starlight scope. A half-kilometer farther down the hill, he could see the Palestinians regrouping near the trucks. As he watched, he could tell by their motions that they were working themselves into a frenzy. Brin knew their style. If they were surprised, as this group had been, they would generally flee. Then would come the embarrassment and the recriminations. Then the working up of rage and courage that he was observing now. When they were sufficiently aroused, they would act, and they could be very resolute when they did. In fact, as he watched, a group of about twenty started up the hill again. Someone took something from a truck. Three rolled up litters. They were coming back for the bodies.

Hausner could not see much in the dark. He tried to maintain a straight line from where he had started. The bodies should be near a geological formation that looked like a ship's sail. He scanned the outlines of the land, but he knew it must look different from down here. He used the approved method of night vision—looking sideways out of the corners of the eyes as the head moved in short motions. He was becoming disoriented in the strange terrain.

As he moved down the slope, he wondered what they were doing back at the airplane. He hoped Brin had let everyone with guns know he was downhill. He thought about what kind of firepower they could muster. There were his five men still on the hill. They each had their own Smith & Wesson .22. In addition, Brin had the M-14 and someone else, probably Joshua Rubin, had the 9mm Uzi submachine gun. He suspected that there were a lot of other handguns on board as well. But handguns were not accurate beyond twenty meters or so. The Uzi and the M-14 were their only hope, but once the ammunition ran out, that would be it. The key lay in recovering those AK-47's. If there was enough ammunition, they could hold out for a day or so on the hill. But Hausner doubted now if he could find the bodies among these jagged, eroded earth formations.

Hausner heard a sound and stopped in his tracks. Kaplan froze against a rock. They heard it again. A low wailing voice, calling in Arabic. "I am over here," said the voice. "Over here."

Hausner responded in whispered Arabic that he hoped wouldn't betray his accent. "I'm coming," he said. "Coming."

"I am *here*," said the voice. "I am hurt."

"I'm coming," repeated Hausner.

He crawled through a shallow gully, then looked up across an open space dominated by the formation that looked like the sail of a ship. Three bodies lay in the light of the newly risen moon. One of them had an AK-47 cradled in his arms. Hausner cursed under his breath.

Kaplan came up beside him and whispered in his ear. "Let me take him. I've got a silencer."

Hausner shook his head. "Too far." If Kaplan didn't kill him with the first round, the bullet might make a sound as it struck, and then there would be AK-47 rounds splattering all over the place. "I'll take him."

Hausner removed his tie and suit jacket. He pulled his blue shirt out from his pants and opened a few buttons at the top. He ripped the white silk lining out of the jacket and tied it on his head in what he hoped would pass for a *kheffiyah*. He began to crawl out to the wounded Arab.

Kaplan cocked his pistol and crouched in a moon shadow.

Brin watched the Palestinians come up the hill. They were less than a hundred meters from the last place he had seen Hausner and Kaplan. The Palestinians were not offering good targets this time. They were practicing cover and concealment techniques like trained infantrymen. Brin swung the rifle and scanned for Hausner. He saw a man crawling over a bare spot between the piles of earth. A man with a dark *kheffiyah*.

Hausner whispered. "I'm here. I'm here."
The wounded Arab squinted into the darkness.
Hausner moved faster toward him.

Brin watched through the scope as the Arab in the slightly irregular *kheffiyah* traveled across the ground like a lizard. He noticed now the wounded Arab whom the crawling man was approaching. The wounded man must be the one he had hit before, the one who had made the sound that alerted the others. He swung the rifle and put his cross hairs on the crawling man. He began squeezing on the trigger. He hesitated. There was something dishonorable about shooting a man who was risking his life to help a wounded comrade. Yet he could see no alternative. He compromised. He would shoot the crawling man, but he wouldn't hit the wounded one again. Why that convoluted decision should satisfy the god or gods of war that put men in these situations, he didn't know. He only knew that it was important that you try to play the game fairly. He scanned the slope again quickly. He couldn't see Hausner or Kaplan. He did see the advancing Arabs who were less than fifty meters from the wounded man and his crawling comrade. But they still didn't present good targets in the terrain they were moving in. Brin aimed at the crawling man in the open.

Hausner whispered. "It's all right." He could hear the sounds of men rushing up the slope.
The wounded Arab picked himself up on one elbow. He forced a smile as Hausner came near. He looked at Hausner from a distance of less than a meter. He let out a surprised sound and raised his rifle. Hausner leaped at him.
Brin eased off on the trigger.
The Arab yelled again. Hausner's hand found a half brick in the dust. He gripped it and swung at the Arab, catching him full in the face.
Kaplan dashed across the open space. He located the two dead Arabs and collected their automatic rifles and several

banana clips of ammunition for each. Hausner took the wounded man's rifle and ammunition.

Brin waited until the lead Arab was into the clear area, then fired. The silencer coughed gently. The man pitched backwards.

Hausner and Kaplan looked toward where they heard the noise of the falling man. They could see the Arabs now, coming over and around the piles of earth and clay not twenty meters away.

Brin fired again, and the Arabs scattered as another of them fell.

Hausner hefted the wounded Arab onto his back and passed the rifle and ammunition to Kaplan. They began running up the hill under their heavy burdens. They wove around ridges of earth and then through erosion gullies, bent down below the hard crust of the slope. Automatic fire suddenly burst out behind them. Earth, clay, and and brick splinters flew up around them.

Kaplan could never forget that distinctive, hollow popping sound that an AK-47 makes, like a string of Chinese firecrackers. His blood ran cold as he heard the whistling go by his ears. Several times he thought he was hit, but it was only flying earth or ricochets, hot but spent. "Put him down!" he yelled at Hausner. They weren't going to make it with the Arab.

"No," panted Hausner. "Need him. Go on ahead."

"My ass!" Kaplan turned and leveled one of the AK-47's. He fired off a complete banana clip of thirty rounds. From the crest of the hill, he could hear the pathetic sounds of Smith & Wesson .22's. Then came the more authoritative sound of the Uzi submachine gun. He turned and caught up to Hausner. They were less than fifty meters from the crest now. Several men ran down the hill. Someone took the Arab from Hausner. Kaplan stumbled and lay, sweating and exhausted, on the ground. Someone helped him up. They ran a zigzag course as the earth kicked up around them. Near the crest of the hill, Kaplan could see Brin slowly aiming and firing with that terrible silent gun. Kaplan felt something hit him. Not a clay chip or a ricochet this time, but something searing and hot. He lost consciousness.

Hausner lay on the ground fighting for air. He put his arms out to each side and felt that he was on level ground. He'd made it. He could hear Dobkin calmly giving orders concerning the placement of the three AK-47's. He heard the gunfire coming up the slope and then the answering fire from their own positions. As soon as the three AK-47's cut in, the Arab fire stopped abruptly. Then all the firing stopped, and as the reports died away there was an eerie silence on the hill.

Dobkin leaned over Hausner. "That was damned foolish, Jacob. But they won't try that again for a while."

"Kaplan?"

Dobkin crouched down beside him. "Hit. But not bad. In the butt."

Hausner sat up. "He called that shot. Last thing he said to me was 'my ass.' Where is he?"

Dobkin pushed him down with one big hand. "Get your breath first. Don't want you having a heart attack."

The big man blotted out Hausner's whole view of the sky. "All right." He felt foolish lying on the ground. "Did we hit any? Take any weapons?"

"We hit a few. But they didn't make the same mistake again. They took their wounded and all the weapons. They've left a few dead, though."

"My prisoner?"

"Alive."

"Talking?"

"He will."

Hausner nodded. "I'd like to get up and check on my men."

Dobkin stared at him. "All right. Easy now."

"Right." Hausner got up slowly. He looked around. "Anyone else hurt?"

"Moses Hess is dead."

Hausner remembered the shattered windshield. "Anyone else?"

"A few people got banged up in the landing. Becker and Hess did an unbelievable job."

"Yes." Hausner took a few steps toward Brin, who was still looking through the starlight scope. Brin's position was the key defensive terrain feature on the east slope. It was a sort of promontory of earth that jutted out from the side of the hill. There was a low ridge of earth around it that would have to be heightened and thickened. It looked like a balcony and was a perfect sniper's perch. Hausner put his foot up on the earth bank and looked out over the dark countryside, then back to Dobkin.

"Where are we?"

"Babylon."

"Be serious."

"Babylon."

Hausner was quiet for a moment. "You mean as in 'Babylon is fallen, is fallen'? Or 'By the rivers of Babylon'?"

"That's the place."

Hausner's senses reeled. A few short hours ago he had been in a comfortable, modern aircraft flying to New York City. Now he was crawling in the dust of Babylon. It was surreal. Dobkin might as well have said Mars. "Babylon," he said aloud. It was one of those evocative names in the lexicon of world geography. A name that was more than just a name. A place that was more than just a place. Like Hiroshima or Normandy. Camelot or Shangri-La. Auschwitz or Masada. Jerusalem or Armaggedon. "Why?"

Dobkin shrugged. "Who knows? Some sort of joke on Rish's part, I suppose. The Babylonian Captivity and all that."

"Odd sense of humor."

"Well, not a joke maybe, but some sort of historical—"

"I understand." Hausner turned to Brin. "You hear that, Nathan? You're a Babylonian captive. What do you think of that?"

Brin lit a cigarette cupped in his hand. "Captive, hell! At sunrise I am personally going down to those sons-of-bitches and give them an ultimatum to surrender."

Hausner laughed and slapped him on the back. He turned to Dobkin. "You see? My men are ready to take on these bastards, General."

Dobkin had little patience with paramilitary outfits like police and security men. He just grunted.

"What's our position?" asked Hausner. "Tactically, I mean."

"It's a little early to tell. I made a quick recon of this hill while you were doing your John Wayne."

"And?"

"Well, this is an elevation of about seventy meters. I suspect that it's not a natural hill at all, but a tell, a mound covering a structure. You can see it's fairly flat on the top like a table mesa—like Masada." The analogy was inevitable. "I think this used to be the citadel on the northern city wall. It's covered with drifting dust, but if it were excavated, you'd see walls and towers. That small hillock over there was probably the top of a tower. And this promontory where Brin is standing was a tower coming out of the side of the wall."

Hausner looked at him. "You know this place." It was more a statement than a question. "How?"

"From maps and models. I never thought I'd ever get to see it. It's a Jewish archeologist's dream." He smiled.

Hausner stared at him through the dark. "I'm really happy for you, General. I must remember to congratulate El Al for taking advantage of an unexpected situation and arranging this excursion. Maybe we'll put it on our regular schedule. Crash and all."

"Take it easy, Jacob."

Hausner let the silence drag out, then let out a long breath. "All right. Can we defend this place?"

Dobkin ran his hand through his hair. "I . . . I think so." He paused. "It's an oblong-shaped mound, about the size and configuration of a standard race track. It runs north and south along the bank of the Euphrates. The river is at full flood this time of year and the waters come up to the western slope of this mound. The Arabs have put some men down by the flood bank. The American, McClure, took a few pot shots at them before. He has some sort of big cowboy six-shooter. Colonel Richardson is with him."

"They are the only ones there?"

"I have lots of sentries posted along the crest, but McClure is the only one with a gun. It's an open, exposed slope and very steep. It was, I think, the river wall of the citadel about 2,500 years ago. What we call in military engineering a glacis. I don't think we can expect a serious attack from there now that we've shown we're watching it and can shoot back."

Hausner lit a cigarette. "How about this side of the hill?"

"That's the problem. From north to south it's about half a kilometer. The slope is gradual down to the road and plain. There are erosion gullies and earth formations in some areas, as you well know. Those are the most likely areas of approach. In other places it's very exposed with clear fields of fire for us. I don't think we could expect an attack from those areas. I've placed the three AK-47's to cover those most likely avenues of approach. Three of your men are handling them. Another of your men, Joshua Rubin, has the Uzi, and Brin here has the 14. Your men have passed their .22's to passengers whom I've designated, and they're supplementing this defensive perimeter. I'm going to place combination observation posts and listening posts further down the slope." He took a deep breath. "Still, it's a thin line. If it weren't for the AK's, I'd have to recommend asking for terms."

Hausner took a long pull from Brin's cigarette and handed it back. He looked to Dobkin. "Do you think they'll attack again tonight?"

"Any military commander worthy of the name would. The longer they wait, the more organized the defense becomes. A half-hour ago the odds against us were overwhelming. Now, we might just make it through the night."

"They wouldn't attack at daylight, would they?"

"I wouldn't."

"Is Becker sending out an SOS?"

"He's operating the radios on batteries. Let's get back to the Concorde. The Foreign Minister wants you at a meeting."

"Even here," said Hausner wryly.

Brin was scanning through the starlight scope. Every few minutes he would shut it off to save the batteries and rest his eyes. Hausner patted him on the shoulder. "I'll have someone relieve you later."

"He's going to have to be very big to take my rifle away."

Hausner smiled. "Have it your way." He followed after Dobkin.

11

The Concorde sat near the middle of the flattened mound. At the north and south extremities of the oblong-shaped mound were the ruins of the river walls that now formed ramps leading up to the mound. It was the southern ramp that the Concorde had taken to the top. Hausner and Dobkin intersected the plowed furrow made by the Concorde's nose cone and walked in it toward the aircraft. Hausner had trouble keeping up with the big man. "Who's in charge?"

Dobkin didn't respond.

"Let's get down to it now, General. Chain of command. You understand that. There can only be one head man."

Dobkin slowed down. "The Foreign Minister is the ranking man, of course."

"Who's next?"

"I suppose Isaac Burg."

"Who's next?"

Dobkin let out a sound of exasperation. "Well, a politician would be next."

"Who?"

"Bernstein. She's in the Cabinet."

"I know that. But that hardly qualifies her here."

Dobkin shrugged. "Don't get me involved. I'm just a soldier."

"Who's next?"

"You or me, I guess."

"I have six men, all armed. They're loyal to me. They are the only effective fighting force on this hill."

Dobkin stopped. "One of them has a bullet in his ass. And it remains to be seen how effective the rest are. Those two actions tonight were only probes. The next time it will be an all-out attack."

Hausner turned and began walking again.

Dobkin came up beside him and clapped him on the back. "All right. I understand. But you've already atoned, Jacob, and you almost got killed in the process. Calm down a little, now. There are going to be a lot of tough hours ahead of us."

"More like days, I think."

"No way. We couldn't hold out much past sundown tomorrow. If that long."

"We may not be rescued by then."

Dobkin nodded. "You're right. This is the worst time of year to be here. The spring floods make the area damn near inaccessible. The tourist season won't start for a month. If Becker can't raise someone on the radio, it could very well be days before anyone realizes we're here. And more time before they act."

"Do you think the Iraqis would attempt a rescue?"

"Who knows? The Arabs are capable of the most chivalrous acts imaginable and the most treacherous—all within the same day."

Hausner nodded. "I think they want this peace mission to succeed. If Baghdad finds out we're here, we can expect help."

Dobkin waved his hand in a gesture of dismissal. "Who can say? The peace may already be lost. But I'm not a politician. Militarily, it would be difficult for them to aid us in this terrain. That's all I know for certain."

Hausner stopped. They were near the Concorde. He could see people standing and speaking in small groups. He lowered his voice. "Why?"

Dobkin spoke softly also. "Well, according to our latest intelligence, the Iraqis have very little helicopter mobility. They have less paratroop capability and virtually no amphibious craft, which would be needed to move troops this time of year. They're well equipped for desert warfare, but there's a lot of marsh and mud flats and swollen streams between the Tigris and Euphrates during the flood season. A lot of armies have come to grief in Mesopotamia in the spring."

"How about regular light infantry? Doesn't anyone use them anymore?"

Dobkin nodded. "Yes. Light infantry could reach us. But it would take a lot of time. There's a small town a little south of here—Hillah—but I don't know if they have a garrison or if they could reach us. And even if they could, would they stand up to the Palestinians?"

"Let's keep all this to ourselves."

"It's military secret Number One. And I'll tell you military secret Number Two. There are whole units of the Iraqi Army made up of displaced Palestinians. I'd hate to be the Iraqi military commander who had to test their loyalty by asking them to fight their compatriots. But we don't want to lower everyone's morale, so that's not for public information, either."

Dobkin and Hausner moved toward the Concorde and stopped near the nose cone. Some meters beyond the nose cone was the structure that they had almost hit. It looked like a ruined shepherds' shelter, but it wasn't stone as Hausner had thought when they were careening toward it. It was baked brick. The baked brick of Mesopotamia. It was partly roofed with date palms. Hausner noted that it was not much different from the shepherds' huts of Israel, or probably anywhere else in the Middle East. It was an ageless monument to the world's loneliest profession. A link with the world of Abraham. He could see through a partly collapsed wall. Men and women were standing inside talking. This was the Foreign Minister's meeting.

Hausner turned toward a sound in the dark. He could make out the majority of the passengers standing under the starboard delta wing. Rabbi Haim Levin was beginning Sabbath services a little late. Hausner recognized the short silhouette of Yaakov Leiber supported by the other two stewards.

Hausner saw something move under the fuselage. Suddenly Peter Kahn dropped down from the wheel well of the collapsed nose gear. He had a flashlight in his hand that he quickly shut off.

Dobkin walked up to him. "How's it look?"

"Bad."

"What's bad?" asked Hausner.

Kahn looked at him and smiled. "That was a hell of a thing you did, Mr. Hausner."

"What's bad?"

"The auxiliary power unit. It got damaged when the landing gear collapsed."

"So what? Are we taking off?"

Kahn forced a smile. "No. But there's still a few hundred liters of fuel left in the bottom of two of the wing tanks. If we can start the APU, we can run the generators and we'll have electricity to broadcast. The batteries won't last forever."

Hausner nodded. Forever might be only a matter of hours for them, in which case the batteries were good enough. "Where's the captain?"

"On the flight deck."

Hausner looked up the sloping nose cone. A greenish glow came through the windshield. He could make out Becker's outline. I'm going to talk to him."

Dobkin shook his head. "The Foreign Minister wants to speak to you." He indicated the shepherds' hut.

Hausner didn't feel up to it. "Not just yet."

"I'm afraid I have to insist."

There was a long silence. Hausner looked up at the flight deck, then back at the shepherds' hut. Kahn became uncomfortable and walked away. Hausner spoke. "In my carry-on luggage, I have an identikit and a psychological profile on Ahmed Rish. I want to get it."

Dobkin hesitated. "Well, I suppose..." Dobkin suddenly looked surprised as it hit him. "Why the hell do you have that with you?"

"A hunch."

"I'm impressed, Jacob. I really am. All right. They'll want to see that."

Hausner jumped up to the leading edge of the delta which was a few meters from the ground. He walked up the sloping wing to the emergency door.

The sloping cabin was dark, but an eerie green light came through the door leading to the flight deck. The seat belt and smoking lights were still on and the Machmeter still functioning. It read MACH 0.00 And always would. The cabin was empty. It smelled of burnt kerosene. Hand luggage, blankets, and pillows were scattered everywhere. Hausner could hear Rabbi Levin's clear voice coming through the split pressure bulkhead where the tail used to be.

He walked into the pitched flight deck. Becker was adjusting knobs on the green-glowing radios. There was the sound of electronic humming and the crackle of static. Moses Hess lay slumped over the instruments where he had died. Becker was speaking in a low voice and Hausner realized he was not speaking into the radio, but to Hess. He cleared his throat. "David."

Becker turned his head but said nothing. He went back to the radio.

Hausner stepped up to the seats. He felt uncomfortable with Hess's body lying there. "You did one hell of a job."

Becker began going through the frequencies again, monitoring but not attempting to transmit.

Hausner moved closer, between the seats, and his leg brushed Hess. He stepped back. If he had his way, the body would be buried in ten minutes. But he knew the rabbi wouldn't allow it on the Sabbath. Unless he or someone else could successfully plead health reasons, Hess's body wouldn't be buried until sundown. "I'll get him out of here, David."

"It doesn't matter." A loud radio whine filled the cabin. Becker cursed and shut it off, then shut down the emergency power. The dim lights went out, and moonlight filled the flight deck. "The bastard is still jamming us. He can't do a very good job of it from where he is, but he's trying."

"What kind of chance do we have to contact someone?"

"Who knows?" Becker leaned back and lit a cigarette. He stared through the windshield, then turned back to Hausner. "The high frequency radio seems to be completely dead. That's not unusual. It's very sensitive. If we can get it to work, we could theoretically call any place in the world, depending on atmospheric conditions. The VHF radio is working fine and I'm broadcasting on 121.5—the International Emergency Frequency. I'm also broadcasting and monitoring our last El Al frequency. But I don't hear anyone, and I'm not getting any responses."

"Why not?"

"Well, the VHF radio works on line of sight only. I haven't

looked, but I imagine there are hills around us that are higher than we are."

"There are."

"And the batteries are not as powerful as a generator. And don't forget that Rish is broadcasting static on every frequency with his broad band transmitter, and he can keep his engines and generator running." Becker blew out a long stream of smoke. "That's why not."

"All right." Hausner stared out the windshield. He could see people moving in the shepherds' hut below him. "But we could probably contact an airplane overhead without much difficulty. Right?"

"Right. All we we need is an airplane overhead."

Hausner noticed the blood-smeared brick that had killed Hess now sitting atop the flight console. In the green glow of the instruments he could make out the ancient cuneiforms pressed into it. He couldn't read cuneiforms, but he was certain that the brick said what most of the bricks of Babylon said: NEBUCHADNEZZAR, KING OF BABYLON, SON OF NABOPOLASSAR, KING OF BABYLON, AM I. The brick was very much out of place and time in the flight deck of the supersonic craft. He turned away from it. "I'll mount an aircraft watch from the top of the fuselage. We'll work out a system to signal you when one is spotted."

"Sounds good." He looked for a long time at his dead copilot, then back at Hausner. "Kahn's working on the APU."

"I saw him. He says it looks bad. How long will the batteries last?"

"It's really hard to say. I can monitor for quite a while, but every time I try a transmission I'm really pulling a lot of juice. I don't know how much more power is being pulled off on the emergency circuit. The batteries are nickel cadmium. They're good, but they don't give much warning that they're on the way out. They perform pretty well right up until the time they die."

Hausner nodded. He knew that. He worried about it. The starlight scope had nickel cadmium batteries also. "Do you think you want to hold off and save the batteries to turn over the APU if Kahn can fix it?"

Becker rubbed his hand through his hair. "I don't know. Shit. Everything we do from now on is going to have to be some sort of trade-off, isn't it? I don't know just yet. I'll think about it."

"Right." Hausner grabbed onto the flight engineer's chair and pulled himself forward toward the door. He caught hold of the jamb and turned. "See you later."

Becker turned in his chair. "Are we going to make it?"

"Of course." Hausner walked up into the steeply tilted cabin and located his flight bag.

Hausner went out into the wing and jumped off the leading edge. He could see that the Sabbath service had just finished. Most of the men and women headed quickly back toward the perimeter. Some were walking toward the shepherds' hut, among them, Rabbi Levin. Hausner fell into step with him. "Can we bury Moses Hess?"

"No."

"We have to begin building some sort of defensive works. Would you object to some work on the Sabbath?"

"Yes."

They stopped by the wall of the shepherds' hut. A few people from the Sabbath service walked past them and into the hut. Hausner looked at the rabbi. "Are we going to work together or are we going to be in conflict, Rabbi?"

The rabbi slipped his prayer book and *tallit* into his jacket. "Young man, it's the nature of religions to be in conflict with rational secular goals. Of course Moses Hess should be buried tonight, and of course you should start working on defenses. So we'll compromise. You order everyone to work over my objections, and I'll take charge of Moses Hess's body and forbid his burial. There are the kinds of compromises Israel has made since 1948."

"And they're damned stupid. It's all a lot of hypocrisy. Well, have it your way for now." Hausner stepped toward the opening of the hut.

Rabbi Levin took Hausner's arm and drew him back. "Survival is often a mixture of stupidity, hypocrisy, and compromise."

"I have no time for this."

"Wait. You're an Anglophile, Hausner. Did you ever wonder why the English stopped for tea at four P.M. in the middle of a battle? Or why they dressed for dinner in the tropics?"

"It's their style."

"And it's good for morale. Good for morale," he repeated and tapped Hausner on the chest. "We don't want people running amok just because we happen to be sitting on a hilltop in Babylon surrounded by hostile Arabs. So we do everyday things in everyday ways. We hold Sabbath services. We don't bury our dead on the Sabbath. We don't work on the Sabbath. And we won't be reduced to eating lizards or something of that sort because lizards are not kosher, Jacob Hausner." He tapped Hausner again on the chest, harder this time. "Nor will we break any other religious laws." He brushed some dust off Hausner's shirt. "Ask General Dobkin why soldiers in combat have to shave every day. Morale, Jacob Hausner. Form. Style. Civilization. That's how to keep this group functioning. Keep the men shaving and the women's hair and lipstick straight. It will follows from there. I used to be an Army chaplain. I know."

Hausner smiled in spite of himself. "That's an interesting theory. But I asked you if we were going to get along."

Rabbi Levin lowered his voice. "I'll rant and rave about The Law, and you rant and rave about military expediency. People will take sides. Internal strife is not always bad. It works to make people forget what a hopeless position they're in when they're arguing about trifles. So you and I will argue over trifles. Privately, we'll compromise. Like now. I'm attending this meeting on the Sabbath. I'm a reasonable fellow. See?" He walked into the hut.

Hausner stood staring at the spot where the rabbi had been. He couldn't follow all the logic. It was a mixture of Machiavellian, Byzantine, and convoluted thinking with a dash of plain Jewish for good measure. He half suspected that the rabbi didn't understand all he was saying himself. The man was definitely eccentric. But what he said had a good gut feeling.

Hausner walked toward the entrance to the hut.

About fifteen people were standing, talking in low voices. Everyone became quiet and heads turned toward Hausner. He paused at the doorway. A blue-white moonbeam shone through the date palms and lit up the spot where he stood. Ariel Weizman, the Foreign Minister, came across the small room and took his hand. "You did a splendid job, Mr. Hausner."

Hausner allowed his hand to be skaken. "Do you mean in allowing the bombs to be placed aboard my aircraft, Mr. Minister?"

The Foreign Minister looked at him closely in the moonlight. "Jacob," he said softly, "enough of that." The Foreign Minister turned around. "Let us begin. We're here to define our objectives and estimate our chances of carrying out those objectives."

Hausner set his flight bag down and looked around the room as the Foreign Minister went on in his parliamentary speech patterns.

Kaplan was lying on his stomach, against a wall. A blue El Al blanket covered him from the waist down. His bloody pants lay on the floor next to him. Two stewardesses, Beth Abrams and Rachel Baum, were looking after him, and Kaplan seemed to be enjoying it. Hausner was grateful that El Al stewards and stewardesses received quite a bit of medical training.

The ten official delegates to the peace mission were there, including the two Arabs, Abdel Jabari and Ibrahim Arif. Miriam Bernstein stood near the cleft in the wall. She looked good by moonlight, reflected Hausner. He found himself staring at her.

The Arab prisoner sat in the corner, his wrists bound to his ankles. His face was caked with dried blood where Hausner had hit him. His fatigue shirt was stiff with blood from his shoulder wound. Someone had opened the shirt and put a dressing on his shoulder. He appeared to be half asleep, or drugged.

Hausner listened as everyone took a turn speaking. A regular Knesset meeting. Arguments and points of order and calls for votes. They couldn't even decide what they were there for, why they had decided to fight, or what to do next. And all the while his five men, with a few other volunteers were manning an impossibly long defensive perimeter. It was a microcosm of Israel: democracy in action, or inaction. Churchill was right, he reflected. Democracy is the worst form of government—except for all the others.

Hausner could see that Dobkin was also becoming impatient, but his training had taught him to defer to the politicians. Hausner interrupted someone. "Has anyone questioned the prisoner?"

There was a silence. Why was this man speaking out of turn? What did the prisoner have to do with anything? A Knesset member, Chaim Tamir, looked down at the prisoner, who was apparently sleeping soundly now. "We tried. He's reluctant to talk. Also, he is hurt badly."

Hausner nodded. He walked casually over to the sleeping Arab and kicked him in the leg. There were a few surprised exclamations, including one from the Arab. Hausner turned around. "You see, ladies and gentlemen, the most important speaker in this room is this young man. What he says about the military capacity of the other side will determine our fate. I risked my life to bring him to you, and you are speaking only to each other."

Hausner could see that Burg and Dobkin looked relieved and anxious. No one spoke. Hausner continued. "And if this young man has very bad news for us, it should not become general knowledge. So, I suggest everyone except the Foreign Minister, the general, and Mr. Burg leave."

The room exploded into shouts of indignation and outrage.

The Foreign Minister called for quiet. He turned to General Dobkin with a questioning look.

Dobkin nodded. "It really should have been the first priority. We must question him no matter what condition he is in. And we must do it without delay."

The Foreign Minister looked surprised. "Then why didn't you say so, General?"

"Well, the prisoner was hurt and the stewardess had given him pain killers, and then you called this meeting—"

Hausner turned to Burg. "Will you do it?"

Burg nodded. "It's my specialty." He lit his pipe.

The Arab prisoner knew that he was the subject of conversation, and he looked unhappy about it.

The Foreign Minister nodded. "We will continue this meeting elsewhere and leave you alone with the prisoner, Mr. Burg."

Burg nodded.

The assembly began filing out after the Foreign Minister. They looked angry and almost rebellious.

Miriam Bernstein stopped in front of Jacob Hausner and looked up at him. He turned his back to her, but she surprised him and herself by grabbing his arm and half turning him back around. "Who the hell do you think you are?"

"You know very well who and what I am."

She tried to bring her anger under control. "The ends, Mr. Hausner, do not justify the means."

"Tonight they do."

She spoke slowly and precisely. "Look, if we get out of here alive, I want us to have our humanity and self-respect intact. In a very short time, you have disbanded a democratic assembly and gotten permission to torture a wounded man."

"I'm only surprised it took me so long." He lit a cigarette. "Look, Miriam, round one goes to us bully boys. And probably every round from now on. So you people just get it through your heads that you're superfluous except as soldiers. I'm going to save this fucked-up situation even if I have to turn this goddamned hill into a concentration camp."

She slapped him hard across the face. His cigarette flew through the air.

The people remaining in the hut pretended not to see or hear the slap in the dark. The room was still.

Hausner cleared his throat. "Mr. Burg has work to do and you're holding him up, Mrs. Bernstein. Please leave."

She left.

Hausner turned to Dobkin. "We'll inspect the perimeter and see how we stand." He stepped across the room. "Isaac, as soon as you get something concrete, send a runner out to us." He indicated his flight bag on the floor. "Here is an identikit and psychological profile on Rish. Take care of it."

Burg stared at the flight bag, then looked up. "How, in the name of God—?"

"Just a very lucky guess. Nothing more." He knelt beside Kaplan. He was almost asleep now, probably drugged. He was not likely to be awakened by the sounds of an interrogation. "Will you be all right, Moshe? Do you want to be moved?"

Kaplan shook his head. "I've seen it before," he said weakly. "Get out to the perimeter. Come up with a good defense."

"What other kind of defense is there for us, Moshe?"

"No other kind."

As Hausner and Dobkin walked, a scream from the hut pierced the still night air. If Brin's first shot committed them to the fight, thought Hausner, then torturing the Arab committed them to a policy of no surrender. They could not ask for better treatment than they gave. There was no turning back now.

They walked along the river side of the hill. Every fifty meters or so men and women stood or sat in pairs or singly, looking down at the Euphrates.

They were mostly the junior aides, Hausner noticed. The secretaries and interpreters. The young men and women of any major diplomatic mission. They had looked forward to New York. Some of them might make it.

Hausner mentioned to Dobkin that they'd have to see to it

that the ten delegates pulled guard duty along with everyone else. "That will cut down on their time for meetings," Hausner said. Dobkin smiled.

They found McClure and Richardson sitting on a sand rise in the ground. Hausner approached them. "Bad luck for you two."

McClure looked up slowly. "Could've been worse. Could've spent my home leave with my wife and in-laws."

Richardson stood. "What's the situation?"

"Grim," replied Hausner. He briefed them, then asked, "Do you two want to leave under a white flag? You're in an American Air Force uniform, Colonel. And you, Mr. McClure, I'm sure have proper identification as an American State Department employee. I'm fairly certain they wouldn't harm either of you. The Palestinians are trying not to antagonize your government these days."

McClure shook his head. "Funny coincidence. I had a great-uncle who was killed at the Alamo. Used to wonder how it felt being under siege. You know? Rejecting offers of surrender. Seeing the Mexos pouring over the walls. That must've been one hell of a fight."

Dobkin understood enough of the English to be confused. "Is that supposed to be an answer?"

Hausner laughed. "You are a strange man, Mr. McClure. But you're welcome to stay. You, by the way, have the only gun on this side of the hill."

"Kind of figured I did."

"Right," said Hausner. "So if someone on this side yells, get over there and pop off some rounds until I can send a few automatic weapons men over from the east slope."

"Will do."

Hausner felt confident with McClure. "Actually, I don't think they will try this side."

"Probably not." McClure looked at the sky, then at Hausner. "You better get some organization in this defense before the moon sets."

"I know," said Hausner. "Thanks, Mr. McClure." He turned to Richardson. "You too, Colonel."

"Call me Tom," said Richardson. He switched to Hebrew which surprised Hausner and Dobkin. "Listen, I'm with you, but I think you should try to negotiate."

Dobkin stepped closer to Richardson and answered him in Hebrew. "Negotiate for what? We were on a mission of peace and half of us are dead now. What are we supposed to negotiate?"

Richardson didn't answer.

Hausner spoke. "We'll take it under advisement, Colonel. Thank you."

McClure seemed unconcerned that everyone was speaking a language he couldn't understand. Hausner felt the tension between the two Americans. There was something wrong here.

12

Hausner and Dobkin continued to walk the perimeter. It was almost a perfect oval, or as Dobkin had described it, the size and shape of a race track, which led Hausner to agree with Dobkin that it was probably not a natural formation. The top of the mound or hill was fairly level, further evidence of a man-made structure underneath. The flat top was broken only by blown dunes and water-eroded gullies or wadis. There were places where a round knoll stuck up from the flat surface. Dobkin explained that these were most likely watchtowers that had risen above the walls of the citadel. Dobkin placed men and women on each one of them.

They counted thirty men and women who had somehow gotten themselves into position. Most of them had just placed themselves instinctively. Dobkin had placed only a few right after the crash.

Hausner stood by as Dobkin considered the problems of cover, concealment, and fields of fire. Dobkin shifted and adjusted the line to take better advantage of the terrain. He issued orders to start piling bricks and dirt for breastworks and to dig foxholes wherever it was possible to dig in the dusty soil. Hausner wondered if it weren't really a useless exercise, since there was virtually no firepower among the defenders.

Burg had given Dobkin his Colt .45 automatic and Dobkin in turn had given it to one of the stewards, Abel Geller, whom he placed in a strategic position. Hausner handed his Smith & Wesson .22 to a young stenographer named Ruth Mandel. "Do you know how to use this?"

She looked at it in her small hand. "I spent my time in the Army."

Hausner counted three handguns of small caliber plus his men's six Smith & Wesson .22's. His own made ten. Then there was Joshua Rubin with the Uzi, Brin with the M-14, and his other three security men, Jaffe, Marcus, and Alpern, with the three AK-47's. The AK's were placed to cover the entire east slope of the hill with intersecting fire. There was an average of one person every thirty meters. It wasn't good, but it wasn't hopeless, either.

Dobkin found a steward, Daniel Jacoby, and asked him to figure out a way of making coffee to take out to the perimeter.

Hausner and Dobkin stopped at Brin's position. A young girl in a bright blue jumpsuit was asleep sitting up with her back to a mound of earth near Brin. Hausner spoke. "Who's she?"

Brin looked up from the scope. "Naomi Haber, a stenographer. She volunteered to be my runner. I'll need someone to pass the word if I see anything."

Hausner nodded. "Have you seen anything?"

"No."

"After the moon sets you will."

"I know."

Hausner and Dobkin stood a distance from Brin and the sleeping girl. They both stared silently down into Babylon.

Hausner lit a cigarette. "Well?"

Dobkin shook his head. "I don't know. It depends on how determined the assault is. A regular infantry unit of platoon size could take this hill if they were good. On the other hand, a five-hundred-man battalion couldn't take it if they were bad. To assault a defensive postion, no matter how lightly defended, takes a special kind of nerve.

"Do you think that bunch has it?"

"Who knows? How charismatic a leader is Rish? Will men die for him? For their cause? We don't even know how many there are. Let's wait for Burg's report."

"Right." Hausner looked eastward down the slope. He could make out ribbons of water shining in the moonlight and large stretches of glistening marsh. Yet the area was basically dead. Sand and clay. It was hard to believe that Mesopotamia had supported millions of people in ancient times. He could see a low wall almost a kilometer away and beyond that the road they had started to land on. "Do you really know this place, Ben?"

"I can probably draw a map of it from memory. In fact, in the morning, when I get my landmarks oriented, I will draw us a nice military map."

"How did these Palestinians get here, I wonder."

"How do guerrillas get anywhere?"

"They had a few trucks."

"I noticed."

"Heavy weapons? Mortars?"

"I hope to God not," said Dobkin.

"They wanted to keep us hostage—captive—in Babylon. That's almost funny."

"It wouldn't have been if we'd landed on that road," said Dobkin. "I wonder if we made the right move?"

"We might never know," said Hausner. He lit a cigarette and put his cold hands in his pockets. "Maybe Asher Avidar made the right move."

"Maybe."

Hausner looked to the north. About three-quarters of a kilometer away was a tall hill that rose dramatically from the flat plain. Hausner recognized it as a tell. "What's that?"

Dobkin followed his stare. "That's the hill of Babil. Some archeologists identify it as the location of the Tower of Babel."

Hausner stared. "Do you believe it?"

"Who knows?"

He looked around. "Can we see the Hanging Gardens from here?"

Dobkin laughed. "I don't give tours on the Sabbath." He put his big hand on Hausner's shoulder. "I'm curious to see what I can identify from here when the sun comes up. The main ruin is to the south. There."

"Does anyone live around here?"

"The Arabs don't like it. They think it's haunted. Do you know the verses from Isaiah?"

"You mean... 'neither shall the Arabian pitch tent there; neither shall the shepherds make their fold there.... But wild beasts... shall lie there.... And dragons in their pleasant palaces....' That one?"

"That's the one."

"Yet, there's a shepherds' hut here."

Dobkin nodded. "And there is a small village located among the ruins, in spite of the Biblical injunction against this place."

Hausner put out his cigarette and saved the stub. "Can that village be any help to us?"

"I don't think so. I used to debrief Army Intelligence men back from Iraq. A lot of Iraqi villages are primitive beyond belief. Some of these people don't even know they are Iraqi citizens. They live like the first Mesopotamian peasants who began civilization here five thousand years ago."

"Then we're not near any type of modern transportation or communication?"

"Hillah to the south. But I wouldn't count on their knowing we're here." He paused and seemed to remember something. "There *is* a small museum and a guest house in the south part of the ruins by the Ishtar Gate."

Hausner turned his head quickly toward Dobkin. "Go on."

"The Iraqi Department of Antiquities built both structures about twenty years ago. I know the curator of the museum. Dr. Al-Thanni. I saw him in Athens only six months ago. We write via a mutal friend in Cyprus."

"Are you serious?" Hausner began pacing. "Could you get there?"

"Jacob, we are what is called in military siege terminology, invested. That means surrounded. Just as we have sentinels and firing positions up here, you can be sure they have the same around this entire mound."

"But if you could slip through—"

"The chances are that Dr. Al-Thanni won't be there until the end of April when the tourist season begins."

"There must be a telephone."

"There probably is. And running water. And I'll give you one guess where Rish's command post must be."

Hausner stopped pacing. "Still, if you could get there—to the guest house or the museum—it's a link with civilization. Al-Thanni may be there. You may be able to get a jeep. Or the telephone might be unguarded. What do you say, Ben?"

Dobkin looked south across the uneven landscape. He could make out the silhouettes of some excavated ruins. It was at least two kilometers to the Ishtar Gate excavation. There would be only a thin line of sentinels surrounding the hill. Still, he'd want to see it by daylight at least once. "I'm game. But if I'm caught they will make me tell them all I know about our setup here. Everyone talks, Jacob. You know that."

"Of course I know that."

"I'd have to have a pistol to . . . to make sure I didn't fall into their hands. Can we spare that?"

"I don't think so, Ben."

"Neither do I."

"A knife," offered Hausner.

Dobkin laughed. "You know, I never understood where our ancestors got the balls to fall on their own swords. That takes a bit of nerve. And it must be very, very painful." He looked off into the distance. "I don't know if I could do that."

"Well," said Hausner, "let's ask around and see if anyone has some kind of medicine that's fatal in an overdose."

"I appreciate the pains you're taking to facilitate my suicide."

"There are over fifty people—"

"I know. Yes, I'll go. But only after I've seen it in the daylight. I'll leave at nightfall tomorrow."

"We may not be alive that long."

"It's worth the wait. I'll have a better chance of success. If I go tonight, I'll only be throwing my life away. I don't want to do that. I want to succeed."

"Of course."

Isaac Burg approached, puffing on his pipe. He walked heavily like someone who has just completed a disagreeable task.

Hausner and Dobkin walked to meet him. Hausner spoke first. "Did he talk?"

"Everyone talks."

Hausner nodded. "Is he . . . ?"

"Oh, no. He's alive. Actually, I didn't have to lean on him very hard. He wanted to talk."

"Why?"

"They're all like that. Dobkin will tell you. You've seen it yourself at Ramla. It's a mixture of bragging, shock, nervousness, and fright." He studied his pipe for a second. "Also, I promised him I'd send him back to his friends."

Dobkin shook his head. "We can't do that. Military regulations. Anyone who sees the inside of a defensive area can't be repatriated until hostilities are ended. It's the same here as anywhere else."

"Well," said Burg, "in my world—spies and secret agents, I mean—we do things differently. I promised. And you can make an exception for medical reasons. Besides, he hasn't seen much. There's no use letting a man die just because we don't have medical facilities."

"I'll think about it," said Dobkin.

Hausner listened to them argue. It wasn't a heated argument but purely a disagreement over the interpretation of the rules. Burg was, at best, an enigma, thought Hausner. One minute he was prepared to torture a man to death and the next he was trying to save his life. And if he did let the Arab go, and they came back and took the hill and captured Burg alive, the Arabs would make certain that Burg died very slowly. If he were Burg, reflected Hausner, he would kill the man and bury him deep. And Dobkin—he was the perfect soldier. Loyal, intelligent, even inventive. But he *did* like his book of regulations. Hausner became impatient with their argument. "Never mind this. What did he *say?*"

Burg knocked his pipe on his shoe. "Say? He said lots of things. He said his name was Muhammad Assad and that he was an Ashbal. You know the word. A Tiger Cub—a Palestinian orphan of the wars with Israel. In fact, that outfit down there is all Ashbals. They were all raised by Palestinian guerilla organizations. Now they are all grown up. And they don't like us."

Dobkin nodded. "War leaves many legacies. This is the worst." He thought about the Ashbals. How many hollow-eyed, tattered waifs had he seen sobbing over the bodies of their parents amid the rubble of Arab villages? War. Now they were all grown up, these young victims. They were nightmares that came back in the day. "They don't like us at all," agreed Dobkin.

"Quite right," said Burg. "They are a dangerous lot. They've been indoctrinated with hate since the day they could comprehend. They reject all normal standards of behavior.

Hatred of Israel is their tribal religion." He patted his pocket for his tobacco pouch and found it. "Also, they've been taught military skills since they could walk. They are a damned well-trained group."

"How many?" asked Dobkin.

"A hundred and fifty."

There was a silence.

"You're certain?" asked Hausner.

Burg nodded.

"How can you be certain?"

Burg smiled. "That's one of the things all soldiers lie about, isn't it, Ben? How many. At first, he said five hundred. I didn't buy that. That's what all the screaming was about. Finally, we agreed on a hundred and fifty."

Dobkin nodded. "Heavy weapons?"

Burg shook his head. "They weren't expecting resistance. Almost all of them are armed with AK-47 rifles, however."

"They must have a base close by," said Dobkin.

"Not so close. In the Shamiyah Desert. That's on the other side of the Euphrates. A good hundred kilometers from here. The Iraqi government suffers the existence of the camp for a variety of very familiar reasons. Anyway, they came here in late January by truck, before the floods. They have been waiting for orders ever since. Then a few hours ago, Rish flew in and called them on the radio. The rest is history—in the making."

"Rish is the boss, I take it?" asked Hausner.

"None other. And his lieutenant is a fellow named Salem Hamadi, another old friend. Hamadi is both a Palestinian and an Ashbal. In fact, he was in charge of the Ashbal program. Rish, as you know, is neither an Ashbal nor a Palestinian. He is Iraqi. His village is not far from here. Anyway, some time ago, they joined forces and began culling both male and female orphans from various camps. About twenty of these Tiger Cubs are tigresses. Muhammad says they trained for years in the Shamiyah Desert for special assignments that never seemed to come off."

"Did they know what they were here for?" asked Dobkin.

"They were told only when Rish's Lear began to make its final approach. There was some confusion as to whether there would be one Concorde or two." He paused as he remembered 01. "They were told they would keep us hostage here for a variety of political reasons, some of which were not too clear to Mr.

Muhammad Assad. He admits they were pretty shaken up by our antics. I suspect that they were not psychologically prepared to fight and lose men. They were prepared to push around two planeloads of Israeli civilians. Then all of a sudden, they had people getting killed."

"But they're crack troops," said Hausner. "That's what you said."

Burg shook his head. "I didn't say they were crack troops. I said they were well trained. There is a difference. None of them has ever seen combat." He seemed to be thinking. "You know, this is not the first time that orphans have been trained from childhood as soldiers. There are a lot of cases of that in history. And you know what? They were never really better or worse than regular draftees. In fact, many times they were much worse. These orphan soldiers, like institutional children everywhere, were a little duller than their peers raised in a home environment. That is the case with the Ashbals, I'm sure. They do not make especially good soldiers. They lack imagination and they have virtually no personal goals in life. They lack any experiences outside of military life, and their emotional development is arrested. They have only a vague conception of what they are fighting for, since they have no home outside the barracks. I'm sure they would fight to the death to defend their comrades and their camps, but outside of that, there's no notion of family or country. Everything is vague when they go beyond their squads, their platoons, and their companies. There are a dozen other reasons why they don't make ideal soldiers. I could see it in our young friend, Muhammad." He looked at Dobkin. "Ben?"

Dobkin nodded. "I agree. But there are still over a hundred of them, and they outgun us. They are not going to pack their tents like your proverbial Arabs and steal away in the night."

"No," said Hausner. "They are not. Because they have two good leaders."

Dobkin nodded again. "That is the key. The leadership." He seemed to be remembering the old fights and nodded to himself several times. He looked at Hausner and Burg. "Here is what I know about the Arabs as soldiers. First, they are romantics whose mental picture of warfare is of men on white Arabian stallions charing across the desert. In truth, the Arabs of today are not known for their successes on the offensive. The days when they carried the banner of Islam across half the civilized world are long gone." He lit a cigarette. "But don't get me wrong. They are not such bad fighters as they are made out to be. They are generally brave and steadfast, especially in a static defensive situation. Like many soldiers from low social and economic backgrounds, they will endure the most extreme hardships and deprivations. But they have flaws as soldiers. They are reluctant to press an attack. They are unable to shift tactics with changing situations. Their officers and sergeants, while not the best, are critical for control and discipline. The average Arab soldier will show little initiative and less discipline when his leader is killed. Also, the Arabs have not completely come to grips with modern military equipment. The Ashbals in particular, from what little I know of them, seem to fit into this description. And further, they are so blinded by hate propaganda that they are not very cool or professional as soldiers."

Burg nodded. "I agree. And I think they *might* run off if they lose enough leadership or if the losses in the ranks become unacceptable—which I admit isn't very likely in this case. On the other hand, *we* can't run anywhere. We are fighting for our lives. All losses are acceptable to us. There is no alternative."

Hausner spoke. "There is an alternative. They'll ask for a conference."

"But not before they try one more attack," said Dobkin. He looked into the sky. "We'll have a chance to see if we can inflict unacceptable losses on them in a short while. The moon is setting."

13

Brin saw them first, even before the two-man OP/LP—Outpost/Listening Post—halfway down the slope saw them.

They came like shadows, wearing tiger fatigues and carrying their automatic rifles. The starlight scope amplified the smallest amount of natural night light so that Brin could see things that even night creatures could not see—things that the men could not even see on themselves. He could see their shadows, cast by starlight. He could see the white skin under their eyes, symptomatic of fear. He could see the most intimate movements made in what was believed to be a shroud of darkness—the lips murmuring prayers, the quick urinations brought on by fear, the pulling of hair locks. A girl squeezed a young man's hand. Brin felt as though he were peeking through a keyhole.

He put down the rifle and whispered to Naomi Haber. "They're coming."

She nodded, touched his arm, and ran off to give the alarm.

The long meandering defensive line on the eastern slope of the hill became alert as the warning moved more rapidly than the swift runner.

144

On the western slope there was silence. The luminescent Euphrates would silhouette anything moving up that slope. Men and women pressed their faces to the ground at the crest of the slope to try to pick out a moving form. But there was only the silver-gray Euphrates flowing silently southward.

Dobkin, Burg, and Hausner stood on a small knoll—one of the covered watchtowers—near the middle of the eastern crest, about fifty meters in back of it.

The knoll had been designated as the CP/OP, the Command Post/Observation Post. From that vantage point, they hoped to direct the fight along the five-hundred-meter eastern slope.

A long aluminum brace from the Concorde's tail section, bent and twisted, was stuck in the hard clay earth atop the knoll. From the top of this unlikely standard flew a more unlikely banner, a child's T-shirt, salvaged from one of the suitcases, an intended gift for someone in New York. The T-shirt showed a cityscape of the Tel Aviv waterfront painted in day-glo colors. The purpose of the CP/OP was to establish command control in the dark—a place where runners could go to impart information and collect orders. It was also to be the last rallying point, the citadel within the citadel from which the last stand was to be made in the event the line was broken or penetrated. It was an old tactic, one that belonged to an age before radios, telegraphs, and field phones. The three commanders took their places on the high knoll, under their flag, and waited.

The two men from the OP/LP, halfway down the slope, fell breathless at the foot of the knoll and reported what was already known from Nathan Brin and Naomi Haber. "They're coming."

Brin watched as the Ashbals continued their silent movement up the hill. They didn't come in file as they had done the last time, but they moved on line along the whole width of the five-hundred-meter slope, approximately a hundred of them, men and women, well-spaced at five meters apart. They kept their line straight like well-trained infantry of another era. There was no wavering and no bunching up. They didn't linger or congregate around areas of natural cover and concealment as their instincts cried out for them to do. They held their AK-47's with fixed bayonets thrust out in front of them. It was an awesome sight to anyone who could see it. But to Brin, it was all show. Parade-ground training. He was interested to see how they would react when the bullets began flying down at them.

Then, he suspected, they would quickly revert to their modern training. They would find what little cover and concealment was available and burrow into it. They would move from rock to gully to pothole. But for now, in the dark, they were putting on a show of the classic infantry attack—more for themselves than for the Israelis who could not see them.

The knowledge that he was the only one who could see them brought Brin to the verge of panic several times. Sweat formed on the rubber eye guard of his scope and ran down his cheek. They were still very far. About five hundred meters. Then four hundred meters.

General Dobkin and Isaac Burg disagreed on tactics. Dobkin wanted to engage them with heavy fire as far out as possible with the idea of keeping them out of assault range of the thin defensive line. With luck, that would precipitate a panicky flight down the hill. The prisoner had said that they had no hand grenades, but Dobkin couldn't be sure of that. He didn't want them in grenade range in any case.

Burg wanted to engage them as near as possible—within handgun range—in order to cause heavy casualties with as little expenditure of ammunition as possible.

Hausner wasn't consulted, but he thought that Dobkin's arguments were more realistic, considering their situation. In the end, however, he knew that Dobkin, soldier to the core, would defer to a civilian government official. It was a subjective type of decision that had to be made, and rank would always carry that type of argument.

Hausner excused himself, jumped from the hillock, and walked the fifty meters to where Brin was kneeling.

Brin was visibly shaking as he watched the wave of Ashbals approach. Hausner couldn't blame him. He spoke softly. "Range?"

Brin didn't look up. "Three hundred and fifty meters."

"Deployment?"

"Still on line. Most are in the open. Bayonets fixed."

Naomi Haber was sitting on the ground breathing heavily from her exertions. Hausner turned to her. "Go to an AK-47 position and tell him to begin the firing." She got up quickly and ran down the line. He turned back to Brin. "Range?"

"Three hundred."

"Commence firing," he said softly.

Brin squeezed the trigger, swung the rifle, squeezed again, swung, and squeezed again. The silenced muzzle coughed faintly again and again. Then the first AK-47 cut in, a signal to begin firing at will. Up and down the line, along the crest of the hill, came gunshots. The hollow popping of the three AK-47's drowned out the small handguns. Above all the other sounds could be heard the sharp staccato of the little 9mm Uzi submachine gun.

The Arabs immediately replied with heavy fire from their own AK-47's. The noise quickly rose to a deafening pitch. Hausner could see the incoming rounds digging away at the improvised Israeli breastworks. He couldn't tell if anyone had been hit yet.

Brin's assignment was to try to identify unit commanders and eliminate them. He swung the rifle and spotted the antenna of a field radio, carried as a backpack by a radio operator. At the end of a corkscrew wire coming out of the radio was a radiophone. A young man was crouched down, holding the radiophone to his face. Brin aimed at the young man's mouth and fired. The phone and the man's face erupted into a scatter of disjointed pieces. He swung the rifle back and shot the radio operator through the heart.

The Ashbal's return fire ceased as their long line broke up quickly into small groups centered around natural areas of cover. Their progress was slowed, but they still moved forward. Brin scanned the area behind the Ashbals, looking for the senior leaders. He thought once that he saw Rish, but then the head disappeared, replaced a second later by that of a young woman. Without hesitation, Brin fired. He could see the head jerk sideways. The beret flew off and the long hair swirled as the girl spun to the earth.

Dobkin could see the fiery bursts as the Arabs moved up the hill. He shook his head. They may have been well trained, but he gave them a low grade on tactics. The approved method of night attack, developed in large part by the Israeli Army, was quite different from what the Ashbals were doing. It was known now that night attacks should begin silently, not with the sound and fury of artillery barrages and screaming men, as in the past wars. The Ashbals had done that at the beginning, but they had moved too slowly and returned fire too soon. The Israelis had, in past engagements, shown that a quick silent run was the most effective method of night attack. The enemy was generally only half-alert, and when they saw what was coming at them in the dark, they only half-believed their eyes. By the time they reacted, the attackers were within hand grenade range, then a second later, they were in the trenches. Even a fully loaded infantryman could cover half a kilometer on the run in less than two minutes.

Dobkin watched as the flashes moved in the darkness. These Ashbals fired on the run and fell behind cover afterward, the exact opposite of what was good sense. The defenders on the hill fired at the flash of the muzzles while the attackers were running. As far as Dobkin could see, the Ashbal's fire was so far without effect on his concealed positions, except for one casualty reported to him. Looking downslope, Dobkin could see what appeared to be muzzle flashes cut short by what he hoped were hits.

It had taken a lot of battles over a lot of years for him to be able to stand on a high place and tell how a fight was progressing by flashes and noises, by sounds of men and the smell of the night air. And most of all, some kind of warrior instinct told him when everything was all right and when it was lost.

In total, despite all the noise, Dobkin knew that casualties would be very light on both sides until the battle was joined up close. That's the way it had always been in the past. This time, however, he felt it was not going to be a victory. He turned to Burg. "They're very sloppy troops. But very determined. We will probably be out of ammunition very shortly. Maybe we should give the order to pull back to this knoll."

Burg shook his head. Long before he had entered intelligence work, he had been a battalion commander in the War of Independence. He had a sense for these things also. "Let's wait. I have a feeling they will break off the engagement."

Dobkin didn't answer.

"At sunrise we will court-martial Hausner," said Burg matter-of-factly.

"We can't be sure he gave the order to fire," said Dobkin.

"You know he did." Burg stood with one hand grasping the twisted aluminum standard. He seemed mesmerized by the flash of weapons and the incessant whistling of bullets. He realized that what was missing was the sound of the heavy weapons that gave a fight a distinctive military flavor. This fight sounded like an American gangster movie—all pistols and submachine guns.

"Well, General? Do you think Hausner gave the order to commence firing against our orders?" asked Burg.

Dobkin didn't feel like arguing. "I suppose he did. It doesn't really make a lot of difference, does it?"

"It makes a great deal of difference to me," snapped Burg. "A great deal of difference."

All along the defensive line, the volume of gunfire remained constant, for to begin conserving ammunition was a signal to the attackers that the end was near if only they would persevere. But the number of rounds left to the Israelis dwindled rapidly and, in fact, a few handguns were already without ammunition. The AK-47's kept up a three-piece symphony of short bursts, while Joshua Rubin with the Uzi fired continuously, stopping only to let the barrel cool. Brin, firing a relatively small amount of ammunition, was the most deadly with ten hits.

The Ashbals were within a hundred meters of the line now, but their casualties went up geometrically with every ten meters they gained.

Someone was running toward the command post from the direction of the west slope. Burg and Dobkin waited for the bad news that the Ashbals had launched a secondary attack up the slope on the river side. The entire line there was held by McClure with his pistol and a dozen men and women with bricks and pieces of aluminum braces fashioned into spears. The runner jumped onto the knoll and caught his breath. "All quiet on the western slope." He grinned.

Dobkin grinned in return and slapped him on the back. "That's the only good news I've had since a lady said yes to me last night in Tel Aviv."

Hausner, kneeling beside Brin, estimated that the end would come within the next few minutes. There simply wasn't enough ammunition to keep up that rate of fire.

As though the defenders read his thoughts, they began increasing the rates of fire in a last desperate gamble to panic the attackers. Hausner watched the oncoming Arabs, who were partially visible now through the darkness. The Ashbals wavered as the increased volume of fire tore into their ranks. They slowed but held firm. The momentum of their attack was stopped, however, but while they were afraid to go forward, they weren't falling back, either. Their commanders yelled and kicked at them and tried to regain the initiative. Some groups moved forward again, reluctantly.

Brin took advantage of the commanders' increased visibility and took two of them out in less than thirty seconds. The others began taking cover when they realized what was happening. Brin then began to search desperately for Rish. He had studied the photo from Hausner's identikit so intently for the past hour that all he could see in his mind's eye was Rish's face on every Arab. But he knew that when he actually saw that face, he would be certain of it.

The Israelis heard the Arabic shouts and could see some of what was happening. They deduced that there was a problem in the Ashbals' ranks. The veterans among the Israelis knew what to do. As Hausner watched, amazed, without any orders from anyone, about twenty men and women began running and screaming down the hill.

Dobkin knew what was happening. With cool detachment, he weighed the possibilities of success. The idea behind a primitive screaming counterattack was to strike fear into the hearts of the attackers. If it were done with enough élan and conviction, and if it were spontaneous like this one, it could make the enemy's blood run cold. They would turn, first the most cowardly among them, then even the most stouthearted would be caught up in the panicky flight as the attackers became the attacked. Lacking prepared defenses, they would run until they dropped.

But would that happen here? What would happen if the Ashbals had another force on the river side? If they attacked on that side, Dobkin could no longer send any reinforcements there. They were all halfway down the eastern slope in an unauthorized counterattack. That's what happened when people didn't obey orders. Dobkin ran toward the crest of the eastern slope.

Hausner took the M-14 from Brin and watched through the starlight scope. For a moment, everything hung in the balance. If the Ashbals did not break ranks, there would be a massacre. The attacking Israelis were outnumbered five to one and lightly armed. They were within fifty meters of the Ashbals and were firing into their ranks with increasing accuracy. Joshua Rubin had gone completely crazy. He ran and fired his Uzi in a long burst that Hausner thought would melt the barrel. Hausner could hear his primeval war cry above the din of the shooting.

Hausner began firing the M-14 at targets around Rubin to try to protect him. He saw what he thought was the first man to break ranks and run. Then two young girls followed. Then others followed. He could hear the Arabic word for retreat shouted by the fleeing Ashbals. A few leaders, officers, and sergeants tried to turn them around. Hausner put the cross hairs on one who was having some success and fired. The man fell. It was already apparent to the leaders that someone with a very good scope was causing them an inordinate number of casualties. Now that they were more conspicuous by trying to organize a stand, they were virtually committing suicide. Hausner aimed again. He had trained with every weapon that his men were issued, but this wasn't his job, and Brin was becoming impatient. Hausner fired, hit another leader, and passed the weapon back to Brin.

Finally, amid the shouts for medics and stretcher bearers for the leaders who were hit, the other Arab officers became disheartened and joined in the flow of retreat.

The retreat became more orderly as the Ashbals put distance between themselves and the Israelis, who by now had lost the madness born of desperation that had made them counterattack.

The Ashbals gathered up fallen equipment, picked up their dead and wounded, and organized a rear guard to allow them more time to get away. As they made their way down the slope, earthslides toppled them over and caused dead and wounded to be dropped.

The Israelis followed close on the heels of the rear guard but finally stopped when a runner sent by Dobkin ordered them back. They gathered what fallen equipment they could find in the darkness and climbed back to the crest of the hill, dirty, sweating, and exhausted. Rubin and a female stenographer, Ruth Mandel, were hit, but not seriously.

There was still no word from the river slope, but Dobkin sent two men with AK-47's there to be certain. A silence fell over the hill and the smell of cordite hung in the still air.

Hausner took the M-14 from Brin and, with the scope, took a last look at the retreating Arabs. They were out of range of the M-14 now, but he could see them clearly. Standing alone on a mound of earth with the body of a long-haired woman slung over his shoulder was a solitary man. He remained motionless as the last of the Ashbals filed past him. The man looked up at the hill that had cost so many of his brothers their lives. He made some sort of movement with his arm—a salute or a motion of damnation. Hausner could not be sure which. He couldn't identify the face at that distance, but he knew for a certainty that it was Ahmed Rish.

14

The Prime Minister of Israel walked, unannounced, into the Operations Room of The Citadel in Tel Aviv. The Air Force personnel allowed themselves one quick glance, then returned to their work.

The noise of telephones, teletypes, and electronic machinery was loud—louder than the Prime Minister remembered it on Yom Kippur, 1973.

The Prime Minister instinctively scanned the big room for General Talman. Then he remembered and walked over to Talman's replacement, General Mordecai Hur. His entourage dispersed throughout the room to gather information and pass on orders.

The Prime Minister stood close to General Hur. "Any survivors from 01?" Hur was a copy of his former boss, British-trained, reserved, correct, well-spoken, and well-dressed. The Prime Minister was none of these things, but he had gotten on well with Talman and he hoped for the same relationship with Hur.

153

General Hur shook his head almost imperceptibly. "No, sir. But we've recovered about half the bodies." He paused. "There won't be any survivors, you know."

"I know." He looked around at the electronic displays. "Where's 02, Motty?"

Hur was slightly taken aback by the diminutive of his name. "I don't know, sir. And every minute that we don't know increases the area where they could be if they have refueled and are still airborne. We're at the limits of our resources now."

The Prime Minister nodded. "How about that American satellite photo in the Sudan?"

Hur took a sheet of paper from a long counter. "Here's a report from our agent on the ground there. The object on the photo turned out to be sheets of aluminum lying on the sand. General size and configuration of a Concorde."

"Ruse or accident?"

"There's a difference of opinion on that. I say a clever ruse. Some people think it was just coincidence. But we've got three or four more photos like that to follow up. We'll have to try to verify with infrared heat pictures and spectrograph analysis if we can't get a reliable agent on the spot. Also, we have radar, radio, and visual reports which seem more like red herrings than anything else."

"This was a well-planned operation. But it needed an inside man, didn't it?"

"That's not my area, sir. Ask Shin Beth."

The Prime Minister had had Mazar on the carpet for over an hour, but Internal Security was just as surprised at the whole thing as everyone else. Mazar, however, unlike a dozen other people, had not offered his resignation. The Prime Minister had to admire a man who said in effect, "Screw you, my resignation is not going to help matters." But he knew that Mazar would have to go eventually.

An aide carried a telephone to him. "The Secretary General of the United Nations, sir."

The Prime Minister took the receiver. "Yes, Mr. Secretary?" He listened as the Secretary General gave the situation report that he had asked for earlier. The Secretary General spoke in guarded terms. The Arab peace delegations were still in New York. No one had been recalled. The mood was apprehensive. Would Israel overreact in some way and put the Arabs in a

difficult position? The Prime Minister would not make any statements one way or the other. They spoke politely for several minutes. The Prime Minister looked at the chronometer displays on the wall. It was midnight in New York. The Secretary General sounded tired. "Thank you, Mr. Secretary. Can you have me switched to the Office of the Israeli Mission? Thank you."

He spoke to his Permanent Ambassador to the UN, and then to the advance personnel of the peace mission who had been working for months to prepare for the Conference. Many had friends and relatives with the lost peace delegation. There was a mixture of outrage, despair, and optimism among them. The Prime Minister could hear his own voice echoing on the amplifiers in their offices. He addressed them all. "You have prepared fertile ground for peace to grow." He was a farmer and he liked these metaphors. "We will plant that seed yet. Keep the ground ready. But *if* it becomes necessary to plow the earth with salt—" he paused. The line was unsecured, and at the very least, the FBI and the CIA were listening and he wanted them—and everyone else—to know, "—then we will plow it with salt and it will lie dead for a decade." He hung up.

He turned back to General Hur. "It will take a few minutes before the American State Department hears the tape of that call and rings us up. Let's have some coffee."

They walk over to the coffee bar and poured mugs for themselves. A nearby counter top was becoming piled with foreign and domestic newspapers showing the same front page picture of a Concorde with El Al markings—the Prime Minister recognized it as an old public relations photo sent out on the occasion of the inaugural flight of 01. They all carried headlines announcing the same news in different ways and different languages. The Prime Minister looked cursorily through a few of the newspapers. "Sometimes I feel we are very much alone on this big planet. Other times, I feel that people care about us."

General Hur looked down into the blackness of his cup. He sensed, rather than actually saw, the red eyes, the puffy skin, the slightly tousled hair. He had never believed in the Peace Conference while it was being talked about. But now he saw how much other people had believed in it, and he felt some guilt over the fact that he had hoped something—something minor, of course—would cause it to be canceled. He looked up at the

Prime Minister. "My experience as a military man has been that people only care about peace at the eleventh hour. By then it's often impossible to reverse the course of events."

"And what time do you figure it is now, General?"

"I couldn't say, sir. That's the thing about the eleventh hour. You never know when it's a quarter to—you only know when it's five after, and counting."

An aide carried another telephone to the Prime Minister. "Washington. State Department."

The Prime Minister glanced at General Hur, then picked up the receiver. "Yes, Mr. Secretary. How is that farm of yours in Virginia? Yes, I know, the Tidewater region has become quite salty since your ancestors settled there. Times change. The tide is relentless. We have similar problems here. The sea has so much room to roam, yet it seems to want the land." They spoke in a roundabout manner for a few minutes, then the Prime Minister placed the receiver back into the cradle and turned to Hur. "Our reputation for overreacting to terrorism has not hurt us, General. Everyone wants to make certain that we are still in a mood to talk."

General Hur forgot his professionalism and his place and asked, "And are we?"

The Prime Minister looked around the Operations Room. He stayed silent for a long time, then said, "I don't know, General. We can't change what happened to 01. But I think the mood of the people will depend very much on what has happened to 02. Why haven't we heard from their captors, General?"

"I can't imagine."

The Prime Minister nodded. "Maybe they are not..."

"Not what, sir?"

"Never mind. Have you seen the report we received from Aerospatiale?"

"Yes. A classic example of closing the pasture gate after the cattle have gone. There's no help for us there."

The Prime Minister nodded again. "The Palestinian mortar men don't seem to know anything."

"I'd be surprised if they did."

"Are we forgetting anything, Motty?"

Hur shook his head. "No. I don't think so. We're doing all we can here. We've linked up with other air force operation centers from Tehran to Madrid, and they're helping. It all depends on an intelligence break now."

"Either that, or Mr. Ahmed Rish will get around to calling us and let us know what is happening."

"I'd rather we found out what is happening ourselves."

The Prime Minister took a last look around the room. "Keep at it, Motty. I'll speak to you later."

"Yes, sir. Where can I reach you if something comes up?"

The Prime Minister considered. Tel Aviv had far superior communication and transportation facilities. It was also less exposed and safer in other ways. A War Ministry study had reaffirmed that Tel Aviv should be the center of all operations during any crisis. Yet, Jerusalem was the capital—not only the political capital, but the heart and soul of Israel. It was a concept, a state of mind, a spiritual and eternal entity. Even if it were just rubble—or salted earth, as the Romans had left it—it would be Jerusalem nonetheless. "Jerusalem. I am going to Jerusalem."

Hur nodded and allowed himself a smile.

The Prime Minister left.

Teddy Laskov stood alone on the tarmac at the military end of Lod Airport. A false dawn lit up the eastern sky and outlined the hills of Samaria rising up from the Plain of Sharon. He stared into the sky for a long time until the light faded and the darkest hour began.

He turned away and looked out across the black runways to where the twelve F-14's stood silhouetted against the lights of the International Terminal in the distance. They stood silent, like sentinels guarding the frontiers of civilization and humanity. People called them warplanes, but they could just as easily have been called peace planes, reflected Laskov. He would miss them. Miss the smell of their leather and their hydraulics. Miss the coffee bar in the ready rooms, the static of the radios. Especially, he would miss the men and women who made the Hel Avir more than just a collection of overpriced metal. From his first aircraft in Russia to his last in Israel—or from chock to chock, as pilots put it—it had been forty years. That was too long, anyway, he thought.

He turned and began walking toward a waiting jeep. He allowed himself one backward glance as he mounted the jeep.

The driver turned on the lights, put the vehicle in gear, and lurched across the runway toward the airport access road.

Laskov removed his hat and tunic and laid them in his lap. The night wind whipped around the windshield and tousled his greying hair. He settled back. He thought of Miriam. Her fate had actually been in his hands for a few minutes. In fact, he had held the fate of his nation in his hands while he held the control column of his warplane. Now he held nothing but his hat and coat. He was ambivalent about leaving the pressure cooker of command. It felt good to leave it, but he felt an emptiness as well. And it felt lonely very quickly, he noticed. Without Miriam, it would feel more so.

The driver ventured a sideward glance.

Laskov turned his head and forced a smile.

The young man cleared his throat. "Home, General?"

"Yes. Home."

15

The beginning of morning nautical twilight—BMNT—was at 6:03 A.M. The sky lightened into perfect cloudless blue. There was a slight chill in the air and the damp morning smell of the river lay over the hill. A mist rose off the water as the air became warmer. Somewhere, birds began to sing in the pale light. At 6:09 the sun rose above the distant peaks of the Zagros Mountains in Iran and burnt off the ground mist.

Hausner wondered what those ancient valley dwellers of the Tigris and Euphrates must have thought of those mysterious snow-peaked mountains as the sun came out of them every day. And then one day, the Persians had come out of them, semibarbarous and full of blood lust, and they had defeated the old civilizations of the Tigris and Euphrates. But eventually, the conquerors were absorbed into the culture of the ancient valley dwellers.

Every century or so, a new group of lean and ferocious mountain men would burst out of the surrounding highlands of what was now Iran and Turkey. The ancient cities and towns

159

and farms would absorb the destruction and pillaging, the rape and the massacres, and then carry on under new rulers after the dust had settled and the killing had stopped. Then came the Arabians from the deserts of the south and swept away the old gods.

But the worst were the Mongols. They had come and wrought such utter destruction on the cities and ancient irrigation works that Mesopotamia never recovered. What was once a land of twenty or thirty million people—the most concentrated population in the world outside of Egypt and China—became a desert with a few million disease-ridden and terror-stricken inhabitants. Land that had been under continuous cultivation for four thousand years turned to dust. Malarial swamps and sand dunes shifted alternately over the land as the twin rivers ran wild over the alluvial plain. Some centuries later with the coming of the Turks, the land and the people declined even further. When the British pushed the Turks out in 1917, they couldn't believe that this was the Fertile Crescent. The legendary site of the Garden of Eden at Qurna was a pestilent swamp. The Tommies would joke, "If this is the Garden of Eden, I'd hate to see hell."

No wonder the modern Iraqis were the way they were, thought Hausner—a mixture of bitterness at their historical fate and pride in their ancient heritage. That was one of the keys to the complex personality of Ahmed Rish. If someone in Tel Aviv or Jerusalem would understand that, then maybe someone would say, "Babylonian Captivity."

Hausner shook his head. No. It was easy to come to that conclusion when you were standing in Babylon. It would not be as obvious to Military Intelligence people who were looking at reports of radio traffic and radar sightings, aerial photographs and agents' memos.

But still, the Israeli Intelligence services were known for imagination and unconventional thinking. If they looked hard at Rish's psychological profile—a romantic with illusions of historic grandeur and all the rest—then maybe they would come to the right conclusions. Hausner hoped so.

Hausner began inspecting the thin defensive line. There were two more AK-47's now and perhaps enough ammunition to hold off an attack such as had been mounted the previous night. Everyone was working on the defensive positions except for a small party that had volunteered to comb the eastern slope again for abandoned equipment. They brought with them aluminum struts and sheets to be used as shovels to bury the two dead Arabs that were left behind.

The Israelis had suffered seven wounded; one, Chaim Tamir, a delegate to the peace mission, was hurt badly. They were all resting comfortably with Kaplan in the shepherds' hut, which Hausner designated as the infirmary, under the supervision of the two stewardesses.

An earth and clay ramp was being constructed up to the leading edge of the starboard-side delta to make access to the Concorde easier. The work was done by sweating, bare-chested men using crude tools made from scraps of the Concorde. Earth was carried in suitcases and blankets and packed onto the ramp by hand and foot.

Hausner stepped onto the partially completed ramp and jumped the remainder of the way onto the wing. He entered the cabin through the emergency door.

Sitting in the back of the aircraft, facing him, were Burg and Dobkin. His court-martial board.

Hausner moved down the aisle. The sun illuminated the small portholes, and a shaft of dusty sunlight streamed in from the gaping hole in the rear bulkhead. "Good morning." He remained standing in the aisle. The smell of burnt kerosene still permeated the cabin.

The two men nodded.

Dobkin cleared his throat. "Jacob, this grieves us very much. But if there is to be any discipline here, we must be brutal with anyone who disobeys orders."

"I quite agree."

Dobkin leaned forward. "Then you concur that we have the authority to try you?"

"I didn't say that."

"It's not important that you do," said Dobkin. "We *are* the law here. Whether you agree or not."

"I agree that *we* are the law. *We* can try people and mete out punishment."

Dobkin frowned. "Jacob, you are drawing a very fine line. Now this is serious. If we try you, it will be in open court, with observers and all of that, but I can tell you already that the verdict will be cut and dry. Guilty. And the only sentence possible under these circumstances is . . . ." He looked toward

Burg for support. Burg had instigated this proceeding, but Burg was a pragmatist and a survivor to the core. He sat back and said nothing. He lit his pipe with a lot of flourish and made noncommittal noises. He wanted to see which way it would go. Dobkin was a military man. He was used to demanding total loyalty and getting it. Burg, in his world, accepted disloyalty and compromises that would make the generals reach for their court-martial manuals.

Hausner looked at his watch pointedly. "Listen, the only thing you have wrong here is the fact that I can't be charged with disobeying an order because *I* am in charge. Now, if anyone else disobeys an order—including either of you—we will convene this group and try him. Is there anything else?"

Dobkin leaned forward. "Are you mutinying?"

"I wouldn't call it that."

"I would. The highest ranking man among us is the Foreign Minister. As an elected member of the Knesset, he—"

"Forget it, General. I have the loyalty of the majority of the armed men out there. The Foreign Minster may be in charge *de jure*, but *de facto* we have taken over and you know it. That's why you didn't even bother to invite him to this little meeting. The only point of contention here is which of us three is the head man. I say it is me. But if you want the orders to come through the Foreign Minister or through either of you, that's fine with me. As long as you all understand who's giving those orders. All right?"

There was a long silence, then Burg spoke for the first time. "You see, it was a classical maneuver, based on the von Neumann-Morgenstern game plan theory, I believe. Jacob usurped the power from the Foreign Minister with our tacit approval. After we had taken that step, there was no going back for us. And now Jacob is finessing *us*. Very Machiavellian." Burg's tone was neutral.

Hausner said nothing.

There was another long silence. Dobkin spoke softly. "Why are you doing this, Jacob?"

Hausner shrugged, "I guess because I'm the only one who understands how to handle this situation. I trust *me*. I'm a little nervous about *you*."

Dobkin shook his head. "No. It's because you got us here. Now you want to get us out. You want to be the hero so you can face life if—when—we get home. And you don't care who gets stepped on as long as you can square this thing with yourself."

Hausner's face turned red. "Whatever you say, General." He turned, walked toward the door, then looked over his shoulder. "Staff meeting at noon sharp. Here in the aircraft." He left.

On the ground, Hausner found Becker and Kahn. They were sitting over a schematic of the APU. He crouched down beside them in the shade of the delta wing. "Why didn't we have any luck with the radio last night?"

Kahn spoke. "We were having trouble concentrating with all the damned noise out here."

Hausner smiled. "Sorry. We'll try to keep it quiet tonight."

"I hope to God we're out of here by nightfall," said Kahn.

Hausner looked at him. "I think that might depend to a large extent on you two."

Becker stood. "On me. I'm the captain. If we make radio contact, I'll take the credit. If we don't, I'll take the blame." Becker's tone was cool.

Hausner stood also. "Of course. Everyone is looking for planes. As soon as someone spots one they have orders to run at top speed back here and tell you. The ramp up to the aircraft will be finished in a few hours. You can be inside and broadcasting within about two minutes of an aircraft being spotted. Is that satisfactory?"

"Sounds good," said Becker.

Hausner looked up at the delta wing. He seemed to come to a decision. "I'm draining off the remaining fuel."

Becker stared. "I need the fuel to run the auxiliary power unit so that we can generate power to run the radios."

"The APU is not working, nor will it ever work. The first priority is to keep the Arabs out of here. Even if you do get the APU working, it will be damned little use to us with Ahmed Rish sitting in the cockpit. I need the fuel to make things that will explode, Captain."

"I can't let you take the fuel."

Hausner stared at him. Technicians got away with a lot more than ordinary mortals. "You're wasting time on this APU. The damned thing isn't worth it. Go back to the flight deck and operate the radios until the batteries are gone. We have no time to worry about generating our own electricity for later. There may not be a later unless we shoot the works with what we've got like we did last night." He looked evenly at Becker, then at

Kahn. He lowered his voice. "Besides, I don't want all that fuel in the wing tanks. One tracer round could set it off and cook you two in the cockpit."

Becker knew that Hausner had a point. But then again, so did he. For every problem that lay ahead, there were several conceivable solutions. "Look," he said, "let us try to fix the APU while radio reception is bad. You take the fuel you need. I think there might be more left than we thought. You can only hold so much in the containers available. The rest will stay in the tanks. Agreed?"

Hausner smiled. "When we were up there, you demanded and got complete obedience from me and everyone else with no arguments and no compromise. You were the captain. Now I am the commander on the ground. Why shouldn't I demand the same?"

Becker shook his head. "It's different up there. That's technical. Here it's all subjective. There's room for discussion."

"Bullshit." Hausner looked up at the Concorde. Its white paint glowed a pale yellow in the rising sun. "I'll make a final decision later. Meanwhile, I'm going to start making Molotov cocktails with the fuel. See you later." He turned and walked away.

Under the damaged tail section of the aircraft, the Foreign Minister sat on the ground with two junior aides, Shimon Peled and Esther Aronson. Also seated with him were two delegates, Ya'akov Sapir, a left-wing member of the Knesset, whom Hausner didn't care for, and Miriam Bernstein, whom Hausner did care for.

Hausner could see that they had taken a break from whatever they had been doing and were engaged in a lively parliamentary debate. He walked over to them.

The Foreign Minister looked up. At first he seemed surprised to see Hausner. Then he nodded to himself. He guessed correctly that Dobkin and Burg had come off second best in their attempt to discipline Hausner. He made a quick eveluation of the situation and stood up to meet Hausner. "I didn't have time to thank you properly for your role in last night's action."

Hausner nodded. "Thank you, Mr. Minister." He looked down at the four people sitting in the dust, trying to ignore him. "I'm sorry I didn't have time this morning to assign you any duties."

"Quite all right. We would be happy to have some direction in the expenditure of our energies and—"

"What I had in mind, Mr. Minister, was this—you should gather all the loose luggage that fell in the wake of the aircraft. Some of it is down the hill, so be careful when you go outside the perimeter. Empty the luggage and sort the contents. Carry all empty bags and clothes to the men and women on the perimeter. They will fill the luggage with sand and clay to make breastworks. Then they will fashion dummies out of the clothes, stuffing them with sand and rags. I want a nice job of it. The dummies will be placed in position at dusk. Save some clothing for bandages and catalogue anything else you find that may be of use, such as liquor, medicines, food, and that sort of thing." He paused, then spoke in a low voice. "Also, I want you to look among the drugs for one that will kill quickly and painlessly if taken in an overdose. But keep that quiet." He said loudly, "Is everything clear?"

The Foreign Minister nodded. "Of course. We'll begin as soon as we adjourn."

Hausner shook his head almost imperceptibly.

"Well, perhaps we should adjourn now," said the Foreign Minister. He turned around and faced the group that was still sitting. "All for adjournment say aye."

A few voices mumbled in return. They all stood slowly and sullenly and walked off, except for Miriam Bernstein.

Hausner turned and began walking in the opposite direction.

Bernstein caught up with him. "You humiliated a fine man back there."

He didn't answer.

"Did you hear me, damn you?"

He stopped but did not turn to face her. "Anyone who insists on playing games with me is exposing himself to humiliations, if not worse. And I don't have the time or patience for one of your lectures, Miriam."

She walked around him and looked him in the face. She spoke softly. "What's come over you, Jacob? I can't believe you're acting like this."

He stepped closer to her and stared down into her eyes. There were tears starting to form there, but he couldn't tell if they were tears of rage or sorrow. It struck him that he could never read her expressions. Sometimes she seemed like a robot programmed to deliver peace and conciliation sermons. Yet he suspected there was flesh and blood there. Passion. Real passion. He had discovered that much while they sat together on the Concorde. But then he had been at a low point and she had become human. She was one of those women who responded warmly to need and weakness. Strength and self-assurance in a man put her off. He supposed it had something to do with the black uniforms of her childhood. God, he would never understand the Jews of the camps. He could understand the arrogant, cocky Sabras, although he wasn't one of them, either. His own peers were a small group and getting smaller every year. He never felt really at home in the new Israel. He never felt at ease with Jews of the camps like Miriam Bernstein. He looked down, against his will, to her wrist where the numbers were tattooed. Many people had them removed by a plastic surgeon. Hers were distorted and lighter than was usual. The result of growth. The numbers of a child.

"Aren't you going to answer me?"

"What? Oh. Yes. What's come over me? Well, I'll tell you, Miriam. A few minutes ago, General Dobkin and Mr. Burg were at the point of putting me in front of a firing squad." He raised his hand to stifle her exclamation of disbelief, then went on. "Don't get me wrong. I'm not angry with them. I agree with the thought processes that brought them to that point. I just didn't agree with their choice of victim. You see, they perceive things a lot more clearly than the rest of you do. They know what has to be done here. I can guarantee you, Miriam, that if this situation lasts another forty-eight hours, you will all be clamoring for the execution of food-hoarders, malingerers, traitors, and people who fall asleep on guard duty. But we don't have the luxury of waiting for a consensus. What seems brutal to you today will seem lenient to you tomorrow."

She wiped away a tear and shook her head. "You have very little faith in humanity. Most of us are not like that. I'd rather die than vote for someone else's execution."

"You *will* die if you maintain that attitude. And for a person who saw what you saw, I don't know how you can have so much faith in the basic goodness of human beings."

"I said *most* human beings were decent. There are always a few fascists."

"What you really mean is that there is a little fascist in all of us. And that's the part of you that will become dominant when things get tough. The part of me that I've called on to survive.

BABYLON 167

Called on knowingly and willingly. The beast. The heart of darkness." He looked at her. She was pale. "You know, for someone who spends so much time with an Air Force general, I would have thought that some of the hawk would have rubbed off."

She looked quickly up at him. Color came into her pale cheeks. "You—" She turned and walked quickly away from him.

16

Hausner sat with Brin and Naomi Haber at their firing position. He looked down the eastern slope, smoking a cigarette and speaking to the young couple. "Are you teaching her to use the scope and rifle?" he asked Brin.

Brin shrugged. "She doesn't want to learn."

Hausner turned to her. "Why not?"

She brushed some dust off her blue jumpsuit. "I can't shoot anyone. I'm a good and fast runner, and that's what I volunteered to do."

Hausner started to answer her, but Dobkin suddenly appeared. Hausner glanced at him quickly and looked for a gun, but did not see one. Brin tensed up, also.

Dobkin seemed to have forgotten the incident in the Concorde. He nodded and sat down on the ground. No one spoke for a long while.

Hausner turned and pointed across the top of the flat mound toward the southwest. "What's that?"

Dobkin looked. The morning shadows lay over the brown

land. Swirls of mist rose out of the scattered marsh. "The Greek amphitheater. Built by Alexander the Great. When he captured Babylon in 323 B.C.E., the city was already ancient and on the skids. He attempted to revive it, but its day was over. Alexander died here. Did you know that?"

"No." Hausner chain-lit a cigarette.

"They'll be coming to parley soon," said Dobkin.

"Who? The Greeks?"

Dobkin allowed himself a smile. "The Greeks I could parley with. It's the Arabs I'm worried about."

Hausner smiled back. There was a little less tension between them. "*Maybe* they'll come." He turned to Brin and Naomi Haber. "Why don't you two take a break in the shade?"

The girl stood. Brin hesitated, then stood also. He took the M-14 and walked off, followed by the girl.

When they were out of earshot, Dobkin spoke. "No maybes about it. They won't try a daylight assault, and they don't want to wait for nightfall to resolve this thing."

"You're right," said Hausner.

"What are we going to tell them?"

Hausner looked at him. "Are you with me?"

Dobkin hesitated. "I . . . the Foreign Minister and Burg are *our* superiors."

"We'll see about that."

Dobkin changed the subject. "I'm going on a one-way mission tonight."

"I know that."

"There isn't much chance for me to get through. I'm going only so that the people here can keep their hopes and morale up."

"That's why I'm sending you. I don't think you'll make it either. There are not many people who would go after figuring that out. You're all right, General." He looked at him. "So, are you with me?"

Dobkin shrugged. "What difference does it make? You hold all the cards. The political leaders are cowed. Your men hold five of the six automatic weapons."

"I just want to know for myself." He pointed to the south. "What's that, by the way?"

"I'm not going to make you feel good by going along with you. Let's just say I'm neutral." He looked to the south. "That should be the Kasr mound. On the other side are the excavations of the palace of Nebuchadnezzar and the ruins of the Hanging Gardens. Close to that is the Ishtar Gate and the museum and guest house." He paused. "I'm looking forward to seeing it tonight."

"Glad to hear it," said Hausner. There was a long silence.

Suddenly, Hausner came to attention. He pointed southwest toward the Euphrates. "Is that smoke? It looks like a village among the ruins."

Dobkin nodded without looking. "It is. The village of Kweirish."

"I wonder if they would be of any help."

"I don't think so. They're peasants. They have no connection with the outside world. Besides, I'm sure the Ashbals are running the place."

Hausner could see the squalid mud huts, huddled like some medieval Italian village in a corner of a ruined Roman city in order to survive.

The whole of the surrounding countryside was a spectacular study of contrasts. Patches of desert and marshland to the east and beyond that the Tigris and then the towering mountains. On the west bank of the Euphrates, endless mud flats stretching to the horizons, wet now, but soon to be cracked by the hot sun like a jigsaw puzzle. A few bulrushes and date palms struggled on both banks of the Euphrates.

In the foreground, around the mound they were on, Hausner could make out bricks and rubble, smaller mounds and marsh. There were the low ridges of straight city walls, punctuated every now and then by higher mounds that had been the watchtowers. Wind, water, sand, and thousands of years of brick quarrying by peasants had combined to obliterate what was once the wonder of the world's cities. Hausner knew that scenes of desolation such as this were common in Mesopotamia. The largest and most opulent cities of the ancient world lay for thousands of years undisturbed beneath the dust. A sense of emptiness assailed him as he looked out across the Euphrates. Flat, bare plains of wet mud were crisscrossed here and there by the fabled irrigation canals, now disused. The very wildlife that should have flourished here seemed to have abandoned the place. This was a strange and somehow malevolent corner of the world. A place where huge temples had been raised long ago to gods that no one remembered and palaces built for kings and kingdoms that had vanished without a trace.

The silence of the place screamed in his ears as if he were hearing the ghostly crashing of Babylonian chariots, the fleeing enemy, and the shouts of her victorious armies. Opulent Babylon. In the Old and New Testaments, a symbol of human pride, carnality, and sin. To modern Jews and Christians, its utter desolation was a symbol of Biblical prophecy fulfilled. Hausner knew that there must be some meaning in all the nothingness that stretched before him. Yet, perhaps the meaning was nothingness. Sand. Dust. Death.

Why had Rish brought them here? The Babylonian Captivity? Hausner imagined that was it. Or maybe it was something less melodramatic. Perhaps it was just convenient for his purposes—close to the Palestinians' camp. But their camp was a hundred kilometers across the desert.... Well, the Babylonian Captivity it was, then. In the libraries of the world there were tomes on Babylon, and when they were revised and rewritten, there would be a footnote with an asterisk and it would read, *a curious incident involving a supersonic Concorde aircraft and....* Hausner put out his cigarette and saved the stub. "Here they come," he said softly.

From the direction of the road, a group of five men were walking up the slope of the mound. The man in front held up a white flag.

Haber and Brin, who had not gone far, came hurrying back. Brin had changed to the ten-power day scope and watched them approach. "I don't think Rish is with them." Brin handed the rifle to Hausner who knelt and sighted through the scope. Hausner put the rifle down and shook his head. "He doesn't trust us. He thinks that we would not honor a white flag. That makes me damned angry. General?"

Dobkin nodded. "It does show a lack of faith on his part." He thought for a moment. "He really doesn't understand us—and *that* scares me."

Hausner stood and turned to Brin and Haber. "Pass the word to hold fire. I want everyone to remain out of sight. No one is to leave the perimeter, Nathan. If anyone tries, stop him." He brushed off his clothes. "General, will you accompany me?"

"Of course." He stood, also, and straightened his uniform. "You know, it's ironic. They want to talk *now*. That's what we wanted to do in New York—and on the Concorde. Now I'm not so sure *I* want to talk."

"I agree," said Hausner. "But I'm sure the peace delegation wants to talk. I don't trust that bunch, Ben. They are professional peacemakers. They are spring-loaded to see the good side of any proposal. Cursed are the peacemakers for they make the next war harder than the last."

Dobkin laughed. "Amen. The generals should negotiate the peaces and the peacemakers should run the armies." He became serious. "Actually, we are not being fair to the delegation. They are not all alike—some—most are very hard bargainers. They are realists as much as we are."

Hausner stepped down onto the slope. "I doubt it. Come on. Let's go before a dozen professional negotiators descend on us." He began making his way downhill. Dobkin followed.

They lost sight of the Arabs for a while as their group descended into a deep draw. A hundred meters down the slope, they spotted the white flag, then they saw the Arabs again. They were armed and advancing fast. Hausner felt a moment of doubt, but he waved a white handkerchief and shouted in Arabic. The Arabs spotted him and responded. Both groups approached each other slowly. The Arabs stopped on a level shelf in the side of the slope.

Hausner walked quickly up to them and stood very close to the leader, in the Arab manner. "Where's Rish? I will speak only with Rish."

The man stared at him for a very long moment. His dark eyes seemed to burn with hate and contempt. Obviously he didn't like this mission. He spoke softly and slowly. "I am Salem Hamadi, lieutenant of Ahmed Rish. He sends his respects and requests your immediate surrender."

Hausner looked at the man. Unlike Rish, Hamadi had never been captured and there existed neither an identikit nor a psychological profile on him. There was not even a comprehensive listing of his activities. All Hausner knew was that the man had started life as a Palestinian orphan and then became head of the Ashbal program for the various Palestinian liberation organizations. Values? Morality? Honor? It was hard to say. You couldn't even count on the strong religious upbringing that most Arabs were exposed to. The man who stood less than a meter from Hausner was short but well proportioned. He wore a neatly clipped goatee and apparently practiced somewhat more rigorous personal hygiene than Hausner had observed among the terrorists at Ramla. Hausner moved even closer. "Where is he? I demand to speak to him."

Hamadi nodded slowly. "You are Jacob Hausner."

"I am."

"Will you accompany me?"

"I might."

Hamadi hesitated. "You have my personal assurances."

"Really?"

Hamadi literally bit his lip to control his growing impatience. "My word." He paused. "Believe me, we want to talk this over as much as you do." He smiled suddenly. "This is not a trap to kill Jacob Hausner. We could do that right here and now. Besides, you are not that important."

"Rish seemed to think I was. He said he would kill me when we landed."

Salem Hamadi looked off into space. "He rescinds that vow."

Hausner turned and waved to Brin, who was watching through the scope. Brin acknowledged. Hausner could see heads staring discreetly over the newly fabricated breastworks of baggage and earth. He noticed that some of the baggage was too brightly colored. He would have to see that a layer of dust was put on everything. He turned back to Hamadi. Hamadi had seen the glint of light from the scope and was committing its location to memory. Hausner bumped him on purpose as he moved past him. "Well, let's go. I have other things to do."

The group started down the slope. They came off the incline and began walking parallel to a meter-high ridge that Dobkin explained was the city's inner wall. Hausner saw the spot where the Concorde's rear bumper wheel had hit it, what seemed like a century before. They turned south and headed toward the main ruins.

The ruins of the city were barely excavated. It took a lot of imagination to picture a teeming metropolis of living souls— young girls with jangling bracelets, soldiers eating and drinking, colorful bazaars, awesome processions, and the famous astrologers of Babylon drawing up horoscopes on wet clay for a few coppers. But Hausner, as an inhabitant of the Middle East, was used to excavations. He could see it all, and more. He could almost feel the presence of the spirits as they jostled him on the busy street. A ringing in his ears seemed to turn into semidistinct voices speaking an ancient Semitic language. Then there was a word or a snatch of a phrase in ancient Hebrew. He suddenly felt that right where he was walking, a Jew had walked and had spoken with his wife. They had their children with them. They were going somewhere. Toward the Ishtar Gate. Out of the city. They were leaving Babylon, and captivity, for good.

Hamadi said something, and Hausner became aware that they had come a long distance. He looked around. The excavations were more thorough here. Hamadi was speaking to Dobkin, who was asking incessant questions about the ruins. Hamadi seemed unsure of his answers and finally told Dobkin to be quiet.

Hausner knew something of the history of Babylon even if he did not know the city itself. He knew Babylon as a name, a symbol, a conception, a state of mind. He hardly credited the fact that it existed as brick and mortar. Dobkin was interested in the brick and mortar. Hausner, if he was interested at all, was interested in something more enduring. And what could be more enduring than total obliteration and destruction? That's what made Babylon a living symbol. Its place in history was secured by the fact that it had fallen as predicted.

So Babylon had died as cities do die, and the dust blew over her endlessly through the centuries, covering it all. The site could hardly be located by modern archeologists, and even local legend, which had kept alive the location of the sites of other buried cities, ceased to mention Babylon, so utter and complete was the desolation.

And now the digging out had begun, as it had in Israel and other parts of the Middle East. Each mound that was excavated was a reminder not only of the transitory nature of man's works, but also of the human peculiarity for self-destruction. For Hausner, the associations with Babylon, with Jews being here again, was both ludicrous and sad. The fact that they had arrived by supersonic transport was beside the point. The point was that they were there—there against their will. The human dimension had not undergone any major changes in thousands of years. Only the externals had changed.

When the small group reached the heights where the Greek amphitheater stood, they turned west toward the Euphrates River and followed a goat path. An emaciated donkey nibbled on the ubiquitous salt-white clumps of thorn. A slight breeze rustled through the yellow-green fronds of a solitary date palm. The heat was growing more oppressive. Hausner was reminded that there was less than twenty-four hours' supply of liquids on the hill. The available food might last twice as long. Sections of the aircraft's aluminum skin had been shaped into basins to collect rainwater, but rain seemed as unlikely here as snow.

They walked silently, Dobkin taking both a military and an archeological interest in the route. They stopped on a small ridge. Hausner could see the hill where the Concorde rested, about a kilometer and a half to the north. The top of the Concorde was barely visible from here. The hill—or the buried citadel—looked formidable from this perspective, and he could see why the Ashbals wished to negotiate.

To the west was the Euphrates, about five hundred meters further down the goat trail. Hausner could see the squalid village of Kweirish, on the bank of the Euphrates, more clearly now. It was a village of *sarifa*—rough mud huts, unwhitewashed and unadorned. As they came closer, he could see women wrapped to the eyes in long black *abbahs* and men in long shirtlike *gellebiahs,* their heads draped in *kheffiyahs*. Someone was scraping a thin music from a stringed instrument. Goats, the color of the earth, grazed the scrub and were herded by Biblical-looking figures in long robes and flowing headdresses, doing the same work under the same conditions as their ancestors had done thousands of years before. The whole scene, Hausner realized, had hardly changed in four or five thousand years. The people were Moslems instead of idol worshippers, they no longer kept swine herds, and Babylon was no more. But otherwise, life on the Euphrates went on and, in fact, changed considerably less than the course of the wandering, restless river.

The group turned off the goat trail and began climbing a huge mound. They reached a flight of steep brick steps and ascended further. On the way, they came to a flat area hollowed out of the side of the mound. Here, mounted on a stone plinth, stood the Lion of Babylon. Nothing was known of it, neither its age nor its significance, but it looked awesome, striding perpetually over a fallen victim. Hamadi spoke. "We search you and blindfold you here."

Hausner shook his head. "No."

Hamadi turned to Dobkin. "It is standard military procedure throughout the world when bringing an enemy into your lines. You know this. It is no humiliation."

Dobkin had to agree.

Hausner agreed reluctantly.

They undressed and were searched thoroughly. They dressed again and were blindfolded and taken slowly up the remaining steps. The ground leveled out, but it was covered with what seemed to be clay bricks. They descended a flight of steps and the air suddenly felt cooler. The blindfolds were removed. Hausner strained to see in the darkened room. He heard voices whispering.

"I am Ahmed Rish," said a soft voice from the shadow in passable Hebrew. "It is an event to see Jacob Hausner—again. And an honor to meet the famous General Dobkin."

Hausner and Dobkin remained silent. They both sensed that there were other men in the shadows along the walls. The ruined chamber had no roof, but the sun was too low to penetrate into it. They looked around slowly, as their eyes adjusted to the darkness.

Rish spoke again. "We are in the excavated ruins of the South Palace. The throne room where Belshazzar, grandson of Nebuchadnezzar, saw the fatal handwriting on the wall. You will be familiar with the story from the Book of Daniel, of course."

Silence.

Rish spoke again from the darkness. "I am standing where the royal throne stood, in a recess of the wall. If you squint into the darkness you may visualize the scene of feasting—the gold and silver vessels taken by Nebuchadnezzar when he sacked Jerusalem, the flickering candle, the apparition of the hand that emerged from the shadows and wrote the words of Babylon's doom upon the wall." He paused for effect. "That is one of the Jews' favorite stories. That is why I brought you here. A special treat."

Hausner and Dobkin did not respond.

Rish went on. "Close by, there has been uncovered a huge furnace. It is no doubt the fiery furnace into which Nebuchadnezzar threw Shadrach, Meshach, and Abed-nego. A miracle was wrought by God and they survived. However, the Jews have not always been saved by such miracles." He paused and the sound of men breathing filled the dark chamber. Rish spoke softly, almost below the threshold of hearing. "Babylon is a place of infinite sadness for the Jews, but it is also a place of miracles. Which will it be this time, Mr. Hausner?"

Hausner lit a cigarette. "You have been very eloquent, Ahmed Rish. I shall be very brief. What do you want?"

"That was foolhardy, landing that huge aircraft on that mound. You could have all been killed."

"What do you want?"

"Excuse me. I neglected to ask you if you would like some refreshments. Water? Food?"

Dobkin answered. "We have plenty of both, Rish."

Rish laughed. "I think not."

Hausner almost shouted. He didn't have any patience with this Arab habit of circumlocution. "Get to the point. What do you *want?*"

Rish's voice sounded a little harder. "I want you all to be my hostages while I negotiate with your government. I want to avoid further bloodshed."

Hausner's eyes were adjusting to the light. He could make out Rish standing in a recess of the wall. He was wearing a simple white *gellebiah* and sandals. He looked about the same as Hausner remembered him from Ramla. He was exceptionally tall and fair for an Arab. Hausner remembered that he was thought to have some Circassian or Persian blood. "You took a bit of a beating last night. You lost about thirty killed and wounded, I suspect."

"I am not here to trade after-action reports, Mr. Hausner. And I am not going to go into a long political harangue about why we did what we did, what our objectives are, or any of that with you. I will take those matters up with your government. I am only going to give you one guarantee and one ultimatum. The guarantee is that no Israelis will be killed if you surrender. The ultimatum is that you surrender before sundown. Is that acceptable?"

Hausner spoke. "What if my country rejects whatever demands you make? How then can you guarantee that we will be safe as hostages?"

"If they call our bluff, I will release you anyway. Only you and I know that, of course. But you have my word on it."

Hausner and Dobkin conferred quietly. Hausner spoke. "I think we know your game, Mr. Rish. Your primary objective was to create an incident to try to wreck the Peace Conference. You may have succeeded there. Maybe not. But your second objective was to grab two planeloads of top-ranking Israelis and interrogate them for political and military intelligence. That intelligence would be worth a fortune on the open market, wouldn't it? And your last objective was to hold us hostage for some unspecified demands. And even if you are willing to let us go if those demands are not met, it would not be before we are vigorously debriefed. Am I right? Do I have your guarantee that none of us will be interrogated or subject to duress of any sort?"

Rish did not answer.

Hausner went on. "How about the Israeli Arabs? I don't think you included them in your guarantee."

Again Rish did not answer, but Hausner could see, even in the bad light, a remarkable change come over his expression. Rish considered the Jews his traditional enemy. But as nonbelievers, by a curious quirk in Arab and Moslem thinking, they were not liable to the ultimate penalty for most offenses. However, a Moslem, especially if he were also Arab, could expect no mercy for transgressions against his people or his religion. Jabari and Arif were dead men as far as Rish was concerned, and Hausner knew it. Rish spoke. "You are making me angry, Mr. Hausner. The lions' den is not the place to be when you wish to provoke the lion. Do it from a distance, Mr. Hausner."

Hausner nodded and looked at Rish closely. He wanted very much to ask Rish about the girl he had seen him carrying away from the battle. But *was* that Rish, and if it was, who was the girl? Was she dead? To ask, however, would confirm what Rish must already suspect about the existence of a night scope. And to ask might send him into an uncontrollable rage. Rish seemed calm enough now, but you couldn't tell with unstable personalities. And that's what the psychiatrists at Ramla had labeled him. Unstable and psychopathic. But like a lot of psychopathic killers, he had a certain charm. The charm could lull you, and then you would make a mistake and that's when he would tear your throat out. "How do I know that you are not so filled with hate that you will not kill us all? What guarantee do I have that you are not... insane?"

Dobkin spoke quickly in a low voice. "For God's sake, Hausner." He grabbed his arm.

There was a very long stillness, during which time Hausner knew that Rish was trying to overcome his urge to murder them. But Hausner knew, as Rish knew, that to murder them was to end all chances of a surrender.

Rish got his emotions under control with considerable

difficulty, then spoke with an even voice. "I can only repeat my guarantee and my ultimatum. You have until dusk. Not one moment longer. After dusk, as we both know, radio reception is better. So don't ask for an extension at dusk." Rish moved a little out of the alcove. "Also, as we both know, it is only a matter of time before the Iraqi authorities discover our little problem here. But don't count on them to act for at least twenty-four hours after they learn we are here. They will hesitate before they move. I can assure you of that. I have friends in the government. They will delay any move and notify me of all decisions. And when the Iraqi Army does move, it moves with painful slowness, Mr. Hausner. Still, I must consider them in my calculations. And so, again I say—at dusk, if we do not hear from you, we attack."

Hausner and Dobkin remained silent. Rish held out his hands in a gesture of solicitation. "Think of the consequences of a defeat. My men are all Ashbals. You know this from your captive?"

There was no answer.

Rish went on. "Well, I cannot be responsible for what might happen in the heat of battle. If my men take the hill tonight, they may be carried away with the madness of killing. They lost many friends last night. They would want revenge. Then there are your women to consider . . . you understand?"

Hausner used one of the most offensive Arabic profanities he could think of.

There was silence except for the sound of men murmuring along the walls.

Then Rish stepped a little further out of the shadows. He smiled. "Your command of the more colorful parts of my native tongue is interesting. Where did you learn that?"

"From you—in Ramla."

"Really?" He moved out of the alcove and stood in the middle of the throne room about two meters from Hausner and Dobkin. "Once I was your prisoner. Now you are about to be mine. When I was in Ramla, you could have had me murdered by my fellow Arabs in exchange for a pardon or an extra privilege. It is done. I know it. But as much as you wanted to have it done, you did not. You had a sense of fair play. Yet I swore to kill you for the insult of slapping me. But really, in a way, I owe you my life. I will be fair with you if you surrender to me now." He looked closely at Hausner, then stepped to within a meter of him. "You know that I still burn with that blow, don't you?" He swung at Hausner and hit him across the face with an open palm.

Hausner was taken aback for a second, then lunged at Rish. Dobkin grabbed him and held him firmly.

Rish nodded his head. "Now that is over. The insult is canceled. *Al ain bel ain al sen bel sen.* An eye for an eye, a tooth for a tooth. Nothing more. Nothing less."

Hausner regained his composure and pulled away from Dobkin. "Yes, I agree, Rish. But there's still the small insult of blowing up a planeload of fifty people."

Rish looked away and spoke. "I won't discuss that. You have an opportunity to save the other fifty." He looked at Dobkin. "From a military point of view you must know it is hopeless."

Dobkin moved closer to Rish. He could hear the sounds of rustling garments in the shadows. Rish made an imperceptible movement with his hand and the shadows retreated back into the walls. Dobkin came within a few centimeters of Rish. "Last night it was indeed hopeless from a military standpoint. Yet we beat you. Tonight the odds will be better."

Rish shook his head. "Tonight we take the hill, General."

Hausner grabbed Dobkin's shoulder. "I've had enough. I want to get back."

Rish nodded. "You will be democratic enough to let everyone vote, I hope, Mr. Hausner."

"Yes. We do everything by vote up there, Rish. I'll let you know before sundown. In the meantime, I'm sending our prisoner down to you. He needs medical attention. Are you equipped?"

Rish laughed. "That is a clumsy way of finding out about our medical situation. But we will take the man. Thank you." He looked slowly from one to another. "Again, I must warn you that if my men take the hill in the dark I cannot control them."

Dobkin spoke. "You're either a bad commander or a bad liar."

Rish turned and walked back into the shadow of the alcove. His retreating voice echoed through the throne room. "I am a realist, gentlemen. Which you are not. Save those people, General. Save their lives, Mr. Hausner."

"I'll do that," said Hausner. He turned to leave.

"Oh. One more thing," said Rish. "This might help you reach

a decision. I have some information that some of your people might find interesting." He paused.

Hausner felt a cold chill of apprehension run up his spine. He did not turn around and he did not respond. Dobkin stood with his back to Rish also.

"Some of your people have members of their families—loved ones—who are in Arab countries. I know the fates of those people. Would *you* like to know them? If you surrender, I will give your people true accounts of each one of them. It would end so much suffering and uncertainty for them. The knowledge of their whereabouts, if they are alive, might help their families to secure their return to Israel."

Silence.

"Abdel Jabari's family, for instance. Or Rachel Baum's brother, missing in action since 1973."

Hausner began walking away. Dobkin followed.

"Wasn't one of your wife's cousins missing in the Sinai since 1967, General?"

Dobkin continued walking without a falter in his step.

"Miriam Bernstein's husband, Yosef. He was in a Syrian POW camp until six months ago. Then one night they took him out and shot him."

Hausner slowed his pace.

"Or was that Rachel Baum's brother? I think Yosef Bernstein is still in a Syrian POW camp. Well, no matter, I have it all written down somewhere. I'll check on it later."

Hausner's body shook with rage and he found it difficult to keep walking. Behind him, Rish's low, taunting laugh echoed through the throne room.

They were led up and out of the chamber into the full sunlight. The escort was slow in putting the blindfolds back on. Dobkin had a glimpse of the towers and battlements of the Ishtar Gate about a hundred meters to the east. Nearby, there was the verandahed guest house and the small museum. The restored gate area gleamed with its blue-glazed bricks in the sunlight. Gold lions of Babylon and mythical beasts shone on the glazing in bas-relief. The walls of the Hanging Gardens stood close by, dusty and cracked with not a trace of vegetation, not even moss.

In the brief time that his eyes were uncovered, Hausner noticed that the mound they were on was approximately the same height as the one the Concorde stood on about two kilometers away, across a small depression in the land. He could see the Concorde from where he stood and his people moving about on the top of the mound.

The blindfolds were put on and they were led away.

After the Arabs left them, Dobkin let out a long breath. "You almost pushed him too far. You're crazy." He glanced back over his shoulder as the Arabs moved further away. "You know, somehow I expected someone more purely evil."

"He's more evil than you can ever imagine."

"I wonder. He's insane. I'm sure of that. But during his moments of sanity, I think that he really wants to be liked and admired."

"He does. And we'll play on that if we get another chance." Hausner was breathing hard from the climb. He looked up and waved at Brin, who waved back. He turned to Dobkin, who was making the climb without any effort. "You're right, of course. To the people up there, Rish is the Devil incarnate, which is fine for our purposes—and theirs, too. But somehow our devils are never quite what we expect when we meet them face to face."

Brin called out. "Are they going to surrender?"

Hausner looked up and smiled. He yelled back. "I gave them your ultimatum." He noticed again how the positions looked from this perspective. He noted the crumbling crust of earth, the treacherous potholes, and the washed-out gullies. In the dark it must be a nightmare. If he were an attacker he would become demoralized very quickly.

The two men reached the crest. Everyone who wasn't standing sentry duty crowded around them. Dobkin briefly related some of what had happened. There were many questions and the discussion began to become heated. Hausner cut off further comment and promised to take a vote before sundown. He asked everyone to go back to work on the defenses, which indicated to a lot of people what they all knew anyway—there would be no surrender.

The men and women of the peace mission continued the work of building defenses for the expected onslaught. They improvised and invented on the spot. There were virtually no tools available except the flight engineer's tool kit, but from this small beginning, larger instruments were fashioned.

The seats and floor sections were removed from the cabin in some areas and the armor mesh was lifted out. The mesh was strung between aluminum braces, like laundry on a line, to absorb gunfire and shrapnel from hand grenades.

A Knesset member recalled the Greek physicist Archimedes' defense of Syracuse. The legend had it that Archimedes constructed giant magnifying lenses to burn the Roman fleet. In the same spirit, but with a different purpose, aluminum sections were taken off the twisted tail and set between aluminum braces around the perimeter. The aluminum served to reflect the blazing sunlight back into the eyes of the Ashbals if they should decide to attack during the daylight hours. It also made it extremely difficult for snipers to focus on a target. It had still another purpose of being used to send heliographic messages to possible sympathizers on land or in the air. A few men and women took turns manipulating different sections of the aluminum sheets to send out a constant international SOS signal.

More cast aluminum braces and crosspieces were broken from the tail section and stuck into the side of the slope, pointing outward. This line of pickets formed what the military called an abatis. Its function was to make it difficult to scale the breastworks without running into one of these impaling stakes in the dark.

Firing positions became more sophisticated as the day progressed. Holes became deeper and breastworks became longer and stouter. Luggage and armor mesh used on the perimeter were camouflaged with the monochromatic dust that was Babylon. At Dobkin's urging men and women also covered their clothes and faces with a paste made from the dust mixed with their sweat and, in some cases, urine.

Fields of fire were cleared downslope by pushing the giant clumps of earth and clay down to the base of the mound. Small walls of earth and clay were built in the erosion gullies so that an attacker using the gullies as an avenue of approach would have to expose himself at ground level to get over the top of them.

The sparse thorn scrub that grew on the slope and offered some pathetic concealment was cut away. The thorn, used as a local fuel, was brought into the perimeter for that purpose.

Clay and earth plaques were hacked out of the hard crust of

the hilltop. Some weighed up to a hundred kilos. They were balanced atop one another to be pushed over the edge of the slope onto attackers below.

Man-traps were dug into the slope and impaling stakes made from the aircraft's aluminum braces were set in the bottom of the holes. The holes were covered with fabric torn from the seats, and the fabric was covered with dust.

Early-warning devices made from wire, string, and cans filled with pebbles were improvised and set out at intervals of one, two, and three hundred meters.

The cannibalization of the aircraft was accomplished with a great deal of difficulty because of the lack of tools. The work went faster when a crude torch was fashioned from the aircraft's oxygen bottles and the aviation fuel. The aluminum was burnt, ripped, pulled, and twisted from the aircraft. Most of the material came from the blasted tail section. The Israelis crawled over and through the great aircraft much as the workers in St. Nazaire had done. They stood on the same cross struts that Nuri Salameh had when he planted his bomb. They saw the twisted, scorched results of that explosion and used the torn material to their advantage.

Small weapons for close-in self-defense, knives and spears, were fashioned from the hydraulic piping. Glass jars from the baggage and the galley were emptied into other containers and filled with aviation fuel. To some jars were added soap from the lavatories and other soap products from the baggage. The result was a crude napalm that would stick and burn.

The men and women of the peace mission took to the work with a mixture of enthusiasm and desperate urgency. Short and informal idea sessions were held. At times, the classical sieges of ancient times were discussed and ideas and innovations gleaned from those past battles. Archimedes and da Vinci were recalled. The sieges of Troy, Rome, Syracuse, Carthage, Jerusalem, and Babylon were dragged out of the memories of school days. What were the elements of the successful defenses? What were the elements that led to the defeats? It was impossible not to think of Masada. There was a similarity that went beyond the tabletop configuration of the terrain.

The question that began to form in the minds of the defenders was: Could a group of intelligent and civilized individuals, given limited resources, stand off a group of less civilized but better armed attackers? Hausner watched as the long line of defensive works took shape. Sitting as they did on a high piece of ground, with the flanks and the western slope almost too steep to climb, the defenses looked very impressive, he thought. An observer looking down from the air—as Ahmed Rish was evidently now doing in his Lear jet—would have concluded that it was too formidable a citadel to storm if there had been any real firepower behind those hastily formed barricades. But there wasn't.

The real question, Hausner knew, was not how long they could hold out. A day might be long enough, yet a week might not be long enough. It all depended on when they would be found. Would they be found in time? What the hell was going on back in Isreal?

17

Lod was hot. Almost too hot to bear. Teddy Laskov sat over a glass of beer at a sidewalk table in front of Michel's. Shops were shuttered and the Sabbath traffic was thin, but Michel's, Christian-owned, was crowded. The *Hamseen* showed no signs of letting up. Laskov looked down at the sweating glass. A puddle collected around it, and a stream wound its way across the marble table top and dripped on his leg. He watched it. The blue civilian pants confirmed that he was Teddy Laskov, private citizen. After almost forty years in one uniform or another, it felt very strange. There was a great difference, reflected Laskov, in wearing mufti off duty and wearing civilian clothes as a civilian. The clothes were the same, but they hung differently somehow.

Michel's brought back memories of Miriam, but he was not there for that reason. It was simply a convenient place to conduct business on the Sabbath. His inactivity and indecision had lasted exactly one hour as he paced the floor of his apartment. Then he had decided to act.

General Talman came down the street with what Laskov

186

thought was his usual jaunty gait. He always looked like an RAF officer in a World War II movie. Even out of uniform, as he was now, he looked as if he were wearing a fifty-mission crush cap and silver wings. But as he approached, Laskov could see that his former boss was in no better spirits than he was. Talman's mustache twitched slightly as he nodded and sat down. "Damn hot."

"I noticed."

"All right, then. Let's get down to it. Is Mazar coming?"

"He should be here."

"Let's begin without him," said Talman.

"Good." Laskov pulled some loose notes from his pockets. "I took all the hunches, all the gut reactions, all the possible and probable radar sightings and all the Israeli and American security agency radio reports that I could collect before I packed it in." He looked down at his papers. "I think they headed east. Due east from the tip of Sinai."

Talman tapped his fingers on the table. "I've spoken to Hur. Off the record, of course. He tells me that the Palestinians have dragged a number of red herrings across their path. But the final consensus of all the Intelligence people is that they went west. Libya. That would make sense politically. A few men in Operations, however, are convinced that they continued south into the Sudan. That might make sense politically, also. They could have put down in the Sahara, refueled, and gone on to Uganda if they wanted. There's little radar in that part of the world and a lot of open space with few people who might spot them visually. It all makes sense politically, logistically, and practically. Libya or the Sudan." He paused and looked Laskov in the eye. "But I don't think so. I think they went east, also."

Laskov smiled. "Good. Now I'll show you why." He went through his notes.

Talman ordered gin and tonic and listened.

Chaim Mazar walked past them and continued down the street. He turned and came back. He looked around as if for a table, spotted Laskov and Talman, smiled in apparent surprise, and went over to them. "Do you mind if I join you?" He folded his tall, lanky frame into a small wire chair.

Laskov shook his head. "I'm glad you're the head of Shin Beth and not an operative. You're the worst actor I've ever seen."

"I try." He looked around. "I just came from a press conference. If you think the hot wind is blowing out here, you should have been in there."

Talman leaned forward. "It's good of you to do this."

Mazar shrugged. "Look, I should probably have resigned or been fired myself."

"Why?" asked Laskov. "You're the hero of the hour after spiking that mortar attack. The government needs a hero now, and you're all we've got."

Mazar shrugged. "For the moment. I'll get the ax when the dust settles. I told you that mortar attack was a setup. The same people who produced and directed that farce also brought you the hijacking. It was like this—if for some reason Rish's Lear couldn't get into position, then they were going to try to let the mortar thing succeed. But the Lear *was* set up, and someone—the Palestinians themselves, of course—tipped us about the mortars. Actually, I already knew about them."

"So how are you responsible?" asked Laskov. "As head of Internal Security you did all you were supposed to do. It was... Hausner... and us...."

"Only partially. You see, in order for the Lear to intercept the Concordes, it was necessary to have the exact time of departure. That information had to go to Rish at Cairo Airport, and that information could only have come from someone in Israel. Someone at the airport. A spy working in our country. That is my area of responsibility. And I can't identify that spy. I don't even have a clue." He lit a cigarette. "Whoever it was had to call a contact from Lod and give him the new flight plan and departure time, not to mention the fact that you both think Rish had the primary tactical frequency. I checked with Cairo. They were cooperative. Rish and his group--under pseudonyms and posing as businessmen—filed a flight plan to Cyprus. But they changed it suddenly. Alexandria Air Traffic Control gave them a hard time about their request for an earlier departure, but I suspect a little *baksheesh* did the trick, as it will do the trick in all the Land of Islam. Anyway, the rest is history."

Talman nodded. "That's interesting, but as you say, history. What matters now is where Concorde 02 is."

"That's what matters to the state of Israel and her external intelligence people and her armed forces. What matters to me as head of Shin Beth is who the spy is. And what makes the job of finding him more difficult is that I have to pull in most of my agents and Arab informers."

"Why?" asked Talmen.

"Because Isaac Burg, head of Mivtzan Elohim, knows one hell of a lot about Shin Beth. That's why. And if they've got him, they are squeezing his nuts, and they could very well have not only his whole organization but mine as well."

Laskov shook his head. "Absurd. He'd kill himself before he'd let them put him through the wringer."

Mazar nodded. "He carried a gun. I only hope he has the time to use it."

Talman ordered another gin. "How about Dobkin? He was actually in the Aman, wasn't he?"

"Yes. Dobkin was closely connected to Military Intelligence. In addition. he knew Cabinet secrets. The Foreign Minister knew . . . everything. And I don't think he will blow his brains out for anyone." Mazar looked down at the table, then stared at Laskov. "Miriam Bernstein was privy to all Cabinet information. I don't think she would stand up well under torture. Do you?" He waited for an answer.

Talman turned to Laskov but could see nothing in his expression. The silence dragged out.

Finally, Mazar let out a long breath. "I'm speaking as an intelligence man of thirty years when I say I hope they're all dead." He paused. "Hausner is, I'm sure."

No one spoke for several minutes. They sipped their drinks and watched the heat waves in the road. Laskov cleared his throat. "What do you have for us on Rish?"

Mazar opened his attaché case and took out a file. "This is insane. Neither of you have any intelligence experience, clearance, or need-to-know. Or common sense." He handed Talman the file. "I don't have any common sense, either."

"We know that," said Talman as he flipped through the file. "The strength of this country is its smallness. The flow of information has always been accomplished in a family-type atmosphere. There is nothing to keep privates from speaking directly to generals and heads of one service from helping the heads of others. But as we get older as a nation, I'm afraid we are going to get bureaucratized and compartmentalized like the rest of the world. You are only helping to delay that dangerous trend, Chaim."

Mazar grunted. "You're full of shit. We'll all wind up in jail if this goes wrong."

Laskov looked impatient. "Did you get any aerial photographs?"

"Yes," said Mazar. "There are thousands of them from the American satellites and the SR-71 recon craft. Here are some suspect ones. The Americans are being very cooperative with the Aman. But I had a lot of trouble explaining what Shin Beth needed them for. Anyway, you can read these as well as any photo analyst, I suppose."

"After forty years, I hope so," said Laskov. He took a stack of photos from Mazar and glanced at the top one. A grease-pencil notation in the margin gave longitude and latitude. The photo was of the Sinai tip. "Lots of cloud cover this time of year."

"It's spring," said Mazar, unnecessarily. "Anyway, they're mostly of Egypt, the Sudan, and Libya. I take it you still suspect points east?"

"We do," said Laskov. "Rish is Iraqi, isn't he?"

Mazar smiled. "I wish it were that easy. Rish's group is almost all Palestinian. They are the wanderers of Islam, like the Jews were the wanderers of the world. Ironic. They could be anywhere from Morocco to Iraq."

Laskov was only half listening. He was looking at a series of high-angle photos taken of the Tigris and Euphrates. They were taken at a height of twenty-five kilometers by the SR-71 recon craft at seven A.M. that morning. There was another series of the Shamiyah Desert in Iraq. The sun was low and cast elongated and distorted shadows over the land. He glanced at Mazar. "Were there any photos of Iraq taken at noon?"

Mazar looked in his notebook. "Only satellite photos. At 12:17. No more recon craft photos scheduled by the Americans until late afternoon tomorrow."

"Get me the satellite photos, then," said Laskov.

"I'll try." Mazar stood. "I've committed a court-martial offense but I don't feel so bad about it." He closed his empty attaché case. "Let me know if you receive a divine message. Meanwhile, I must look for our traitor."

Talman looked up from Rish's psychological profile and background dossier. "Have you questioned the three Palestinian mortar men?"

"Yes," said Mazar. "They really don't know anything, of course. At least they thought that they didn't. But we were able to interpret little things that seemed irrelevant to them. You know the procedure."

"Learn anything?" asked Talman.

"I'm convinced it was Rish who set them up, poor bastards. There are a few other clues, but I have to run them down before I can draw any conclusions. I'll keep you both informed."

Laskov stood and took Mazar's hand. "Thank you. You're a fool to do this."

"Yes." He wiped the sweat from his forehead with a handkerchief. "You owe me. And I'll be around to collect someday."

"How about right now?" Laskov scrawled something on a wet cocktail napkin. "Here's your payment." He handed Mazar the wet paper.

Mazar looked at it and his eyes widened. "Are you sure?"

"No. That's your job. To be sure."

Mazar put the napkin in his shirt pocket and walked quickly into the square toward St. George's, where he hailed a cab.

18

The Lear jet came in low, but not too low.

"Let's shoot it down," suggested Brin.

Hausner shook his head. "We've agreed to a truce until sundown, and we can well use the break. So don't mess it up, Brin."

"Bullshit. They wouldn't attack in the daylight, anyway. They didn't give us any break."

Dobkin looked up from a range card he was drawing. "That's not completely true. They could be sniping all day and causing other unpleasantness. I don't like having to accept a truce any more than you do, son, but let's be realistic." He went back to the card. He drew in rises and depressions in the slope in front of him. A gunner using that position at night or in other times of limited visibility should be able to place effective fire downrange by using the information written and drawn on the range card in relation to aiming stakes placed directly in front of the firing position. He handed it to Brin. "Here."

"I don't need it. General. I have the starlight scope."

"The batteries are almost gone. Also the lens could get broken."

"God forbid," said Hausner. "That's our early warning and best weapon, all in one."

"That's why I'm handling it," said Brin. He took the range card reluctantly.

Naomi Haber sat against the packed earth parapet with a towel wrapped around her head in the style of a *kheffiyah*. "You're very modest."

Brin ignored her.

Dobkin looked at her. The towel hid her long black hair and covered her forehead. She looked familiar now. "Your last name is Haber, isn't it?"

She looked at him warily. "Yes."

"Well, no wonder you teamed up with Davy Crockett here."

"Who?"

"Never mind." He turned to Hausner. "This girl used to be on the Army match-shooting team."

Brin looked honestly surprised. "Why didn't you mention that?"

She stood up and turned to Dobkin. "General . . . I . . . I mean, I just volunteered to be his assistant . . . his runner. Well, maybe I came to this position because I knew there was a rifle and scope here. But . . . shooting at targets and shooting at human beings are worlds apart, aren't they? I don't think—"

Dobkin looked sympathetic and began to speak. "Jacob—"

Hausner stood and grabbed her roughly by the arm. "Look, young lady, not one of my men is anywhere near the marksman that Brin is, and no one else on this hill came forward when I asked if anyone had this kind of training. You kept information from me, and by God, you'll answer for it! But for now, consider yourself a sniper. When you see one of those young buck Ashbals coming up the hill tonight, think of what he's going to do to you if he makes it to the top."

The girl turned away and stared down the hill.

Brin looked embarrassed. "I'll take care of it, boss."

"Do that," said Hausner. He walked away in the direction of the Concorde. Dobkin followed.

The work had not let up all morning, but now at midday, when the sun was at its hottest, most of the people were stopping for a break as they did in Israel and throughout the Middle East.

They sat under the Concorde, the big delta wings protecting them from the blinding sunlight.

The garbage disposal unit on board gave up the previous day's partially eaten meal, and it was being reheated on aluminum sheets over fires of thorn. Liquids of all types were stored separately in a hole dug under the aircraft. There were bottles of sweet wine from the luggage and cans of juices and drink mixers from the galley. The extra baggage allowance had enabled everyone to bring a lot of packaged Israeli foods as gifts or for personal consumption. Still, the tremendous work load had resulted in big appetites.

Yaakov Leiber was put in charge of the stores by Hausner, and he seemed to be functioning well. Hausner put his hand on the little man's shoulder. "What's the situation, Steward?"

Leiber forced a smile. "We can eat and drink like kings . . . for one day."

"What can we do for, let's say, two more days?"

"We can go hungry and thirsty . . . but survive."

"Three days?"

"*Very* thirsty."

Hausner nodded. If the physical labor continued and the heat kept up, dehydration would begin setting in within three days. Maybe a lot sooner. Then no one would be able to think rationally. All thoughts would be of water. That would be the end, even if the defenses held. How many sieges had ended like that? Water. Food was not the problem. Humans could go for weeks on almost nothing. Besides, there was an abundance of lizards and scorpions. He'd heard jackals the night before. They could be snared with bait . . . the buried Arabs. . . . To hell with Rabbi Levin.

Leiber was speaking to him. "I've measured the water tanks carefully. There's enough for half a liter a day per person."

"Not enough."

"No, sir." He looked at the ground and kicked a clump of clay. "We could dig."

Hausner called to Dobkin, who was near the shepherds' hut. "Is this a tell or isn't it?"

"I'm certain it is," he called back. "A crumbled citadel. Covered with dust and debris." He came closer. "Why?"

"I want to dig for water," said Hausner.

Dobkin shook his head. "You'd find some interesting things down there, but not water. Not until you reached the level of the

Euphrates." He walked up to Hausner and Leiber. "Why don't
we send a water party down the slope?"

Hausner shook his head. "They have sentries, as you know."

"Tonight. It can be done if they don't attack up the river
slope. I'll lead the party."

"You're going to make a telephone call from the guest house
tonight."

Dobkin laughed. "I don't have a local coin."

Hausner smiled back.

Dobkin looked down at the ground and then at the
Euphrates below them. "They would put the mud and slime into
wooden forms and lay them in the sun," he said, apropos of
nothing. His voice became distant. "The brickyards would
stretch to the horizons in every direction. The sun would bake
the bricks and they would use slime from the Euphrates for
mortar. They would press designs into the brick. Lions and
mythical beasts. And the kings would press their cuneiform
inscriptions into each brick. NEBUCHADNEZZAR, KING OF
BABYLON, SON OF NABOPOLASSAR, KING OF BABYLON, AM I. Over
and over again. And sometimes they would fire-glaze the brick
with reds and blues, yellows and greens. They built one of the
most beautiful and colorful cities that man has ever seen. It sat
like an iridescent pearl in the green silk of the Euphrates valley."
Dobkin kicked at the brown dirt, then walked a few paces. He
stared west across the endless mud flats into the sinking sun, as it
burned reddish-yellow, still high on the horizon. "And they
captured Israel and led Israel away to live by the rivers of
Babylon. Right here, Jacob. A Jew stood right here and laid
brick with slime to strengthen this citadel against Cyrus of
Persia. Over twenty-five hundred years ago. But Cyrus took
Babylon, and one of his first acts was to let the Jews go. Why?
Who knows? But they went. Back to Israel. And they found
Jerusalem in ruins. But they returned to it. That's what's
important." He looked up and seemed to come out of his reverie.
"But what's more important to us is that not all of them
returned."

"What do you mean?"

"There may still be Jews of the Captivity living by the rivers
of Babylon."

"Are you serious?" asked Hausner.

Leiber seemed a little confused by Dobkin. He stood a few
meters off and listened politely.

"I'm serious," replied Dobkin. "Unless they've been moved to Baghdad by the Iraqi government, which is a distinct possibility. I'm talking about the Iraqi Jews who we've been trying to get the hell out of here. About five hundred of them all together. That was to be one of the points in the peace proposal."

"Do you think they're still here?"

"They've been here for twenty-five hundred years. Let's hope they still are. Their main village was on the opposite bank of the Euphrates. A place called Ummah. About two kilometers downstream. Almost across from Kweirish, the Arab village that we saw."

"Would they help?"

"Ah. That's the question. What is a Jew? Who is a Jew? Why did the ancestors of these Jews choose to stay in sinful Babylon? Who knows? They *have* remained Jews after all these years, cut off from the mainstream of Judaism. We know that much. Though God knows what kind of Hebrew they speak . . . if any." He opened his tunic. "But they'll know this." He pulled out a silver Star of David.

Leiber spoke. "I wonder if they know we're here."

Hausner put his hand on Leiber's shoulder. "You can be sure, Steward, that everyone knows we're here except the people who count—the Israeli and the Iraqi governments." He patted Leiber's shoulder. "But they'll find us soon. Now, I want you to comb every centimeter of this place and find more supplies."

Leiber nodded and moved off.

Dobkin spoke. "From what I saw this morning, I don't think I can make it to the Ishtar Gate alone at night. The terrain is bad and unfamiliar, there are deep unmarked excavations all over, and there will be sentries along the way, I'm sure."

"Then, what do you propose?"

"The land on the other side of the Euphrates is flat and presumably without Palestinians. I'll go down there tonight—with a water party if you want. They'll collect some of the Euphrates—I'll swim it."

"The sentries," said Hausner.

Dobkin shrugged. "Once the shooting starts on the east side of the hill, the sentries on the river bank won't hear much or even care about much. By two or three in the morning, they will be cold and tired and thanking their stars they're not part of the assault. I could make it."

Hausner looked doubtful. "And if you make it across the

river and then down to this village of Jews, then what? What do you expect to find there?"

Dobkin didn't know what to expect. Even if they had a communal farm vehicle of some sort, the roads were impassable. There was certainly no telephone. A donkey would take days to get to Baghdad. Hillah was a possibility, but then he'd have to recross the river. A boat maybe. A motorized boat could get upriver to Baghdad in five or six hours. An unmotorized boat could be downriver to Hillah in less than an hour. Then what? Hello, I'm General Dobkin of the Israeli Army and . . .

"What are you smiling at?" asked Hausner.

"A private joke. Listen, I didn't just remember about this village. I thought of it the moment I knew we were in Babylon. But do we want to drag these people into this? Don't they have enough problems?"

"No more than we do," said Hausner. "And I'll advise you not to hold back that type of information in the future, General. As I see it you have two choices—the guest house at the Ishtar Gate or the Jewish village of Ummah."

Dobkin nodded. There was a good possibility that Ummah was no longer inhabited. There was also a chance that it was occupied by Palestinians. The third possibility was that the Jews there wouldn't help. But *was* that possible? Was it possible for him to walk up to a primitive Jew who lived in a squalid mud hovel on the banks of the Euphrates, claim kinship, and demand help? Dobkin thought it was. And would Rish take retribution against those miserable wretches if he found out? Of course he would. But what were the alternatives? There were none. "I'll try Ummah tonight."

"All right. I would have preferred that you take a shot at the guest house, but it's your decision." He turned and walked toward the shepherds' hut with Dobkin. He turned to the big man as they walked. "I still can't spare a gun."

"All right."

They walked on for a few more paces in silence. Hausner cleared his throat. "I asked the Foreign Minister to—"

"Yes," interrupted Dobkin. "I've got it. Digitalis. The Foreign Minister's aide, Peled, has a bad heart. He has a month's supply with him. I took two weeks of it."

"I hope that's enough."

"Me too."

Burg came out of the shepherds' hut with the two

stewardesses, Rachel Baum and Beth Abrams. Their light-blue uniforms were soaked with sweat and what looked like blood and iodine. They gave Hausner an undisguised look of something that resembled a mixture of fear and disgust and kept walking.

Burg shrugged. "They look at me like that, too. They were doing so well with their patient, Muhammad, until I sent him into remission. No one understands us, Jacob."

"Has he said anything new?" asked Hausner.

Burg chewed on his empty pipe. "A few things." He watched as the Lear headed west over the Euphrates. "I wonder if he's going to base camp to get mortars and grenades?"

Hausner watched as the Lear disappeared into the sun. "That would make it a little tougher tonight."

Dobkin lit a cigarette. "I'm glad I won't be around."

"You're going, then?" asked Burg.

"Right. I'll be eating matzoh and roasted lamb and dancing the *horah* tonight while you're ducking bullets."

"I think you've had too much sun, General."

Dobkin told Burg about the Jewish village.

Burg listened and nodded. "Pardon the joke, but it doesn't sound kosher, Ben. Stick with the original plan."

"I have a better feeling about this."

Burg shrugged. Either way, it was suicide. "By the way, Muhammad says that Rish's lieutenant, Salem Hamadi, is a homosexual. That would be consistent with institutional upbringing."

"Who cares?" said Hausner.

"Salem Hamadi will when we broadcast it at top volume over the plane's PA tonight."

Hausner smiled. "That's low."

"All's fair. Did you get the PA boxes strung out to the perimeter yet?"

"It's done," said Dobkin.

Hausner moved into the shade of the delta wing. The earth and clay ramp was completed and he leaned back against the side of it. He felt the first stirring of a hot wind. Becker had reported that the Concorde's barometer had been dropping rapidly all day. "Does anyone know the name of the east wind here?"

"The *Sherji*," said Dobkin. "Do you feel it?"

"I think so."

"That's not good. I understand it's worse than the *Hamseen* in Israel."

"Why is that?"

"It's hotter, for one thing," said Dobkin. "And there is only sand and dust here. It picks up the dust. It can choke you. Kill you. Especially on a hill like this. That's how Babylon and all of Mesopotamia disappeared. Someone once said that a civilization would always survive if everyday people did everyday things every day. Well, that was true in Mesopotamia throughout every invasion—except the Mongol invasion. As soon as the women stopped sweeping the streets and the farmers stopped cultivating the land, the dust built up as the *Sherji* came out of the Persian mountains and carried the desert with it."

Hausner looked across the landscape toward the distant mountains. Dust devils began to form around the drifting sand dunes. They swirled across the hillocks and disappeared into the wadis, then appeared again, heading west toward them.

Dobkin followed Hausner's gaze. "From a military point of view, I honestly don't know to whose advantage a dust storm would be."

"We have enough problems," said Hausner. "I could do without another one." He looked at Burg. "We'll get rid of the prisoner if you're through with him."

"I assume you mean let him go."

"Yes."

Dobkin objected.

Hausner offered him a cigarette. "Let me tell you a story or two." He settled back against the cool earth ramp. "During the siege of Milan, in the twelfth century, the inhabitants filled grain bags with sand and used them to reinforce the battlements. The besiegers under the German Emperor, Barbarossa, thought the bags were filled with grain and became disheartened. Actually, the city was starving, but Barbarossa didn't know that. Some years later, Barbarossa besieged the Italian city of Alessandria. A peasant took his cow out of the city for pasture and was captured by Barbarossa's forces. When they slaughtered the cow for food, they saw that its stomach was filled with good grain. The peasant explained that hay and fodder were in short supply in the city, but there was so much grain that it was fed to the livestock. Barbarossa again became discouraged and lifted the siege. Actually, the Alessandrians were starving and the peasant and the cow were a ruse."

"You're trying to make a point," said Burg.

"Yes. First we have a party. A little singing and dancing. Some feigned eating and drinking. Store every weapon we've got in the shepherd's hut. Put a single round in all the spare magazines so that they look fully loaded. Look casual about food and ammunition. Set up a mock machine gun far enough away so that it will pass. Come up with more *ruses de guerre*. Make it look as if we have the Third Armored Division up here on rest and recreation. Then let Mr. Muhammad Assad loose."

Dobkin looked thoughtful. "It's kind of obvious."

"To Rish and his officers. But the Ashbals will think about it." He looked at Burg.

"Why not?" said Burg. "I'm through with him."

The three men went into the hut. Kaplan was still on his stomach, but looking well. Four other lightly wounded men, including Joshua Rubin, were playing cards. The wounded stenographer, Ruth Mandel, was wrapped in blankets and looked feverish. The Palestinian looked fearfully at Burg. Hausner could see that his nose was broken. He didn't like the idea of keeping the man with the wounded, but the hut was the only enclosed area except for the Concorde, which was like an oven in the sun. The wounded, between them, could keep watch on him. And all in all, casualties were very light, so Mr. Muhammad Assad could report that piece of intelligence as well.

The stewardesses were back and one of them, Beth Abrams, uncovered Kaplan's wound. It was starting to fester and it smelled very bad. The whole mud-brick hut smelled of ripe bandages and sweating bodies. Beth Abrams put some sort of yellow pulp on the open gangrenous wound. "What's that?" demanded Hausner.

Beth Abrams looked up at him for a long second, then spoke. "It's a local plant that is astringent. Like a witch-hazel bush."

"How do you know?"

"I read it in an Army medical manual when I was in." She dabbed it gently on the open wound as she spoke. "The fruit are lemon-yellow, about the size of tennis balls, and smooth. They lie on the ground tethered to long stalks. I forget the name, but these fit the description. They grow on the slope. I'm using the pulp on everyone. There's no alcohol left." She covered up the wound and moved away.

"All right." Hausner turned to Kaplan. "How's your ass?"

Kaplan managed a laugh. "These two stewardesses keep putting that yellow slime on it. When they say fly El Al and be treated like King Solomon, they're not kidding."

Hausner smiled. Kaplan reminded him of Matti Yadin. He'd have to see that Kaplan got a good promotion. "The smaller one, Beth Abrams, is a bit of a bitch, but she keeps looking at your ass in a non-medical way. Keep that in mind when you get back to Lod."

"I'll keep that in mind tonight."

Hausner noticed that Chaim Tamir, badly wounded the previous night in the counterattack, was sleeping fitfully.

Hausner crossed the small room to where the lightly wounded men were playing cards. He spoke to Joshua Rubin. "You never told me you were psychotic."

Rubin, a small red-haired man of about twenty, folded his cards and looked up. "You never asked. Who's got my Uzi?"

"It's retired. There were only three rounds left in the magazine when they brought you in."

"Give it back, then. I want it here. In case we get overrun. I want to take the first bastard who comes through that door."

"All right. I'll get it for you." Hausner looked around at the men, who went back to their cards. They were ordinary men, civilians, who had gone off the deep end for a few minutes the night before. Now they looked normal—were normal, arguing over a game of cards. What did Miriam Bernstein think of that? Did she understand that nice people were killers and killers were nice people? Did she understand that a man like Isaac Burg could smile and fumble around disarmingly with his pipe, then break a wounded prisoner's nose and still be a nice guy? The bottom line was survival. If it had to be done in order to survive, it was done.

19

The sun seemed hotter than usual as it reflected off the skin of the Concorde. Hausner and Burg stood with their eyes shielded from the glare, watching the tail section being disassembled. Hausner wondered again why he had never thought of checking the inaccessible parts. The Concorde had been X-rayed once for metal stress, but no one had thought to look for shadows that didn't belong there. Why hadn't *he* thought of it? If you accepted a job such as his and people got killed because of an oversight on your part, how much was your fault? How much was the fault of your subordinates? How much did you have to do to atone for the resulting tragedy? Did you have to atone at all? Weren't there some things that no one could reasonably be expected to foresee?

The one man he couldn't blame was Ahmed Rish. Rish was just doing *his* job as he saw it had to be done. It was Hausner's job to stop Rish from doing that job. Hausner knew that what bothered him most, although he tried to keep it in its proper perspective, was that Ahmed Rish had outfoxed *him*. That was very personal. Like a slap in the face. Was he leading these people to their certain death because of his excessive pride?

Excessive pride was always considered a sin in Jewish thinking. Babylon was a symbol of excessive pride, and Babylon was cursed. Babylon was brought to her knees. Was he acting out of wounded ego? No. He was following precedents set by Israel over the years. No negotiation with terrorists. Hard line. Unbending. It happened to fit his mood and personality, but it was not personal. Yet the thought nagged at him. He turned to Burg. "Is there anything else that is urgent?"

Burg turned away from the tail section and pointed to a depression in the earth about two hundred meters away. Abdel Majid Jabari and Ibrahim Ali Arif were digging a latrine trench. They used the same tools as everyone else: lengths of aluminum braces to break up the hard crust and aluminum sheets to scoop out the broken clay and dust. Their hands were wrapped in clothing to protect them from the jagged aluminum. "I questioned them," said Burg. "They are both Knesset members and it was not my place to doubt their loyalty, but the situation called for it. They were a little hurt and very angry. Maybe you can smooth it out."

Hausner watched the two Arabs for a while. "Yes. We'll all have to answer for our actions if we get back, won't we, Isaac? Here, Jabari and Arif are just two Trojan horses inside the walls of Troy, if you'll pardon the metaphor. Back in Jerusalem, they could have you in front of a Knesset committee in a second, couldn't they?"

Burg shot Hausner a dark look. "I did what I thought had to be done. Do you back me up?"

"Of course." He watched the two men as they straightened up and wiped the sweat from their faces. Their *kheffiyahs* kept the sun off their heads better than any of the headgear most of the other people were wearing. "They are in an awkward position. But I don't think turning traitor would help them with Rish. They don't want Rish on this hill any more than we do. Less. He will do more than kill them. You know what they do to traitors."

Burg nodded. "It's unpleasant." He reamed out his pipe. "Incidentally, your friend, Mrs. Bernstein, gave me a hell of a hard time about casting aspersions on the loyalty of Jabari and Arif. And also about my methods of questioning our prisoner. She said that we have all turned into perfect barbarians. She's right, of course. But we don't think that's so bad—do we, Jacob?

But she does. Why is it that bleeding hearts refuse to see this world as it is?"

"They see it fine, Burg. They just can't pass up an opportunity to play the moral superiority game with bastards like us who have to slug it out in the shit so they can go do seminars on world peace and disarmament."

"Well, I don't think as unkindly as you do of that type. Anyway, she's causing trouble and I think you should do something."

"Like what?" He stared at Burg.

Burg stared back. "That's up to you."

Hausner wiped his palms on his pants. "I'll see."

As Hausner walked away, he noticed that the ground sunk into a shallow depression near the south ridge. Dobkin thought that this was the courtyard of the citadel and the south ridge was actually the city wall that ran from the citadel along the river to the Kasr mound in the south. The north ridge was similarly a covered wall. If the ridges weren't so narrow-backed, they would have made likely avenues of approach for the Ashbals. Hausner admitted that neither ridge looked like a natural formation, but how Dobkin could see walls, citadels, watchtowers, and even courtyards was beyond him. It all just looked like dirt. It was much more completely obliterated than anything he'd seen in Israel. Dobkin said to picture a thick shroud over a corpse. If you had a previous knowledge of human anatomy, then it was not difficult to pick out legs, arms, face, stomach, and chest by the rises and falls of the shroud. So it was with cities. Courtyards and watchtowers. Walls and citadels.

The two Arabs looked up at Hausner as he approached. Jabari spoke. "I didn't have an opportunity to congratulate you on your defense of Babylon last night."

"That's rather a dramatic way to put it," said Hausner.

Arif tried to catch his breath. He was bare-chested, and his stomach quivered as he panted. "I wish to congratulate you, also."

Hausner nodded. He stayed silent for a long while, then spoke. "Is there any reason for me to doubt you?"

Jabari came close. A few centimeters from him. "No."

"That's all you'll hear on it, then. I suspect Mr. Burg would like to apologize, but his training makes that impossible." He

looked around. "I have a very important job for you two
tonight."

"Even more important than digging the latrine?" asked Arif.

"I hope so," said Hausner. He sat with his feet dangling in the
unfinished trench. They sat with him as he explained.

Dobkin and Burg called for another work break. They
passed the word around to put on a show for the prisoner.
Everyone complied, although the dancing and singing took
more energy than anyone had to spare. The five AK-47's and
about ten pistols were stacked carelessly in the shepherds' hut, as
if they were extra weapons, and ammunition was left lying on
the dirt floor. A security man, Marcus, came into the shepherds'
hut with the Uzi submachine gun slung on his shoulder and gave
it to Rubin, who put it ostentatiously under his blanket. He
spoke with Rubin for a while and left. Another security man,
Alpern, came in to visit with Kaplan and Rubin. He, too, had a
Uzi, a little dustier then the other. It was the same one—the only
one—passed through the cleft in the mud wall by Rubin.

The M-14 with the daylight scope was paraded into the hut
by Brin. Muhammad Assad looked at it. He stared at the scope.
Brin saw him staring at it. The only secret weapon they had was
the starlight scope, and Hausner ordered that it not be shown.
Brin spoke to Assad in Hebrew, which the man couldn't
understand. "No, my friend, this is not the scope that put the
bullet into you. We have another. But you'll just have to wonder
about it."

Assad was given a very big lunch of airline food and
packaged delicacies from the luggage. He seemed mystified by
some of it, but tried everything. One of the stewardesses poured
water from a galley pitcher into plastic glasses for the wounded.
They sipped at it. Joshua Rubin drank half of his and threw the
rest out the cleft in the wall. If Assad had noticed that they
weren't as careless with water before, he did not show it.

Assad was taken out of the hut by two security men, Jaffe and
Alpern. Before he was blindfolded, he saw the dozens of glass
jars that held the aviation fuel stacked in a hole dug next to the
hut. A steward, Daniel Jacoby, was filling more jars from an
aluminum pitcher filled with fuel. One of the aides, Esther
Aronson, was fashioning wicks made from strips of cloth. This
was no ruse, and Muhammad Assad was duly impressed.

Alpern yelled to Esther Aronson to throw him a strip of cloth for a blindfold. She was slow about it—as she was told to be—and Alpern yelled angrily to hurry it up.

In the interim, Jaffe spun Assad around and pointed him toward the perimeter. Assad glimpsed what he took to be a heavy machine gun on a tripod, but was only a broken strut from the front landing gear, blackened with soot and sitting on a truncated camera tripod recovered from the luggage. Spent shell casings tied together with string gleamed in the sunlight like links of belt ammunition. If Assad wondered how the Israelis came to be carrying a heavy machine gun on board, he didn't ask. He saw all he was supposed to see in those few seconds, then the blindfold was quickly tied around his head. He was led to the edge of the perimeter where he was guided between two big aluminum reflectors and over the trench and earth wall. Halfway down the slope, the blindfold was removed and he was given a white handkerchief fixed to a length of aluminum hydraulic tubing. Jaffe, with the same tone in his voice that the Lord must have used with Lot's wife, told Assad not to look back. Despite his wound, Assad made good speed down the slope.

Hausner called an end to the festivities and found Burg and Dobkin standing on the high mound—the buried watchtower—that was the previous night's Command Post/Observation Post. They were looking over the progress of the work. The Tel Aviv waterfront moved slightly as the hot wind picked up the T-shirt flag. "What's the next priority?" he asked.

Burg suggested, "We should speak with Becker again. He's on the flight deck."

They walked back to the Concorde. A flattened platform of earth had been raised up under the collapsed nose wheel assembly, and Kahn was lying on it, supine, with his arms thrust up into the wheel well. He was covered with grease and sweat. Hausner wondered if his energies couldn't be better spent digging man-traps, but said nothing.

Dobkin called to him. "Any luck?"

Kahn slid out and stood up. "No. Not yet. But I think I'm getting closer."

Dobkin nodded. "Good."

"I only hope we have enough batteries and enough fuel left to turn it over and run it if I fix it." He looked pointedly at Hausner.

"Why?" asked Hausner. "So we can run the air conditioners?" He stepped onto the ramp. "If you two can't make contact with the radio using the batteries, I don't think the generator will make any difference."

Kahn didn't answer.

Hausner began walking up the ramp. He looked back toward the nose. "Technicians are tinkerers by nature. If something is broken you want to fix it. Your ego is involved with that goddamned APU, Kahn, but what good it's going to do us fixed is beyond me."

Kahn was red-faced but remained quiet.

Hausner took a few steps and shouted over his shoulder. "The radio is a quick ticket out of this place, but you two don't seem to have the touch with it." He jumped onto the delta wing.

Dobkin and Burg stayed behind and spoke quietly with Kahn.

The cabin was like an oven and Hausner, in spite of having gone without water for some time, began to sweat. There were sounds coming into the cabin from the work being done on the dismantling of the tail. As he passed the galley, Hausner could see that it was stripped bare. The Machmeter was lit, indicating that Becker was using the emergency power. It still read MACH 0.00, which somehow annoyed Hausner. What bright electrical engineer in France had wired the passengers' Machmeter into the emergency power? Why would the passengers want to know how fast they were going during an emergency situation? It occurred to him that the passengers on 01 must have watched the speed bleed off after the explosion. He wondered how it read in the cabin of 01 when the craft was somersaulting across the sky.

Hausner was assailed by the smell from the flight deck before he reached it. He looked inside. Hess was still sitting slumped over the controls, but rigor had set in and Hess's body had shifted and looked very unnatural. A hot wind blew in through the hole in the windshield. Becker was listening at the radio with earphones.

Hausner stopped in. "I want him out of here," he said loudly.

Becker removed his earphones. "He's my responsibility. I'll keep him here until they're ready to bury him."

Hausner didn't know what was going on in Becker's mind and didn't want even to begin to try and fathom it. What difference did it make where the body was kept? Maybe it was better that the rest of the people didn't see it. If only that damned rabbi wasn't . . .

Levin was an enigma. Religious people were all enigmas to Hausner. They wouldn't fly El Al; they wouldn't eat lizards even if they were starving; they wouldn't bury bodies on the Sabbath. In short. they wouldn't come to grips with the twentieth century. They let people like Hausner break The Law so that the water flowed into their homes on the Sabbath and the radar was manned and surgery was performed. Levin was just another version of Miriam Bernstein, Hausner decided. They were sure they were on the way to Heaven, and Hausner was in training for Hell. It occurred to him that either he was making very astute observations or he was becoming a paranoiac. But was there a despot anywhere who wasn't.

"I *said,* do you want to fool around with the radio yourself?" said Becker.

"What? No. I don't. Did you hear anything? Did you try transmitting?"

"As I said before, it's very difficult to transmit in the daytime."

"Right. Maybe we'll have more luck tonight."

"No, we won't."

"Why not?"

"Well, I did get one transmission."

Hausner came closer. "Who?"

"Fellow by the name of Ahmed Rish. Before, when he was flying overhead. He said that he hoped Jacob Hausner considered all the lives at stake and all that. He also complimented me on my flying. Nice guy." Becker allowed himself a laugh. "He also said that he'd be back at dusk to circle overhead and jam me if we weren't surrendering."

"Son-of-a-bitch."

"He's certainly full of surprises. All bad." Becker turned off the radio. "Could you shoot him down?"

Hausner wiped the sweat from his neck. "How high could he fly and still jam you?"

"As high as he wants. He has the power, and it's line of sight through the clear sky."

"Then we can't shoot him down unless you have a SAM on board that you're keeping under wraps."

Becker stood and pulled at his wet clothes. "Incidentally, I want final authority concerning what is taken off this aircraft, Hausner. A little while ago two of your men tried to take the goddamned wiring that connects this radio to the batteries."

Hausner nodded. "All right." He saw that Becker was sallow

and his lips were cracked. "Get some water."

Becker moved toward the door. "I think I'm going to dig the grave." He left the flight deck.

Hausner stared at the radio. After a few minutes he also left.

He didn't want to run into her, but it was inevitable. She was standing on the delta wing with some other men and women from the peace delegation. He had noticed how all the peer groups had stuck together. She didn't mingle with the junior aides or the flight crew.

They were all going up to the tail to help with the work. She stood with her hands wrapped in cloth to protect them from the jagged metal. She was covered with sweat and dust. She walked slowly across the unbearably hot wing as the others went on up the fuselage. She stood with her legs spread to keep her balance on the pitched wing. "Everyone seems to think you're a hero."

"I am."

"So you are. No one really likes heroes. They fear—detest heroes. Did you know that?"

"Of course."

"Have you made amends for the sin of overlooking a bomb planted in that tail section," she pointed to it, "over a year ago in France? Can you rejoin the human race now?"

"You almost make it sound inviting."

"Then do it."

He didn't answer.

"What else did Rish say?"

"He just wanted to talk about old times at Ramla."

"We have a right to know."

"Let's not start this again."

"What terms did he offer?"

"Would you consider surrendering under any circumstances?"

She hesitated. "Only to save lives."

"Our precious lives are not worth the national humiliation."

She shook her head. "What is it that I thought I found likeable in you? You are a loathsome person, really."

"Don't you want to tame the beast, Miriam? Aren't you a doer of good deeds?" He remembered her warmth on the plane when she thought he needed someone.

She seemed confused. "Are you playing with me?"

He took out a cigarette stub and stared at it for a long time. She suddenly seemed so defenseless. He looked up. "Listen,

Burg is complaining about you. He says you're bad for morale. So shape up and keep your opinions to yourself until you have the floor in the Knesset. I'm serious, Miriam. If he decides to charge you with causing dissension, I can't help you."

She looked at him, but it took some time before the words registered. Her mind was on what he had said before. She suddenly flushed red. "What? What the hell kind of charge is 'causing dissension'? I won't be bullied like that. This is a democracy, damn it."

"This is Babylon. This is where the law of retaliation—the law of an eye for an eye, a tooth for a tooth—was codified by Hammurabi long before Moses gave it to us. Our origins are brutal and cruel, and there was a reason for that—it was a brutal world. Then we became the world's professional pacifists, and look what happened to us. Now we're raising young men and women who are fighters again after all these centuries. We may not like their manners, but they don't care. They don't much like our European background and all it connotes. If my parents had stayed in Europe, they would have gone into the boxcars like yours. They were the type. Asher Avidar was a damned fool—but you know what? I like that type of damned fool. People like you scare the hell out of me."

She began to shake and her voice came in short breaths. "If... if your parents had stayed in Europe—you would have grown up a Nazi. They would have recognized one of their own."

Hausner hit her with his open palm. She fell onto the wing and rolled a few meters down the incline before she came to a stop. She lay there with the metal burning her bare legs. She refused to stand up, although she was able to do so.

Hausner finally reached down and yanked her to her feet.

The people on the tail section were staring openly.

Hausner held her up by her arms and pressed her face near his. "We're never going to get it together if we keep knocking each other around, Miriam." He stared into her eyes and saw the tears well up and roll down her cheeks. "I'm sorry," he said.

She pulled away from him with surprising strength. "Go to hell!" She raised her fist, but he caught her by the wrist and held her.

"That's the spirit, Miriam. Now, doesn't that feel better than turning the other cheek? You'll be a fighter yet."

She pulled loose, walked quickly across the shimmering delta wing, and disappeared through the emergency door of the fuselage.

20

Hausner walked slowly down the earth ramp. Burg was waiting for him. Hausner sighed. "Well, what's next?"

"I feel like your adjutant."

"Yes. And my intelligence officer. Dobkin is my executive officer. Leiber is my supply sergeant. Everyone has a function, or will have within the next few hours."

"Even Miriam Bernstein?" ventured Burg.

Hausner looked at him. "Yes. She has a function, also. She keeps us honest. She reminds us that we are civilized."

"I'd rather not be reminded of that now. Anyway, she's only an amateur guilt-producer. The professional wants a word with you. That's what's next."

"The rabbi?"

"The rabbi. Then I think you should speak with McClure and Richardson. As your intelligence officer, I think there is something there that is not entirely kosher."

"Like what?"

"I'm not sure. Anyway, as your adjutant, I think they could

use some morale boosting, being the only foreigners with us. If I were them, I would have taken a walk long ago."

"McClure is steady as a rock. Richardson is a little shaky, I think. I'll speak to them. Anything else?"

"Not that I can think of, unless you want to take that vote about accepting Rish's terms. It's getting late."

Hausner smiled. "We'll take it in the morning."

Burg nodded. "Yes. We'll sleep on it."

"Where's Dobkin?"

"The last time I saw him, he was giving a class in breastworks, trenches, foxholes, and parapets."

"Is that a graduate course?"

"I think so. And the final exam is tonight."

Hausner nodded. "Tell him that before nightfall I also want him to give a class in weapons training. I want as many people as possible cross-trained. If a gunner falls, I want anyone to be able to pick up the weapon."

"All right. If you need me I'll be at the shepherds' hut. I promised those two stews I'd pull a few hours of orderly duty."

"If we do nothing else right up here, we'll do our best for them. See that they have everything they need."

"Of course."

Hausner found Rabbi Levin speaking with Becker. Becker was digging a grave on a little knoll that overlooked the Euphrates.

Hausner stood some meters off until the rabbi saw him.

The rabbi said something to Becker, then walked over to where Hausner stood. "Jacob Hausner, the Lion of Babylon. Did you see your namesake on your journey to the Ishtar Gate?"

"What can I do for you, Rabbi?"

"You can begin by telling me precisely the terms that Rish offered."

"What difference does it make? We're not accepting them."

"You're not and I'm not and most people here are not. But there are some people who wish to. The Law teaches us that each man should make his own decision as to his fate in situations like this."

"I don't remember that in the Bible or the Talmud. I think you make these laws up to fit your needs."

Rabbi Levin laughed. "You're a hard man to fool, Jacob Hausner. But I'll tell you what The Law does say. It says suicide is a sin."

"So?"

"So? You should keep better informed. There are about six
young interpreters and secretaries—two girls and four boys, I
think—who are members of the hardcore Masada Defense
League."

"And?"

"And they are running around proselytizing a Masada
solution if we can't hold out. I won't have that, and I suspect you
won't either." He looked at Hausner sharply.

Hausner wiped the sweat from his neck. The wind was
creating swirls of dust across the top of the mound. On the far
side of the Euphrates, the flat mud plain stretched forever. There
had been trees there once and fields of high grain, but still it must
have been possible to see Babylon as you approached with a
caravan from the Western Desert along the ancient Damascus
road. That's how the Jews of the Captivity came. Across the
burning deserts of Syria. Then they would have seen the
cultivated alluvial flood plains in the distance, not at all the way
Hausner had seen it from the flight deck of Concorde 02, but it
must have looked inviting, even though they knew it was the
place of their bondage. And the Babylonians would have stood
in the fields and on the walls of the city and watched their great
army approach with Israel in chains and with carts loaded with
the silver and gold from the sack of Jerusalem.

"Well?"

Hausner looked at him and spoke slowly and softly. "The
Captivity...the camps...the pogroms....You need warm
human bodies to commit atrocities against....I mean, when
resistance becomes impossible...*physically* impossible...then
you just...you just end it, damn it. You don't deliver yourself
up for humiliation, rape, and slaughter. You end it yourself
before they—"

"God decides who dies and who doesn't! Not man. Not Jacob
Hausner. I won't have this! We have no moral right to end our
own lives. And I'll tell you something else about Masada. It was
brave beyond comprehension, but not everyone there wanted to
commit suicide, either. There were some who were slain by their
own kin before the mass suicide. That's murder. And I think that
is what is going to happen here if those hotheads get control.
What the hell kind of young men and women are we raising,
anyway? I've never seen such recklessness."

Hausner thought of Avidar again. Then of Bernstein. There
must be a compromise between the two philosophies. "In the

end, when the situation is beyond saving, those who wish to be taken captive will find a way to surrender. Those who wish to fight to the end will do so. Those who wish to take their own lives will arrange it. Is there anything else, Rabbi?"

Rabbi Levin looked at him with a mixture of pain and disgust. "The wisdom of Jacob Solomon Hausner. Here's another little piece of unconventional wisdom for you. If those two women had called Solomon's bluff and agreed to let the baby be split in two, then that would have put King Solomon in the position of murderer and not a revered judge. That's what you will become—a murderer. Your compromise is not acceptable to me." The rabbi waved his arm and his voice became louder. "I insist that you let those who wish to surrender do so now, and that you forbid suicide and talk of suicide!"

Hausner noticed that the rabbi was holding something. He stared at the object as it made its way through the air in the rabbi's hand. Levin was still shouting, but Hausner had tuned him out. He suddenly put his hand on Rabbi Levin's shoulder and spoke softly. "I don't know." He lowered his head. "I just don't know, Rabbi. I'm getting tired of this. I don't think I want to be in charge here after all. I don't feel up to it. I . . ."

Rabbi Levin took Hausner's hand gently. "I'm sorry. Look, let's let it rest for now. You look very tired. Listen, you have my word that I won't bother you for a decision until later—when you're feeling better."

Hausner recovered very quickly. He took his hand away from the rabbi's. "Good. Then that's the last I expect to hear about it—until later." He looked down at the object in the rabbi's other hand. "What the hell is that?"

The rabbi knew he'd been taken by a sharp operator. He was angry, but impressed. "What?" He looked down at his hand. "Oh. This. It's an abomination. I hate to touch it. A false idol." He held it up to the sunlight. "Becker found it in the grave he's digging."

Hausner moved closer. It was some sort of winged demon fashioned out of what appeared to be terra cotta, although Hausner thought for a wild moment that it was something mummified. It had the body of an emaciated man with an oversized phallus and the most hideous face Hausner could ever remember seeing represented in any type of art. "I think this should make old Dobkin's day complete. He's been annoying everyone about sifting through the rubble on their breaks. Let me have it."

The rabbi turned it in his hand so it faced him. "It's really too obscenely ugly to be exposed in the sunlight of God's world. It belongs to another time. It should have stayed in darkness." He gripped the clay figure tightly until his knuckles went white.

Hausner stood transfixed. A gust of scorching wind picked up the fine dust around him and obscured everything in front of him for a second. He yelled through the wind and dust. "Don't be a damned fool. We don't do that in the twentieth century. Give it to me!"

Rabbi Levin smiled and loosened his grip on the demon. The wind dropped and the brown cloud settled to the earth. He held the figure out toward Hausner. "Here. It's meaningless. God would laugh at my superstition if I smashed it. Give it to General Dobkin. My compliments."

Hausner took it. "Thank you." They stared at each other for a few seconds, then Hausner turned and walked off.

Hausner strode quickly along the crest of the steep slope overlooking the Euphrates. He looked down. It was about a hundred meters to the river, and he wondered how Dobkin thought he was going to descend it without being seen, even at night.

At the base of the slope, once the foot of the citadel, a few dusty little bushes that looked like castor oil plants grew along the bank. There were also clumps of bulrushes, and Hausner knew that Ashbals were posted there.

The Euphrates looked cool and inviting. Hausner licked his parched lips as he made his way south along the perimeter. Men and women stopped digging at their positions to look at him as he walked by. He moved faster.

Hausner stopped at McClure and Richardson's location. He noticed that they had erected quite an elaborate position. There was a chest-deep firing position with a crenelated wall of earth around it like a miniature castle. There was a small sun shield fashioned from seat covers and straightened seat springs. It blew in the growing wind and looked as though it might not hold up. "It looks like the Alamo."

McClure bit a matchstick in half and spit out one end. "It *is* the Alamo."

Both men were covered from head to foot with grime and sweat. Richardson's blue Air Force tunic lay in a hollowed shelf of the hole, neatly folded and partly wrapped in a pair of women's panties. Hausner wasn't angry to see that Richardson was thinking ahead. He gave him credit for it. Hausner assumed a more formal attitude. "We have been offered terms, as you have probably heard. We cannot accept those terms. *You* can, however. And you can accept them with no shame and no fear. Rish will hold you only as long as it is necessary to keep this location secret from the world. No matter what happens, you go free. I'm fairly certain he will live up to that. They don't want any trouble with your government. I ask you to please leave here. It would be better for everyone."

McClure sat down on the edge of the hole and swung his long legs in front of him. "I feel kind of important here. I mean, being the only gun on the west side of the hill. I was the first one here last night, and I think I might have stopped those fellers from trying this slope. Besides, I put a lot of improvements into this real estate. I think I'll stay here."

Hausner shook his head. "I don't want you two here. You're a complication."

McClure looked down at his shoes for a while. "Well, if you want to know the truth. I don't want to be here myself. But I don't want to take my chances with that Rish feller, either. If you start beating the shit out of him tonight, he'll forget we're neutrals damn quick and start squeezing our nuts for information about the weak points in this setup. Think about *that*."

Hausner thought about it. He looked at Richardson. "Colonel?" He could see that Richardson looked unhappy. Clearly, something was going on between these two.

Richardson cleared his throat. "I'm staying. But, goddamn it, I think you might try to parley again before sundown."

"I'll take your advice under consideration, Colonel. And if either of you change your mind . . . then I'll have to think about it in light of what Mr. McClure has said."

"You do that," said McClure. "And send over some of them kerosene bombs you're making. I can chuck one right down into those bushes and bulrushes tonight and light up the whole river bank."

Hausner nodded. "I'd like that. Incidentally, General Dobkin is leaving the perimeter tonight after sundown and before moonrise. He will be exiting here from your position. Try to observe the patterns and habits of the sentries down there. Give him whatever help you can."

McClure didn't ask any questions. He just nodded.

• • •

Dobkin was standing near a large, round black ball that came up to his chest.

Hausner, walking back from McC'ure and Richardson's position, saw him examining it under the tip of the port-side delta. He walked up to him. "Where the hell did that come from?"

Dobkin looked up. "It was thrown out of the tail section when it blew. It was lying there on the southern ridge, hidden by the terrain. Leiber found it when he was looking for stores. I had it brought here."

"That's nice. What the hell is it?"

Dobkin patted it. "Kahn says it's the compressed-nitrogen bottle."

Hausner nodded. The bottle was a backup to the hydraulic system. The compressed gas performed hydraulic functions in an emergency, until it ran out. "Can we use it?"

"I think so. It's a muscle. Energy waiting to do something."

"Is it full?"

"Kahn says it is. There's a lot of raw energy here if we can tap it. It has a valve, see?"

Hausner tapped on it with his knuckles. "Put the word out that I want some inspired thinking on this. Another little problem to keep our group of super-achievers busy. Idle minds are the playthings of the Devil.... Which reminds me..." Hausner held up the winged demon, "What's this?"

Dobkin took it carefully and held it cradled in his hands. He looked at its face for a long time before he spoke. "It's Pazuzu."

"I beg your pardon?" He smiled, but Dobkin did not smile back.

Dobkin scratched some dirt away from the enlarged penis with his thumbnail. "The wind demon. It brings sickness and death."

Hausner watched Dobkin examining it for a minute. "Is it ... valuable?"

Dobkin looked up. "Not as such. It's terra cotta. And it's not an unusual example, but it's in good condition. Who found it?"

"Becker. He's digging a grave for Hess."

"Appropriate." He cleaned off the face with a bit of saliva. "I really didn't expect to find much here. This was the top of the citadel. The battlements and watchtowers. There must be meters of dust piled on top of them. Strange to find anything in so shallow a hole." He looked up at Hausner. "Thank you."

"Thank the rabbi. He overcame an irrational urge to smash it."

Dobkin nodded. "I wonder if it was irrational."

The remainder of the afternoon was spent in fatiguing labor. Trenches grew longer and deeper and snaked toward each other. In some places they joined, and, in fact, the object was to join them all—if they were to be there long enough—to make up an integral system, stretching from the Euphrates at the north ridge to the Euphrates at the south ridge. The defenses along the western slope consisted only of individual foxholes.

Before dusk, Hausner ordered a rest period for personal grooming. The men were ordered to shave. Hausner expected an argument, but got none. The shaving water was reused to make mud for face camouflage.

The nitrogen bottle posed a diversionary problem for the mechanically minded. It rose out of the brown earth like a monolith, black and mute. Hausner offered a half-liter of water to anyone who could find a use for it.

The *Sherji* grew stronger and hotter, and dust began to cover everyone and everything. People with respiratory problems had difficulty breathing.

The sun set at 6:16. The truce was over, and their fate was again in their own hands. Hausner watched as the blazing red circle sank into the western mud flats. Overhead, where the night met the day, the first stars showed in the darkness. In the east, the sky was already black as velvet. By the ancient Hebrew conception of measuring time, the day was nearly finished. The Sabbath was ended. The rabbi's influence would be slightly reduced.

Hausner walked toward the lightly guarded western slope. He found a small depression in the earth, away from anyone else, and lay down in the dust. He stared up at the changing sky. The air rapidly cooled as it does on the desert, and the *Sherji* dropped to a soft breeze. Hausner stared without blinking at the marvelous black sky studded with stars brighter and closer than he had seen them since childhood. Then, the days were all sun-splashed and the nights were all starlight and magic. It had been a long time since he had lain outdoors on his back under the stars.

He stretched sensuously in the warm, yielding dust. The dark half of the sky fell westward and pushed the light half down further into the west. It was all so incredibly beautiful. It was no wonder, he thought, that the desert peoples of the world had always been more fanatical than other groups about their gods. You could almost touch them and see them in the stunning interplay of terrestrial and celestial phenomena.

Out on the mud flats, a pack of jackals howled. Their howling got closer very quickly, and Hausner guessed that they were running toward the Euphrates. They were pursuing some unfortunate small prey that had ventured out to drink under cover of darkness. They howled again, long and malevolently, then came the awful shrieks and sounds of struggle, then quiet. Hausner shuddered.

The strange dusk of the desert lasted only a few minutes after the sun set, followed by what pilots and military people euphemistically called EENT, end of evening nautical twilight—darkness.

The moon would not rise for hours. Would Rish attack, like the jackals, during this period of darkness, or would he wait until much later when the moon set? Brin had not seen the Ashbals moving from the Ishtar Gate area toward their attack during this period of darkness, he would move his men into the attack positions. There was only the thin line of sentries at the base of the hill. But that didn't mean anything. If Rish were going to attack positions after dark. Any commander would. That gave the Israelis about half an hour before an attack could be launched. Enough time to bury Moses Hess.

Hausner considered not going to the funeral. It was meaningless. He could draw more spiritual strength from staring at the heavens than from looking into a hole in the ground and listening to Rabbi Levin talk about them.

Hausner tried to pick out the constellations, but it had been a long time. Ursa Major was easy and so were Orion and Taurus, but the rest were meaningless groupings. He had more luck with the individual stars. Castor and Pollux. Polaris and Vega.

It was the Babylonians who were the primary astrologers of the ancient world. Like the inhabitants of modern Iraq, they slept on the flat roofs of their houses at night. How could they fail to develop a vast amount of lore concerning the heavenly bodies? Their learning was jealously guarded and at first did not spread to the other civilizations. But after the downfall of Babylonia, they traveled the ancient world as professional astrologers. Long after Babylon was forgotten by the ancients, the name Chaldean, synonymous with Babylonian, became another name for astrologer, magician, and sorcerer. The fate of Babylon as a state was to be remembered for her haughtiness and corruption. The fate of her people was to wander the world, selling their ancient mysteries for bread, and in the end to be remembered only as magicians. But the world gained a profound knowledge of the stars in the process. It was strange, reflected Hausner, that of all the learned people of the ancient world, only the Jews never took an interest in astrology or astronomy. He could probably develop an entire theory as to why that was so, but he felt too lazy and too tired to bother.

She knelt down next to him and stared at him in his shallow hole. "That's morbid. Come out of there."

"It's a womb." He couldn't see her at all. How in the world did she find him, and how did she know it was he? She must have been close by when it was light.

"It's far from that. It's dry and dead. Get up. The funeral is beginning."

"Go on ahead."

"I'm afraid. It's totally black. Walk me there."

"I never go to funerals on a first date. We have about fifteen minutes. Let me make love to you."

"I can't."

"Laskov?"

"Yes. And my husband. I can't bear another complication."

"I am a lot of things, Miriam, but a complication is not one of them." He could hear her breathing. She was very close, probably less than a meter. He could reach out ...

"It's wrong. Teddy, I could justify. You, I could not justify to—to anyone. Least of all to myself."

He laughed, and she laughed and sobbed at the same time. She caught her breath. "Jacob, why me? What do you see in me?" She paused. "What do I see in *you*? I loathe everything about you. I really do. Why do these things happen to people? If I loathe you, why am I here?"

Hausner reached out and found her wrist. "Why *did* you follow me?" She tried to pull away, but he would not let go. "If you follow a dangerous animal," he said, "you should know what you are going to do when you track him to his lair. Especially when you turn to leave and you find him standing at the entrance. If he could talk, he would ask you what you had in mind when you followed him. And you should have a good answer."

She didn't speak, but Hausner could hear her breathing getting heavier. Some kind of animal reaction subtly passed through her body, and Hausner felt it in those few square centimeters of her skin that were pressed to his. The pitch of her breathing changed, and he could swear that he could smell something that told him she was ready. In the dark, without any visual message, he knew that she had gone from alert and guarded to passive and submissive. He was surprised at his own heightened perceptions—and very confident of their accuracy. He pulled gently on her wrist and she rolled, unresisting, into his dusty resting place.

She lay on top of him and he helped her undress, then they lay on their sides facing each other and he undressed. Her skin was smooth and cool, as he expected it would be. He pressed his lips onto her mouth and felt her respond. She lay back on their crumpled clothes and raised her legs. Hausner lay between them and felt her firm thighs come around and grip his back with surprising strength. He went into her easily and lay still for a second. He wanted to see her face and was sorry he couldn't. He told her so. She replied that she was smiling. And when he asked her if her eyes were smiling, too, she said that she believed they were.

He moved slowly and she responded immediately. He could feel her nipples harden on his chest, and her breath blew in a rhythmic hot stream on his cheek and neck.

He put his hands under her buttocks and lifted her. She let out a little sound of pain as he thrust too far. He picked up his head and stared at her face, trying to see it. It was an incredibly black night, but the stars were growing stronger and he could finally see her eyes—black as the sky itself—pinpoints of reflected starlight. He thought he could read the expression in them, but he knew that it must be only a trick of the remote starlight.

She began to move spasmodically beneath him. Her buttocks rolled sensuously into the warm dust. Hausner heard his own voice speaking softly to her, saying things he would never have said except in total darkness. And she answered him in kind,

protected also by that invisibility, like a child who covers his face
while disclosing his deepest secrets. Her voice became rich and
throaty and her breath came in short convulsive gasps. A soft
ripple passed through her body, followed by a long spasm.
Hausner's body tensed for a second, then shuddered violently.

They lay still, holding on to each other. The wind passed over
them, cooling the sweat on their bodies.

Hausner rolled onto his side. He ran his hand over her
breasts, feeling them rise and fall. His thoughts were not clear
yet, but they included the knowledge that he had compromised
his position. In Tel Aviv, this would have been fine. Here, it was
not. But it could only have happened here. Strategic and tactical
considerations aside, he was fairly certain that he loved her, or
would love her very soon. He wanted to ask her about Laskov
and about her husband, but these were things that had to do with
the future. Therefore, they were irrelevant now. He tried to think
of something to say that he thought she would like to hear, but
couldn't think of anything. So he asked, "What would you like
me to say? I don't know what to say."

"Say nothing," she said and held his hand to her breast.

The stars were stronger and there were more of them now.
The Euphrates magnified the thin, cold starlight, and Hausner
could see the group of about twenty dark shapes standing
around the grave and silhouetted against the wide river. He
moved closer but stayed behind the group. Miriam stood beside
him for a second, then moved among the people to the graveside.

Moses Hess was lowered gently into his grave. The rabbi said
the *El Male Rachimim*, the Prayer for the Dead, in a loud, clear
voice that rolled down the slope, across the river, and onto the
mud flats.

Becker also stood back from the ring of people around the
grave, and Hausner could see that he was visibly upset.

How strange, thought Hausner. The bones of thousands of
Jews were buried at Babylon. How strange to be burying
another today. The rabbi's voice reached him from the edges of
his mind. "...*yea, we wept, when we remembered Zion. We
hanged our harps upon the willows in the midst...*" Hausner
realized that those famous willows no longer existed. He had not
seen one.

Miriam Bernstein spoke quietly with the rabbi. He nodded.
She turned and spoke softly, almost inaudibly, to the people
gathered in the darkness. "Many of you know what has come to

be called the Ravensbrück Prayer," she began, "written by an
anonymous author on a scrap of wrapping paper and found at
the camp after it was liberated. It is proper that we hear it now, at
this service, so that we remember, whether we be in Babylon,
Jerusalem, or New York, that we are on a mission of peace." She
turned and looked down into the open grave and began.

> Peace be to men who are of bad will,
> and may an end be put to all vengeance
> and to all talk about punishment and chastisement.
> The cruelties mock all norms and principles,
> they are beyond all limits of human understanding
> and there are many martyrs.
> Therefore, God
> does not weigh their sufferings on the scales of your justice,
> so that you would demand a cruel account,
> but rather let it be valid in a different way.
> Rather, write in favor of all executioners, traitors, and
>   spies,
> and all bad men, and credit to them
> all the courage and strength of soul of the others. . . .

Miriam's voice wavered as she continued reciting the prayer.
Then, as she came to the end, her voice strengthened.

> . . . All the good should count and not the evil.
> And for the memories of our enemies,
> we should no longer remain their victims,
> no longer their nightmare and their shuddering ghosts,
> but rather their help, so that they may cease their fury.
> That is the only thing that is asked of them,
> and that we, after it is all over,
> may be able to live as humans among humans,
> and that there may be peace again on this poor earth
> for the men of good will
> and that this peace may come also to the others.

Hausner only half-listened as the last sounds of Miriam's
voice died in the darkness. It was a senseless prayer—a
dangerous prayer for people who were going to have to live with
revenge and hate in their hearts if they were to survive. Miriam,
Miriam. When will you learn?

The funeral service was ended. Hausner realized that

everyone was gone and he was alone. He looked out across the Euphrates, out across the black mud plains, out to where the black velvet sky met the black horizon, out toward Jerusalem. He fancied he saw the lights of the Old City, but it was only a star setting on the horizon. It disappeared, and in that moment, he knew he would never go home again.

BOOK THREE

BABYLON
THE ISHTAR GATE

Go ye forth of Babylon,
  flee ye from the Chaldeans,
with a voice of singing declare ye, tell this,
  utter it even to the end of the earth;
say ye, The Lord hath redeemed his servant Jacob.
  And they thirsted not when he led them through the deserts: he caused
the waters to flow out of the rock for them:
  he clave the rock also, and the waters gushed out.
      Isaiah 48:20–21

21

They came soon after the funeral service was ended. They did not come on line as they had the night before, but in small squad groups and fireteam groups—in threes and sixes and nines. They moved quickly and silently from one area of cover and concealment to the next. They picked out the best avenues of approach, having found them the hard way the previous night. They were surprised to find the low walls built across the gullies, but they crawled up and over them like snakes and continued in the erosion gullies upward, toward the crest. Noise control and light discipline were excellent, equipment was taped down, faces were blackened, and the death penalty was in force for any breach of orders.

Ahmed Rish crawled with his lieutenant, Salem Hamadi, some distance behind their advancing army. Both of them knew that this might be their last effort. If they failed, it would mean humiliation and eventual death at the hands of their own men or at the hands of a tribunal made up of other Palestinians. Worse yet, they might be hunted for the rest of their lives by Mivtzan

227

Elohim. They might spend the remainder of their lives at Ramla. The irony was that the head of Mivtzan Elohim, Isaac Burg, was within their grasp, as was fame, fortune, and glory. For Rish and Hamadi this was the most important night in both their lives. Rish covered his eyes as a swirl of sand blew in his face. He put his mouth to Hamadi's ear. "The ancient gods are with us. Pazuzu has sent us this wind."

Hamadi wasn't sure *whom* the wind was sent for. He spit some sand out of his mouth and grunted.

Nathan Brin rubbed his eye and looked again, then shut off the scope. He put his arm around Naomi Haber, who was nestled next to him. "My eyes are strained. I've been seeing things since sundown." He pushed the rifle sideways across the earth wall. "Here. Take a look."

Naomi ran her hand through his hair and wiped the sweat and camouflage dirt from his forehead. The inevitable had happened, after hours of forced company and a high state of nervous tension, combined with the fact that neither of them knew if they would be alive very much longer. She doubted if she would look twice at him in a café in Tel Aviv. But this was Babylon, and perhaps some of the wantonness of the place hung in the air like a vapor.

Their lovemaking, accomplished between sunset and the end of the funeral service, had been as hurried as Hausner's and Bernstein's, but much more frantic. It was interrupted whenever either of them had had a premonition or a panicky moment and they had stopped to scan the slope. They had laughed over the clumsy affair. But that was before, when there was little chance of the Ashbals being in the area. Now they were dressed, and the threat of attack was very serious.

Naomi Haber put the scope to her eyes and scanned. This was much different from match shooting. Much different. She could hit moving and still targets with uncanny accuracy, but she never was much good at picking out targets from a cluttered background. She was not yet familiar with the night view of the terrain. The eerie green glow further confused her.

"See anything?" asked Brin.

"I don't think so. That damned wind."

"I know," said Brin. The *Sherji* was picking up dust and sending wispy shadows across the land that could only be seen in the powerful scope.

She cursed silently and handed the rifle back to Brin. "I'm not good at this."

Brin took the rifle and pointed it straight into the air. He scanned for a full three minutes before he spotted the Lear overhead. He estimated its altitude at better than two kilometers. Well out of range of his rifle. Hausner had told him to look for the Lear and to try to knock it down. He considered sending one round at it, but decided against wasting the ammunition. They were jammed, and that's all there was to it. He switched off the scope and sat back. "Let's give us and the batteries five minutes rest." He lit a cigarette in his cupped hands.

The Ashbals took their time, resting between areas of concealment, then moving quickly to the next. They knew that the Israelis would have put out early warning devices and outposts, and they were on the lookout for both. In addition, they were under orders not to return any probing fire. But had they practiced the tactic of the quick, silent run just then, they might have been over the Israeli breastworks and into the Israeli trenches within minutes. But they continued to move in short, silent rushes.

Far ahead of the main body of Ashbals was a two-man sniper-killer team. One man, Amnah Murad, was armed with a Russian Dragunov sniper rifle. Mounted on the rifle was an infrared scope. Murad cradled the rifle carefully in his arms as he moved. The other man, Moniem Safar, carried a compass and an AK-47. Murad and Safar had trained as a team since they were five years old. They were closer than blood brothers. They were bound by the brotherhood of the hunt and the kill, and each could anticipate every move and every emotion of the other. They could literally communicate without speaking. A touch, a raised eyebrow, an imperceptible twitch of the mouth, a breath. The Lear had flown them in that afternoon from the desert base camp.

The two young men followed a compass heading that they were told would bring them to the promontory where the suspected Israeli night scope was located.

The two men looked up the slope and picked out the outline of the black ridge against the star-studded sky. They estimated the distance at half a kilometer. Murad knelt down, turned the scope on, and sighted through it as he adjusted the knobs. The hillside appeared red-glowing, and it reminded him of blood or of hell and made him uneasy for a moment. He scanned and spotted the promontory. He looked for the telltale light of a night scope, but saw nothing. He lay on his belly and rested the rifle on a small rise in the ground. He relaxed as he continued to stare.

Outpost/Listening Post, OP/LP No. 2, was located in the central section of the slope, almost a half-kilometer down from the promontory. It was manned by Yigael Tekoah, the Knesset member, and Deborah Gideon, his secretary. Tekoah thought he heard something to his front, then to his left, then, with a frightened start, to his rear. He touched the girl's shoulder and whispered into her ear. "I think they've gotten around us."

She nodded in the dark. They had both been too frightened to move when they first heard the noises, and now they were behind the enemy lines with no way to get back to their own. They were lost.

Tekoah knew that in a real military unit he would have had sound-amplifying devices, night-seeing devices, weapons and radios or line phones to speak with the main body. But here, OP/LP was tantamount to suicide. They were sacrificial lambs. Still, it had not been difficult to find six volunteers for the three posts.

Tekoah felt he had failed. He had not done his duty of alerting the others. There was still no fire coming from the Israeli positions, and he knew that the Arabs were making a successful surprise attack. They might very well infiltrate the Israeli positions before a shot was fired. "I am going to shout and warn them."

Deborah stayed frozen like a small rabbit.

"I'm sorry. I must."

She seemed to come out of it. She touched his cheek. "Of course."

Tekoah could hear footsteps very close now. He stood in their shallow foxhole, cupped his hands to his mouth, and faced the top of the slope. He took a deep breath.

An Ashbal tripped a wire that had hanging from it cans of pebbles and metal filings. The pebbles and metal rattled noisily in the still air. There was complete silence on the slope. Tekoah froze in mid-breath.

•   •   •

Brin grabbed the M-14, turned on the scope, and sighted. Nothing moved downslope, not even the cloud and dust shadows. All along the defensive perimeter the Israelis held their breath, and all across the slope the Arabs did the same. Brin wondered if it was the wind rattling the cans or an animal or a small earthslide. There had been a lot of that all day. He relaxed but continued to scan.

The two-man sniper-killer team came alert. Murad stared intently at the promontory now. He saw the light of the Israeli scope as it went on. He noticed that it was green. An American starlight. He knew it would be. The starlight picture was better than his, but that didn't mean that the man who had it was a better shot than a man with an infrared. Murad felt confident. He sighted on the green light and waited to see the head behind it.

Brin leaned out further over the small earth balcony. He whispered to Naomi Haber. "You might as well pass the word that I don't see anything yet."

She nodded and ran silently, barefoot, back toward the Command Post/Observation Post.

Murad saw Brin's reddish-white skin where Naomi Haber had wiped the sweat and camouflage from his forehead. Murad fired three times in quick succession. The silencer coughed very gently like a weak old man clearing his throat.

Brin felt nothing but a tap on his forehead, then nothing at all. He pitched backward and lay in the dust, the rifle thrown out and down the slope in his death throe.

After a few minutes, the Ashbals began advancing again. Another man hit another wire, and cans again rattled in the night.

Hausner stood with Dobkin and Burg at the CP/OP.

Naomi Haber had had trouble finding the CP/OP in the dark, but she finally spotted the phosphorescent banner. She ran up to the three men and reported.

Hausner listened again for the rattling, but heard nothing He turned to Haber and the two other young runners at the

Command Post. "Go down the line and tell them to fire a mad-minute when they hear my whistle. But make the minute only ten seconds," he added.

The runners took off in different directions.

After a short interval, Hausner whistled. Those closest to him heard the whistle and began firing at full rates of fire, which was a signal for everyone down the line to begin.

The Ashbals froze, then stretched themsleves out on the ground. A few were hit, but they did not call out in pain for fear of being strangled by their officers. The officers and non-coms whispered frantically to hold fire. "It is only probing fire. Probing fire. Do not shoot," they said through clenched teeth. But as the seconds dragged out, each second seeming like a year, and with the five Israeli AK-47's pounding automatic fire down the slope, even the most disciplined among them began to feel for their safety catches and triggers. Just as one young man was about to return the fire, the Israeli fire ceased as suddenly as it had begun. The "mad-minute," ten seconds long for want of ammunition, was over.

The smell of burnt cordite blew away with the east wind, and the last of the gunshots reverberated off the surrounding hills and died in the ears of the defenders. There was not one among them who believed that the Ashbals were disciplined enough to hold their fire under that barrage, or to choke down a cry of pain if they were hit, or to stifle a panicky scream as the earth churned up around their faces.

Hausner turned to Burg and Dobkin. "I think we're getting jumpy."

Burg spoke. "I hope the OP/LP's are not hurt."

Dobkin answered. "If everyone followed his range cards and the OP/LP's stayed where they were supposed to, then they should be all right." He looked toward the eastern slope. "And speaking of outposts, if they haven't heard anything, then I don't think there is anything out there. Animals, wind, and earthslides. That's the bane of trip-wire devices. Once a sparrow landed on a trip flare wire in Suez in '67 and—but who gives a damn about Suez in '67?"

"Nobody," Hausner assured him.

Micah Goren and Hannah Shiloah, typists, manned Outpost/Listening Post No. 1 on the north end of the slope. They also knew, too late, that they had been surrounded. They sat huddled in their small foxhole until the mad-minute ended.

They contemplated their next move. Out of the darkness, three young Ashbals jumped with flashing knives and cut the throats of the two unarmed Israelis.

Reuben Taber and Leah Ilsar, interpreters, sat at OP/LP No. 3 toward the south end of the slope. They also knew what had happened. They moved out of their hole and began making their way back to the top of the slope.

Murad spotted them with the infrared scope not forty meters from where he was lying. The Arab raised his silenced rifle and shot each of them neatly through the head.

The Ashbals began crawling now, feeling ahead for trip wires. Their progress was slow but nonetheless unrelenting. The closest squad was within three hundred meters of the crest.

Tekoah realized what the mad-minute was and knew that the Israelis had not seen anything. He turned to Deborah Gideon. "Good luck." He swung and hit her on the jaw. She fell silently to the bottom of their foxhole. He quickly pushed clay and dirt over her from the rim of the hole, then jumped out of it and began to run up the slope. He cupped his hands to his mouth again and shouted. "TEKOAH HERE! OUTPOST NUMBER TWO! THEY ARE ALL OVER THE SLOPE!"

Whether it was an Arab or Israeli-fired AK-47 that cut him down, he never knew, nor would it have mattered to him if he had.

The Ashbals charged. The first of the man-traps collapsed under the weight of one of them, a young girl. She fell onto the stakes and became impaled but did not die. Her screams were much louder than the guns at first but soon faded.

The Israelis were somewhat demoralized to hear the Ashbals so near. What had happened to the outposts? To the early warning devices? Why didn't the mad-minute work? Where was Brin and that marvelous scope?

A three-man fire team of Ashbals made it to the crest but ran into the abatis. One was impaled in the neck, another in the chest. Abel Geller, a steward, shot the third man at close range with Dobkin's Colt .45.

The man-traps were taking their toll, but there were not as many of the arduously dug holes as there should have been. Once they were collapsed, the screams of the victims kept everyone else away. The dead absorbed the stakes in their bodies and rendered the traps useless.

The Israelis had five AK-47's now and there were fewer

Ashbals than in the first attack, but the Arabs had achieved surprise and that was always a critical factor. And there was no Joshua Rubin with his Uzi. Neither was there Nathan Brin with his M-14 and starlight scope, though no one knew that yet.

A squad of Ashbals made its way toward the promontory over ground that was not covered by any weapon. They keyed on the green glow of the starlight scope lying in the dust at the base of the promontory.

All along the line, as the Ashbals got closer they positioned themselves between the Israeli gun positions, which they could spot from the muzzle flashes. The Israeli guns had to swing farther right and farther left to cover these dead spots with effective fire.

The Ashbals had another advantage: This night they were veterans. The previous night they were untried young men and women who were taken by surprise by the Israeli resistance. Incoming gunfire held no irrational terror for them now, only the healthy fear that comes with experience. They had lost many brothers and sisters, and they wanted revenge. Hamadi had promised them that, with victory, they could use the Israelis—men or women—as they pleased. Ahmed Rish had promised all of them personal wealth after the ransom. Another difference between this night and the previous night was a long inspirational talk by Hamadi. Everyone knew, or thought he did, what he was fighting for now.

Hausner's man, Jaffe, leaped over the breastworks and went between the impaling stakes of the abatis to recover the AK-47's of the men who had become impaled. He threw the rifles into the perimeter but was hit as he tried to get back and rolled down the slope. Another of Hausner's men, Marcus, recovered the AK-47's and ammunition of the Ashbal whom Abel Geller shot with the .45.

The three extra rifles were given to two men and a woman trained by Dobkin. Still, the Ashbals had the initiative and they were in that peculiar situation that happens sometimes in battle, where there would be more casualties in retreating than in advancing. They were too near the crest.

The Israelis had cleared the slope well in front of their positions and they had leveled the land and flattened the clay mounds, but the Ashbals were so close that they were able, with their superior firepower and almost unlimited ammunition, to pour overwhelming fire into the breastworks on the crest. The defenders spent more and more time keeping their heads down and less and less time returning the fire. Each time they raised their heads, they saw that the muzzle flashes had gotten closer than the last time.

Bullets ripped into the breastworks, eating away at them and causing small earthslides as they fell away, leaving exposed holes in the defensive walls. Bullets also ripped into the aluminum reflectors, knocking most of them off their posts. The armor mesh from the Concorde was effective, but after several thousand hits, the nylon began to fray and the posts holding the sections were cut in two and toppled over. The aluminum impaling stakes were severed or uprooted by rifle fire, leaving openings in the abatis. To those Israelis who had never seen battle, there was amazement at how much damage small arms fire could do.

Hausner, Burg, and Dobkin stood at their posts and received reports from the runners. Dobkin knew that the Ashbals had the initiative and that the next few minutes might bring them over the top. He put his hand on Hausner's shoulder. "I'm staying."

Hausner roughly pushed his arm away. "You're going, General. Now. That's an order."

Dobkin's voice rose, which was a rarity. "Now you listen—you need a military commander here. There's no need for me to go for help any longer."

"That's right," said Hausner. "It's all over. But you were willing to go when it looked safer up here. So now I want you to go in order to save yourself. And I want someone out there so that the survivors here can have hope during their captivity. Now, go!"

Dobkin hesitated.

"Go!" shouted Hausner.

Burg spoke. "Go, Ben. The best commander in the world couldn't save this situation. It's in the hands of the troops—and God. So go."

Dobkin turned and jumped off the small knoll. Without a word of parting to anyone, he made his way toward McClure's position on the west slope.

On the east slope, two Ashbals managed to make it to the breastworks where there were no AK-47's or pistols. The two

Israelis there, Daniel Jacoby, a steward, and Rachel Baum, a stewardess, hurled makeshift aluminum spears and shouted a warning. The Ashbals ducked the spears and opened fire. Jacoby and Baum were both hit. The two Ashbals slid between the impaling stakes of the abatis and jumped the breastworks and trenches. They were inside the perimeter.

Alpern, another security man, ran down the line with his AK-47 blazing. The two Ashbals fell into the Israeli trench. Alpern jumped into the trench and finished them with one of the homemade spears. Two men, carrying a makeshift litter made out of alumimun spears and carpeting, collected Daniel Jacoby and Rachel Baum and carried them back to the shepherds' hut. Alpern called to two unarmed women and handed them the Ashbals' weapons. They had been lucky this time, but Alpern, a veteran of the 1973 war, knew that it was coming close to the end unless their last desperate defensive plan worked.

22

On the flight deck of Concorde 02, Captain David Becker sat back in his chair and lit his last cigarette. He thought about his children in the States and about his new Israeli wife. The radio gave off a high, piercing squeal, but he did not seem to notice it. Occasionally, a bullet struck the fuselage and made a popping sound as it broke the thin skin. A few ricochets bounced around the cabin. Two bullets had come through the windows of the flight deck and caused spider-web shatters in them. Becker crushed out his cigarette and threw it on the floor. He reached to turn off the emergency power, but remembered that they wanted it left on for some last minute ruses they had planned. He shrugged. All the resourcefulness in the world meant nothing against hordes. The hordes. That had been an American infantryman's joke during the Korean War. A Chinese squad was made up of three hordes and a mob, or something like that. Funny. The hordes were taking over the civilized world. Little by little. Like the end of Rome. He got up to leave.

The radio went silent, then hummed pleasantly. A voice in

bad Hebrew came out of the speaker. "You must give up," said the voice quickly. "Tell H he must give it up." Becker stared at the radio. The Arab spoke quickly and cryptically in the event the transmission was being monitored somewhere. In a second the jamming was back on. "Fuck you," said Becker. He left the flight deck and went out to join the flight.

The Ashbal squad under the promontory was within a hundred meters of the green-glowing starlight scope. The two-man sniper-killer team near them had set up a position, and Murad was firing silently and accurately at heads looking over the breastworks on the ridge.

Burg turned to Hausner. "They're close enough, I think."

Hausner nodded. Dobkin had told them to hold off on what was termed their final protective measures and their psy-warfare until it was absolutely necessary. Hausner knew it could not get any more necessary than it was now. He gave the order to his runner to set in motion the last defensive measures. He turned to Burg. "I'm going to see how Brin is doing. You are the commander. Stay here."

Burg acknowledged. As Hausner moved off, a young girl, one of the runners, came up behind him. "They're coming up the river slope," she reported.

Burg lit his pipe. Directing battles from hilltops was not his strong suit. It had been over thirty years since he was a soldier. Dobkin had left, and Hausner had gone out to the perimeter to commit suicide—he had no doubt about that. No one had heard anything from the Foreign Minister for some time. He was dead, wounded, or fighting for his life like everyone else. And he, Burg, was left holding the bag. He would have to negotiate the surrender if there was a chance to negotiate. He, who was always careful to remain detached and on the fence. But this time he was on the spot, and he was alone on that spot. No more runners were reporting the course of the battle. They were all fighting on the perimeter, he supposed. There was no staff to consult, no meetings to be held. He had a glimpse of how Hausner must have felt, and he was sorry for him. The runner stood beside him. He looked at her closely. It was Esther Aronson, one of the Foreign Minister's aides. She was shaking and her voice was breaking as she gave a fragmentary appraisal. "What are we going to *do*?" she asked.

Burg pulled on his pipe. He heard at least ten AK-47's on the east slope now. He had no doubt that they needed every one of them, but he couldn't let the Arabs come up the west slope unopposed. The Foreign Minister was in charge of that side of the perimeter, and Burg supposed that he knew he was unqualified for the task. The line was held by only about eight people. Then there were Richardson and McClure. He pointed out to the east slope. "Go out there and beg, borrow, or steal two AK-47's and at least two loaded pistols. Take them back to the west slope. Tell Mr. Weizman to begin all the last defensive measures as soon as you get back. All right?"

She nodded quickly in the dark.

Burg looked at her. That was a lot of responsibility for one person, he decided. Alone, it was up to her to appropriate weapons and ammunition, then take them several hundred meters in the dark and place them where they would do the most good, and at the same time pass on orders to the Foreign Minister, who was probably beside himself with doubt by now. And all this had to be done before the Arabs could make the climb up the slope. He patted her shoulder. "It'll be all right. Just take it one step at a time."

"I'm all right."

"Good. Did you happen to see General Dobkin over there?"

"No."

"All right. Just go ahead, then. Good luck."

She ran off toward the sound of gunfire.

Dobkin stood in the foxhole with McClure and Richardson. "I knew they'd try this slope eventually."

McClure leaned forward and held out his pistol with both hands. He aimed cross-slope to the right and fired twice, then fired twice more to his front, then fired his final two rounds cross-slope to his left. He drew fire before he got the last round off. He leaned back. "Hard as hell to hold a five-hundred-meter front with a six-shooter." He fished around in his pockets for loose rounds.

"They'll send something over here from the other side," Dobkin assured him.

"I sure hope so," answered McClure. He began to reload.

Richardson looked down over the steep slope when the gunfire stopped. At short intervals a tin of pebbles would rattle, or the sound of an Arab cursing as he slipped would carry up the slope. "When the hell are they going to begin the final protective defenses? Where the hell did that runner go? Where are our AK-47's?"

Dobkin lifted himself out of the hole. "Ask General Hausner. I don't work here anymore." He crouched down in a runner's stance. "Adios, Tex," he said to McClure. "See you in Haifa or Houston." He sprang out of his crouch and took a long step that brought him over the crest. He seemed to hang in the air for a long moment. He looked down and realized how steep the drop was. It was a wall, he remembered, a glacis. A sloping wall built up from the river bank. His fall intercepted the slope and jolted him with a shock. His next step was ten meters further down the almost perpendicular slope, the next, twenty meters. He ran, dropped actually, almost vertically to the ground below. He covered half the slope in less than three seconds. To his front, two surprised-looking Arabs suddenly appeared climbing out of the dark. They reacted instinctively and held their AK-47's, with bayonets fixed out in front of them.

Hausner found Naomi Haber cradling Nathan Brin's mutilated head in her lap. He knew now what at least part of the problem had been with the defenses. "Where's the rifle?" he snapped.

She looked up. "He's dead."

"I can see that, damn it! Where's the goddamned rifle?"

She shook her head.

Hausner crouched on the promontory. He half-felt and half-saw where Brin had rested his rifle on the ledge. There was a furrow in the soil where a bullet had ripped through. There was something warm and wet there as well. He wiped his hand. It was no stray shot, he decided. The Arabs had at least one sniper rifle now. They'd have another when they recovered Brin's gun. Were they still keeping this sniper's perch under observation? He'd find out very soon. He leaped over the earth wall and slid down the slope below. He saw the green glow very easily and dived at it.

Murad saw him in his scope. He called out to the nine-man infantry squad that was moving toward the rifle, but they could not see Hausner.

Hausner picked up the rifle, rolled to another position, and raised it. He saw the squad less than thirty meters off and fired five rounds in quick succession. He hit one or two men, and the rest scattered. They were no match for the starlight scope in the dark and knew it.

Murad drew a bead on Hausner. He had had his heart set on owning that scope. Now this madman might get it damaged when Murad shot him. He fired.

Hausner was already moving. He heard the round kick up dirt near his feet. He flattened himself on the sloping hill and scanned the terrain to his front. The Arab knew where he was, but Hausner didn't know where the Arab was. If he couldn't spot him in the next few seconds, he would be dead.

Murad had Hausner directly in his cross hairs. He squeezed the trigger. It was an impossible shot to miss.

The Ashbal infantry squad directly behind Murad began firing blindly at the scope, their streams of green tracer rounds making crisscross patterns in the blackness. Burning tracers lodged in the earth and glowed like dying fireflies while ricochets shot off at all angles.

Murad squeezed the trigger as the picture in his infrared scope began disappearing. The major disadvantage of the scope in battle was that it whited-out when it was aimed at burning phosphorus. The tracers of his backup squad arched across his red picture and left white streaks that thickened and bled into each other. That was why he had wanted the starlight scope. He cursed loudly and fired blindly. "Stop, you fools! Stop!" He fired blindly again and again. His teammate, Safar, shouted over the sound of the AK-47's, and the squad ceased fire.

Hausner knew what had happened. Another man would have said that God was with him again. But Hausner felt that he was being toyed with. The bomb. The crash. The recovering of the AK-47's. Now this. He wasn't charmed, he decided. He was cursed. Why wouldn't it end?

Murad's picture returned, and he scanned the spot where Hausner had been but saw nothing.

Hausner had found a very shallow depression in the slope, under the steep rise of the promontory—the watchtower—and had fallen into it. Like infantrymen everywhere, he knew how to shrink. Every muscle contracted, the air left his lungs, and he seemed to deflate into his pitiful hole. His chest, thighs, and even his loins collapsed in some metaphysical way known only to men under fire, and the bottom of the depression seemed to drop a few more precious centimeters.

Murad suddenly became frightened. He felt naked, exposed. He, too, found a cavity in the earth and burrowed into it.

The sounds of battle along the ridge filled the air, but in that spot, there seemed to be silence. Hausner and Murad waited for each other. The two night scopes. Two flash suppressors. Two silencers and two fine rifles. Silent, invisible, and deadly.

The main body of the Ashbals was within a hundred meters of the perimeter, but a few squads of trained sappers, infiltrators, had penetrated to positions directly beneath the breastworks and abatis. They lay there, silent and frozen, armed only with knives and pistols, every inch of their exposed skin blackened, waiting for the main group to make the final assault. Had they had hand grenades, bangalor torpedoes, or satchel charges, as sappers are supposed to have, they could have wreaked havoc on the Israeli lines. But no one had expected that they would have to storm a hill to take these hostages. They felt ill used in this attack. They were professionals, the elite of any infantry unit. It was a suicide mission to crawl up to the enemy lines in front of the main advance. And here they were, but they could do nothing until the main body got within final assault range. Then they would jump into the Israeli trenches and kill with knife and pistol. But if only they had those explosives to send in first...

Dobkin leaped and flew past the two astonished Arabs. They swiveled and lay with their backs on the slope, and their heels dug into the shifting clay and sand. They pointed their AK-47's downward and fired. The reports from the automatic weapons shook their bodies and they slid down the glacis, breaking off the crust of age and exposing the original brickwork.

Dobkin literally flew forward. He heard the pop and zip of the bullets as they went by him. His feet came down again and he sprang off again. His heels crashed through the castor oil bushes and his feet hit the flood bank. He leaped again like a high diver and sailed into the air.

An arch of green tracers followed him. He seemed to somersault around and through the long, deadly green fingers. He hung in mid-air for what seemed like an eternity. Above him was the starry black sky of Mesopotamia. Then the ridge line sped past in a blur, then below was the luminescent Euphrates, then, as his body spun again, the mud flats flashed past his eyes, and then again the sky. Out of the corner of his eye, those green phosphorus streaks, like death rays in a science fiction movie, came closer and closer, following him, and those hollow staccato sounds grew louder as more and more guns joined in. He wondered why he wasn't falling, why he seemed to be suspended above the river. Then a sharp green light hit him with searing pain and everything resumed normal speed as if he had just awakened from a dream. He heard a splash and the muddy Euphrates closed over him.

Hausner decided he was not going to make it back to the Israeli lines. It was too open, and the Arab sniper had his position fixed now. Yet from where Hausner lay, he could not deliver effective fire anywhere except to his front. The scope was not being utilized to its fullest advantage, and in any case, he was almost out of ammunition.

A round knocked off the heel of his shoe, and his leg jerked spasmodically. He cursed as he stuck his head up. He took aim, but the Arab was invisible in his hole. The infantry squad had switched to non-tracer rounds and began firing in his general direction. He spotted the sniper's teammate traversing the terrain toward the infantry squad—bringing them a definite fix on his position. Hausner fired, and the man, Safar, went down holding his side.

Murad fired, and Hausner felt a sting on his ear. He swung toward the sniper and fired at his form as it disappeared into the hole. He felt a warm wetness on his ear as he settled back in his shallow concavity. He thought, briefly, irrationally, of Miriam.

Hausner had had enough. He wasn't accomplishing anything, and he could sense that the Ashbals on both sides of him were approaching the crest. He called out behind him, above the sound of the shooting. "Haber!"

There was no answer.

He called again. "Haber!"

She looked up. Brin's bloody and brain-splattered head still lay in her lap. She remembered that Hausner was there a few minutes before, but didn't know what had become of him. She heard him shout again, but didn't answer.

Hausner ripped off his shirt and wrapped it around the starlight scope. He reversed the rifle and gripped its red-hot silencer/flash suppressor. He stood and swung the rifle around his head and released it into the air. It sailed upward and over the top of the ruined watchtower above his head. It fell into the soft dust some distance from Naomi Haber. She heard it fall and knew instinctively what it was and what she was supposed to do. She lowered her head and placed a kiss on Nathan Brin's shattered forehead.

The order for the final protective defenses had gone up and down the perimeter, and the carefully rehearsed operations began to be set in motion. All the ruses and all the makeshift weaponry that looked so clever and inspired in the daylight were about to be put to the test, and there were many doubts now in the dark.

An Arab voice shouted loudly a hundred meters to the north of the promontory. "Here! There is a hole in the lines here! Here! Follow me!"

Two Ashbal squads, eighteen men, converged on the voice. They charged upward, following the commanding voice. No one fired at them. They came within fifty meters of the apparently deserted breastworks. Another few seconds and they would be inside and the fight would be virtually over.

The voice called again. "Here! Quickly! Over the top!"

If the Ashbals noticed in the din of the firing that the voice had a slightly metallic quality, or that the Palestinian accent was not quite right, they did not act on that knowledge. One of their commanders must be using a bullhorn. They kept coming on toward the voice which was so close to the Israeli defenses.

Ibrahim Arif lay in back of the breastworks in a small dugout and shouted into the PA microphone again. "NOW, UP AND OVER!"

The PA speaker box, thirty meters in front of the breastworks, beckoned the Ashbals forward. "NOW, UP AND OVER! SHOUT! SHOUT! DEATH TO ISRAEL!"

The Ashbals stood straight, ran forward, and shouted: "DEATH TO ISRAEL!"

Kaplan, who had checked himself out of the infirmary, Marcus, and Rebecca Livni, a young stenographer who had just acquired an AK-47, opened fire. They each poured two thirty-round magazines into the Ashbal ranks.

The Ashbals stood in the glare of the muzzle flashes, paralyzed and bewildered. The 7.62mm rounds ripped into them. They collapsed on top of one another like a pile of jackstraws. It was their single biggest loss so far, and it left a sizable gap in their frontal attack.

• • •

Esther Aronson had been pleading with everyone she ran into in the dark to listen to her. Burg said to beg, borrow, or steal. And begging wasn't working. Everyone was too involved with his own survival to worry about the strategic problems of an attack from the rear. Everyone who listened to her sympathized, but that was all she got. She searched desperately for Hausner. Hausner could give a simple order, and she would have what she wanted. But no one knew where he was. Missing, presumed dead.

She saw and heard the ruse of the PA box and knew that the last desperate tricks and defenses were beginning. On the west slope there was hardly anything of that sort. She needed arms. She ran over to where Marcus and Rebecca Livni were cautiously making their way through the breastworks and abatis to recover the rifles of the slain squads. Kaplan was covering them. Esther Aronson ran past Kaplan, vaulted over the trench and over the top of the breastworks, and slid through the stakes of the abatis past a surprised Marcus and Livni. "Sorry," she yelled. "I need guns for the west slope. They're attacking." She stepped quickly among the carnage, among the dead and still living, and quickly and expertly stripped off bandoliers and web gear that were loaded down with ammunition pouches. She grabbed at the AK-47's in the dark, more often than not finding their hot barrels instead of their stocks. Her hands and body burned as she slung them one after the other over her shoulders.

Marcus and Livni had run to Aronson and were helping her. Marcus kept shouting to watch out for live men, but Esther Aronson didn't seem to care or hear. Marcus shot a man who appeared to reach for his rifle as it was being pulled away.

Aronson yelled, "Thank you," and disappeared over the breastworks under that incredible load.

Marcus and Livni quickly gathered up the remaining rifles under cover of Kaplan's AK-47. The PA box was screaming, "BACK! BACK! STAY AWAY, COMRADES! THE JEWS ARE WELL ARMED OVER HERE." The Ashbals kept their distance.

Naomi Haber put a fresh magazine into the M-14 and sighted. The entire slope was covered with crawling, crouching figures. She scanned the area directly below her perch. She spotted Hausner lying very still in his hole. Had he been hit? She couldn't tell. He must have stood up to throw the rifle that distance. The Arab sniper would certainly have gotten him.

A bullet brushed the knuckles of her right hand and she let out a scream and almost lost the rifle. She crouched below the earth wall until the shock wore off. She licked at the wound like an animal, and this seemed to have a calming effect on her. She knew that the man who had almost killed her was the same man who had killed her lover. And she knew that for that reason, more than any other, he must die. She got up slowly and peeked over the earth wall.

Murad realized by now that Safar was dead. Safar, his childhood friend. His only real friend. His lover. And that Jew had killed him. Had he hit the Jew when he threw the rifle up? And the rifle and scope were gone. Who had it? He scanned between Hausner's hole and the sniper's promontory. The danger was on the promontory now, but his emotions wouldn't let him take his eyes off the last place he had seen the cursed Jew.

Haber sighted slowly as she took a breath. She could see the sniper's full body lying prone below her about eighty meters away. A shot toward the head area would, with luck, destroy the scope as well as the head, but a shot at the back was more certain. She put the cross hairs over the small of his back and fired twice.

Along the perimeter, the Israelis were setting up the dummies that had taken so long to construct. As they were set up, they drew fire, were knocked down and set up again.

A dozen unarmed men and women held up aerosol spray cans and ignited their vapor mists in short spurts, simulating muzzle flashes. The Arabs fired at these flashes, which they could see all along the ridge. Their estimation of the number of weapons captured by the Israelis went up considerably.

Meanwhile, the real AK-47's, newly captured with sufficient ammunition, were beginning to operate.

Two unarmed women, who had spent the last half hour tape-recording the sounds of battle on the peace mission's two dozen cassette tape recorders, now began placing those recorders at various points and pushing the playback buttons. The volume of fire from the Israeli lines seemed to increase.

Things were beginning to function again. Runners were coming to the CP/OP and reporting to Burg and asking for orders. Burg gave orders as though he had been doing it all his life. The final protective defenses were apparently working and morale was going up. But Burg knew that it was still a very close thing.

Esther Aronson staggered in the dark toward the west slope. She called out, but no one seemed to hear.

The Ashbals, temporarily confused by Dobkin's one-man charge, had stopped moving for a while, but eventually they began crawling up toward the top of the wall again. They could make out the top against the starry sky, less then fifty meters off. Their commander, Sayid Talib, couldn't believe their good luck. Except for the single pistol shooting intermittently at them, there was no one on the crest. But that wouldn't last forever. He exhorted his men to move faster. He had believed this to be a suicide mission for himself and his forty men, but Ahmed Rish had calmed him, with a story about an English general who took his army up a cliff more impregnable than this one and captured Canada for the English. And it was true. No one could have expected an attack here.

Talib's blood flushed his face as he climbed. He could not wait to get among the Israelis. He touched his half-mutilated face. When he had lived in Paris he had received a letter from the French Ministry of Immigration. He had opened it and discovered that it was in fact from Mivtzan Elohim. That carelessness had cost him the right side of his face, and life had never been the same since. Women let out a little cry when they saw his once handsome features. Even men looked away.

Talib prayed that he would find Isaac Burg alive. Of all the torture fantasies he had played out in his mind, he had decided that flaying would be ideal for the head of Mivtzan Elohim. He would strip his skin off over a period of twenty-four hours—maybe longer. He would feed it to the dogs while Burg watched. He looked up. They were less than twenty-five meters from the top.

McClure put his last six rounds in the chamber of his pistol. He turned to Richardson, who was standing very still. "How do you say, 'Take me to the American consulate,' in Arabic?"

"You should have asked Hausner that yesterday."

"You don't speak any Arabic, then?"

"No. Why should I?"

"Don't know. Just figured you did." He leaned out of the foxhole and looked downslope. He could see men, like lizards, crawling up out of the darkness. He aimed at one and fired.

Miriam Bernstein and Ariel Weizman found Esther Aronson crawling along the ground. They took the eight AK-47's and ammunition without any formalities and ran along the half-kilometer-long perimeter in opposite directions. At each position, they dropped off a rifle and ammunition. Bernstein skipped McClure's foxhole. At the south end of the perimeter she found herself alone with the last AK-47. An Ashbal girl lifted herself up onto the flat ground and stood five meters away with her AK-47 slung. She saw Bernstein and unslung her weapon, slowly and deliberately.

Bernstein did not have any idea of how to use the AK-47 and didn't know if she wanted to use it in any case. Was the safety off? Was it loaded? Did it have to be cocked? The previous owner, of course, had it cocked with the safety off for the attack, but she did not think of this. All she knew for certain was that the gun had a trigger. She found it and hesitated.

The Ashbal girl fired a full burst at her at point-blank range.

Miriam Bernstein saw the muzzle flashes and they blinded her. She thought of a blindingly sunny day in a café in Jerusalem. A young infantryman was telling a story of how an Arab had popped out of a house on the Golan Heights and fired a submachine gun at him from a distance of a few meters. The young infantryman had been standing in front of a tree, and the tree, directly behind him, was hit again and again and bark and wood splinters flew off and hit the young man all over his head, neck, and back. Then the Arab disappeared. The infantryman had said, "An angel was standing in front of me that day."

Bernstein heard another burst of fire and the automatic rifle jumped in her hands. The young girl appeared to leap backwards over the edge.

Miriam Bernstein sank to her knees and covered her face.

In the Concorde, Yaakov Leiber sat and watched an American war movie. He'd seen the movie that afternoon and had made notes. The projector was set on "fast forward." When a portion with authentic war sounds came on, he returned it to normal speed and turned up the volume. The movie sound speakers, set up on the perimeter, reproduced the deep throaty sounds of a heavy machine gun. Rumors of this heavy machine gun had run rife in the Ashbal camp ever since Muhammad Assad had been released by the Israelis. Before his execution for treason, Assad had apparently told his guards many stories of Israeli strengths.

The Ashbals were wavering now. Flashes of gunfire twinkled up and down the Israeli line. More and more sounds of increasingly rapid gunfire rolled down the slope. Above the sounds of the small arms came the rumble of the heavy machine gun. It seemed as though the Israelis had more weapons than they had people. The Ashbal fighters smelled defeat in the air. They began throwing anxious glances at their commanders.

Naomi Haber watched as the Arab sniper's body bounced. Her whole body shook as she realized that she had actually put two bullets into the man's back. She called out, trying to keep her voice even. "Mr. Hausner! He is finished. I will cover you!" She looked down on Hausner's still body below her. "Mr. Hausner! He is finished! I will—" She saw his arm move slightly in a wave. She turned the rifle downslope and began firing at the targets. Forward-moving target at eighty meters. Fire! Hit! Stationary target at ninety meters. Fire! Hit! Right-to-left at fifty meters. Fire! Miss. Adjust for range. Fire same target. Hit! Next target.

Hausner clawed at the steep sides of the overhanging watchtower, but there was no way up. He moved to his right where the slope was gentle and began running uphill. Ahead of him, to the left, he could hear the metallic operating rod of the M-14 slide back again and again. To his front, the Israeli breastworks rose up. There was not supposed to be anyone there—the M-14 was supposed to cover the entire area—but he could see an incredible number of muzzle flashes along the defensive perimeter. Where the hell had they found all those rifles? Or were they all aerosol cans? Flashes appeared in front of him, and he knew they were not aerosol cans. Bullets went buzzing past his ears from behind as well. He yelled out above the gunfire. "For God's sake, stop firing! Hausner! Hausner!" The sand gave way under him and he crawled and stumbled directly into the Israeli guns, shouting at the top of his lungs between gulps of air. Then he found himself at the bottom of a trench. A young man and woman with AK-47's looked down at him curiously. Hausner stood up. "You're the worst goddamned shots I have ever seen."

"Lucky for you," said the girl.

The unarmed fighters began pushing the stacked plaques of clay over the side. The heavy plaques tumbled down the slope, breaking off the hard crust as they went and picking up more mass and energy. The earth slides tore into the Ashbal ranks and snapped legs and crushed ribs as they hit.

Suddenly, torchlike flames illuminated the Israeli lines as dozens of Molotov cocktail wicks were lit. The incendiary devices arched high into the air and began landing among the Ashbals. To make sure that they burst on impact, the Israelis used half bricks, tied with thongs onto each device, to act as clappers. The jars and bottles broke on impact and the kerosene or the more deady crude napalm ignited, splattering flames over the side of the slope.

For greater distance, brassieres were used as slings to hurl the bombs down the slope. The side of the slope lit up, and the Israeli gunfire became more accurate as the Ashbals stood revealed against the flames.

The Ashbals became confused and milled about. Some ran for dark areas where the burning kerosene would not illuminate them. Occasionally, a man would be splattered with burning fuel, and his screams would carry above the other ghastly sounds of battle.

The last few man-traps that had not caught anyone were soon occupied. A half-dozen young men and women screamed and squealed their lives away when the impaling stakes drove deeper into their rumps, their necks, their bellies, and their genitals as they squirmed to get off of them.

The sappers, who were playing dead directly beneath the Israeli breastworks, knew that they were in fact dead men. Their own army's fire had already killed some of them, and the chances of their men assaulting the Israeli lines were diminishing. They were caught almost in the jaws of the enemy. But their training had provided for almost every contingency. Slowly, a few at a time, they rolled downhill, stopping every few meters and playing dead again. They knew that the defenders' attention was riveted elsewhere. Meter by meter, they closed in on the main body of their comrades. It was slow and torturous, and almost every one of them was hit at least once, but half of the twenty-man elite team eventually made it back to their comrades. They were by no means out of danger there, however.

The fight on the west slope was over within sixty seconds of the time the first Israeli AK-47 opened up. Molotov cocktails incinerated the entire line of castor oil bushes, silhouetting the climbing Ashbals. Clay plaques and AK-47 fire swept the flat, steep slope clean. The glacis was as unassailable as when Darius first saw it over twenty-five hundred years before, or when Alexander remarked on the defenses some years later. Almost every man was killed outright or burned to death in the castor oil bushes below. The few who fell into the Euphrates, like most Arabs, could not swim and drowned in the deep, muddy waters.

Sayid Talib, his dreams of flaying Isaac Burg now forgotten, ran screaming through the burning bushes. The searing pain of two bullets almost made him lose consciousness. He stumbled and crawled and finally saw the Euphrates below him. He threw himself in. Swimming was one thing he had learned in Europe, and he let the river carry him southward. A few of his men splashed and shrieked around him and finally drowned. He believed he was the only survivor.

Hausner walked up to Burg who was standing on the CP/OP. "You are either the best commander since Alexander the Great or you had the good sense to stand here and do nothing."

Burg was surprised to see Hausner alive but didn't remark on it. "A little of both, I think." He could see that Hausner was bare-chested and missing both his shoes. Blood was smeared across his face. "Where the hell were you?"

"Downslope." He stood on top of the rise and looked out toward the perimeter. "Brin was killed by a sniper."

"I see." Burg lit the pipe that had been hanging dead in his mouth for some time. "We took a lot of casualties. The outposts are done for, I'm afraid."

"I suppose they are," said Hausner. Two girls approached the CP/OP from the direction of the west slope. They each had several rifles slung on their shoulders. One of them was Esther Aronson. She spoke. "It's all over for them over there. No casualties for us. One missing, though."

"You did a marvelous job," said Burg.

"I think these rifles could be put to better use on the east slope," she continued.

"Yes," said Burg. "Who's missing?"

"Miriam Bernstein. They're looking for her."

Hausner didn't seem to react.

The two young women hurried off into the darkness.

Hausner put out his hand. "Give me a pull on that damned thing."

Burg handed him the pipe. "Was this a miracle?"

"It doesn't qualify," said Hausner. His hands were shaking.

"Why not?"

"Because I didn't hear the voice of the Lord."

"*You* have to hear it? Only *you* are supposed to hear it?"

"That's right."

Burg laughed.

Hausner handed back the pipe. "Dobkin?"

Burg shrugged. "There's the miracle—if he's alive."

"Right. Listen—I'm going over to the west slope."

"No need. It's all over there."

"Don't tell me how to run this battle, Burg." He jumped down off the rise and walked very quickly west.

Burg stared after him.

Ibrahim Arif spoke into a PA microphone. He pitched his voice to carry above the deep bass sounds of battle and at the same time made it sound mocking. "Go home, little children. You have been soundly spanked. Now, go home and hide your faces! Salem Hamadi! Can you hear me? Go home and go to bed with your young boyfriend! Who is it this week? Ali? Abdel? Salman? Or is it Abdullah? Muhammad Assad said you were making love to Abdullah this week!"

Arif went on, taunting in that high wailing manner peculiar to the Arabs. As he spoke his heart thumped heavily in his chest, and his mouth, already dry from lack of water, felt like the sands of the desert. Between him and Rish's cruel, mutilating knife was a handful of Jews whose weapons were again running out of ammunition. And even if, by some miracle of Allah, he did get out of this alive, he would be hunted for the rest of his life with a renewed vengeance by the people he had once called brothers and sisters. But that was tomorrow's worry. Tonight's worry was staying away from Rish's knife and carrying out the orders of Jacob Hausner. "Or is it a camel or an ass for you tonight,

Salem? Or perhaps it is your lord and master, Ahmed Rish?"

The young Ashbals, in their confusion and misery, shouted back. Two got up and charged the crest and were shot down. Some held the triggers of their weapons like a man in a helpless rage clenches his fists, and the barrels of the AK-47's overheated and the weapons exploded.

Ahmed Rish squatted in a gully with his radio operator. Salem Hamadi sat a few meters off. He appeared, in the dark, to be weeping or praying, or perhaps just muttering to himself. Rish called to him. "Get up! We must make one last effort. Their ammunition must be low. The moon is not yet risen. One last effort. Come! We must personally lead it."

Hamadi stood and advanced alongside Rish. Most of the remaining Ashbals followed mechanically.

Molotov cocktails rained down on the stalled attackers and bullets ripped their ranks. Earthslides knocked their feet out from under them or covered their prone bodies.

Finally, the call to retreat came loud and clear from behind them. "Back! Back! It is finished! Fall back!"

Abdel Jabari sat near the shepherds' hut and spoke authoritatively into the PA microphone. "Back! Back! It is finished! Fall back!" The PA speaker, its wire miraculously unscathed, blared from the hole of Outpost No. 2 "Back! Back!" Deborah Gideon awoke to its sound. She brushed the clay off her face and looked up out of the hole at the sky. An incredibly beautiful cluster of dazzling blue-white stars sat right above her. Footsteps hurried past her, heading downslope. She closed her eyes as a silhouette blotted out the stars above her.

"Back!" shouted Jabari. Though by now the young Ashbals knew it was yet another ruse, they pretended they did not and fell back as ordered by that strong voice. Another voice, as strong and as compelling, the voice of Ahmed Rish (or was it another ruse?), ordered them forward. The voice called out in the darkness and, in fact, it even crackled over the few functional field radios. "Forward! Attack! Follow me!" But the other voice, further down the slope, said, "Back! Go back!" And it was certainly easier to direct one's footsteps downslope than up—and less deadly. In fact, the Israeli fire seemed to abate as though they were waiting to see how it would go. The meaning, as the Ashbals saw it, was clear. The Israelis seemed to be saying, "You are no longer trapped on the slope. The back door is open. Go."

●   ●   ●

Near the center of the eastern defensive line and twenty meters behind it, Peter Kahn and David Becker stood by the big nitrogen bottle. Attached to its nozzle was a telescoping strut from the front nose wheel assembly. Balanced on top of the strut was a seat from the Concorde. On the seat was a tire from the nose assembly. Kahn gave the signal and Becker put a match to the kerosene-soaked seat and tire. They burst into flames and Kahn released the pressure valve. The nitrogen shot into the hollow strut and pushed its telescoping section into the air. The seat and wheel hurled upward and arched over the breastworks like a fiery image from the Book of Ezekiel. It hit the slope and bounced high, spewing burning particles and throwing off its flaming wheel. The seat and the tire bounced again down the slope through the ranks of the Ashbals.

Kahn and Becker retracted the strut and fastened another seat and the second and last tire to it. They lofted the burning, bouncing missile into the air, then put a third seat on the strut, pointed the wheel assembly farther southward, and fired again.

The Ashbals turned back, only a few at first, then all of them, including their remaining officers and sergeants. They moved quickly, but did not run or break into a disorderly route. They picked up the wounded when and where they could, but left the dead and near-dead for the buzzards and jackals. The unaided wounded crawled and rolled down the slope.

The Israelis had ceased firing even before Burg's runners got the order out to the line. The unspoken understanding called for an unhampered and unharassed line of retreat for the Ashbals. The Ashbals were recovering a lot of loose equipment because of the lack of Israeli fire, but it seemed a small price in exchange for their ending the attack. And it was the Ashbal rank and file, not the officers, who had tacitly accepted the Israeli deal. Burg felt this was an important point.

There was a stillness on the hill and down the slope, a stillness that penetrated into the dark, out to the mud flats, and into the surrounding hills. The steady east wind blew off the smells of cordite and kerosene and impartially covered the living and the dead with a film of fine dust. As the din cleared from everyone's ears, they noticed that the stillness was only a temporary postbattle deafness. Now the east wind could be heard as well as felt, and it carried with it the sounds of crying and moaning men and women from the littered slope. The jackals began howling in the night—howling like a Roman crowd that had just witnessed an excellent fight in the gladiator pits—like a crowd mesmerized into a temporary silence, then suddenly bursting forth with approval at the slaughter.

Burg looked at his watch. The whole thing had taken just thirty-nine minutes.

23

Dobkin lay bleeding on the west bank of the Euphrates. He heard the silence and wondered what it meant. It had two interpretations, of course. He tried to replay the sounds of the past fifteen minutes in his mind—to interpret them like the old campaigner that he was. But the pain in his thigh bothered his concentration. Still, he felt certain that he would hear the Arabic victory shouting if that was the way it had gone. He listened intently through the pain. Nothing. Silence. He let the pain and fatigue take him into unconsciousness.

Hausner found her near the south end of the west slope. She was staring over the edge of the drop, down into the river. She held a rifle by one hand at her side. Hausner stood a few meters to the side of her and stared at her face, illuminated by the reflection from the river. "You killed someone."

She turned her head quickly. "I . . . but you're all right. You're all right." She let the rifle fall and turned toward him.

He seemed to hesitate. Making love was one thing. Showing

256

affection on the morning after implied a deeper commitment. He didn't know if he was ready for that. "You...you're an MIA."

She hesitated also. "I'm here. Not missing." She laughed softly, a nervous laugh.

"Me, too," said Hausner with what sounded like a touch of disbelief. "We made it."

"I killed a young girl."

"Everyone who fires a gun in battle for the first time thinks he has killed someone."

"No. I really did. She fell down the slope."

"She may have been nicked a bit and run off."

"No. I hit her in the chest... I think."

"Nonsense." But he knew it was not. He wanted to say, "Good for you, Miriam. Welcome to the club," but he couldn't bring himself to say it. "You fired the gun and you thought you killed someone. Did you hear her yell?"

"I... I don't know. It happened..."

"Come with me. I have to get back."

She picked up the rifle and followed. She wanted to say something neutral like, "Thank you." Instead it came out, "I love you." She said it again, louder. "I love you."

He stopped but would not turn. He knew that he was not going to make it. He knew that with more certainty then he'd ever known anything. But maybe she was fated not to make it, either. If she were to die and he hadn't told her that he loved her, too, then that would be a tragedy. But if she lived, then his "I love you" could only cause her further grief. He began walking again and he could hear her soft footsteps in the dust, falling further and further behind.

Rabbi Levin ministered spiritually and physically to the wounded. He helped carry bodies from the line to the hut, then assisted in dressing wounds. He looked like a casualty himself, smeared with blood and hollow-eyed, and he smelled like a charnel house.

After the wounded were all assembled in and around the hut, the rabbi began making an accounting of them in a small book. He added the wounded of the second night to the wounded of the first night and made notes on their progress or lack of it. Tamir, unchanged. Hausner's three men—Rubin, up and around; Jaffe, unchanged; and Kaplan, bleeding again. Brin was dead, they'd told him, leaving only Marcus and Alpern still fit for full duty out of Hausner's original six men. Ruth Mandel was still feverish. Neither Daniel Jacoby nor Rachel Baum, wounded together, was doing well. Abel Geller, the steward, lay bleeding to death all over the floor of the hut, his white uniform an incredible red. A pool of mixed blood had collected on a low point in the ancient brick floor, and it made a splashing sound whenever Rabbi Levin walked through it. There were six other wounded whom he didn't know by sight, and he gave them numbers until he had time to identify them.

The rabbi needed air. He walked outside, but there was only more carnage there. Shimon Peled, the Foreign Minister's aide, lay dead against a wall of the hut. He had died not of his moderate wound but of a heart attack. He'd been ruled unfit for combat duty, but had insisted on being given a rifle. Levin shook his head. There would be a lot of stupidity and stubbornness that would pass for bravery in the hours and days ahead. He found some towels and covered Peled's face with one of them. Strange custom, this covering of the face of the dead. There were two girls lying against the wall, dead also. He arranged their bodies in a more restful position, closed their eyes—another strange custom when you thought about it—and covered their faces with towels also. He'd get their names later.

The biggest loss was the six men and women on the outposts. Rabbi Levin entered their names in his book. Deborah Gideon, Yigael Tekoah, Micah Goren, Hannah Shiloah, Reuben Taber, and Leah Ilsar. He'd say a prayer as soon as he had a minute or two.

And where was Hausner? He'd been reported as missing, as dead, and as alive. Even Jacob Hausner couldn't be all three at once. Levin wondered if they would be better or worse off without him. And General Dobkin? Did Ben Dobkin make it? He'd have to say a special prayer for Ben Dobkin.

As the rabbi walked back into the hut, Beth Abrams collapsed from the heat and the stench, and Levin carried her outside. She revived before he even set her down and insisted on going back to her nursing. The rabbi sighed and let her go. Yes, it *was* going to be a long and terrible night. The rabbi had an unorthodox thought: If everyone looked out for himself first, then everyone would have at least one person looking out for him. That didn't sound as if it should come from a rabbi, but he liked it. He took a deep breath and went back into the hut.

•   •   •

There was no celebration among the Israelis this night. Although they had accomplished the incredible feat of arms, not only was the price high, but they knew that the worst was yet to come. Now would set in the hunger and the thirst. The wounded were consuming vast quantities of water. Their moans and cries carried across the still hilltop, wearing away at the morale of the others.

A party went downslope and began looking for abandoned equipment. Three other teams went off to search for the outposts. When they brought back the hacked-up bodies of Micah Goren and Hannah Shiloah, there was a great deal of weeping among the defenders. The bodies of Reuben Taber and Leah Ilsar, each with a neat hole in the head, were added to the dead in back of the shepherds' hut.

Occasionally, a shot would be heard on the slope. The men and women on the hill pretended not to notice the shots, but they could not help noticing that there wasn't as much moaning from the Arab wounded left behind.

The Israelis badly needed a morale booster, and they found it in Yigael Tekoah. He was already a hero—presumably a dead one—for disregarding his own life to shout the warning. Now he was a live hero, found with multiple, but not mortal, wounds. He was brought back into the perimeter. Between periods of unconsciousness, he told them what he had done to try to save Deborah Gideon and asked about her. He was assured that she was fine and a runner was quickly sent out to pass on to the search parties what Tekoah had told them about her.

At Outpost No. 2, they could see where she had lain in the dust, but she was no longer there. They called for her and searched the area, but it was apparent that she had been taken prisoner.

Jacob Hausner stood with Burg on the promontory and watched the full moon rise in the east. If the full moon really made lunatics restless, then Ahmed Rish would be howling tonight. The entire slope turned blue-white, and the full extent of the carnage could be seen clearly now. "That's it until moonset," said Hausner.

Burg nodded. The next period of darkness between moonset and the beginning of morning nautical twilight would be about an hour and a half long. He wondered if Rish would attempt an attack then. Twilight might catch them on the slope, and then that would be the end of Ahmed Rish and company. "Maybe they've had it," he said aloud.

The awful post-action sounds hung in the night air: the moaning, the cries of pain, the weeping, the labored breathing from the necessary exertions, the heavy, shuffling footsteps of people fatigued beyond their limits, the sounds of retching, and the occasional sharp report of a *coup de grâce* being administered on the slope.

These sounds were far more unsettling than the sounds of the battle that had created them, reflected Hausner. He stared at the body of Nathan Brin, not yet removed from the place where he had fallen. He wanted to say something aloud or touch the man, but Naomi Haber, on duty with the starlight scope, was already tottering on the edge of hysteria. His low reserve of compassion was better expended on the living, he thought. He said a silent good-bye to the young man who had been such a fountainhead of optimism and strength, then walked over to the girl and put his arm around her. He marveled at how young people became so attached to each other in so short a period of time, but then remembered his own situation. "A lady who means very much to me was also forced to kill tonight. She is a professional pacifist, but she is coping with it."

Haber put down the rifle. "I'm all right. I can cope with that. Let me do my job." She wiped her eyes and went back to her protective scanning.

Hausner walked away and began his lonely circuit of the line.

As the night wore on and the shock wore off, most of the defenders on the hill returned to a more normal state of mind. Everything began functioning again. The dwindling supplies of water and ammunition were distributed, the wounded were cared for, and repairs were made on the defenses wherever possible.

After Hausner completed his inspection of the defenses, he found Burg and they both moved to the cockpit of the Concorde. As they entered, Becker was workjng the radio. Its squeal shot through the still cockpit. He switched it off and spoke to the two men behind him. "The Lear is still on station. Probably won't have to go and refuel until daylight."

"Well, we'll try again at daylight, then." Hausner took a long drink from a bottle of sweet Israeli wine that was Becker's ration. He made a face. He couldn't see the label, but he knew it wasn't a Trockenbeerenauslese. He sat in the jump seat, took Rish's psychological profile from the floor, and flipped through it absently. "One of our brilliant Army psychiatrists says here that Ahmed Rish would respond to treatment. He didn't say what kind of treatment, but I presume he meant decapitation." He looked up. "If you were Ahmed Rish, Isaac, what would you do next?"

Burg swiveled around in the flight engineer's seat and crossed his legs as he drew on his pipe. "If I were a paranoiac I think I would be so filled with desire for revenge that I'd lead those poor bastards back up the hill."

"But would they *follow*?" asked Becker.

"That's what we were trying to resolve before," said Hausner. "I think Rish will convince them that we are through. He can do that. He has a prisoner now, and no matter what she says about us, Rish will translate it to fit his own needs."

There was a long silence in the cockpit. Each man conjured up his own image of Deborah Gideon at the mercy of Ahmed Rish—naked, brutalized, broken, alone... dying. Hausner hoped that she would save herself a lot of pain and tell them everything she knew. It wasn't much and it wasn't worth the torture to keep it secret. But he feared they might torture her anyway, just for the pleasure of it. He found it hard to work up anger for Rish, just pity for the girl. Anger at Rish would have been the purest type of hypocrisy, as Muhammad Assad would attest to.

Becker rolled a cigarette from some of Burg's pipe tobacco and weather-map paper. He cleared his throat and broke the silence. "How are the odds now?"

Hausner knew that Becker was discreet. "The same, really." He seemed to be thinking out loud. "We have almost thirty guns but no more ammunition per gun than before—about a hundred rounds apiece, I think. Our defenses are in a shambles, and we don't have the water or energy to rebuild them. We've shot all our ruses and they won't be fooled by the same ones twice. Brin is dead, and the scope may be at the end of its life, too. Anyway, there are only ten rounds left for the M-14. I have two men trying to adapt the scope to an AK-47." He took another long pull from the wine bottle and swallowed it before it ran over his tongue. "By the way, how is the kerosene holding out?"

Becker smiled. "It's hard to believe that the instruments were that inaccurate. I don't know where the stuff is coming from."

Hausner nodded. "Don't let the rabbi know, or we'll get a sermon on the miracle of the holy oil. Anyway, we are completely out of containers and almost every Molotov cocktail is gone." He finished the wine and let the bottle drop to the deck. "But you asked about the odds. The odds are still dependent on the Ashbals. We still are not the odds-makers here. We can only wait for their next move." He looked down at the portfolio in his lap. He stared at a picture of Rish. "Ahmed," he said softly, "if you had an ounce of sanity, you would get the hell out of Babylon before it becomes your grave. But of course you won't."

24

Teddy Laskov looked down at Rish's picture. "Speak to me, Ahmed."

Itzhak Talman sipped on a glass of port and flipped through his own portfolio of Rish. "Why haven't we heard from him yet? What does he want?"

Michel's was noisy and crowded, and almost every conversation had to do with the peace mission. It seemed unpatriotic to speak of anything else. Everyone in the café recognized the two ex-Hel Avir generals, but no one stared at them or made them uncomfortable.

Laskov sipped a vodka. "I don't believe he has them under his control. If they were captives, then we would have heard from Rish."

"If they are not captive, then they are dead, Teddy."

Laskov leaned across the table, spilling the vodka from his glass. "Alive! I know it. I feel it."

"Captive where, then?"

"Babylon." The word surprised him as much as it did

Talman. Perhaps it was because they had been using the Hebrew word, *shrym*—"taken captive"—instead of an expression like "held hostage" or "held prisoner." The association of words was inevitable. Perhaps the vodka helped. Or perhaps it was more than just an association of words mixed with alcohol. "Babylon," Laskov repeated and felt it was so. "Babylon," he said again, standing up and overturning his chair. "Babylon!" he shouted, and heads turned toward him. Talman took his arm, but Laskov pulled away. He stuffed his papers into his case and ran into the street, leaving Talman to throw a handful of pound notes on the table.

Outside, Talman jumped into a cab alongside Laskov, just as it began moving.

"Jerusalem!" Laskov shouted to the driver. "National emergency!"

Talman pulled the door closed as the driver, who was not unfamiliar with breaking the speed laws when someone yelled "national emergency," accelerated across St. George Square and turned onto the Jerusalem road.

"Babylon," said Laskov, more quietly this time.

The driver glanced over his shoulder, then watched his passengers' faces in his mirror.

"Babylon," said Talman with not as much conviction. "Yes. Maybe. Babylon."

"Babylon," said Jacob Hausner. He stared at Rish's psychological profile. "Babylon in all its desolation is a sight not so awful as that of the human mind in ruins." He had read that somewhere. Hausner had found Kahn's half-bottle ration of wine and picked it up from the floor. "Nice. Appropriate." He took a long drink from the bottle but could not stomach it any longer and spit it out. "If I ever get back to Haifa, I'm going to devote my energies and wide-ranging talents to the development of a good local wine."

Becker was unimpressed with both Hausner's erudition and his plans for the future. "What really galls me," he said, "is that we have to wait here for this lunatic. We are not the odds-makers."

"Perhaps we should be," said Hausner. "Perhaps it's time *we* went on the offensive."

Burg caught a danger signal. He sat up. "Meaning?"

Hausner stretched out in the jump seat. "They're probably

back at their bivouac around the Ishtar Gate by now. If they are going to attack again at moonset, they will first come back here and assemble at a staging area, a jump-off point, some distance from the base of the slope. That's military procedure. The most distinguishable landmark for that purpose would be the city wall. We can place an ambush there. About ten or fifteen men should do it."

Burg shook his head. "For God's sake, Hausner, don't start thinking you're a general. It's all we can do to hold them off from up here. We can't send anyone out of this perimeter. If the ambush party didn't find them, then we'd be ten or fifteen men and guns short when the attack began."

"Then the ambush party could attack from the rear," said Hausner. "Or attack their bivouac, kill their wounded and the orderlies, smash their communications equipment, burn their stores, and maybe even rescue Deborah Gideon."

Burg stared over his glowing pipe for a few seconds. "Who are you, Hausner... Attila the Hun or head of El Al Security? Kill their wounded—burn their stores—have you gone mad? Stay out of the moonlight."

Becker spoke. "He's been mad at least as long as I've been with El Al," he said, not altogether jokingly.

"We have to *do* something," said Hausner. "The least we could do is send a party down the west slope for water."

Burg shook his head again. "If there is even one Ashbal left there, that water party will never make it. That slope—wall, really—is suicide. We can find plenty of volunteers to go, I'm sure, but I really have to object to sending anyone outside of this perimeter again. And that includes, I'm afraid, observation posts. That was a massacre." Burg felt more confident in his ability to lead men now. Also, Hausner had abandoned him, in a way, and he felt that his position was stronger because of it. The people had seen him on the hill as the commander, and he rather enjoyed the sensation. He was not satisfied with being non-committal any longer. He could butt heads with Hausner, and Hausner would have to listen to his point of view. "A tight defense. No excursions. The water will have to last. No OP's. We pull in like a turtle in a shell and hang on until someone realizes that we are here."

Hausner rose from the jump seat. He stared at Burg for a long time. "You know, I thought that converting our pacifists to dedicated killers was a miracle. The bigger miracle, I see, was transforming Isaac Burg from a shadowy, wispy, translucent little intelligence man into a man of substance. Flesh and blood. Opinions, even. Field Marshal von Burg. So you liked it, did you? It's nice to be king of the hill, master of your own fate, and to hold so many other fates in your hands. If you had made a mistake tonight you wouldn't be any more dead than if I'd made the mistake. But if you win—ah—that's the thing, Isaac. If you win, they'll parade you through the Jaffa Gate like a Roman emperor."

Burg stood up. "That's a lot of shit. I just think you could use some input here. My God, Hausner, don't you want help?"

Becker turned back to his log book and busied himself with it.

"The only help I can accept," said Hausner, "is from competent military people. That would be Dobkin. Not you." He lowered his voice. "I like you, Isaac, but don't get in my way."

"I'm in your way whether you like it or not. And I mean to have a say in the decision-making process around here." His pipe twitched in his mouth.

Hausner could see that he meant it. He suddenly laughed. "You bastard!" He moved toward the cockpit door. "All right, then, as long as you want it badly enough to stand up for it, it's yours. Welcome to the top of the pyramid. If I jump off, you're alone again." He laughed as he walked through the cabin, out the emergency door, and onto the wing. He shouted back into the aircraft. "You poor bastard!"

Benjamin Dobkin looked up into the faces of six or seven Arabs who were all bent over staring down at him. One of them bent further and shook Dobkin's shoulder. They were speaking to him in broken Arabic. Why should Arabs speak in broken Arabic?

He remembered crawling along the river bank, passing out, and crawling again. He had no idea of how much time had gone by since he left the perimeter. The moon was high and it was cold. He moved his hand slowly so as not to alarm them. He reached into his pocket and felt for the digitalis. It was gone.

One of the Arabs dangled the plastic bag containing the pills in front of his face. He grabbed for it, but the man pulled it away. The man said, in bad Arabic, "Medicine? Need?"

"Yes," said Dobkin. "Medicine. Need."

This caused some mumbling. Another man bent over and held something up to his face. "Pazuzu. Evil."

Dobkin stared at the blurry demon a few inches from his eyes. In the moonlight, the feral grin seemed wet and obscene. He supposed that having that with him was not going to get him on the right side of these Moslems. He said the Arabic word for archeologist, but they seemed not to be listening. The man dropped the demon on the ground and turned away.

They began talking among themselves now. It was with a slow realization that Dobkin recognized that they were using Hebrew words mixed with their strange Arabic.

He thrust his hand into his shirt and felt for the star. It was still there. He pulled it out and held it up by its chain. It gleamed in the cold, blue moonlight. "Shema Yisroel Adonoi Elohenu Adonoi Echod."

The effect was as if he had dropped out of the sky in a space suit—which in a way he had. The men stopped talking to one another and looked down at him wide-eyed.

He spoke in slow Hebrew, sticking to the classical words that he knew they would recognize from the Scriptures. "I am Benjamin Dobkin, *Aluf"*—he used the ancient Hebrew word for general—*"Aluf* of the Israelites. I came with the—" They would not understand that Hebrew construction, so he used the Arabic word for aircraft. "I need help. The Jews on the hill—in Babylon—need your help. Will you help?"

The oldest among them knelt beside him. He was what Dobkin would have expected of a Babylonian Jew—swarthy, white-bearded, dark-eyed, and dressed in a flowing robe that was not quite a *gellebiah*. "Of course we will help an *Aluf* of the Israelites. We are kin," he added.

"Yes," said Dobkin. "You have not forgotten Jerusalem."

Hausner walked the perimeter again and again. He was alone. He was tired, thirsty, hungry, and in pain from a dozen cuts and bruises. His ear was mangled from the bullet and felt as if it were on fire. The wine was whirling around his head, and he felt nauseous.

He stared up at the stars, then down at the moonlit landscape. There was something compelling about those expanses of blue-white terrain. He was sick to death of the hilltop, the big broken Concorde sitting with its torn tail, mocking his tragic error. He was sick of the people, the smells, the closeness of everyone and everything. He was suffering from what so many men in fortresses suffer from—claustrophobia mixed with contempt, born of familiarity, for everyone around him. Yet he had been there only a little more than twenty-four hours. But in his mind he had been there forever. The hilltop was big enough, physically. The people made it small. Their eyes followed him wherever he went.

He came around to the west side and looked out at the endless mud flats. He threw his hands into the air. "God, I want to go home! I am tired and I want to go home!" He thought of the famous question, "Why me, God?" and the sardonic answer, "Why not?" He laughed and shouted, "Yes, why not? Jacob Hausner is as good as anyone else to bully around! Thanks, God! I'll remember this!"

He laughed again, then broke into soft sobs and sank to the warm earth. Through his tears he could see the domes, spires, and towers of Jerusalem suffused with the warm golden glow of sunset. He was standing on the heights above the town, and lambs were being shepherded home by young boys outside the walls of the Old City. It was Passover and Easter Sunday as well, and the city was filled with people. Then, suddenly, he was home in Haifa on the terrace of his father's villa, overlooking the blue bay. It was autumn now—Succoth, the thanksgiving festival. His father's house was decked with harvest decorations and the tables were laden with food. He was a young man about to leave home for the war—to work with British Intelligence. Life was good. It always was. The war was great fun. Lots of girls. There was one who looked like Miriam, he remembered. Miriam. Miriam was a child then. While she and her family were being herded around naked by the Nazis, he was sitting in his father's house in Haifa reading German philosophers. Or he was playing war between leaves. That wasn't his fault, of course, but it was a fact. For every victim there is a wife, a husband, a son, a daughter, a friend, or a lover who lives.

But why feel guilty? Everyone has his turn at suffering sooner or later. For him it had come much later, but when it came it was complete—disgrace, humiliation, guilt, physical suffering, futile and furtureless love, and . . . death. Death. When and how? Why not now? He looked down at the wide Euphrates and stood up. Why not just step off this ridge? But he wanted to go *home*. He wanted to take Miriam home to his father's house and sit her down to Passover dinner and fill her with food—all the food she had missed as a child—and he wanted to explain to her that life was not really that pleasant for him during the war, either. His mother's family had been killed. Did she know that? That's what he wanted—to sit Miriam down to dinner, to invent some retroactive suffering so that she would accept him as a fellow victim, and then to declare that the suffering was finished.

He wiped his eyes and face. He wondered how much of his sudden sentimentality was the alcohol, how much was Miriam Bernstein, and how much was battle fatigue. In any case, he didn't believe he would ever again be in Haifa for Passover, and if by some miracle he were, it would not be with Miriam Bernstein.

The wind rose noticeably and picked up great quantities of sand and dust. The *Sherji* was coming in force. Hausner could hear the wind whistling through the dead aircraft. He could hear it moan as though it were taunting the suffering men and women in the shepherds' hut. If God had a voice, it was the wind, thought Hausner, and it said anything you wanted to hear.

He turned eastward and saw it coming toward him. He could see it coming out of the hills, carrying more dust for Babylon. Under the blue-white moon, huge dust devils chased headlong down the mountains and over the foothills. Behind the twisters, clouds and sheets of dust blotted out the hills and mountains. He spun around. The Euphrates was unsettled, and he could hear its waters lapping against the banks. The dark pools on the mud flats stirred restlessly. Jackals became quiet and flocks of night birds flew east by the thousands, across the flatlands. The water lilies of the river were swamped, and the frogs became quiet as they abandoned them and found their mud holes on the banks. A herd of wild boar made grotesque sounds as they gathered on the far shore. Hausner shivered.

He looked up at the sky and wondered if the wind would throw up enough earth to blot out the full moon.

25

Teddy Laskov stood at the end of a long table in a long, plain room. The wind rattled the window panes and shutters. Full-length portraits of Theodor Herzl and Chaim Weizmann hung on the wall. On another wall was a color photograph of Israel taken by the American astronaut, Wally Schirra, from an Apollo spacecraft. The conference table and the floor around it were cluttered with attaché cases. The Prime Minister sat staring at the two interlopers. The room was as quiet as anyone ever remembered it to be during a combined session of the Cabinet, the Chiefs of Staff, and the National Security Committee.

The Prime Minister spoke. "Babylon?"

"Yes, sir."

"Not the pyramids along the Nile, now, General? Babylon?"

"Yes, sir."

"Just a hunch? A feeling? A divine inspiration?"

"Sort of." Laskov licked his lips. In Israel it was still possible to go right to the top if you screamed and yelled at the aides and lackeys long enough. In any event, the Prime Minister's provisional office in Jerusalem was small enough for the man himself to have heard Laskov screaming at the portal. Laskov glanced at Talman standing next to him. The man was trying to look very dignified—very British—although it was obvious that he was uneasy and not quite certain of his right to be there. Laskov spoke again to break the silence. "Some of the electronic data that we have—radar sightings, radio transmissions, and that sort of thing—points, I think, to Iraq."

"Really? And where did you get that information, General?"

Laskov shrugged. There was a lot of mouth-to-ear whispering in the long room. Laskov waited and looked over the heads of the assembly. The small red-tiled building had seen a lot of history. It had originally housed the Knights of the Order of the Temple. During World War II, the British used the building to intern German civilians who were suspected of Nazi espionage or sympathies. Jacob Hausner had sent his share of Germans there, but Laskov was not aware of this. After the war the building was a British military headquarters during the Mandate period. Coincidentally, Laskov had been questioned in the very next room as a suspected member of the underground Israeli Air Force. Now he was here again, and the dryness in his mouth reminded him of the kind of life he had led. Some people would call it exciting and romantic. He called it worrisome and dangerous. Why didn't he accept his forced retirement and fade away? Let the government worry about the whereabouts of the peace mission. He might have done that if Miriam weren't among the missing.

"All right, General," said the Prime Minister. "We'll come back to the question of your sources of information later." The Prime Minister put a handkerchief into the open collar of his sport shirt and wiped his neck. He was a tall, thin man with nervous habits, one of which—tearing pieces of paper—he was engaged in at the moment. "Well, what do you propose we do with your information—or should I say, inspiration?"

Laskov spoke loudly and clearly. "I propose that we send a low-level reconnaissance craft to Babylon now—tonight. Take pictures and make visual sightings, if possible. If they're there, we'll try to show them our colors, fly low, give them hope. Behind the recon craft should be an airborne strike force—the F-14's for preparatory fires and behind them C-130's with commandos, if there's a place where they can land, or C-130's with airborne troops if they can't land. Maybe troop helicopters instead. That's for the army to worry about. If the recon craft can confirm their presence, then the strike force goes in."

The Prime Minister tapped a pencil on the table. "Would you object violently if I called the King of Jordan and told him I was sending an air armada over his sovereign kingdom?" There was a lot of laughter, and the Prime Minister paused with the timing of an accomplished performer. He leaned forward. "Surely you wouldn't be too hard on me if I called the President of Iraq and told him, by the by, that I was invading his country—shooting up Babylon, for old time's sake?"

Laskov waited for the laughter to subside. The Prime Minister had an acerbic sense of humor, but after he had his fun with Knesset members or generals, he became more attentive and was actually more open-minded than the average politician. "Mr. Prime Minister, surely a contingency plan of this sort exists. Where did we expect to find the peace mission? On Herzlya beach? And what did we intend to do when we found them?"

The Prime Minister settled back in his chair. His expression darkened. "Actually, rescue plans do exist. But Iraq is on that list of countries not friendly enough to get full cooperation from . . . and potentially unfriendly enough to declare war on us, I might add."

"I'm sorry, Mr. Prime Minister, but like all generals, I don't understand politics."

"Like all generals, you understand politics damn well, and you don't want to be bothered with them. Don't play the innocent with me, Laskov. You know the situation with Iraq. Now, the first thing I must do is place a call to Baghdad."

Laskov nodded his head enough to acknowledge the deserved rebuke, but he wasn't willing to concede the whole point. "Mr. Prime Minister," he said, his voice filled with emotion, "since when have we left the safety of Israeli citizens to foreign governments?"

"When they are in foreign lands, General Laskov."

"Uganda."

"A different time, a different place."

"The same old cutthroats." He took a deep breath. "Look, sir, the West German commandos did it in Somalia. We did it in Uganda—and we can do it again in Babylon."

The Prime Minister made a sound of exasperation. "I really must call first, if you don't mind." He leaned forward. "Anyway, if they are in Babylon, we have no idea of their condition. Dead? Alive? Captive? Really, General, I'm meeting you more than halfway on this. We've been in session for thirty hours and we're damned tired—and you come busting into this meeting yelling Babylon, and we give you the damned floor. Any other government would have had you thrown out on your ass—or worse." He took a sip from a cup of coffee.

The sound of the wind filled the quiet room, and the shutters began clattering again. The Prime Minister raised his voice over the noise. "But what you say makes sense. And I believe in God and I believe that He has whispered in your ear, Teddy Laskov—although why you and not me is a great mystery. Anyway, we will call the President of Iraq at once and then *he* will send a recon craft and his air force people will call us after they've interpreted the data from the craft. All right?"

"No, sir. Too much wasted time."

The Prime Minister rose. "Damn you, Laskov—get out of here before I call you back to active duty and put you on permanent latrine detail." He turned to Talman. "Do you have anything to say before you both leave, General?"

Talman swallowed and his mustache quivered. He took a deep breath and his voice escaped with the exhale. "Well, sir, I think that we should really do the reconnaissance ourselves, you know—I mean, we are rather good at it and the Iraqis may not be as accomplished, you see, and we have no direct data link with them and these things do get fouled up and at least we can ask the American SR-71 to take a high-level photo in the meantime—they won't go down low, but maybe they can get a clear shot and—"

The Prime Minister held up his hand. "Hold on." He turned to the members of the Joint Chiefs who were becoming fidgety. He beckoned to them, and they crowded around the Prime Minister's chair and spoke in whispers. The Prime Minister looked up. "Thank you, gentlemen. We'll handle it from here. Thank you. Yes, you may leave. Please."

Laskov walked slowly behind Talman toward the door. It felt strange—worse than strange—reflected Laskov, to be asked to leave a room when state secrets were about to be discussed. That was one of the consequences of leaving the halls of power. Your need-to-know was limited to monthly memos in the mail telling you what was being taken off the classified list. In exchange for the loss of power you got tranquillity and peace of mind. And boredom. Laskov reached the door and turned. He didn't know what the Joint Chiefs were whispering about, but he was somewhat eased to see that they, rather than the Cabinet, had the Prime Minister's ear. He felt obligated to deliver a parting shot. "They are in Babylon and they are alive. I can feel it. We have no right to play it safe. Whatever you decide to do must be based on *their* welfare and the long-range welfare of this nation. Don't make a decision based on your own immediate career goals."

Somebody—Laskov didn't see who—called out, "That's easy to say when your own career is finished, General."

Laskov turned and left.

The Prime Minister waited until Laskov and Talman were out of hearing range. "I don't know where Laskov got his information on this, and as you just reminded me, we don't know where Chaim Mazar got his information, either. But if Mazar is correct about our American air attaché—Richardson—then the Americans owe us one, I think." He looked at the color photograph on the wall—a gift from the Americans. "Yes, we can ask them to make a special SR-71 flight over the Euphrates for us. Then we can see if Laskov is correct." He took a sip of coffee. "Apparently there is an angel or some other celestial entity flying around whispering in the ears of certain people. Has anyone here received a piece of intelligence in this manner? No? Well, we are not among the chosen, then. Ten-minute break, ladies and gentlemen."

26

The *Sherji* swept across Babylon, carrying tons of dust and sand with it. Trenches and foxholes that had been laboriously dug into the clay were filled to the brim in minutes. Man-traps were covered and early warning devices blown away. The pit containing the remaining stores of Molotov cocktails was covered with sand, and the aluminum reflectors and crude sunshields flew away with the wind. Many of the palm fronds on the roof of the shepherds' hut blew off and sand began raining in on the wounded. Weapons had to be wrapped in plastic or clothing to protect their moving parts. Men and women pulled clothing around their faces like desert Bedouins and walked bent into the dustladen wind.

Only the Concorde stood upright on the hill, enduring yet another indignity with the same haughty indifference it had shown since the beginning of its ordeal. The wind screamed through its torn skin and left deposits of dirt throughout its interior.

Hausner and Burg looked in on the wounded and spoke to

the rabbi and Beth Abrams. Most of the wounded were stable, explained Rabbi Levin, but infection and other complications would kill most of them if they did not receive medical care soon.

Hausner and Burg left the hut and began walking the perimeter again. Burg shouted into Hausner's ear. "I know the Arabs. They'll take this wind as an omen to attack."

Hausner shouted back. "I should think they'd take it as an omen to get the hell out of here." He looked up at the sky. The moon was near its zenith and would begin to set soon. The dust clouds nearly obscured the moonlight. Occasionally, the dust would rise high enough to actually blot out the moon itself, and for a few seconds there would be almost complete darkness across the hilltop. It occurred to Hausner, as he looked down the east slope, that the Ashbals could be ten meters away and no one would see or hear them.

Burg pulled a T-shirt closer around his face. "Even if by some miracle someone knows where we are, a rescue is impossible under these circumstances."

Hausner was more interested in the subject of being overrun. "Unless we put out some sort of listening posts we are going to be taken by surprise."

"It's suicide to send anyone down there."

It felt odd sharing authority, thought Hausner. Not odd, actually—annoying. "All the same, Field Marshal, I'm sending at least one man—or woman—downslope. In fact, I may go myself."

Burg wondered if that wouldn't be a good idea. He remained silent.

As they turned west across the flat hill, the wind pushed them so that they had to strain in order not to be forced into a run. At the first position they came to, overlooking the river, they found what appeared to be two women sleeping in the remains of a foxhole. A blue El Al blanket lay over them and sand drifted over the blanket and their partially exposed limbs.

Hausner was reminded of Dobkin's lecture on the similarity between buried cities and people under shrouds. He stared down at the two restless forms. There was little chance of an Ashbal attack up this slope. In fact, there might not be any Ashbals left on the west slope. And if there were, could they negotiate the slope in the wind? But that was irrelevant. As soon as he had seen the two sleeping figures, Hausner's heart had made a small flutter. On all his inspections, he, like a million officers and sergeants-of-the-guard before him, had hoped that he would never see a guard asleep. Sleep, natural and innocent in civilian life, was a capital offense for a man or guard in probably every army in the world.

Hausner crouched down beside the two figures and cleared his throat. He hoped they would jump up so he could pass it off lightly, but neither seemed to be aware of his presence. He felt Burg's eyes on him. The two were unmistakably sleeping. He reached out and pulled back the blanket. Esther Aronson. He pulled it back further. Miriam.

One of the two sleeping women had the duty. The other was legitimately sleeping. One would live to share the fate of them all, the other might be shot within the next hour. "Miriam." Neither figure moved.

Burg moved around into Hausner's view and crouched down also. He gently picked up the AK-47 lying near the two women. Hausner knew this was prescribed military procedure, and he also knew that the situation was going downhill fast.

He looked closely at Burg but could not read anything in his face. The man had assumed his inscrutable expression. Was Burg willing to let it go? Hausner wondered if he himself would let it go if he were alone, as he usually was. Of course he would. Hausner put his hand on Miriam's shoulder and shook her. "Miriam." He noticed that his voice was tremulous and his hand was shaking. "Miriam!" He was suddenly angry—angry at having to be put in this position—angry at having another dilemma thrown at him by fate. "Miriam, God damn you!"

She sat up quickly. "Oh!"

Burg moved in and grabbed her arm. "What are your hours for guard?" he demanded suddenly.

She was still half-asleep. "What? Oh! Guard. Midnight to two—four to dawn. Why?" She looked around bewildered and saw Hausner, then saw Esther Aronson sleeping next to her. She understood.

Burg looked at his watch quickly. It was a quarter after twelve. "Did Esther Aronson wake you for duty?" he asked loudly. "Well?"

She stared hard at Hausner, who looked away.

"Did she wake you for duty?" repeated Burg as he shook her. "Yes."

"Then I place you under arrest for sleeping on duty. I must warn you that this is a capital offense, Mrs. Bernstein."

Miriam rose to her feet and stood in the wind. Her hair and clothes billowed and sand pelted her face. "I see." She straightened up and looked at Burg. "Of course, I understand. I've endangered the lives of everyone else and I must pay for it."

"That's correct," said Burg. He turned to Hausner. "Isn't it?"

Hausner fought back an impulse to knock Burg over the side of the glacis. He looked down at the sleeping Esther Aronson, then at Miriam. His unpopularity, past and present, was due largely to what people called his Teutonic discipline. That had never bothered him in the least. In the civilization that he lived in, there were always people who stepped in to soften his tyranny. Now he had met a man who was either calling his bluff or, in fact, really wanted to shoot Miriam Bernstein as an example to the others. It was incredible, but anything was possible here. Hadn't they made threatening noises about shooting *him*?

"Isn't that correct?" Burg repeated. "Isn't that correct—that Miriam Bernstein must pay for jeopardizing the lives of close to fifty men and women?"

Hausner stared at Miriam, clothed in darkness and dust, a scarf held up to her face like a lost child. "Yes," he said. "We must try her—in the morning."

"Now," said Burg. "There may be no morning for us. Discipline in the field must be sure and swift. That's how it's done. Now."

Hausner moved close to Burg. "In the morning."

General Dobkin lay on the straw pallet in a mud hut. The wind came in through the closed shutters and deposited fine sand over his body. The oil lamp flickered but stayed lit. The man lying next to him stirred, then groaned. Dobkin could tell he was awake. He spoke to the man in passable Arabic. "Who are you?"

"Who are *you?*" asked the man.

Dobkin had been told that the man had been taken out of the river also. He was shoeless and shirtless, but wore what looked like tiger fatigue pants. Dobkin had been asked by the old man, whose name was Shear-jashub, if this injured man was also a Jew. Dobkin had lied and said he did not know. He was fairly certain now that the man he was speaking to was an Ashbal, but he could not be positive. Shear-jashub, who was a rabbi in the older sense of the word—an unordained teacher, a master—had asked Dobkin if there was any reason why the injured man should not be cared for or should not be placed in the hut of the Aluf. Dobkin had told the rabbi that there was no reason why these things should not be done.

Now, he regarded the man for a long time before he spoke. "I am a fisherman whose *dhow* overturned in the wind and I was injured. These Jews found me and helped me."

The man lay on his side and faced Dobkin. The oil lamp flickered across his face and Dobkin almost gasped when he saw it. He kept his eyes fixed on the grotesque man's eyes. The mutilation, he noticed, was old and scarred, not a part of his recent injuries. He saw that the Ashbal—he was sure of it now—was sizing him up: his haircut, his hands, his bare arms, which lay outside the blanket. Dobkin's boots were off and lying in a shadow, and the man seemed not to see them, but Dobkin could tell that he'd seen enough to know he was not a Euphrates fisherman.

The man rolled casually on his back. "Well, fisherman, this is quite a thing—being obliged to these Jews for our aid and comfort."

"Misfortune makes strange bedfellows," agreed Dobkin. He glanced at the man. Yes. He had seen him on the glacis. He remembered the face as a blurred nightmare—but it was real. He *had* seen it. "How shall I call you?"

"Sayid Talib. And you?"

Dobkin hesitated. He had a perverse desire to say, Benjamin Dobkin, Israeli Army, General of Infantry. "Just call me fisherman." His Arabic was not good, but he had to keep it passable so that Talib could find reason to continue the farce. Each of them was only waiting for the chance to rip the other's throat out, and a wrong word would do it. He wondered if Talib had gotten a good look at his face on the glacis.

How badly wounded was the man, Dobkin wondered. How badly wounded was *he* himself? He flexed his muscles under the blanket and took a deep breath. He seemed to have regained some of his strength.

The clay oil lamp, a dish with a wick floating in some fat, flickered on the floor between them. Dobkin looked around him slowly. There was nothing but his blanket. He felt casually over his body. His knife was gone. He should have gotten a knife from someone. He felt something hard inside his top pocket. Pazuzu. They had given him back his obscene little statue.

Dobkin and Talib lay on their sides staring at each other, listening to the wind blow and watching the lamp flicker.

"How is the fishing, fisherman?"

"It was good until tonight. What did you say your trade was?"

"I am a buyer of dates."

Occasionally, the mask would slip and each could see in the other's eyes the hate and the fear and the threat.

"How did you come to be in the river?"

"The same as you."

The conversation died and neither man moved for a very long time. Dobkin could feel his mouth becoming drier and his muscles fluttering.

Then the wind blew open a shutter and the lamp went out, and each man let out a long animal scream as he lunged for the other's throat in the dark.

Deborah Gideon lay naked on the tiled floor in the manager's office of the guest house. Long welts from a whip and small burn marks from a cigarette covered her back. There was blood on her thighs, legs, and buttocks as well, from wounds caused, apparently, by some animal.

Ahmed Rish washed his hands and face in a bowl of water. "Have her shot," he said to Hamadi.

Hamadi called out to the duty man at the front desk. "Kassim."

Rish dried his hands. What the girl had told him about Israeli numbers, defenses, and dispositions was not much more than he had already found out the hard way. But now he could fabricate his own intelligence report and his men would believe him. "We can be on that hill within an hour, Salem, if the *Sherji* stays with us. It will literally propel the men up that slope and hide their movements and sounds as well."

Hamadi nodded. The wind must have been sent by Allah, for if it hadn't come, he knew that he and Rish would have been murdered by their own men. Strangely, only Rish seemed unaware of this. "I will assemble our people."

"Good." He looked down at Deborah Gideon, then at the duty man who was staring at her. "Yes, yes, Kassim, you may use her. Then shoot her and burn the body and throw the ashes in the river. I want no evidence." He turned to Hamadi. "A military operation is one thing. Torture and murder are another. We still have to negotiate for the hostages with Israel tomorrow."

Hamadi nodded. Rish drew fine and meaningless lines as only an insane man could. If he weren't a hero to the whole Palestinian people, Hamadi would himself have murdered him long ago. The image of Rish, on his hands and knees biting that girl, turned his stomach. He, Hamadi, had tortured before, but this thing that Rish had done was something quite different. The whips and cigarettes had undoubtedly hurt the girl more than the bites, but it was the sheer animal terror of the madman snapping and howling and ripping into her flesh that had made her scream out everything he wanted to know. Hamadi could hardly blame her. He only hoped that the men outside did not understand what was happening. Hamadi turned and walked out of the room and through the small lobby onto the veranda.

The last of his men and women, about fifty of them, sat crosslegged, huddled under their open pavilions, holding up the supporting poles. Hamadi blew his whistle and the Ashbals struck the tents and came scrambling toward the veranda. They stood in the wind with long trailing veils wrapped around their mouths and their *kheffiyahs* pulled low over their eyes. Hamadi held up his hand and shouted above the wind. "Allah has sent us this *Sherji*," he began.

Hausner stood on the delta wing and watched the people swathed in all sorts of strange garments, walking like phantoms in the wind and dust, making their way under the failing moonlight.

He turned and went into the cabin. The noise of the wind through the rent skin and the sand grating against the craft made it difficult to hear or speak inside. Holes that had been punched in the roof to let the heat out during the day now let the sand sift in, and there were little hills of it in the aisles. He made his way to the rear of the cabin through the door that led to the aft galley. Across the aisle from the galley was the small baggage compartment that abutted the split pressure bulkhead. The compartment was a shambles and still smelled faintly from the kerosene, melted plastic, and burnt garments.

Miriam Bernstein had made a pallet of some half-burnt clothing and sat on the floor with her back against the hull and her legs pulled up to her chin. She was reading a book by the illumination of a small penlight that someone had given her. There was also a small emergency light on overhead. Hausner could see through the split bulkhead out to the twisted aluminum skin and braces in the tail. Swaying electrical wires and hydraulic tubing lent a phantasmagoric touch in the cold, blue moonlight. There was a grotesque sort of beauty in any ruin, thought Hausner—even this technological ruin which stood as a monument to insult him and remind everyone of how they got there. He looked down at Miriam.

She glanced up over her book. "Is it time?"

He cleared his throat and spoke above the wind. "She said she did not wake you. She said she fell asleep on her watch and never woke you."

Miriam closed the book gently and rested it on her knee. "She's lying to cover for me. She woke me and I fell asleep."

"Don't be noble, Miriam." He looked at the book on her knee. Camus's *The Stranger*.

"Why not?" She shut off the penlight. "It would be a change of pace for this group."

"Don't criticize what we've done here or how we've done it."

"Condemned people may criticize anything they wish. Well—is it time?"

"Not yet."

They both let the silence drag out. Finally, she spoke. Her voice was belligerent and taunting. "I'm sorry. I shouldn't criticize. I'm one of you now. I mean, I killed that girl."

"Yes. You probably did."

"I had no choice, of course. You have a choice in this case."

"No, I don't. Self-defense is many things to many people. To some of us, it's shooting someone who threatens us. To others it's shooting someone only after they shoot at you first. This case is also a case of self-defense, Miriam. Society defending itself against slackers and malingerers. It's just a matter of projecting the facts. It's a matter of what your perception of immediacy and exigency is."

She understood, had understood all along, really. "So, who goes on trial?"

"Both of you. Unless whoever was at fault confesses."

"I've already confessed."

"You know what I mean."

"We'll both lie."

"I'm sure you will. There's an army procedure for that, too. It's happened before. You'll both be found guilty on the testimony of Burg and myself."

"Is this all show or do you actually intend to shoot one or both of us?"

Hausner lit a cigarette. He wondered if he could even get anyone to sit on a court-martial board, let alone form a firing squad. What, then, was the purpose of this exercise? To show the rank and file that the game had to be played by the rules right to the end? To instill fear in all the fatigued men and women who wanted to sleep on guard duty or who might be slow in obeying orders in other situations? Or was this Burg's way of bringing him down a peg or two?

"Well? Do you intend to shoot us or not? If not, let me out of here. I have things to do. If you're going to have a trial, have it now and don't keep us waiting until morning."

Hausner threw his cigarette on the floor and looked down at her. Moonlight from the porthole illuminated her face. She was staring up at him, and her face did not look as angry or hard as her voice sounded. It looked open and trusting, ready to accept whatever he said. He suddenly realized that any meeting could be their last.

"Would you pull the trigger yourself, Jacob?" The voice was inquisitive, as though she were asking his views on capital punishment in general.

Hausner stepped toward her. He seemed undecided about what to do or say. He suddenly knelt in front of her and put his hands on her bare knees. "I . . . I would kill myself before I would harm you. I would kill anyone who tried to harm you. I love you." The words didn't surprise him as much as they seemed to surprise her.

She turned her face away and stared out through the hole in the bulkhead.

He grasped her knees and shook them. "I love you."

She turned her head back and nodded. She put her hands over his. Her voice was low and husky. "I'm sorry I put you in a compromising position, Jacob."

"Well . . . you know, one's lifelong beliefs don't amount to a hell of a lot when it comes to these decisions—decisions of the heart, as they say." He forced a smile.

She smiled back. "That's not true. You've been pretty consistent. A consistent bastard, I might point out." She almost laughed. "I *am* sorry I put you in this position. Would you have had an easier time shooting Esther Aronson?"

"That's enough of that. I'll get you both out of this."

She squeezed his hands. "Poor Jacob. You should have stayed in your father's villa. Idle and rich."

"Would you come to my father's house for Passover?" He suddenly felt that if he asked her that question, he might make it there himself.

She smiled, then took his hands and pressed them to her face.

He felt a heaving in his chest that he hadn't felt in many, many years. He waited a moment before he trusted himself to speak. "I ... I'm sorry I ... walked away from you before."

Her voice was deep and soft. "I understand."

"Do you?"

"The future. We have no future." She put her cheek against his chest.

He pulled her closer. "No. We don't." He wanted to live. He wanted a future. But even if he lived, he knew he would lose her. Laskov or her husband. Or someone else. This was not a match that was destined to last. Then he would wish that he had died in Babylon.

She was weeping now, and she sounded to Hausner like the wind, overwhelming and perpetually sad.

He felt her tears against his face and thought at first they were his own, and then they were. It was all so sad, he thought; like waking after a bittersweet dream of your childhood and finding that you had a lump in your throat and your eyes were misty. It made the whole day sad and there was nothing you could do about it because it was a dream. It was that kind of sadness that he felt with her.

They both clung to each other and she cried uncontrollably. He couldn't think of anything to say to make her stop because, he thought, she had every right to cry if she wanted. That's right, he thought, scream, cry, do anything you want, Miriam, only don't suffer silently. That's for fools. That's the Miriam that everyone knows in Tel Aviv and Jerusalem. Let the world know your pain. If everyone howled at every injustice, every act of barbarism, every act of unkindness, then we would be taking the first step toward a real humanity. Why should people walk, unprotesting, to their deaths? Scream. Cry. Howl.

As if she could read his thoughts, she threw back her head and let out a long wail.

That's right, Miriam. Scream. They've extinguished your blood, slaughtered your family, stolen your childhood, taken your husband, killed your son, murdered your friends, and left you here alone with a man like Jacob Hausner. You have a right to cry.

Her sobs became louder, louder than the wind, and Hausner knew that Becker could hear her and that they could probably hear her outside, and he didn't care if they did. "If I could do something to make it a little better, I would, Miriam."

She nodded to show that she understood, then suddenly she grabbed his head in her hands and kissed him the way she had kissed her husband on the day he went to war. "Yosef," she sobbed his name. "Jacob." She mumbled something else that Hausner could not make out.

He put his lips to her face and neck and tasted her tears. Yosef. Teddy. Jacob. What difference did it make? As long as they brought her comfort and did not hurt her any further. Hausner wished that her husband would turn up alive. Should he tell her that Rish knew? No, never. He would never tell her that. But while she waited for Yosef Bernstein, he hoped that Teddy Laskov, or anyone, could give her what she needed. He wished it could be he, but he knew it could not be. He would not see Jerusalem again, and even if he did, he would be no comfort to her outside of Babylon. He licked her tears the way an animal licks another's wounds.

Dobkin had never tasted blood, or another man's sweat, for that matter, and he was surprised at how salty they both were. The Arab had him by the testicles and he had his teeth in the Arab's windpipe. They both meant to kill the other, but without weapons, they had been uncertain at first of how to go about it. They had begun by battering each other about and striking at the obvious places—the head—the chest. Talib had smashed the oil lamp on Dobkin's head, and blood and fat ran over the big man's back and neck. But these spots had been protected by nature's armor. Then the old instincts, buried so deep in the psyche, returned. Each man felt a tingling down his spine, and his neck hair raised and his testicles drew up as each became aware of what he had become. They found the weak spots that nature had inexplicably left exposed.

Dobkin concentrated on forcing his jaws closed and tried to ignore the searing pain. He had missed the Arab's jugular, but he knew that the cartilage of the windpipe would collapse if he persevered.

Talib was trying to get a better hold of Dobkin's testicles, but the big man's knees kept battering at him as they rolled across the mud floor. Talib reached around and poked at Dobkin's eyes, but Dobkin squeezed them tight and buried his face deeper into Talib's neck. Each man was fighting the battle of his life in almost absolute silence. Neither man ever once considered asking for mercy.

In another hut, across the crooked lane, the two appointed attendants made herbal tea over a crackling fire of thistle and told stories to keep each other amused. They heard nothing unusual, just the whistling of the wind and the slapping of the shutters.

Dobkin could take the pain no longer. His thigh wound was open and hemorrhaging, and he felt that he was going to lose consciousness. He found the terra cotta figure in his pocket and brought it down hard on Talib's ear. The wing of the wind demon shattered as it struck. The Arab's scream was lost in a sudden loud rush of wind that threw open the shutters.

Talib, stunned, loosened his grip long enough for Dobkin to pull away. Dobkin raised his huge hand and smashed the jagged edge of the Pazuzu down on Talib's good eye. The man let out a long scream and covered his face. Dobkin took the sharply pointed fragment of the demon's wing and plunged it into Talib's jugular. A stream of blood spurted up into Dobkin's face.

Talib thrashed across the room holding his throat with his hand and making gurgling sounds. The two men collided several times in the small, dark room, each time letting out primal noises as they touched. In his death throes Talib splattered blood across the floor and walls.

Finally, Dobkin fell back into a corner and remained still. He listened until he was certain the Arab was dead, then he lay back, fighting to remain conscious. He spit and spit to get the taste of blood out of his mouth, but he knew he never would.

27

Laskov and Talman were as surprised as anyone to have been invited back to the Prime Minister's meeting.

Laskov listened to the photo-analyst, Ezra Adam, as the young man gave his report. The analyst spoke apparently without passion, but Laskov could tell that the man was saying, "I have found the missing Concorde. Believe me. Go and get them." Laskov had heard too many photo-analysts over the years to mistake the tone. The man went through each of the dozen high-altitude SR-71 infrared photographs that the Americans had taken only hours before at the Israelis' request.

The various ministers and generals, most of whom could not discern anything from the light and dark blotches, followed Adam with their own set of photographs as he spoke.

Adam laid down another photograph and looked up at the Prime Minister. "So you can see, sir, it's somewhat difficult to read night photos with the—what do you call it?—the *Sherji* kicking up dust, and the high altitudes and all. We really should have our own low-level shots, but of course I understand there are political—"

"Get on with it, young man," snapped an air force general. "Let the PM worry about that."

"Yes, sir. Well, here—photo number ten, then. Similar to the others. I've seen this pattern before. Small scattered and random residues of heat. Suggestive of a battle, perhaps."

"Or a shepherd's encampment," said an army general.

"Or a village," added a Cabinet minister who didn't know anything about infrared photography an hour before but was catching on fast.

"Yes," agreed Adam. "It could be any of those. But one gets a feel for these things after a while. First of all, there is no known village on this spot. Please look at your transparent overlays of the archeologist map of Babylon. The village of Kweirish is a kilometer to the south of these heat sources, near the Ishtar Gate. Also, villages look different. And the cooking fires and lamps of a village or an encampment leave a different heat residue. You can see this in Kweirish. Based on a spectrographic analysis of these photos, I have reason to believe that there was phosphorus burned here on this slope. And here, in quadrant one-three—look at the size of that heat source. It's dim, you see, but it must be large. See? An aircraft whose engines haven't been running in perhaps twenty-four hours or more. Then a series of streaks here like trucks moving—or a light aircraft taking off. See these spots on each photo? That may be a small aircraft flying over the mound."

Laskov knew that to the laymen in the room it was all very suspect. But to his surprise, the Prime Minister suddenly stopped Adam in mid-sentence. "I believe you, Sergeant Adam. God knows why, but I do." Then more surprisingly, he turned to Laskov instead of to his military aides. "Well, Laskov, tell me a story based on these ridiculous smears."

Laskov looked around the room. "It would appear—that is, we can only surmise—"

"No. No," interrupted the Prime Minister. "No suppositions. I want one of your divine flashes. What does this—" he waved a particularly cryptic photograph in the air, "—what does *this* mean, General?"

Laskov wiped his face with a handkerchief. "Well, it means, sir, that the Concorde was forced down in Babylon—by the Lear—we know how that was done. There was no hijacker on board, of course, so the pilot of the Concorde—Becker—after a

vote, I'm sure—put the craft down outside of the area controlled
by the terrorists, who were waiting on the ground."

Laskov closed his eyes. He seemed to be thinking. After a few
seconds, he opened his eyes again, but they were far away now.
He continued. "At that point, the passengers had the choice of
fleeing or fighting. No, they didn't have the choice. The
Concorde appears to be against the Euphrates. So they were cut
off—unable to flee except into the river. The terrorists would
have immediately surrounded them to seal off all escape routes.
So they decided to stay and fight. They are on a buried citadel.
Not a bad defensive position. Look at the maps. And they had
one Uzi and one M-14 with a starlight scope and perhaps a
half-dozen handguns. The terrorists would come up that slope,
perhaps not expecting anything, and would be fired on. The
Arabs would become confused. Perhaps they would leave a
weapon or two in their retreat. They would try again, of
course...."

Laskov paused. "The Concorde radio is jammed. They can't
signal. We know from our sources that there is a transmitter
causing radio interference somewhere near Hillah. That's not
unusual in itself—we have dozens of such reports. But now, that
one takes on a special meaning." He paused again and looked
around the room. "So they hang on and wait—wait for someone
to come to their aid." He looked at the Prime Minister.

The Prime Minister looked back at him. "That's quite a
story, General. See if you can get me into that celestial radio net
that you're tuned in to." He paused and tapped a pencil on the
table. "So there are only a few terrorists then? Few enough for
the people on the Concorde to defend themselves against
successfully?"

The photo analyst spoke up. "Sir, if this was a battle that we
see on these photographs, then it was one hell of a fight. The
whole slope area for a length of a half-kilometer shows heat
residues."

"Well, then," said the Prime Minister, "it was not our people.
They could hardly have fought a full-scale battle with a large
Arab force. Perhaps what we're looking at here," he tapped his
pictures, "is a local insurrection of some sort."

"The large aircraft, sir," Adam reminded him. "And the
aircraft overhead."

"Large aircraft, my ass," shot back the Prime Minister.

"Blurry, streaky nonsense." He pushed his stack of photos away. He tapped his pencil awhile, shredded some paper, then sat back and sighed. "All right. Large aircraft. Big battle. Why not?" He turned to his communications man sitting in an alcove and called to him. "Do we have Baghdad yet?"

"Baghdad is on station, sir. Their President will be on station in one minute."

There was a silence in the room as the seconds dragged out.

The communications man called out. "The President of Iraq. Line four."

The Prime Minister looked around the room and picked up the receiver. He hit the number four button and spoke in passable Arabic. "Good morning, Mr. President. Yes, sir, it concerns the Concorde, of course. Babylon, Mr. President. Yes, *Babel.*"

Miriam Bernstein and Esther Aronson were kept, technically still under arrest, in the cabin of the Concorde. Hausner had stalled Burg's plans for an immediate court-martial, but the man was insistent—insistent, Hausner knew, on using the incident to bring him down. Hausner suspected that Burg no longer had faith in his, Hausner's, ability to lead. Burg believed that he was acting in the best interests of the group, and, thought Hausner, if that included shooting one or two women, while at the same time taking from him the last two things that were keeping him going—Miriam and his position as leader—then that was perfectly justifiable. Burg knew about him and Miriam, but that seemed not to change his attitude in the least, and Hausner could only respect him for that. Hausner was unhappy that he couldn't develop a healthy hatred for Isaac Burg. It was Hausner's misfortune that he liked the man. If he hadn't, Burg would never have gotten as far as he had.

To add to the internal problems, the Foreign Minister was making his own belated power play, and he had a lot of followers, not only because of his position as legal head of the group, but because he had a compellingly attractive solution to their problems. It was Ariel Weizman's theory that there were no longer any Arabs on the banks of the Euphrates. Therefore, the Israelis could escape down the west wall and flee across the Euphrates. The Concorde's life jackets would be given to the wounded and the nonswimmers.

Hausner and Burg had agreed to a short conference to

discuss the Foreign Minister's proposal. The meeting convened in the littered cabin of the Concorde. The Foreign Minister presided.

Hausner spoke. "I admit that the idea has a certain appeal, but I very much doubt that Ahmed Rish would neglect the most fundamental military tactic of cutting off the enemy's line of withdrawal." He tried to explain this to the most civilian-minded of the group, but there was increasing resistance to anything he said.

Hausner's original power base was his six fanatically loyal men: Brin, Kaplan, Rubin, Jaffe, Marcus, and Alpern. Brin was dead, and Kaplan, Rubin, and Jaffe were wounded. And his men were no longer the only armed people on the hill. Now, even when he gave good advice, it generated negative responses.

Burg came to Hausner's defense and pointed out that if they did manage to cross the river, they would not get far if Rish discovered their absence. "You would be run down on the open mud flats and massacred like rabbits caught in the open by a pack of jackals—or worse, you would be forced to surrender."

Yet more than half the people wanted to flee Babylon. Hausner knew that he had to do everything in his power to keep the group together. It would be a pity—a tragedy—to see all their sacrifices and bravery wiped out in a precipitate flight.

The Foreign Minister insisted on discussing the question of Miriam Bernstein and Esther Aronson with Burg, but Burg refused. The women would remain under arrest until he, Burg, got around to selecting a court-martial board. Rabbi Levin called him an ass and walked off in disgust. The short conference was adjourned with no provision made for convening again.

Neither Hausner nor Burg nor a lot of others regretted the quick subversion of the democratic process. They knew, for example, that a vote taken just then would probably authorize the Foreign Minister to lead them out of Babylon and that this exodus would end in disaster. Ariel Weizman was not Moses and the waters were not going to open for him and swallow the army of Ahmed Rish. If Hausner and Burg agreed on anything, they agreed that the successful conduct of a war was too important to be left to politicians.

Ahmed Rish and Salem Hamadi led the remains of their army through the Ishtar Gate and up the Sacred Way until they reached the temple of the goddess Ninmakh, where they turned west toward the Greek theatre. They walked in the bed of an old canal and passed through the inner city wall. A kilometer further west, they intersected the outer city wall and followed it north, toward the Northern Citadel.

Rish came up beside Hamadi and spoke into his ear. "We will walk right into their midst before they even know we are there."

"Yes." Hamadi listened to the wind coming down out of the hills. They were walking on the lee side of the wall, but nowhere were the ruined defenses more than two meters high and the sand and dust were choking the hard-breathing men as they tried to keep up with Rish's pace. "We must slow down, Ahmed."

"No. The wind may die at any moment."

Hamadi was no desert Arab, and the blowing sand was as alien to him as it was to the Israelis on the hill. He looked around at his men moving like specters through the swirling darkness. Many wore bandages and some were lame. It was obvious that they were no longer completely disciplined or reliable troops. If the fight did not go their way, Hamadi knew they might mutiny and kill their commanders. If the fight did go their way, they would massacre the Israelis and take no hostages. Without hostages, he and Rish would have no power to negotiate. Either way, Hamadi knew that it was over for him and Rish. But Rish seemed not to understand this and Hamadi would not tell him.

Rish increased his pace and the Ashbals did the same. They were almost running now, and Hamadi had the sense that they were all rushing headlong toward their fate, toward a collision with history, toward their personal destinies, and toward a clash that would affect the relationship between the Jews and the Arabs for the next decade or more. Hamadi had been listening closely to Radio Baghdad during the past twenty-four hours, and he knew that if they had accomplished nothing else, they had at least seriously jeopardized the Peace Conference. But the possibility of changing world history paled when compared to personal passions and motivations. He thought of Hausner during the body search—Hausner standing naked under the burning sun beside the Lion of Babylon. He remembered how his skin felt as he ran his hands over him. He was filled with an overwhelming desire to rape—to sodomize Jacob Hausner. To humiliate him and finally to torture and mutilate him.

Hausner walked away from the Foreign Minister's conference alone, hunched into the *Sherji*. The sand blew in his face and the wind billowed his tattered clothes. The incessant noise of the wind was driving him slightly mad and he wanted to shout against it.

He found Kaplan huddled in the spot that Brin had occupied for so long. The starlight scope had been adapted to an AK-47, but it was no more an aid in seeing into that wild night than the obscured moon was. Kaplan was shivering with fever from his wound, but he had insisted that he was the best qualified night-scope man on the hill.

Naomi Haber was looking over the parapet wall, trying to spot movement in the dust. She wore one of the newly fashioned windscreens on her face. The device was made of plexiglas from the Concorde's portholes and had foam rubber, taken from the seats, around the edges to keep out the sand the way a diver's mask keeps out the water. The device was secured to her head with a band of elastic.

Hausner drew Kaplan to the side. "They don't have to wait for moonset with this dust storm, you know."

"I know." And Kaplan also knew Hausner. He knew his tones of voice and his mannerisms, and he knew something was coming, and he knew it was not going to be pleasant.

"There are no more OP/LP's or early warning devices. We are blind."

"I know," He saw it taking shape now.

"My assistant commander—Burg—has absolutely forbidden anyone to leave the perimeter."

"I know that, too." Hausner had come to him out of the blackness and dust and touched him like the Angel of Death. And now he was going to die.

"But the best defense is a good offense, as they say. We can't wait here like a herd of frightened deer hoping that our numbers will be sufficient to make the wolves think twice before they attack. And if they do attack, then all we can do is stand shoulder to shoulder like the deer and kick. We must carry the fight to them. Take the offensive. Like last night."

"Yes."

"If we don't they will come out of that dust and be on this hill before we can do a thing. Take a look out there."

Kaplan looked obediently out into the swirling dust. The defenses were covered with drifting sand, and visibility was not more than five meters beyond the perimeter. They could be out there now for all he knew—six meters out, and he wouldn't know. A sudden apprehension, almost panic, came over him and he tightened his grip on his rifle. He had an overwhelming impulse to run out into the night, to penetrate the blackness with his body and see what was on that slope.

"What's out there, Moshe? What's out there?"

"I don't know."

"Wouldn't you like to know?"

Kaplan didn't answer.

Hausner waited, then went on with his evaluation of the situation. "The most effective military strategem at this point would be to send an ambush patrol downslope. I would place such an ambush by the outer wall. The Ashbals would have to follow that wall from the Ishtar Gate to get here. Not only would an ambush decimate their attacking force, but it would alert us well in advance." He sighed. "But Burg refuses to risk any more people or to split our forces. It's a subjective decision, and I have to go along with it." He paused. "On the other hand . . . on the other hand, if one person with an automatic weapon and a few hundred rounds of ammunition were to be lying out there as the Ashbals walked along that wall, he could take out about a dozen of them before they even fired back." He paused again. "You know?" Hausner lit a cigarette in his cupped hands and passed it to Kaplan, a gesture more intimate than Kaplan could ever remember seeing or hearing of from Jacob Hausner.

Kaplan took a long pull on the cigarette and did not pass it back. "I . . . I suppose that's right—if they are not already halfway up the slope."

"Yes," agreed Hausner. "There's that. And there are undoubtedly sentries still posted at the base of the slope. But a single man should have no difficulty slipping by them in this darkness."

Kaplan had no doubt that Hausner would go himself if necessary. If Hausner had decided not to do it himself, it was only because he felt he had a more important mission to complete on the hill. But Kaplan, after risking his life once for Hausner, had developed an overwhelming desire to live to a ripe old age. Hausner was trying to undermine that desire. "A man who went down there would have damned little chance of getting back."

"Damned little."

"Especially if he had a wound that limited his mobility."

Hausner nodded. "You know, Moshe, there were only a few

real soldiers on this hill. Your six men, Dobkin... a few other veterans... Burg. The number is dwindling. Professional soldiers know that someday they will be called on to do something that the conscripts would not be asked to do. You understand?"

"Of course." Kaplan wondered why Hausner had not gone to Marcus or Alpern. They were not wounded. He supposed it was the classical "this is an honor" type of thing. There were other reasons, he was sure, but Kaplan could not fathom the motives of Jacob Hausner.

"Well... thanks for listening to my ramblings, Moshe."

"Don't mention it." He hesitated. When he saw that Hausner made no move to leave, he said, "Actually, a person could get some good ideas of his own by just listening to other people's ideas."

"That's right."

Kaplan hesitated again, then turned and took a step. He felt Hausner's hand on his shoulder and heard Hausner's voice saying something appropriate, but the exact words did not register. The hell of it was that he couldn't even say any good-byes to the people who had come to mean so much to him over the past twenty-four hours. He felt very much alone walking out into the night.

28

The Prime Minister sat upright as he held the telepnone to his ear. His eyes darted around the room toward the other men and women who were monitoring on earphones. The call to Baghdad was not going well. The Iraqi President had run the gamut of emotions from surprise at the call, to incredulity at the information, and finally to a lack of commitment on the Israeli Prime Minister's suggestions. The Prime Minister spoke evenly and firmly. "Mr. President, I *cannot* divulge to you the source of my information, but it is a *usually* reliable source." He looked across the room as if to confirm the reliable source.

Teddy Laskov and Itzhak Talman stood near the door. The Prime Minister's gaze seemed to be reevaluating them.

The Iraqi President sighed, which the Prime Minister knew in Arabic meant, "It's a great pity, but we're not getting any closer to a deal," or words to that effect. The Iraqi spoke. "In any case, a low-level reconnaissance is out of the question. The *Sherji* is blowing. However, I am sure your American friends have made an illegal overflight with one of their high-altitude craft. That should be sufficient."

"I wouldn't know anything about that."

The Iraqi President ignored the denial and began recounting his objections to adopting any hasty measures.

The Prime Minister listened to the wind rattle the shutters as he half-listened to the Iraqi. He knew that between the floods, the sandstorm, and the darkness, any land transportation, as well as air flights, were out of the question. The more he prodded the Iraqi, the more he knew that the inadequacies of Iraq's transportation and communication network would be revealed, not to mention the inadequacy of their armed forces in navigating through their own country. To have to admit to those problems only made the President more irascible. But Hillah was so close and it was a fair-sized town, thought the Prime Minister. He said, "Isn't there a garrison in Hillah?" His intelligence had told him there was.

There was a long pause. The Iraqi President seemed to be speaking to his aides. He finally spoke into the telephone. "That is classified information, I'm afraid."

The Prime Minister's fingers tightened on the telephone and his knuckles went white. "Mr. President... what do *you* suggest?" He glanced at his watch.

"Wait for the storm to end or at least wait until daylight."

"There may not be time."

"Mr. Prime Minister—it is the old question of risking lives to save lives. You tell me there are fifty Israelis under siege at Babylon, and you want me to risk an operation that could cost as many lives in accidents alone... not to mention money.... Anyway, we have *no* idea of what—if anything—is going on in Babylon."

"But you know that there *is* something going on there. Don't you?"

The Iraqi hesitated. "Yes. Something. We have just confirmed from our government office in Hillah that something is going on around the ruins of Babylon."

There was an immediate rustle of excitement in the room when the Iraqi made this admission.

The Prime Minister leaned forward over the telephone. He saw no reason to play his cards carefully any longer. He spoke abruptly. "Then for God's sake, send the Hillah garrison."

There was another long pause. When the voice came back it sounded almost apologetic, embarrassed. "The Hillah garrison is the 421st Battalion—your military intelligence will know them. They are a unit composed almost entirely of Palestinians. They fought against you in 1967 and 1973. The officers are Iraqi, but the men are refugees and sons of refugees. It would be unfair to put them in a position where their loyalties would be divided. You understand."

The Prime Minister understood. He looked around him. The people who were monitoring looked angry. A hard-line attitude was forming in the room. "Mr. President, could you speak to Hillah now—I'll hold. Ask your government people there—or your loyal officers—to find out exactly what is happening in Babylon."

"There is unfortunately much difficulty with the land lines at the moment. The storm and the floods. We will raise them by radio and see what they can discover."

"I see." The Prime Minister had no reason to believe that the Iraqi was lying about the land lines. He had one more card to play with the Iraqi. "Mr. President, my military people inform me that it is entirely possible to reach Babylon by river. An expedition from another garrison town on the Euphrates could be at Babylon within hours."

The Iraqi President's voice came back, hard now and impatient. "Do you think the Euphrates is like your little River Jordan? This is a great, mighty river. This time of the year it wanders like a lost sheep across the plain—it joins with lakes and swamps and with many, many small streams which are now swelled in size and are mistaken for the river. There are many false rivers to get lost on tonight."

The Prime Minister already knew this. In fact Babylon itself was no longer on the modern Euphrates but on the ancient, narrower course of the river. Still, a modern army or river unit should be able to navigate it. The ancient Mesopotamians had mastered it. "Mr. President, we are all aware of the great tribulations your country goes through each spring, and we know that any other time of the year we could count on a quick and sure response to our request. We know that one of the reasons these..." he didn't want to say terrorists, "...these guerillas picked your country was because of the inaccessibility of Babylon for these few weeks. However, Mr. President, I know that you will provide every assistance that is in your power to provide."

There was no answer.

The Prime Minister was aware that the Iraqi had already had

to swallow a lot of pride in admitting to potential disloyalties and the inability to move armed forces around the country, to say nothing of the fact that a Concorde could have been hijacked into the middle of the country without his knowledge. Added to that was the fact that a small private army of Palestinians was operating in his sovereign state. The Prime Minister sensed that the Iraqi President was, understandably, not in a good mood. The only thing left to do was to add insult to injury and try to provoke him into some sort of action. "Are you aware, Mr. President, that there is a Palestinian base camp in the Shamiyah Desert? That is probably where these Palestinians in Babylon come from."

Again, there was no answer.

The Prime Minister looked around the table. A psy-warfare colonel, who had spent some time over the years studying the Iraqi President, scribbled a note and slid it down the table. The Prime Minister read it. *As long as you've goaded him this far, finish it. Too late to be diplomatic.* The Prime Minister nodded and spoke into the telephone. "Are your armed forces *capable* of mounting an expedition at this late hour, Mr. President?"

There was still no response. Finally the President's voice came back. He sounded very cold. "Yes. I will give the orders to mount a river expedition. But they will not disembark until dawn. That is the best I can do."

"That will be fine," said the Prime Minister, knowing that it was anything but fine and yet not wanting to jeopardize what little he had gained.

"What do you expect us to find there?"

"I have no idea."

"Well, neither do we. For your sake, I hope there is something there. It will be somewhat embarrassing for you if there isn't"

"I know." The Prime Minister paused. It was time for the big question. "Would you allow us to assist you? We can make this a joint operation."

There was not even a small pause this time. "That is absolutely out of the question."

There was no use arguing that point. "All right. Good luck to you."

The Iraqi let the silence drag, then he spoke softly. "Babylon. The Captivity. Strange."

"Yes. Strange." You couldn't make a political or diplomatic

move in the Middle East without tripping over five thousand years of history and bad blood. That was something the Americans, for instance, never understood. Events that took place three millennia ago were brought up at international conferences as though they had taken place the week before last. Given all that, was there hope for any of them? "But not so strange."

"Perhaps not." The Iraqi paused. "You must not think we are unsympathetic. Terrorists do not do us any service, either. No responsible Arab government endorses what they have done." He paused again, and the Israelis could hear a noise over the electronic speaker like a deep melancholy sigh. It was so Arabic, and at the same time so Jewish, that many people in the room were overcome with feelings of empathy, even kinship. The Iraqi President cleared his throat. "I must go."

"I'll call you before dawn, Mr. President."

"Yes."

The phone went dead. The Prime Minister looked up. "Well, do we go in now or not?" He looked at the wall clock. There was a little over six hours until first light in Babylon. "Or do we wait for the Iraqis?" He lit a cigarette and the striking match sounded loud in the quiet room. "You understand this is the first dialogue an Israeli Prime Minister and an Iraqi President have ever had. Do we want to jeopardize what might come out of this? Do we want to jeopardize the whole climate of peace that launched those Concordes?" He looked around the room and tried to read the faces at the long table. Many of those faces had been at the Entebbe conferences, but this was much more complicated than the Entebbe situation, and *that* had taken days before a military solution was agreed upon.

One by one the generals and the politicians got up. Each was allowed two minutes to present his views. The room seemed fairly evenly divided and the division was not along military and civilian lines. Fully half of the military cautioned restraint and fully half of the civilians were in favor of a military solution. If a vote were taken, the result would have been very close.

Amos, Zevi, Deputy Minister of Foreign Affairs, now Acting Foreign Minister, stood. He pointed out that if Foreign Minister Ariel Weizman and Deputy Minister of Transportation Miriam Bernstein were present, they would vote for restraint.

General Gur stood and quipped, "That might be true if they were *present*, Mr. Minister. But if they could send in a proxy vote from Babylon, I'm sure they would vote for an air attack without delay." This brought the only laughter in an otherwise somber debate.

There were those who still believed that Ahmed Rish was in control of the Israelis and that he would make his demands known very soon. This splinter group wanted to be prepared to negotiate when the terms of the ransom were announced.

One of the ministers, Jonah Galili, stood. He reminded the conference that at the time of Entebbe two of the chief rabbis in Israel had interpreted the *Halacha*, the collection of legal precedents in Jewish religious tradition, as allowing for the exchange of terrorists for hostages.

The Minister of Justice, Nathan Dan, himself a rabbi and a lawyer, jumped to his feet. "I take exception to that interpretation."

The Prime Minister slammed his hand on the table, causing his little pile of shredded paper to jump. "That's enough. This is neither a Yeshiva nor a café in Tel Aviv. I'm not interested in ancient *Halachas* or ancient Hebrew or semantics. I'm interested in here and now. Laskov! Your turn. Two minutes."

Teddy Laskov stood at the end of the long table. He spoke in general terms, citing the classical military arguments for action, but he saw he was not making an impression. It was clear that the lack of resolution was based on the fear of mounting an airborne assault on Babylon and finding no one there but the wild beasts of the desert. In a parliamentary government, one fiasco like that could send the whole government and half the Knesset home to write their memoirs. If the government acted and they found the Concorde with the peace mission missing—or God forbid, all dead—then at least they could justify their attempt to the world on humanitarian grounds. But if he, Laskov was wrong—if the photo-analysts were wrong—if there was nothing there . . .

Laskov decided to gamble. "I see what the problem is. All right, then. If I can prove conclusively that our people are at Babylon, can anyone then have any objection to going in there and getting them?"

The Prime Minister stood. "That is the crux of it, General. If you can prove to me conclusively that our people are there, I will vote for going in."

Here was an out for everyone. If later events showed that they should have authorized a raid, they could explain their inaction to the Israeli people on the very solid grounds of faulty and incomplete intelligence. They could state categorically that they never *knew* that the peace mission was at Babylon. It was more than just an excuse. It was the truth.

"And where do you propose to get this conclusive evidence, General?" asked the Prime Minister. "We really can't accept another divine message, I'm afraid, unless we are all permitted to tune in."

Laskov ignored the scattered laughter. "Do I have full authority to act in your name?"

"That's rather a lot to ask."

"Until dawn."

"Well, you can't do much damage in that short a time, I suppose. All right. In the meantime the airborne operation will be standing by on full alert. If you come back here before 5:30 A.M. and show me incontestable proof that at least the Concorde is at Babylon, then I'll push the red button and we'll all cross our fingers and hope for the best. However, if we hear from the Iraqis before then and they state that they have obtained intelligence that there is no one at Babylon, then whatever proof you bring me will be *ipso facto* no longer incontestable. In any case, after dawn, I will have to rely on the Iraqis to keep their word that they will send a force to Babylon. I don't want our forces bumping into theirs, so 5:30 is the cutoff time for mounting an operation. Fair enough?"

"I'd like to lead the fighter wing that goes in."

The Prime Minister sat down and shook his head. "What incredible balls. You're not even in the armed forces any longer. Why did I just give you the full authority of my office? I must be insane."

"Please."

There was a stillness in the room. The Prime Minister seemed to be lost in thought for a long time, then he rose again and looked at Laskov. "If you convince me to go, then I'd like it very much if you would lead the fighter wing. I can't think of anyone else I'd rather send," he said ambiguously.

Laskov saluted, turned, and strode briskly into the hall. Talman followed quickly.

Talman spoke in a low voice as they walked past people in the crowded hall. "What the hell kind of information could you possibly obtain in so short a time?"

Laskov shrugged. "I don't know."

● ● ●

They stepped outside and passed through the columned façade, through an iron gate, and into the street. They both walked in silence. Jerusalem was quiet except for the hot, dry wind. The night, in spite of the heat, was spectacular in the way that only Jerusalem can be in the spring. The air was sweet with the smell of blossoms and the sky was crystal clear. The waxing moon was nearly full overhead. Its light was yellow and warm. Flowers, vines, and trees grew in all the empty spaces as in a country village. The street itself was paved with ancient stone and the houses could have been anywhere from twenty to two thousand years old. It didn't seem to matter in Jerusalem. Everything was ageless and ancient at the same time.

Talman spoke. "What the hell did you say it for, then? There was an outside chance they would have voted to go. Now you've given them an out."

"They would never have voted to go."

Talman looked at Laskov in the weak light. "Are you having doubts?"

Laskov stopped abruptly. "I have absolutely no doubts. They are in Babylon, Itzhak. I know it." He hesitated, then said, "I can *hear* them."

"That's nonsense. You Russians are incurable mystics."

Laskov nodded. "That's true."

Talman reasserted his old authority. "I insist on knowing what you had in mind when you said you'd bring conclusive proof."

Laskov began walking again. "Let's suppose that you wanted to get a message to a high-level recon craft. How would you do it without a radio?"

Talman thought a moment. "You mean a photographic message? Well, I'd make a big sign on the ground—you know. Or if that were impossible, or if the craft were very high and it was dark or overcast—or if there was a sandstorm, then I'd—I'd create a heat source, I suppose. But we saw those heat sources. They are not conclusive."

"They *would* be if one of them were in the shape of the Star of David."

"But there was no such shape."

"But there was."

"There wasn't."

Laskov seemed to be speaking to himself as he walked. "With all that brain power, I'm surprised no one thought of it. But that's an arcane field—high-level infrared reconnaissance, I mean. Maybe they have a star waiting to be ignited if they *see* an aircraft. They don't understand that if they lit it, it could be photographed from an aircraft for some time after it burned out. Dobkin and Burg should have thought of that. But I'm being too critical. It may very well be that there is no kerosene left, or for one reason or another they could not do it, or the kerosene was critical to make bombs. And why would they think anyone would make a recon over Babylon? I mean, why—"

Talman interrupted him. "Teddy, the point is that they did not ignite a Star of David or a message that said, 'Here we are folks!' or anything of the sort. Maybe they had no time before..." His voice trailed off. "Anyway, there is no such sign or mark."

"If there *were*...?"

"I'd be convinced. And so would most people."

"Well, then we'll have to look at the pictures that Air Force Intelligence didn't think were worth sending over to the Prime Minister. I'm sure we'll see the residual heat from a burning kerosene Star of David. It's just a matter of knowing what you're looking for—then you'll see it."

Talman stopped suddenly. His voice was low, almost a whisper. "Are you insane?"

"Not at all."

"Do you mean you would actually try to alter one of those photos?"

"Do you believe they are—or were—in Babylon?"

Talman believed it, but he didn't know why. "Yes."

"Do the ends justify the means?"

"No."

"If your wife were there—or your daughters—would you think differently?"

Talman knew about Laskov and Miriam Bernstein. "No."

Laskov nodded. Talman was not lying. He'd spent too many years among the British. Emotions played little or no part in his decision-making process. That was a good trait most of the time. But Laskov thought he should be a little more Jewish sometimes. "Will you promise to forget what I just said and go get some sleep?"

"No. In fact I feel it's my duty to place you under arrest."

Laskov put his big hands on Talman's arms. "They're dying in Babylon, Itzhak. I know it. The Russians *are* mystics and the Russian Jews are the worst of the lot. I can *see* them, I tell you. Last night I saw them in a dream. I saw Miriam Bernstein playing a zither—a harp—and crying by a stream. It was only before, in the café, that I understood what that meant. Do you think I'd lie to you about that? No. Of course you don't. Itzhak, let me help them. Let me do what I must do. Forget what I told you. When you were my commander, you looked the other way for me once or twice—yes, yes, I know you did—don't be flustered. Go home. Go home and sleep until noon, and when you wake up it will all be over. It will be a national celebration—or, yes, a tragedy—maybe even war. But what choice is there? Let me do this. I don't care what happens to me afterwards. But let me walk away now." He grasped Talman's arms tightly at his sides.

Talman was uncomfortable with Laskov's sudden intimacy, both physical and emotional. He made a small movement to indicate that he'd rather not be held, but Laskov would not release his grip. This was a crossroads for Talman, and he thought he could make the decision better if Laskov were standing off a bit. The Israelis stood too close, not as close as the Arabs, but close enough. Too close for Talman's comfort. "Well..." But Laskov's nearness made him... what? He could feel the man's warmth, his breath... he could feel something pass through Laskov's fingers and into his body. "I really..." This was terribly awkward. The man's face was less than half a meter from his. And he could ... feel what Laskov was feeling. "I ... think I'll go home.... No.... I'll come with you. Yes, damn it! It's insane, you know ... insane, really ... but I'll help you. Yes!"

Laskov smiled slowly. Yes, he knew Talman as well as he thought he did. Even Talman could be moved. The dream was a nice touch. "Good." He released Talman and stepped back. "Listen. I know an Air Force photo lab tech in Tel Aviv. We can pick him up on the way to the Citadel. He can make a storage dump look like a nude of Elizabeth Taylor if we want. He'll do anything I say, with no questions asked."

Talman nodded and they began walking again, almost running, back to the taxi rank outside the Prime Minister's office. They jumped into a cab. "Tel Aviv," said Laskov, out of breath. "National emergency!"

29

Benjamin Dobkin took the hand of Shear-jashub. They stood on the mud quay that jutted into the Euphrates. The entire village of a few dozen persons stood at the foot of the quay and watched them quietly. The moon revealed the dust clouds on the opposite shore. On this shore, the wind blew, but most of the dust fell into the river. The river itself was choppy, and small waves lapped against the quay. It would not be an easy crossing, nor would it be an easy journey on the land. Dobkin looked back at the old man. "Carry him out onto the mud flats for the jackals, and in the morning go about your business."

The old man nodded politely. He didn't need any instructions on how to survive. His village had survived for over two thousand years through episodes that were second to the European Holocaust only in scale. "May God go with you on your journey, Benjamin."

Dobkin was wearing the bloodstained tiger fatigues and the *kheffiyah* of the dead Ashbal. The man himself would soon be in the bellies of the jackals, but Dobkin couldn't get out of his mind the troubled feeling that Rish would eventually come to this village to avenge Talib and would swiftly complete the job that two millennia of attrition had not completed. "Would your people want to come—to come home to Israel—if that could be arranged?"

Shear-jashub looked at Dobkin. "Jerusalem?"

"Yes. Jerusalem. Anywhere in Israel. Herzlya beach, if you want." He could dimly understand what was going on in the old man's mind. Israel to him was just a Biblical name, along with Judah and Zion. It was hardly a real place and had not much more meaning than Babylon had had to Dobkin two days before. "It's a good place," said Dobkin. "The land is good." How the hell could he possibly bridge two millennia? Not only was the Hebrew different, but the concepts and values were worlds apart. "You may be in danger here."

"We are always in danger here."

What right did he have to hold out the promise of return to Jerusalem anyway? How could he deliver if they accepted? But he continued. "You have been in Babylon too long. It is time to go home." He'd have to be insistent. They were like children, and they did not know how good it could be for them in Israel. And he did not like to see Jews living in subjugation. When he traveled and saw Jews in some countries keeping a low profile, it angered him and he wanted to scream to them, "Come home, you idiots! Come home and hold your heads up. There is a place for you now. We bought it for you with our blood." He tightened his grip on the old rabbi's hand. "Come home."

Shear-jashub placed his free hand on Dobkin's shoulder. "*Aluf*," he began. "Have you come to lead us out of the Captivity? Or are you to be the unwitting instrument for our final destruction? Wait. Let me finish. In the Book it says, 'Then rose up the chief of the fathers of Judah and Benjamin, and the priests, and the Levites, with all them whose spirit God had raised, to go up to build the house of the Lord which is Jerusalem.' But God did not raise the spirit of my forefathers and they stayed. But let me tell you this, Benjamin. When this house of God of the returned exiles, the Second Temple, was also destroyed and the populace was dispersed and wandered the world, it was the Jews who had remained in Babylon who kept the flame of learning lit. Babylon, not Jerusalem, was the first city of Jewish learning and culture in those years. Israel will always need her exiles, Benjamin, in order to insure that there

will always be someone left to carry on the Law and to return to
Jerusalem if it is ever again destroyed." He smiled and his shiny
brown face wrinkled in the moonlight. "I hope the spirit of God
moves you someday to build the Third Temple. And if you do,
remember this—if Jerusalem falls again, then there are always
the Jews of the Diaspora, and even us of the Captivity, to return
and build the Fourth." He squeezed Dobkin's hand and
shoulder, then gently pushed him away. "Go, Benjamin. Go and
complete your work. And when it is done, then perhaps we will
speak again of Jerusalem."

Dobkin turned quickly and walked to the end of the quay. He
looked back over his shoulder and gave a half wave to the robed
figures standing motionless in the moonlight. A sense of
unreality came over him, not for the first time. The sights,
sounds, and especially the smells of this place made it difficult
for him to think rationally—to think like a twentieth century
military man.

Dobkin stared down into the Euphrates. An odd-looking
craft called a *gufa* sat in the river. It was no more than a large
round basket, coated with the famous bitumen of Babylon. It
looked as if it had just been freshly coated with the slime. It may
have been a few days or a few thousand years old. Dobkin
lowered his big frame into it, and it sank almost to the gunwales.
A young man named Chislon jumped in after him, apparently
without worrying about the few centimeters of freeboard
remaining. The *gufa* bobbed dangerously low in the water, but
finally settled with about ten centimeters of freeboard on
Chislon's side and about five on Dobkin's. Chislon took a long
pole from the quay, cast away the mooring rope, and pushed off.

Dobkin guessed correctly that the *gufa* was never used when
the Euphrates was at high flood as it was now. Within minutes
his guess was confirmed when he noticed that the pole was no
longer touching bottom no matter how far over Chislon leaned.
Chislon looked up and smiled at him several times.

The *gufa* picked up speed. Dobkin knew that they had to
make a landfall on the opposite bank within two kilometers or
they would overshoot the southern end of Babylon and he would
have to backtrack on foot. He didn't feel strong enough for that.
He smiled at the young man who was trying to look very calm,
but Dobkin could see that he was scared.

Another possibility that had nagged at Dobkin's mind was to

go on to Hillah. They might help in Hillah. He could go directly to the Hillah garrison and explain the situation. They would call Baghdad. But the Hillah garrison or the local government people must know that something was going on in Babylon. Why, then, weren't they investigating? He thought about it. The Jews had never completely trusted any outside group to show them charity or give them aid. They expected treachery and were not often disappointed. No, he should not go to Hillah. He should go to the guest house or the museum and get his hands on a telephone and call Israel That was where he could expect help. That was where there were people who cared if he and the rest lived or died—cared very much, in fact.

The *Sherji* blew over the water and what it lacked in sand, it made up for in velocity. The *gufa* bobbed and swayed and waves splashed over the gunwales on all sides. The round craft began to spin around like a top, and Dobkin was becoming nauseous. His groin ached and his thigh was on fire. He put his head over the side and vomited up his meal of hot lemon tea and an unidentifiable fish that was called *masgouf*.

He felt better and leaned over the side and washed his face in the river. Chislon looked a little unwell also, he noticed.

Dobkin could see a few lights on the far bank and pointed to them.

"Kweirish," said Chislon.

Dobkin was certain now that the young man was clearly worried about the weather. Westerners always had an inordinate faith in native guides, but the truth of the matter was that natives rarely or never did the things that Western adventurers expected they did as part of their routine. Undoubtedly, Chislon had never before had any reason to cross the Euphrates at full flood in the middle of the night when the *Sherji* was blowing.

Dobkin looked at both banks as they spun past him. On the east bank, great masses of dust veiled the land and blotted out the moon. He knew that this meant the last act would be unfolding on the hill long before the moon set.

The river bent below Kweirish and the *gufa* gathered more speed as it came out of its turn. The small craft was caught in the high-velocity water between narrowing banks. Chislon continued to feel for the bottom with the pole and almost caused the craft to be swamped as he leaned farther over the side.

Dobkin tried to estimate when their course would intersect the far shore. Ahead, the river made a turn westward, and if the *gufa* didn't sink first, they might make landfall there. That should put them in the vicinity of the southernmost wall of the city. He would have to backtrack at last two kilometers to the Ishtar Gate and guest house. He wondered what he was going to do if he got there.

"Disasters and victories are very closely related," observed Hausner.

Burg stuffed a few cigarette stubs into his pipe and lit it as only a nicotine addict can light tobacco in a driving wind.

Both men huddled in what was left of the trenches on the east slope. Sand drifted into the cut in the earth, bringing it slowly and inexorably back up to grade level.

"Where is Kaplan?" asked Burg, for the second time.

How Burg knew that Kaplan was gone was anyone's guess, thought Hausner. Maybe Naomi Haber. Burg had his followers. "You know, not too far from here, at a place called Kut, a whole British army was besieged by the Turks during the First World War." He lit a full cigarette. "The British Expeditionary Force came from India and landed on the Persian Gulf at the mouths of the Tigris and Euphrates. They were going to wrest ancient Mesopotamia from the Turk. The Arab populace—the desert Arabs and the marsh Arabs—were like vultures. After every clash between the two armies, they would strip the dead and finish off the wounded. They harassed both armies and killed stragglers for their clothes and equipment. There's a lesson there and the lesson is, don't go out on the mud flats. If we do and the Ashbals don't get us, marauding Arabs will."

Burg pulled a scarf closer around his face and stuck his pipe into a fold and drew on it. He looked at Hausner. "I absolutely agree with you there. We'll tell the Foreign Minister that story later. Meanwhile, where is Kaplan?"

"This story has another part and another lesson to be learned, Isaac."

Burg exhaled his smoke on a sigh of resignation. "All right."

"Well, after a large battle with the Turks, the British had to hole up at this town called Kut. They had outrun their supplies. The Turks laid siege to the town, and the siege lasted for months. The relieving British force actually got within a kilometer of Kut, but the Turks drove them back again and again. The British in Kut finally had to surrender when their supplies ran out. One of the most severe criticisms of the British commander—this was stated in the War Office report—concerned his lack of forays and sallies from Kut into the encircling Turkish ranks. The report called for an end to static defenses and recommended mobile and fluid defenses. No more walls. Fire and maneuver. Military science has accepted that now. Why don't you?"

Burg forced a laugh. "I hardly see the parallel in your parable. Where is Kaplan? Downslope?"

"There *is* a parallel, and it is that good tactics are good tactics whether it is at Kut, Khartoum, or Babylon. And speaking of Khartoum, Burg, don't forget that the British relief force was only one day late in arriving *there*. But that didn't make General Gordon and his men and the civilians any less dead. If outside help does not reach us in the next few hours, we will suffer the same fate, Burg. While we sit here and no one is trying to hack us to pieces we lull ourselves into a false sense of security. But when that slope comes alive with screaming, bloodthirsty Ashbals, we will all be saying, 'Why didn't we try this?' or, 'Why didn't we try that?' Well, I'm telling you now, Burg that any desperate method to buy more time is worth the risk."

"Where did he go? The Ishtar Gate?"

"No. Only down to the outer city wall. That will be the route they take."

"How can you be sure?"

"All field problems have only a finite number of solutions."

"I'm going to get you a job at the War College when we get back."

Hausner lay back against the side of the trench and closed his eyes as he smoked.

"When are we trying Bernstein and Aronson? Before or after *your* court-martial?"

Hausner had had enough of humility and deference. It didn't suit him. He didn't like sharing anything, least of all his authority. He sat up quickly and tapped Burg on the chest, "Don't push me, Isaac, or it will be you in the dock, not me. If it goes to a vote, they will pick the genuine bastard to lead them out of the wilderness, not the ersatz bastard like you or the statesman like Weizman. They can trust a real bastard to drive them on. They know they can't trust you or Weizman to make unpopular decisions or to enforce them. So back off. I'll be out of your way—and out of your life—soon enough."

Burg stared down into the glowing bowl of his pipe. "I don't trust you, Jacob. Anyone who thinks victories and disasters are very closely related is the kind of man who calls for another card when he already has twenty points on the black-jack table. That's not the way we play it in intelligence. We accept minimum gains in exchange for minimum losses. We never go for the big gain if there's a chance of a big loss. That's the way all armies, intelligence services, and foreign ministries play the game today. You're the last of the big gamblers. But you shouldn't do it with other people's lives. Even the life of one man—Moshe Kaplan—a brave man—shouldn't be gambled away—thrown away—on the outside chance that the loss of his life may do us some good."

"You know damn well that one life is considered a small risk. By the rules of your own damn game theory, that was an acceptable loss for a possibly large gain."

"It's very subjective, I suppose. I don't consider the loss of one life a small loss."

"You're a damned hypocrite, Burg. You've done worse than this in your lifetime. And don't pretend that you weren't glad I asked Dobkin to go. That mission is almost certain death, you know, and you didn't seem so goddamned upset about that."

"That was different. Dobkin is a professional. A man like that knows that a time like this comes at least once in his life."

"That doesn't make it any easier for him or any easier for me. Do you think I enjoyed sending either of them down there?"

"I didn't say that. Lower your voice. I'm only playing Devil's Advocate here."

"I don't need any-more devils or their advocates, Burg. I do what I think I have to do. And I hope to God that the people in Jerusalem and Tel Aviv forget about their game plan theories, because if they're not willing to take that big gamble on us, if and when they find out where we are, then we are all dead."

Burg looked off downslope and spoke in an offhand manner. "Well, better dead than that we should be the cause of another war or that our rescue should jeopardize the Peace Conference."

Hausner saw it all in a flash of insight. Burg was willing to sacrifice them all for what he thought was a higher good. He would rather they die bravely—and quietly—than see them used as an instrument to put Israel in a difficult position. It was a matter of degree, if you thought about it. He, Hausner, was willing to sacrifice Kaplan, himself, or anyone else for higher goals. But where did the sacrifice stop? If Israel were being overrun, would she refuse to use her atomic weapons "for the sake of humanity and the higher good"? Did anyone, nation or citizen, have the right to say, "Higher good, my ass. I deserve to live and I'll kill anyone who tries to put an end to my life"?

But people did make sacrifices for higher goals; Kaplan was doing that now. Kaplan, lying so very alone in the dark—he could count his remaining time on earth in minutes. And Burg was willing to let them all—including himself—die rather than force Israel to make a decision.

Hausner thought about it. He was willing to sacrifice his life. But that was because fate had put him in a position where to continue to live might be worse than dying. And he had put Kaplan in that position. Kaplan could never have lived a normal life after refusing Hausner's kind of invitation to lay down his life. But it wasn't the lives or the deaths that bothered him, he realized. It was the principle of aggressive intervention that was at stake. The Jews of Israel couldn't let themselves slip into that passive role that had been the cause of the death of European Jewry.

It went against Hausner's personality to accept Burg's argument. If he, Hausner, were asked directly by the Prime Minister, he would say, "Damn right I want you to blast your way in here and get us. What the hell is taking you so long?" Certainly Burg believed that, too. Burg was only playing Devil's Advocate again. Burg was speaking like the Foreign Minister—and Miriam—would speak. Burg, the spy, had many personalities and spoke many tongues. But if Burg really believed what he said, then Burg was wrong. Burg would have to be watched. Burg might have to go.

Hausner sat alone in the trench. The dust and sand sifted into the slit and began covering his legs. The place where Burg had sat opposite him was already obliterated. Soon everything that they had constructed would also be obliterated. The Concorde, too, would be covered someday and only its vague outline would remain. Their bones would lay buried in the dust and all that would remain of them and their deeds would be another written record of suffering and martyrdom to go into the Jerusalem library. He grabbed a handful of dust from his leg and flung it into the wind. Babylon. He hated the place. He hated every square centimeter of its dead dust and clay. Babylon. Corrupter of men. Killer of souls. A million acts of moral depravity had been committed here. Massacres. Slavery. Illicit couplings. Blood sacrifices. How could his love for her have flowered in such a place?

He'd sent for her, but there was no guarantee that she would come. His heart beat heavily in his chest. His mouth, already dry, became sticky, and his hands trembled. Miriam, come quickly. The wait became insufferable. He looked at his watch. Five minutes since Burg had left. Three minutes since he had sent a runner to the Concorde. He wanted to get up and leave, but he couldn't bring himself to move from the place where she would come looking for him.

He heard two voices and saw two silhouettes. One figure pointed, turned and walked off. The other came toward him. He licked his lips and tried to steady his voice. "Here."

She slipped into the trench and knelt beside him in the dust. "What is it, Jacob?"

"I ... just wanted to speak to you."

"Am I free?"

"No. No, I can't do that. Burg—"

"You can do anything you want here. You are King of Babylon."

"Stop it."

She leaned toward him. "A little bit of you is in complete agreement with Burg. A little bit of you is saying, 'Lock the bitch up and keep her locked up. I'm Jacob Hausner and I make the tough decisions and I stick to them.'"

"Don't Miriam..."

"Don't misunderstand me. I'm not concerned about me—or Esther, for that matter. I'm concerned about *you*. Part of you will die if you let this farce continue. Every minute you allow it to go on you become less of a human being. Take a stand for kindness and compassion for once. Don't be afraid to let everyone know the Jacob Hausner I know."

Hausner shook his head slowly. "I can't. I *am* afraid. Afraid things will fall apart here if I show mercy. Afraid—"

"Afraid *you* will fall apart if you show mercy."

He thought of Moshe Kaplan. How could he have done such a thing to that man? He thought of other Moshe Kaplans over the years. He thought back on Miriam reciting the Ravensbrück Prayer.

As if she read his mind, she said, "I don't want to be your victim, your nightmare, your shuddering ghost. I want to be your help."

He drew his legs up and rested his head on his knees. It was a posture he hadn't assumed since he was a child. He felt himself losing control. "Go away."

"It's not that easy, Jacob."

He picked his head up. "No. It's not." He stared at her through the darkness.

He looked so lost, she thought. So alone. "What did you want with me?"

He shook his head. His voice cracked. "I don't know."

"Did you want to tell me you love me?"

"I'm shaking like a schoolboy on his first date and my voice is an octave higher."

She reached out and ran her hand across his temple and through his hair.

He took her hand and brought it to his lips.

Hausner wanted to kiss her, caress her, but instead he only took her in his arms and held her tightly. Then he moved her away gently and knelt on one knee. He reached into his shirt pocket and removed something. He held it out toward her in his open palm. It was a silver Star of David. It was fashioned from two separate triangles riveted together. Some of the rivets had apparently broken off and the triangle had shifted. He tried to sound nonchalant. "I bought it in New York on my last trip. Tiffany's. Drop it off for me and have it fixed. All right?"

He handed her the Star of David. She smiled. "Your first gift to me, Jacob—and you have to pretend it isn't even a gift. Thank you."

Suddenly her expression became very serious. She knelt in the bottom of the trench and stared down at the silver star in her open hand. "Oh, Jacob," she whispered, "please don't throw your life away." She made a fist over the star and clutched it to her breast. The points of the star dug into her hand until it bled. She lowered her head and fought back the tears until her body shook. "Oh, damn it. Damn it!" She pounded her fists against the ground. She shouted into the wind. "No, damn it. I won't let you die here!"

He said nothing but there were tears in his eyes, too.

With unsteady hands she removed a silver chain from her

neck. On the chain were the Hebrew letters ﬡﬡﬡ —life. She clasped the chain around his neck and pulled his head toward her. "Life," she said, through her sobs. "Life, Jacob."

Moshe Kaplan lay in a small ravine and scanned with the starlight scope. The moonlight was weak and the dust was thick, but he had no trouble seeing the file of Ashbals in tiger fatigues against the low wall less than twenty meters away. He was reminded of a nineteenth-century print called *The Gathering of the Werewolves*. It showed grotesque semi-humans gathering against the wall of a churchyard cemetery in the moonlight. It was a frightening picture, but far less frightening than the greenish picture in his scope.

As he watched, the picture suddenly dimmed and he knew the batteries had finally given out. He took one last look before the picture became darker and pulled back on the trigger.

On the hill, everyone knew that the time had come.

30

Dobkin pushed Chislon forcibly back into the *gufa*, then shoved the craft away from the shore. There was considerably more freeboard now, and Chislon was far better off taking his chances with the Euphrates than sharing Dobkin's fate. Also, Chislon was the only connection between Dobkin and the village of Ummah, and Dobkin did not want that connection known by Rish should they be caught. He watched the *gufa* float downriver toward Hillah until he lost sight of it. He turned inland.

Dobkin was totally disoriented and could not be sure exactly where he was in relation to the Ishtar Gate. He walked through the blinding dust storm, keeping count of his paces. There were unmarked excavations everywhere and he almost fell into a few of them. At least their presence confirmed that he was indeed in Babylon. He navigated across that peculiar blanched, nitrous soil which had been produced from the walls of ancient buildings and which stunted and destroyed vegetation, making the site of Babylon an awful and naked waste.

When he had traveled three hundred meters, he climbed onto a high piece of ground and peered out at the surrounding terrain. He assumed that the guest house would have lights and looked for them through the darkness, but saw nothing.

He heard a noise behind him and spun around. Something moved in the dark. He saw it move again and saw its slanted yellow eyes glowing through the darkness.

The jackal stood on a crumbled wall, its hindquarters to the wind and its face pointing at Dobkin. Its eyes were half-closed and it stood stoically, accepting its miserable lot. Dobkin suddenly felt an empathy with this predator. "I don't know what you're looking for here, old hunter, but I hope you find it—as long as it isn't me."

The jackal moved gracefully along the wall toward Dobkin, sized him up, and stopped. He raised his muzzle and howled. There was no answer from his pack, and the jackal leaped from the wall and disappeared into the night.

Dobkin also came down from the high place and took tempory shelter in a partly excavated house. There were owls in the dark corners and they hooted at his presence. Dobkin settled onto the floor and fought down the numbing pain and fatigue. He let his eyes close, and his mind drifted.

Babylon. What an incredibly dead place. And the dead city was trying to kill him and add his bones to its bleached earth. "And Babylon shall become heaps, a dwelling place for dragons, an astonishment, and an hissing, without an inhabitant." Jeremiah's prophecy had been as accurate as Isaiah's.

In the fourth century, recalled Dobkin, a Persian king had turned the city into a royal game reserve. Its incredible walls, sometimes listed in place of the Hanging Gardens as the Second Wonder of the World, still stood in those days, though most of the 360 watchtowers along its ramparts had fallen. This bizarre fate, the transformation of the largest city in the world into a place for wild animals—a zoo, really—recalled even more dramatically to Dobkin the prophesies of Isaiah and Jeremiah. A dwelling place for wild beasts.

By the beginning of the fifth century the Euphrates had changed course and Babylon had become a vast marsh, and the final prophesies of Isaiah and Jeremiah were fulfilled when, as Jeremiah wrote eight hundred years before the fact, "The sea is come up upon Babylon: she is covered with the multitude of the waves thereof."

Dobkin felt himself slipping off and lurched to his feet. He took some water from the goatskin and cleared his eyes. It was a strange world that he had been catapulted into, and he suspected that there was some meaning in all of it, but he could not begin to fathom what it was.

He climbed out of the half-buried house and onto a trail that ran over the sunken ruins. He turned north and picked his way along the flood bank of the Euphrates. He walked on for nearly a kilometer, his body hunched over against the wind and his face wrapped in his *kheffiyah*.

The wind dropped briefly, and he thought he heard a noise and lifted his head. An Arab stared at him from the alcove of a doorway. Dobkin realized that he was in Kweirish. He stared back at the Arab, then approached him. "The guest house," he said in what he hoped was Palestinian-accented Arabic.

The man believed that he was speaking to an Ashbal who had lost his way in the darkness. He had little love for these Palestinians, but they seemed to be the local authority at the moment. He had never seen an Ashbal without a rifle and he wondered about that. He stepped out of the alcove and walked past Dobkin, looking closely at him as he brushed by.

As Dobkin followed, he reached into his belt and took out the knife that the Jews of Ummah had given him. They walked up a crooked street for a few minutes, then the man disappeared into an alley between two buildings.

Dobkin followed carefully. He looked down the alley, but the Arab had disappeared. Dobkin put his back to the wall on his right and sidestepped in, the knife at his side ready to move.

The Arab suddenly stepped out of a niche in the wall opposite him and held out his arm. "This is the way."

Dobkin was certain this was the goat path down which Hamadi had taken him and Hausner and which led to the Ishtar Gate. He nodded and made an appropriate expression of gratitude, adding a mild benediction. He realized he would have to pass very close to the man to get by. He tightened his grip on his knife and walked, his right shoulder slightly out front, until he was abreast of the Arab.

The Arab gripped his own dagger. He meant to murder the Ashbal for his clothes and boots and whatever else he happened to have in his pockets. The Ashbals would never trace the man back to Kweirish.

Dobkin passed within a meter of the man and fixed his eyes on him.

The Arab realized how big the Ashbal was and saw also that he was alert. In fact, he wondered if the man had plans to murder *him*. His eyes glanced downward and he saw the big man's knife. Should he strike first or should he stand back and pray to Allah that the big man had no murderous designs on him? Certainly the man would not murder him for his poor *gellebiah* and his old sandals? "Allah go with you," he said and bowed his head, leaving himself at the big man's mercy.

Dobkin hesitated. All the reasons for murdering the man and not murdering him flashed through his mind. "And with you," Dobkin answered. He slid by and disappeared up the goat path between the houses.

Again, as before, a feeling of déjà vu came over him as he walked up into the city. He knew it was only a combination of fatigue and stress coupled with all those old maps and conjectural restorations he had seen of the place, but nevertheless it was haunting. He supposed that like most Jews—if the stories of the Captivity were substantially correct—he had had ancestors living in this place. But his ancestors had not tarried when Cyrus said "Go." They went, only to be dispersed again by the Romans some centuries later. From then until 1948 there had been no place to call home. Somehow the family known as Dobkin, after two millennia of wandering, had come to live in Russia, and from Russia they completed their journey and returned to Palestine. And from Palestine—Israel—Benjamin Dobkin had come back to Babylon. It remained to be seen if he would return to Jerusalem.

Dobkin found the ancient bed of the Euphrates, and from there it was easy to follow the old river wall into the palace area. Within a quarter of an hour, he found himself staring up at the glazed lions on the towers of the Ishtar Gate. He passed through the gate and followed the Sacred Processional Way until he saw the lights of the guest house. There appeared to be no sentry. Across from the guest house was a bivouac of struck tents. Some distance off he could make out the small museum. The Ashbals appeared to be gone. Gone to attack the hill again. As he stood and caught his breath, he heard a long burst of AK-47 fire coming from the direction of the hill, then silence. He wondered who had fired the burst. An outpost, he imagined. Another martyr to add to the very long list.

He thought for a moment of trying to find Dr. Al-Thanni in the museum, but decided against that. Time was crucial now. Besides could he trust Al-Thanni? And if he could, did he want to involve him in this? He realized that he had no specific plans beyond making a very important telephone call, and in fact he did not want to think too long about making any plans. The whole incredible operation could only work because of boldness, daring, and luck. So far he had been very lucky. He had found the village of Ummah and had acquired a set of tiger fatigues. He had found the guest house, and the Ashbals seemed to be gone from the tents. Now all he had to do was go inside and kill the duty man and anyone else left behind. But the wounded would probably be in there, and that meant orderlies, too. Perhaps a lot of them.

He walked up to the front veranda and opened the door into the small lobby. He blinked his eyes to adjust them to the light. A young Arab in tiger fatigues sat behind the clerk's counter reading a newspaper. It was all so commonplace, thought Dobkin. The young man looked up, and Dobkin could see his features straining as he tried to place him.

"Yes?" The man, Kassim, had just decided to rape the Jewess again—if she wasn't dead yet. Now this interruption. "Yes?" There was something wrong—those ill-fitting fatigues. They were wet and the dust was plastered on them with dark blotches that looked like blood. No rifle—a goatskin—the *kheffiyah* didn't sit quite right. Kassim stood up.

Dobkin walked to the counter quickly, but not too quickly, reached over and grabbed the young man by the hair with his left hand as his right hand thrust his knife into the man's larynx. He twisted the knife, then let the man slide down gently to the floor. He wiped his hand on the newspaper, then blotted the counter with it and dropped the paper behind it. He could still hear a bubbling sound from the other side of the counter. He turned and walked to the door marked in Arabic "Manager's Office," and opened it.

The small office was lit by a single floor lamp, and in the pool of light on the floor lay a naked women—or a girl—on her stomach, covered with blood and apparently dead or close to it. Dobkin knew by the skin and haircut that it was no local peasant girl who had been abducted for the obvious reason. He walked quickly over to the body and turned it over. She looked familiar even though her face was battered. His worst fear—that she was one of his—was realized as he slowly recognized Yigael

Tekoah's secretary, but he could not remember her name. He knelt down and put his ear to her heart. She was alive. He looked at her bloody body. It appeared as if they had let some kind of wild animal attack her.

He picked her up and laid her on a small ottoman against the wall. A long woolen *gellebiah* hung on a coat hook on the door and he took it down and slipped it over her. He found a pitcher of water standing next to a basin of bloody water on a sideboard. He poured the water from the pitcher over the girl's face. She stirred slightly. Dobkin put the pitcher down. He could not spare one more second for the suffering girl. He walked to the desk and picked up the telephone. The single, commonplace act felt strange, the way it had during the Sinai Campaign when he had once found a working telephone in a destroyed village. He had called the next village—still in Egyptian hands—and announced his imminent arrival. That had been a lark. This was not. He waited impatiently for a dial tone. Overhead, he could hear the sound of footsteps and groaning. Orderlies and wounded. On the other side of the wall he heard men speaking. Outside, the wind shook the louvers and rattled the window panes. Dobkin wondered if the line was dead. He looked down at the telephone. There was no dial face. It was completely operator-controlled, but how did one raise the operator? He tapped on the cradle for what seemed like a very long time.

Suddenly, a man's voice came on, annoyed and churlish. "Yes? Hillah exchange! Yes?"

Dobkin took a breath. "Hillah, get me the international operator in Baghdad, please."

"Baghdad?"

"Baghdad." Dobkin knew that he would have to route this call with all the care and patience of a man building a house of cards. One slip and the connection could be broken.

"Who is calling Baghdad?"

Dobkin never fully appreciated his own country until he traveled to controlled societies. He hesitated, then spoke. "This is Dr. Al-Thanni." No. The Hillah operator would certainly know that voice. A bad mistake. "That is, I am Dr. Omar Sabbah, a *house guest* of Dr. Al-Thanni of the museum, Baghdad please."

There was a pause. "Wait."

Dobkin wondered if Al-Thanni was in his quarters in the guest house, or if he was staying at the museum. Or was he home in Baghdad? He held the receiver to his ear and waited. A clock on the wall ticked away the minutes. He found himself staring into the bowl of bloody water and turned away. His eyes burned and his whole body felt as though it wanted to fall. He carried the telephone across the room and knelt beside Deborah Gideon. He wet her lips from his goatskin and let some water slide between them. He felt her pulse and her pale skin and forced back her eyelid. She was in shock, but she was young and healthy looking enough to come out of it. He touched some of her wounds and looked at them closely. He did not feel so bad about killing the duty man now.

He ministered to her as best he could while he waited, the receiver cradled between his shoulder and ear. The clock ticked off a quarter of an hour. The voices on the other side of the wall got louder. A card game. Overhead there was a thump on the floor. A patient fell out of bed—or died and was thrown onto a stretcher.

Someone walked into the lobby and shouted. "Kassim! Kassim! Where are you?"

That was probably the dead man's name, thought Dobkin. Would anyone think to lean over the counter and look on the floor?

Footsteps approached the door. The doorknob turned. Dobkin kept the receiver to his ear and reached up and shut off the lamp. The door opened, and a shaft of light from the lobby passed a meter away from him and illuminated the place on the floor where the girl had lain. The edge of the shaft fell on her bare foot hanging over the sofa. "Kassim! Where are you, you son of an ass?"

The Hillah operator spoke. "Babylon? Babylon? Baghdad is on. Babylon, are you there? Are you there?"

Dobkin stood motionless, not even drawing a breath.

The Hillah operator spoke to the Baghdad operator. "Babylon is gone."

The door closed and the room went dark.

Dobkin spoke softly. "Babylon is here."

"What? Speak up. Speak up."

"Babylon is here."

"Can you hear Babylon, Baghdad?"

"I hear Babylon, Hillah," said the female operator to the male Hillah operator.

They are very up to date in Baghdad, thought Dobkin.

"Go ahead, Babylon," said the Baghdad international operator.

Dobkin thought again about asking for an Iraqi government office, or explaining to the operator who he was and what he wanted, but he would then have to have the international operator get him a regular operator. And what government office was open at this hour? And what reaction would the operator have to his story? Several scenarios played themselves out in his mind and each one ended with a dead telephone.

"Go *ahead*, Babylon."

"Get me . . ." There was no way that a call from the Land of Islam was going to reach Israel. Istanbul would call Israel, but he didn't speak Turkish so he would have to speak to an Arabic-speaking international operator in Istanbul. And if Baghdad or another exchange were still listening they would become very suspicious when he asked for Tel Aviv.

"Babylon. Are you *there*?"

"Yes. Athens. Get me Athens."

"Why are you calling Athens? Who are you?"

Bitch. "I am Dr. Omar Sabbah, young lady, and I wish to call an associate in Athens. Put me through without delay."

There was silence for some time, then the voice said, "That will take some time, Doctor. I will ring you back when I complete the call."

"No." Why not?

"Why not?"

"The . . . bell doesn't work properly here. I can never tell when I have incoming calls."

Silence.

"Did you hear me, Baghdad?"

"Yes. Yes. Wait. I will route your call. Stay on the line, then."

"Thank you." He heard Baghdad speak to Damascus and Damascus speak to Beirut. Beirut, the big exchange in the Middle East, reached Istanbul quickly. There was a time—and in fact there were still days—when Beirut would have rung Tel Aviv only two hundred kilometers down the coast. But today might not be one of those days, and he didn't want to risk it. The easy flowing Arabic became halting Turkish and equally bad Arabic as the Beirut and Istanbul international operators spoke to each other. The clock ticked on. Dobkin could not believe that he had gotten this far. He waited for the connection to be broken or the door to open. Sweat ran down his face and his mouth turned dry. He listened to his heart beat in the dark.

The card game in the next room was ending. There was another shout for the duty man. Some crying from the wounded. Dobkin thought he could hear automatic weapons fire to the north. The girl on the sofa cried out in her sleep, and Dobkin held his breath.

Istanbul spoke to Athens. Athens spoke better Turkish than Istanbul spoke Greek. Istanbul spoke to Beirut. Beirut bypassed Damascus and spoke directly to Baghdad. Hillah was no longer on station and Baghdad spoke directly to Babylon. "Athens is connected."

"Thank you." The last Athens operator spoke Turkish, but they automatically switched him over to an Arabic-speaking operator. "Number, please?"

Was anyone in Islam still on the line? He wanted to ask for an English-speaking operator but didn't want to cause any confusion. He stalled to give the way stations time to get off the line. Operators were nosy and would listen until they had another call or until they were bored. "Is this Athens?" he asked in Arabic.

"Yes, sir. Number, please."

"Can you look up a number for me?"

"Certainly, sir. Who is the party?"

Dobkin paused. He thought of an archeological acquaintance. "Dr. Adamandios Stathatos. He lives in the Kipseli district." He spelled it out slowly.

"Hold on, please."

Dobkin was certain that by now the Arabic operators had hung up, but there was still a chance that there was a security man on the line somewhere along the way. International phone calls were not that common in this part of the world and certainly not at that hour. Even in Israel, international calls were spot-monitored by Shin Beth.

The operator came back. "Dr. Stathatos in Kipseli. I'm ringing."

"Stop the call."

"Sir?"

"Stop the call. I just remembered another call." He could have spoken to Dr. Stathatos and perhaps accomplished his mission, but he wanted more than anything in the world to talk directly to Tel Aviv, and he was so close. "Cancel that call."

The Athens operator stopped the call. She was obviously annoyed. "Yes, sir."

"Get me... Tel Aviv."

"Tel Aviv?" There was a pause. This had happened before. It was no concern of hers. Greece and Israel were on good terms. Politics were silly. But that poor man had better be careful though, calling Tel Aviv from Iraq. "Hold on, please." There was another transfer of operators and more clicking, buzzing, humming, and ringing down the line.

A new voice came on and said, "Tel Aviv is on the line, sir."

A girl's voice in Hebrew, brisk and efficient, came through very weak. "Number, please?"

Dobkin's heart pounded in his chest. He wanted to crawl into the receiver and come out in Tel Aviv. He wanted to shout into the mouthpiece and tell this girl all there was to tell.

"Number, please."

He controlled his voice. "Wait." There were several numbers. His own, for one, but his wife would be with one of her innumerable relatives. There were lots of numbers. Friends, officers, politicians. But if he spoke to an intermediate party, there would be unnecessary confusion when that person spoke to the government.

"Sir, you—"

"The Prime Minister's office in Tel Aviv." He could not give the secure number on an international line, and he would have to speak to the regular office operator. He wondered if the government was in Tel Aviv or Jerusalem. At the very least he would be able to speak to a responsible duty officer in Tel Aviv. Dobkin heard noises in the lobby again. It was only a matter of time before they found the lost Kassim. He could hear the phone ringing on the line.

"Prime Minister's office," said a female operator.

"Yes. Is the security meeting there or in Jerusalem?"

There was a pause. That information was in the newspapers, so there was no reason not to answer. Still... "Who is this, please?"

"General..." He didn't know what her reaction would be to his name. "General Cohen."

She paused. "I'll have the Tel Aviv operator ring you through to the Jerusalem operator... General."

"Thank you." He heard a busy signal. Everyone in Israel must be calling the Prime Minister's office tonight with advice and complaints. That happened during every crisis. Everyone in Israel thought they were Prime Minister material.

"All the lines to Jerusalem are busy, sir."

"I'm calling long distance. Government business. Copy this number." He gave her the secure number for Jerusalem.

The phone rang almost immediately.

"Yes," said a tired-sounding male voice without identifying himself or his office. "Who's calling?"

Dobkin could hear the regular operators in the background. It was a busy night there. He drew some comfort from the fact. "Listen to me carefully and don't hang up."

"No, sir." The man had taken a lot of calls that evening and few of them had been pleasant, but he never considered hanging up on anyone who called on the VIP line.

"I am General Benjamin Dobkin." He gave his code name and number.

"Yes, sir." The man hit a button, and one of Chaim Mazar's Shin Beth men picked up in another room.

"I am calling from Babylon. Iraq. The place where they forced the Concorde down."

"Yes, sir."

"Have you authenticated my code?"

"Yes, sir."

"But you still don't believe it's General Dobkin?"

"No, sir."

"I don't blame you, son. Now listen, I must speak to someone who knows my voice and can authenticate it."

"Yes, sir."

Dobkin spoke slowly and clearly, but not too loudly. "Write down the names of these generals. If one of them is there, put him on so that he can identify my voice."

"Yes, sir."

Dobkin rattled off the names of a dozen army and air force generals. "If you put one of them on, he can verify my identity." He wondered if his connection would be broken somewhere along the line. Would the operator listen in just to confirm if he was still on and hear the Hebrew? What would an operator do in that case? "All right, young man?"

"Yes, sir."

The Internal Security man spoke to one of the Prime Minister's aides in the conference room over an intercom while he monitored.

The aide quickly scribbled a note and handed it to the Prime Minister.

Teddy Laskov opened his attaché case and pulled out six high-level photos, each showing a blowup of a blurred Star of David, put there by an expert airbrush. He felt strangely numb and indifferent about what he was about to do. One way or the other, the ruse would be discovered sooner or later, of course. His career was already over, but after this his name would be discredited and he might very well wind up in jail. But as long as his deception was discovered *after* the operation he didn't care. But *would* they discover it? Or would people believe that the photo was just a fortuitous illusion . . . or a miracle? In a way it was, the way it came to him that they were in Babylon, the way he was still so certain of it—so certain that he would risk jail and disgrace to make everyone else believe it. He picked up the stack of photographs on the table and straightened them. Talman, standing across the room, caught his eye. He looked sad, thought Laskov. Sad, frightened, guilty, and confused. But Talman stared at Laskov and managed a smile and a nod.

The Prime Minister pushed the note aside, unread. "Well, General? What do you have there? Color pictures and map coordinates of the Concorde delivered to Teddy Laskov by Gabriel from God? Come on. Let's see it."

Laskov seemed not to hear.

The Prime Minister's aide tapped his finger insistently on the note, and the Prime Minister finally looked down at it. He picked up and read it.

Benjamin Dobkin could hear them calling for Kassim again. The girl cried out again. An Arab on the other side of the wall heard her and made an obscene remark and laughed. The sound of rapid-fire weapons rose above the wind, and Dobkin knew there was not much time. He heard a click on the line. "Jerusalem? Jerusalem? Are you still there?"

31

Kaplan's ambush was deadly, but more than that, it gave the Israelis on the hill a warning.

The Ashbals nearly broke and ran under the withering fire, but the few remaining leaders, including Rish and Hamadi, kept their heads and returned the fire.

Kaplan might have been able to withdraw, but a madness overcame him as he slapped magazine after magazine into the hot AK-47. The sound and the smell and the vibration combined with the orange-red muzzle flash to mesmerize him. At the rate of about two hundred rounds a minute, he sent nearly a thousand rounds downrange, tearing into the Ashbal ranks. Hausner had not been stingy with the ammunition, and Kaplan meant to use it all.

Rish, Hamadi, and a few others had the presence of mind to notice that there was only one man firing at them. They maneuvered around and came up behind Kaplan. They rushed forward under the cover of the noise from Kaplan's gun and the whistling of the wind and fell on him from behind.

The Israelis on the hill heard his screams above the wind as clearly as if he had been in the next trench. He was taking a long time to die, and his screams had the dual effect—as is usually the case—of strengthening the resolve of the defiant ones and shaking the will of the faint-hearted.

Hausner took the PA microphone and screamed into it. His voice carried into the wind and down to the city wall. "Rish! Hamadi! You are animals! You are subhumans! I'll rip your balls off, Rish! When I get you, I'll rip your balls off!" Hausner's screams became shrill and took on a frenzied quality, almost indistinguishable from the agonized shrieks of Moshe Kaplan or the wild baying of the jackals which had begun again around the base of the mound.

Men and women on the hill looked away from one another as Hausner howled, bellowed, and roared with primeval sounds mixed with the most vulgar and obscene threats and invectives that anyone could imagine. The man had clearly lost control.

Someone—it sounded like Burg—took the microphone from Hausner and shouted words of encouragement and comfort to Kaplan. It did little good. The man continued to die slowly and horribly.

The Israelis began probing fire down the slope. The few remaining Molotov cocktails were thrown out into the night to try to illuminate the slope, but the wind and the sand smothered them before they could burn for very long.

The last of the Ashbals, fewer than forty, came up the slope in pairs, spread far apart. The wind pushed at their backs, driving them onward. The sand and dust masked their movements, while the noise of the wind covered their sounds. Even their muzzle flashes couldn't be seen clearly in the blinding dust.

The Israelis bailed sand from their shredded defenses and began returning the fire. AK-47's began jamming almost immediately, but specially trained teams ran up and down the line field stripping the malfunctioning rifles and swabbing them with lubricants from the Concorde. Still, the sand took its toll of guns on both sides, but more so among the defenders who lacked the cleaning and protective paraphernalia of the Ashbals.

The odds appeared to be even for this round, but Hausner, Burg, and for that matter just about everyone else knew that the *Sherji* was going to be the Israelis' downfall. Also, the defenses were weakened, the ruses were used up, and the ammunition was running out. Hunger and the intermediate stages of dehydration completed the job of reducing Israeli fighting effectiveness. There also seemed to be a crisis in leadership, and it was infectious down to the last man and woman.

In addition, many believed, along with Ariel Weizman, that the back door was open, that the west slope and the Euphrates were unguarded. But, in fact, Hamadi had sent a party from the east slope to the river bank within minutes of losing radio communication with Sayid Talib. Those Ashbals at the base of the west wall had been anxiously waiting for an attempted retreat down the steep slope and were still waiting.

The Ashbals used ammunition as though it were sand, spraying it into the Israeli lines. They fired long bursts as they angled horizontally over the side of the slope, advancing a few meters upward each time they made a sideward run.

Hausner stood on his command mound with Burg. He had calmed down considerably, and Burg thought he looked all right. But to Burg's annoyance and discomfort, he had asked Miriam Bernstein to act as his special messenger and aide. Technically, she and Esther Aronson were still under arrest, but no one objected when Hausner removed any restrictions on their movements. Miriam did not mention Kaplan or the scene with the PA microphone.

Hausner spoke above the noise. "When the ammunition is almost gone, some of our people will make a run for the west slope."

Burg nodded. "And I'm certain there are Ashbals there waiting for that very thing. We have to reiterate our orders to stand fast and fight hand to hand."

"They're not soldiers," Hausner reminded him. "They will do whatever their instincts tell them to do, in the end." He lowered his voice so that it was barely audible. "Some of them have formed a suicide pact.... After what happened to Kaplan, suicide looks inviting... I can't blame them...."

There was a long silence on the small mound. The makeshift banner stood out straight in the steady wind, but brown dust had muted the colors of Tel Aviv's waterfront, and the aluminum staff tilted farther and farther downward.

Miriam began to say something, then stopped.

"What is it?" asked Hausner.

She began again. "Well... while we still have the ammunition and while the Ashbals are still some distance down the east slope, perhaps we should . . . withdraw quickly, cross the hilltop, and drop down the west slope—in force and organized—not a disorderly retreat. We should be able to break through whatever small force they have placed at the river bank. We can take to the river and float away in the darkness."

Hausner and Burg looked at each other, then at her for a few seconds. Hausner spoke. "Aren't you forgetting the wounded?"

"They will be just as lost in an orderly retreat as in a disorderly flight. We have a responsibility to the majority."

Burg spoke. "You've come a long way. But which way?"

"Why does it sound so awful coming from me?" she asked rhetorically. "Yet it does, doesn't it?" She paused. "Anyway, I would stay behind with other volunteers to look after the wounded, of course. I am practically under sentence of death anyway. Aren't I?"

Hausner shook his head. "Even when you make hard decisions, you somehow make them sound soft. The hard fact is that if we retreat—orderly or disorderly—or if we are being overrun and are fighting hand to hand—the first thing we do is shoot the wounded." He put his hand up to quiet her. "Don't be a fool, Miriam. You heard what they did to Kaplan. God knows what they did to Deborah Gideon."

"But . . . they want hostages."

"Maybe," interjected Burg. "But maybe not anymore. Maybe all they want now is revenge. Anyway, if Rish and Hamadi—if either of them is still alive—could stop them from massacring everyone, then the best we can hope for is to be subjected to a slow, more refined torture until we give up whatever state secrets we possess. No, we are not leaving wounded or nurses behind, and we are not going to try to move in the dark. The best trained and most disciplined armies are wary of night maneuvers. If *we* try it I'm convinced it will be a disaster."

"Then what *are* our options?" asked Bernstein. "You refuse to order a retreat or a surrender, and you are not encouraging mass suicide. What is going to become of us then?"

Hausner turned away from her. "I don't know," he said. "The best ending I can envision, outside of rescue, is that each and every man and woman dies in battle. That won't happen, of course. There will be surrenders and captures. There will be suicides, and there will be murders. Maybe some of us will be overlooked in the dark and escape. It will be very much like every other siege when the besiegers break through."

No one spoke. The sound of battle settled into an orderly pattern. Both sides were tired and both sides sensed that this was the last fight. Everyone moved mechanically as though it were a formalized dance—a ritual whose end would come at a fixed time regardless of what they did to hasten it.

The Ashbals kept a respectable three hundred- to four hundred-meter distance and maneuvered mostly laterally, trying to keep the Israelis off balance and at the same time seeking out their weakest sectors.

There was still over three hours left until dawn, but actual daylight would come somewhat later unless the wind dropped and the dust settled.

This was to be a battle of attrition and logistics, and the Ashbals still had a small advantage in manpower and guns and an overwhelming superiority in ammunition, food, medical supplies, and water. They had only to remain deployed and draw fire until they were certain that the Israelis were at the end of their ammunition. They gambled on the principle that even with strict fire discipline the Israelis' ammunition could not hold out until dawn.

Burg tried to formulate several plans in his mind. Flee now? Counterattack? Wait until the end and fight hand to hand? Kill the wounded? Kill Hausner? Would they be rescued at the eleventh hour? Not likely. "What happened to Dobkin?"

Hausner turned and looked southwest, out to where the village of Ummah was supposed to be. He stared as though he were trying to make contact with Dobkin. He turned again, due south, toward the Ishtar Gate. "I have a feeling he is all right."

Miriam was holding onto his arm, openly showing Berg how matters stood. "I wonder if he's made contact with anyone?"

"Well," said Burg. "I can tell you this—even if by some miracle he is speaking to some kind of authority right now, I don't believe help would arrive in time." He looked at Hausner as if for confirmation, but what he was really inviting now was one of Hausner's contradictions.

Hausner turned his back to the wind and looked west. He pointed toward the invisible horizon. "I can't help but think that Teddy Laskov will be as good as his word—that he is out there now with his squadron of fighters, looking for us, getting closer. . ."

Burg looked at Hausner, pointing into the sky. "That's a

rather optimistic statement for you, Jacob," he said carefully. "I hope you're right."

Hausner folded his arms across his chest. "You know, Burg, I can't seem to accept the idea that all those very clever fellows in Tel Aviv and Jerusalem could still be sitting around with their fingers up their asses. I expected more from them. Is that patriotism? I suppose. Well, perhaps I'm expecting too much. After all, I was one of those clever fellows, too, and look how I fouled things up, Isaac. They're entitled to a few days off, too."

Burg couldn't help but laugh. "Not today." Whenever he started doubting Hausner's reasoning, the man showed a flash of insight.

A runner approached, and Burg walked to meet her.

Miriam had been standing off a few meters listening silently to Hausner and Burg. She came up beside Hausner now and took his arm again and squeezed it tightly. She thought of Teddy Laskov. She had been thinking of him less and less lately. After they crashed, she pictured him doing just what Hausner had said—swooping down in that big steel charger and rescuing her ... everyone. But in reality she knew that he was probably in disgrace, and she knew that she was partly responsible for that. At first she refused to make the connection between her influence on him and his actions in the air, but the connection was there for anyone who knew them both, and she had finally faced up to it at about the same time she had faced up to a lot of other realities.

Hausner made realities real for her as no other man ever would or could. Other men in her life went along with her conception of the world in order to flatter her or be polite. That was the type of man she attracted. Thin men with glasses who sat next to her at seminars and committee meetings. Men who spoke in party jargon and repeated clichés and bromides as if they had made them up that morning.

Laskov had been different from most of the men she had known, and so had her husband. They were somewhat alike, and in her mind she characterized them both as noble savages. Jacob Hausner was another variation of the type but more extreme. She might have gone through this whole experience in Babylon without having changed her perceptions of the world very drastically. Hausner had *forced* her eyes open. She didn't like what she saw, but now she could objectively weigh the pros and cons of a proposal to shoot the wounded without going into fits of moral outrage. Was that good or bad? It was neither. It just *was*.

"Do you know Teddy Laskov well?" she asked Hausner.

"Not well. Our paths cross now and then."

She nodded. After a few seconds she said, hesitantly. "Do you like him?"

"Who?" He let the silence drag out. "Oh. Laskov. I suppose. He's easier to deal with than you political types."

She smiled in the dark. After a while she said, "He reminds me of you."

"Who? Laskov? Is that so?"

She squeezed his arm tighter. Friends her age who remembered the camps were bitter and disillusioned with mankind. Many had psychological problems. She was determined not to be scarred, and she had overcompensated. She was well adjusted and optimistic to the point where a psychiatrist friend had jokingly called it a neurosis. Yet she was scarred, of course. People said they saw it in her eyes, and she saw it herself in the mirror. "I'm certain he thinks this is all his fault."

"Well, then, we do have something in common."

"You're both egocentric, and you think that all the good and all the bad that happens around you is a result of your actions."

"Isn't it?"

"Teddy Laskov and I were lovers," she said suddenly.

Burg overheard her as he walked back toward the mound. He was still annoyed at her presence. Now this. It was really too much. He turned his back on them and walked away.

"And you will be again," said Hausner.

"I don't think so."

"The question is irrelevant right now, Miriam." He sounded impatient.

"You're not—?"

"Not at all. Listen. You go on to the Concorde and see how Becker is doing with his radios. If there's nothing to report—and there won't be—stay there."

"Why?"

"Just stay there, damn it! I don't have to explain my orders to anyone else, and I don't have to explain them to you."

She took a step, then turned. "I won't see you again, will I?"

"You will. I promise."

She looked up at him. "I won't see you again."

He didn't know what to say.

She reached up and took his head and pulled it down to her and kissed him.

He took her hands and disengaged himself. "Don't leave the aircraft," he said softly. "No matter what happens, promise?"

"Will I see you again?"

"Yes."

They stood looking at each other for some time. She reached up slowly, touched his face, then turned quickly and ran off into the dark.

Hausner watched her until he could not see her any longer.

He coughed some dust up out of his throat and wiped his running eyes. If there was any divine meaning or message in this senseless ordeal, if there was any secular lesson to be learned here, he couldn't think of what it could be. It was the same old human circus of bravery and cowardice, selfishness and selflessness, cleverness and stupidity, mercy and heartlessness. Only the clowns were different. How many times did the show have to be performed for whoever was up there watching? And why didn't it all end quickly? Why did God give them the cleverness and strength to prolong their own suffering when the end was preordained? Hausner had that uneasy feeling again—that it was a great cosmic joke directed at him. He turned toward Burg and shouted. "This is God's way of punishing me for not giving up smoking as I promised my father I would." He laughed into the wind.

Burg put his hand in his pocket and fingered the small .22 pistol there.

32

"Are you *there*, Jerusalem?"

"Still here . . . General. Stand by," said the duty operator.

The Prime Minister tapped his pencil on the table for several seconds and looked down at the note again, then looked up. "I assume many of you could recognize General Dobkin's voice if you heard it." He tried to control the edge of excitement in his voice.

There was a loud outburst of questions and exclamations, and people rose to their feet. The Prime Minister slapped the table for silence. "Be quiet and listen carefully." He signaled to the communications man in the alcove, and a loud rushing sound came over several speakers in the room. The Prime Minister pressed a button on the console in front of him and spoke into a microphone mounted on the console. "Who is this?"

Dobkin recognized the slightly mocking voice at once. His senses reeled for a second, then he steadied himself and swallowed. "This is General Benjamin Dobkin, Mr. Prime

Minister." He paused. "Do you recognize my voice?"

"No." But it was obvious to the Prime Minister that there were people in the room who thought they did.

Dobkin tried to bring his voice under control, to sound as natural as possible. "Is there anyone there who can recognize my voice, sir?"

"You better hope there is." The Prime Minister looked around the table. A few heads nodded tentatively. A general who had been a colonel under Dobkin added, "Or a very good impersonation."

"Go ahead, General," said the Prime Minister, still not fully convinced, but very excited. "Where are you calling from?"

Teddy Laskov held the forged photographs tightly in his hands. Slowly, he began moving them back toward his attaché case.

"Babylon," said the voice over the speaker.

The room exploded with exclamations and most heads turned toward Laskov and Talman. The Prime Minister hit the table for silence, but he could not quiet the room. He spoke loudly into the microphone. "Where are you calling from, General? The telephone, I mean? Are you at *liberty?*"

"Yes, I'm at liberty. I'm calling from the guest house here, sir. Near the museum." Dobkin tried to control his voice, but it wavered slightly.

The Prime Minister tried, also, to sound composed, but his voice was becoming tremulous. "Yes. All right. Can you give us a situation report, General? What the hell is going on?"

Dobkin knew that the entire Cabinet, and most of the important men in the military were listening. He collected his thoughts and gave a clear, concise recapitulation of everything that had happened since they were lost over the Mediterranean.

A half-dozen aides ran in and out of the conference room with army ordnance maps of the area, facts and figures about flight times to Babylon, ground elevations, weather, time of first light and sunrise, and a hundred other items of input that had been assembled ever since Laskov had made his statement about Babylon. It would all have to be considered before any final operational decisions could be made.

As Dobkin spoke, he could hear men and women passing through the lobby outside his door. The walking wounded going somewhere. A door opened and shut off the lobby. A radio went on in the room where the card game had ended. A woman's husky voice came out of the radio singing one of those interminable Arab songs. A few of the Ashbals joined in. The noise masked his voice, but it also kept him from hearing if anyone was near the door.

"What do you suggest, General?"

Dobkin recognized the voice of General Gur. "Suggest? I suggest, General Gur, that you come and get us the hell out of here."

"How are those mud flats on the west bank?" asked Air Force General Katzir.

"Still wet," said Dobkin truthfully. "But it looks drier farther from the river."

"The road you landed on," said Katzir, "do you think it would support a C-130?"

"I can't say, General. I think we ripped it up when we put down."

"We may have to use helicopters," said an unidentified voice.

"No," said Dobkin. "No time for that. They're being attacked right *now*."

Another voice said something about sending a squadron of fighter craft in first. Dobkin could hear several voices being picked up by the microphone now. He heard Teddy Laskov's name mentioned. He'd thought that the man would be in retirement by now, but apparently he was at the meeting. Dobkin answered a few more questions as he listened to the debate heat up. Suddenly, he interrupted in a loud voice, "Mr. Prime Minister. I'm afraid I have to go. There are three gentlemen here with AK-47's, and when they comprehend what is happening, they will surely want me to get off the telephone."

In Jerusalem they heard what sounded like a scuffle, then a sharp crack like a gunshot, or perhaps something breaking. Then the telephone went dead.

Miriam Bernstein sat in the copilot's seat next to David Becker. "You don't think *anyone* heard your SOS, then?"

"No." He turned the radio down but left it on so that he could monitor. "The Lear is still up there, but I suspect he's in trouble."

"Why?"

"Why?" The fact that Hausner had sent a messenger to get a report from him and not come himself was an indication of how little faith everyone had in his end of this operation. Miriam Bernstein was, however, the Deputy Minister of Transportation and, therefore, both Hausner's and Becker's boss. But that didn't seem to matter anymore. "Why? Because he can't land in this dust, that's why. He will have to land and refuel somewhere where the dust is not so thick. Then *maybe* I can get a call through." He glanced sideways at her. "Do you want to go and make your report? That's all I have."

"Later." She stared out the shattered windshield. "Are you afraid to die?" she asked suddenly.

He turned his head and looked at her in the glow of the instrument panels. He hardly expected such a question from this very reserved woman. "No. I don't think so. I . ... I'm afraid to fly again . . . but not to die. Funny . . ." He had no idea why he let himself be drawn into such intimacy. "And you?"

"Almost everyone I've been close to is dead." She changed the subject. "What do you think of Jacob Hausner?"

He looked up from the book that he had begun to write in. He suspected that Hausner and Bernstein had become very close. But that didn't change his public or private opinion of Jacob Hausner. "A Nazi."

"He likes you."

Becker didn't understand where the conversation was going or why. Apparently she was overwrought and just wanted to talk. People did funny things when they were staring death in the face. He had just admitted that he was afraid to fly, and he wouldn't have admitted that to his psychiatrist. "Don't get me wrong, Mrs. Bernstein. I'm glad we had him along for the ride. Things would probably have been all over for us by now without him." He kept looking at her. She didn't *look* overwrought. She appeared to be . . . happy, excited. He looked down and began writing again.

"I'm in love with him."

Becker broke the point on his pencil. "Oh." The gunfire seemed to grow louder, and Becker looked up. The night looked more frightening, more hideous and ominous through the glass of the flight deck than it did when he was outside in it. Every frightening thing he had seen he had seen through a piece of plexiglas, and he was increasingly associating horror with plexiglas, danger with plexiglas. Death with plexiglas. When he looked through a car windshield or even a house window, his stomach would churn, and he had never been consciously aware of the reason until now. That was an interesting discovery, but it was a little late. "Oh. That's . . . I'm . . ."

"What are you writing... David... may I call...?"

"Yes. Of course." He closed the book. "The log. The ship's log."

She leaned toward him. "A log? You mean you've been keeping a record of all that's happened?"

"Well, only in a very dry, officialese way."

"May I see it?" She held out her hand and he passed it to her. She sat back, opened it, and flipped through the pages. She read a random entry. *1602 hrs: Switch to alt. tac. freq. Gen. Laskov broadcast last message: E-2D will keep us on radar. Laskov leaves decision to use Phoenix to us. Squadron turns back.* She flipped a few more pages. *18:31 hrs: Flt. off. Hess dead from skull fracture caused by brick through windshield during rollout. Pilot should have had supersonic visor raised sooner in prep. for crash land. Might have averted death.* She stared at that entry for a few seconds, then closed the book and looked up. She forced a smile. "We are called the People of the Book, and we are also a bookish people. The written word has kept us together since the Diaspora. It's odd that no one else thought to keep a chronicle of what we did here."

"Well..." Becker found a cigarette stub and lit it. "It's hardly a chronicle, Mrs. Bernstein—"

"Miriam."

He hesitated. "Miriam, It's just my job to—"

"But that's the point, David. It's always someone's job. A scribe. A keeper of the books. A scholar. A ship's captain. Throughout history someone has always had the job of keeping the written records, and sometimes those records have been powerful and illuminating documents. Ezra was a scribe, and he has left us the only account of the repatriation of the exiles from Babylon. In modern circumstances, it can be an airline captain who performs this function." She smiled at him.

"I suppose."

She leaned toward him. "I can't convince you of your own importance, but can I convince you to hide this book in some way?"

"I suppose that's a good idea."

She started to pass the book back to him, but hesitated. "Would you mind if I sat awhile and wrote my own account of what has happened here? I'll try not to take up much space."

Becker forced a laugh. "Take as much space as you like. I made what I believe was the final entry just now."

"Thank you. Do you have carbon paper? I'd like to make a second copy of what I write. We can bury the book and leave the copy of my writing on the craft."

Becker found a piece of carbon paper in his flight kit. "The book itself has to remain on board. We can bury your copy."

"All right." She took the carbon paper. "Thank you."

"No one is going to see either of them, you know."

She looked up at him. "The Ravensbrück Prayer was written on a scrap of paper, David."

"That prayer has a lot of meaning for you."

"It did." She looked out the windshield for some time. "It was unsigned, you know, but the camp was mostly for women, and so perhaps that can give us a clue to the author." She passed a hand over her face. "They told me that . . . that my mother died at Ravensbrück. And so I like to think that perhaps she wrote it." She lowered her voice, and it was barely audible above the noise outside. "The words once had greater meaning for me, but what still does have meaning is that the human being who wrote it had faith. Faith that it would be found, but more importantly, faith that there would be free people left in the world after that terrible time who would find something of value in those words. And so it survived on a scrap of paper, although the author probably did not survive. It has been reproduced a million times, and it will survive the next holocaust." She smiled again at Becker. "Genesis was originally written with lampblack on papyrus, David. If that first scribe had listened to someone like you, we would never have known how the world began."

He forced a smile. "I'm convinced."

"Good." She took a pen from him and bent over the logbook. She wrote in quick, flowing Hebrew characters.

Suddenly she looked up, and there were tears in her eyes. "That prayer *had* meaning for me, but it has very little now because it was a prayer of forgiveness—a call to turn the other cheek. The person who wrote it was tested in the extreme for those qualities and was not found wanting. I have been tested here—not very hard, mind you, not the way the testing was done at Ravensbrück—and I am no longer forgiving. The fact is, I'm happy the way it has turned out. I look forward to shooting the first enemy soldier who puts his head in here. If I make widows and orphans and childless parents and grieving friends before I die, I'll be sorry for those unfortunate people, but it's nothing personal. Do you understand that? Does it sound so terrible?"

He shook his head. "An eye for an eye."

"Yes. And a tooth for a tooth." She turned a page in the logbook and continued writing.

Hausner sensed, without looking at his watch, that it was close to dawn. The battle was nearly finished, and only a few Israeli rounds were being fired downslope.

The Ashbals were advancing cautiously yet casually, laughing and shouting to each other through the blowing sand. They were not unaware that this apparent exhaustion of Israeli ammunition might be yet another ruse, but if it were, then the Israelis were playing it very close. In fact, an advance party of sappers had actually breached the perimeter at the south end near the promontory and had found the trenches deserted.

They moved slowly through the windblown darkness. They could sense the kill now and they were savoring it. They came through the fallen abatis and over the crest. They paused curiously at the trenches, then moved over them. They experienced that strange, subdued exultation that comes with violating the long-forbidden lair of the enemy.

Occasionally, a round or two of Israeli fire sent them scattering and slowed down their movements, but for the most part, except for the steady wind, which no one consciously heard any longer, there was an eerie silence on the hilltop.

In military terms, resistance was light and scattered. The Ashbals were having everything their own way, but patience and caution were still called for. After coming so far, none of the survivors wanted to meet his end within minutes of the final victory. They all wanted to share in the fruits of that victory.

The Ashbals refrained from answering the scattered Israeli fire for fear of drawing return fire on themselves. They signaled quietly to one another in the dark and tried to join up and form a single search line to sweep across the flat terrain. They did not want anyone slipping through their advance. The Ashbals in the center of the evolving line could begin to distinguish the outline of the Concorde whenever there was a break in the dust clouds.

The Israelis moved back slowly and quietly, firing only enough to keep the Ashbals at a distance and slow down their advance. There was no final plan, no last orders from the command post, but the retreat was orderly. About half the Israelis had decided to try to escape down the western slope and half had decided to stay and meet their fate where they stood.

The wounded were moved out of the shepherds' hut and into the Concorde where it was felt they might have a better chance to survive a massacre if they were temporarily out of the way during the worst of it. There were, however, persistent rumors that the wounded were to be killed before the Áshbals could get to them. There seemed to be some confusion on that point.

The Israelis on the west slope fired down toward the Euphrates to try to determine if there were any Ashbals there.

Ahmed Rish spoke on his field radio and ordered his small force there to return the fire. He didn't want the Israelis to run inadvertently into a massacre down there. He wanted them for himself on the hill.

The Ashbals on the river bank fired up the glacis, and everyone's heart sank as they discovered what they really had known all along—there was no escape route. There was a great deal of confusion, and some of the people who had counted on escaping that way began to weep.

Hamadi took a call over the radio from the officer in charge of their rear area, Al-Bakr. "Hamadi here. What? Who is he? Well, find out! Did he complete the call? The Baghdad operator confirms that? What was he saying? Yes, I know you don't speak Hebrew, damn it! I'm sure he speaks Arabic. After you take his first eye out, he will speak it for you. Yes. Keep me informed." He handed the phone back to the operator. He looked at Rish. "Ahmed."

Rish turned to him as they advanced slowly through the dust. "I understood enough of it. It is of no importance."

"But if he got through—"

"No importance!"

Hamadi turned away. More and more he felt that their fate was sealed. They were being hemmed in on all sides by forces over which they had no control. If he were to turn around and walk away into the night, he would live to see the sun come out of Persia. But he could not do that any more than he could kill Rish.

John McClure watched the green tracer rounds arc up from the base of the glacis and pass in front of his foxhole. "Well, we're not going to get down that way." He put his last two cartridges into his Ruger. "Well, Colonel, did you learn how to say 'take me to the American ambassador' yet?"

Richardson carefully put on his blue tunic and buttoned it.

"We're going to have to be very careful in the next few minutes, McClure. Our lives may hang on a misunderstood word or gesture."

McClure placed the first loaded chamber to the right of the hammer. "Why'd you do it, Tom?"

Richardson straightened his tie and uselessly brushed some dust from his shoulders.

"I said, why'd you do it?"

Richardson looked at him across the small foxhole. "Do what?"

McClure cocked the pistol, and the cylinder turned left so that the cartridge was under the raised hammer.

Richardson found his cap and poured sand out of it. He looked down the big open muzzle. "Money. I have a weakness for expensive things."

"How much money, Tom?"

"A cool million. American."

McClure gave a low whistle. "Not bad."

"No. Safely deposited in a Swiss bank, I should add. I was supposed to get another mil afterwards, but I don't think so now."

"Maybe they'll still come across, Tom. Those people have lots of it."

"That's right, John. Those people have more petrodollars—our dollars—than they know what to do with. The West is hemorrhaging money and getting transfusions of oil."

"Interesting figure of speech, Tom. But we're not talking about that or about Israel, either. We're talking about you, Tom—a Colonel in the United States Air Force—selling out to a foreign power. That's still against the law—even in America."

Richardson straightened the cap on his head. "Well, I haven't been home in some time so I can't verify that, John. It used to be all right to publish classified Pentagon papers. Are you sure it's still against the law to sell out to a foreign power?"

"Don't temporize, Tom."

"Right. Well, I'll take my punishment when I get home. I wish you'd put that thing down. I'm not running off."

"People talk better when they're looking down a muzzle, Tom." McClure spit out a matchstick. "I thought you liked these people."

"It's not very fashionable to be an open anti-Semite these days."

"I see."

Richardson's face underwent a remarkable change. His mouth hardened and his eyes became narrow slits. "So, I went and had a celebration drink down at the Officers' Club with Israeli flyers who I was training at Travis in 1967. And I commiserated with them in 1973 after the near disaster. The next thing I know, someone puts in a good word for me and I'm posted here. I almost vomited when I got the assignment."

McClure did not respond.

After several long seconds, Richardson looked up at McClure. "Anyway, no one was supposed to get hurt," he said softly.

"But we're not talking about them, Tom. I may not like them either, but I'd hold out under torture before I'd betray them. Know why, Tom? 'Cause that's what Uncle says I got to do. That's what I get paid for . . . Tom."

Richardson ignored the entire exchange. His face softened again. "That reminds me, John," he said brightly. "Can I purchase you? A hundred thou?"

"Sorry."

"Half?"

"Nope." McClure found his last match.

"Plus the whole second mil if I get it?"

McClure seemed not to be paying attention. He chewed on the matchstick and spoke as he chewed. "You said no one was supposed to get hurt. But a lot of people got real hurt, Tom. Real hurt."

"I know. And I *am* sorry about all of this, John. None of this was supposed to happen. Who could have foreseen this? That's my real regret. All these casualties." He stared out into the dust.

"If no one was supposed to get hurt, Tom, why'd you *pick* 02?"

Richardson licked his dry lips. "Well . . . all right . . . *if* there was to be any trouble, then 01 was to be the . . . demonstration. We knew any trouble would come from Avidar. Not Becker."

McClure let out a short laugh. "*Knew*? How can you know these things? Suppose that against all we know about human nature and that kind of thing, Becker had gassed it and Avidar had played your game? That would have left you trying to tread sky at a couple thousand meters, my boy."

"Calculated gamble, John. You see, I gamble with my own life, too. I'm no coward." He continued to stare out into the dust.

"I hear voices. Should we go out and surrender or should we sit tight and wait for them to get here?"

"You're awfully goddamned anxious to surrender to these young gerbils or whatever the fuck they call themselves, Tom. Do you think they're going to give you a hero's welcome, Richardson? They're going to murder you, you stupid son-of-a-bitch. And then they're going to murder me to make sure no one knows about you."

Richardson shook his head and smiled. "No, they won't kill me. Rish has a boss, and that boss and I worked out a guarantee for my safety. We foresaw problems with Rish. If I'm killed, then a letter in my safe at the Embassy will be opened, and it names names—Arab terrorist agents in Israel, including my contacts and others. I think ahead, John." He paused. "I won't let them harm you, either."

"Thanks, Tom. You're better than the American ambassador. Well, I wonder if Rish is in control of these guys . . . or in control of himself. I think maybe they're all so worked up they'll shishkebob you. . . . But maybe they won't." He seemed to be thinking. "You know, Tom, American justice *is* very lenient these days. That's why you don't care if I get you home. In most countries they'd hang you up by your left nut in a dungeon and forget about you. In the good old U.S. of A., a general court-martial or a Federal trial will get you ten to twenty—if we can get a conviction at all—and you'll walk in six . . . or less. Walk right to Switzerland. And the U.S. won't turn you over to Israel afterwards because that would raise one hell of a squawk."

"I don't make the rules." Richardson looked wary.

"No, but I do, sometimes. When I'm authorized to." He paused. "Did you say if you died, that would blow the cover on a whole lot of terrorists?"

"Wait! There's no need for any wet stuff, John. There's lots of things to consider here."

"Yes, there are, and if we had more time, then maybe we could work something out. But time is something we don't have."

"Hold it!" Richardson instinctively put his hands out in front of him. "I can guarantee your safety. These people—"

McClure thrust out his big .357 Magnum between Richardson's hands and fired a few inches from his heart. The impact sent Richardson's head snapping back and his officer's hat flew off and was taken up into the wind and sailed westward.

•   •   •

David Becker moved quickly down the ramp. In his hand was a metal can that contained a carbon copy of Miriam Bernstein's short chronicle, wrapped in oil rags and plastic. He picked a spot at the base of the earth ramp and dug a quick hole with a length of aluminum brace. He thought it was a useless exercise, but she seemed so intent on it. She appeared to be brave enough about death and didn't show any signs of hysteria, but she also seemed a little irrational about this chronicle, so he thought it best to go along with her. He placed the can in the hole and covered it quickly. The logbook itself, containing the original of her chronicle, was tucked under a loose floor section in the cabin. There *was* a chance that Israel would repatriate the Concorde someday, and so perhaps a worker would find the log. But as for the buried chronicle he wondered if it would ever be uncovered. Perhaps it would. After all, he had uncovered Pazuzu.

He straightened up and wiped his hands. He could hear two Arabs shouting to each other above the wind. They weren't more than two hundred meters away. An Israeli took a shot at the voices, and one of them let out a sound of pain. No, thought Becker, they will not be in a good mood when they get here. Yet he never once regretted the decision to fight, and he had never heard anyone else say they regretted it, either.

He moved over to the front wheel well and spoke to Peter Kahn, who was still working on the auxiliary power unit. "Come on, Peter. It's a little late for that. Come onto the flight deck."

Kahn took his head out from the well. "What the hell for? Look, when they get here, I want them to see Peter Kahn breaking his ass on this son-of-a-bitching power unit. Maybe they'll feel sorry for me and give me a ticket to Lod."

Becker smiled. "All right. . . . I . . . I'll see you around."

Kahn looked at him. "Right. See you around, Captain."

Becker turned toward the ramp and slowly mounted, oblivious to the rounds whistling through the air around him.

He walked across the wing and passed into the cabin. He had to pick his way through the wounded to reach the flight deck.

Inside the flight deck he took his seat next to Miriam. "It's done."

"Thank you."

There was a long silence. Becker finally spoke. "I always knew I'd die in this thing."

Miriam reached out and touched his arm. "I think you're the bravest man I've ever met."

Becker looked down at the control panel. He felt that he should be doing something, but he had orders from Hausner to stay in the cockpit no matter what happened. He turned the radio up and began scanning the frequencies. He would do that until someone put a bullet in his back. He felt sorry for Miriam—for all the women. He was certain the Ashbals had a special fate reserved for them. "Do you want to stay here? I mean . . ."

"I'm under orders, too." She smiled.

He looked out the windshield. "There are people gathering in the shepherds' hut. I think they are going to—"

"Yes, I see them. I'll stay with you, if you don't mind."

He hesitated, then reached out and took her hand and squeezed it.

The group of Israelis who were intent on suicide gathered in the blood-soaked, fetid shepherds' hut after the wounded had been removed.

Arabs, as a people, did not often take their own lives, but no one in the hut was surprised when Abdel Majid Jabari and Ibrahim Arif entered. It was understood that these two, above everyone else, were far better off dead.

The hut was completely dark, and that made things easier for everyone. There was little talking, only some dangling, whispered half-sentences as someone new entered.

After a few minutes, it became apparent that no one else was coming, but no one present knew what to do next, and a stillness fell over the hut.

In all, there were eleven men and women gathered in three small groups in separate corners. In one group was Joshua Rubin, who was the prime mover behind the suicide pact. Lying on the floor near him was Yigael Tekoah. Tekoah was bitter over the fact that he had not died when the Arab bullets cut him down as he shouted the warning from his outpost. Now he had to face death again. With Rubin and Tekoah were four young Knesset aides, two men and two women, all members of the Masada Defense League.

In another corner was the steward, Yaakov Leiber, and the two stewardesses, Beth Abrams and Rachel Baum. Beth Abrams had spent the last two days caring for the wounded and watching them suffer. She had changed from a happy girl to a despondent one in a very short time. Rachel Baum was lying on the floor between Lieber and Abrams. She, like Tekoah, had refused to be moved to the Concorde with the rest of the wounded. She was in terrible pain from her wounds and didn't see much sense in waiting on the Corcorde for more pain. She had nursed Kaplan and had heard him die, and she was frightened enough to take this way out.

Yaakov Leiber had considered his three children before he made his decision, but Rubin had convinced him that no one would survive what the Ashbals had planned for them. Still, he was having second thoughts about it. He could see that the two stewardesses needed him there. He spoke softly to them in the dark. Beth Abrams was crying but Rachel Baum was quiet. He knelt next to her and took her hand. Beth Abrams also knelt and took both their hands.

In the third corner, Abdel Jabari and Ibrahim Arif sat back on their haunches. They had lived alone among these people for over thirty years, and now they were to die alone among them.

Jabari lit his last cigarette and whispered to Arif. "You know, Ibrahim, I always knew that I would not die a natural death."

Arif was pale and shaking. He, too, lit a cigarette in the black room and drew heavily on it. He tried to make a joke. "I may die of a heart attack yet." He drew again on the cigarette. "How are we going to work this?"

"I think there are two or three pistols. They will pass them around."

Arif's hands were shaking so badly he could barely hold the cigarette. He didn't see how he was going to hold a pistol. "I don't think I can do it, Abdel." He stood.

Jabari grabbed his arm and pulled him violently back into the corner. "Don't be an idiot," he hissed. "Did you hear what they did to Moshe Kaplan? Can you conceive of all the things they will do to *you*? Save yourself from that, old friend."

Arif began to cry, and Jabari comforted him. Jabari's only regret was that he had not said good-bye to Miriam. In fact, he had hardly seen her at all in the past two days. He had not wanted to burden her with his company, but now he wished that he had spent more time with her. He suspected that she was in love with Jacob Hausner, and he had been concerned over her choice. Jabari believed that there was an actual place called Heaven, as the Koran so vividly described, and he believed he was going there, but he could not believe that Miriam Bernstein would not be there, too. "Come, Arif. Calm yourself. It's a better world on the other side. Cool gardens, fountains, flowing wine, and virgins. Is that a reason to weep?"

Yigael Tekoah, who did not like Arabs and did not like the idea of having them on the peace mission, called softly across the room. "Abdel. Ibrahim. Courage."

Jabari called back. "We are all right, Yigael. Thank you." Jabari was still troubled that he could not see Miriam before he died. He was tempted to leave the hut and look for her, but he did not want to leave Arif alone. The Ashbals were too close. He wanted to make certain that he cheated Rish of his fun. But this waiting was not good for anyone. Finally, he broke the silence and asked what was the procedure. No one answered.

The sounds of firing got closer, and the Israelis who were still returning fire took up positions not far from the hut. A burst of rounds slammed into the mud wall outside. This acted as a catalyst for action, and Rubin walked into the middle of the hut. He cleared his throat and spoke. "We must act soon." He waited. "If it will be easier, I will do it for you. I have the two pistols."

Jabari stood quickly and walked to the center of the room. "If you please. Quickly."

Rubin did not answer, but raised one pistol and held it up between the two points of light that he knew were Jabari's eyes. He kept the pistol from touching Jabari and fired a single bullet into his forehead.

When the loud report died away the sound of praying could be heard along with soft sobbing.

Rubin was covered with wetness and instinctively wiped it from his face and arms. He began to shake and couldn't trust himself to speak. He didn't know what to do next. His resolve to finish the job for everyone left him, and he turned the pistol and shot himself through the heart. He fell backwards into the corner and landed among the four young aides. One of the girls screamed and fainted. The three others laid him gently on the floor. The two young men recovered the pistols. They whispered hurriedly between themselves, then rose and walked over to the corner where Leiber, Abrams, and Baum were huddled together. They lit cigarette lighters and aimed the pistols, then extinguished the lighters and began squeezing on the triggers. Beth Abrams let out a sob and Leiber threw his body between the two girls and the men. One of the men fired but didn't appear to hit anything. The other young man lit his lighter again to fix his aim.

Rabbi Levin burst into the hut and saw all he wanted to see before the cigarette lighter went out. He grabbed the two young men by the collars and threw them to the floor. He screamed and swore as he delivered kicks and punches in the dark. "Did you think you could outwit me? I found you! I knew what you were up to! Out! Out! Get out!" He ran around the small hut in a frenzy, kicking and punching blindly in the dark. He tripped several times over the bodies of Uri Rubin and Abdel Jabari. He repeatedly kicked both bodies until he realized they were dead. "Out! Out! Get out of here! How dare you! How dare you do this! Take the wounded into the plane! Out!"

As soon as he had entered, his presence broke the strange spell that had hung over the room, and everyone who could move quickly ran out.

Rabbi Levin was left standing alone in the center of the hut, his body shaking and tears streaming down his face. He had done what he had to do, but he was in no way certain that he was right and they were wrong. He wondered how he was going to get the two bodies buried in the short time remaining. He wondered who they were.

The Foreign Minister, Ariel Weizman, assembled a small, lightly armed group on the west side of the perimeter near McClure's foxhole. Weizman saw Richardson lying at the bottom of the hole, a layer of dust already covering his blue uniform, but he did not have time to speculate on the meaning of that or on McClure's absence.

Ariel Weizman was determined to lead his small group down the steep glacis. His plan was to drop quickly down the slope and vault into the river the way Dobkin had done. Without wounded, it might be possible. He wished that Miriam Bernstein would reconsider and join him, but she was very much under Hausner's influence and would not budge from the Concorde. He lined up his group of men and women, all of whom were wearing the orange life jackets from the Concorde, at the edge of the steep drop. He crouched in a runner's stance and instructed them to do the same. "When I count to three, we go. Steady. Wait for my count, now."

Few orders were coming from the command post. The runners who were still operating brought only bad news to

Hausner and Burg and carried away no commands, only suggestions and encouragement.

Hausner and Burg had agreed that there came a time when the best orders were no orders, and so they let the civilian instincts for individual action and survival take over.

Hausner turned to Burg. "Would you want to take complete charge now, Isaac? I'm ready to step down."

Burg smiled wryly and shook his head. "No, thank you."

"Do you believe there was anything that I could have done that I did not do?"

Burg thought a moment. "No. Frankly, you did an excellent job. You might have been a touch more diplomatic ... maybe not." He listened to the approaching gunfire. "Our people were marvelous, too."

"Yes. They were."

The last two of Hausner's men who were in action, Marcus and Alpern, came up to the command post. Marcus gave a half salute. "What should we do now, boss?"

Hausner didn't know what to tell him. He felt obligated to say something, but couldn't think of an order to give or an expression of gratitude to pass on. "Just take as many of the bastards with you as possible." He paused. "And thank you. You were the backbone and the heart of this defense. You did a hell of a job here. No one who survives will forget that."

The two men nodded and moved off into the darkness.

Burg put his hand on Hausner's shoulder. "I think you'd better get to the Concorde before you get cut off. You promised, and she's waiting for you. I'll stay here and try to do what I can."

Hausner shook his head. "No. I don't want to see what they're going to do to her any more than she wants to see what they're going to do to me. She knows that and she's not expecting me."

"I see. Are you going to—you know."

"No. I'm not the type. I have a few things I want to say to Ahmed Rish before I go."

Burg nodded. A crooked smile passed across his face. "We did do one hell of a job, didn't we?"

"Yes, we sure as hell. ... Listen!"

"What?"

"Did you hear—?"

"Yes. Yes!"

Hausner stared upward. He thought he saw a flash of light. He could hear the distant shrill whining of jet engines. He yelled to Burg. "They found us, Isaac. They found us, damn it!"

Burg began gesticulating wildly. "Here! We're here!" Hausner forced a smile. "They're too late to help us but not too late to blow away Rish and his gang." He turned to Burg. "My faith in Israeli military intelligence is restored."

Burg was so excited he could hardly comprehend what Hausner was telling him. Then he understood. The air force had arrived—Israeli or Iraqi—but they were too late. Burg calmed down and his body seemed to sag. He nodded. "I hope Dobkin made it," was all he could think to say.

Hausner and Burg stared upward and saw the fiery trail of a missile cut across the sky.

33

The first thing Laskov did was the last thing he had promised Becker he would do. He fixed the Lear on his radar and engaged it with the long-range Phoenix missile at 160 kilometers.

The Lear pilot yawned as he looked sleepily out the windshield. The automatic pilot had kept the craft in a continuous left bank for longer than he cared to remember, and he thought he was developing vertigo. Below, the ground was obscured by the dust, but up here everything was very clear and moonlit. The dawn was creeping out of Persia, and it looked as if it would be a good day to fly. In a while he might have to fly to their camp in the Shamiyah Desert, refuel quickly, and come back—unless those fools on the ground could get it over with. He yawned again.

He glanced out of his left window and noticed a flame streaking across the sky. A second later he realized with astonishment that the light was coming toward him. He tapped the sleeping copilot on the shoulder, and they both watched the thing change course and follow them as they moved in their circle. The pilot let out a long shrill scream when he realized what it was. The Phoenix flamed up at them and seemed to hang outside their cockpit. The Israeli armorers had painted a likeness of the beautiful phoenix on its terrible namesake. The great bird seemed to smile in the first rays of sunlight, and an eye on the warhead appeared to wink at the two pilots in that split second before it consumed itself and its prey in an awful orange ball of flame. Unlike its namesake, however, there was no chance that it would rise up from its own ashes and begin a new life.

Laskov had guided his squadron in with radar. Their computers had enabled the automatic pilots to hug the terrain during the entire night flight, and they had flown under Jordanian and Iraqi radar. They had very little time to familiarize themselves with the terrain, but each pilot knew what he lacked from the briefing could be made up in skill and desire. The Mach 2 flight across Jordan and western Iraq, a thousand kilometers' distance, had taken less than forty-five minutes. Except for Laskov's craft, which carried two Phoenix missiles, the fighters carried only air-to-surface ordnance.

As soon as the Lear disappeared from his radar, Laskov spoke into his mouthpiece. "Concorde 02, this is Gabriel 32. Can you hear me?"

Miriam Bernstein heard the explosion overheard as she sat alone in the flight deck and couldn't imagine what it was, but didn't really care, either.

"Concorde 02, this is Gabriel. Do you hear me, Concorde?"

She thought she heard a faraway voice. It sounded vaguely familiar.

"Concorde 02, Concorde 02, do you *hear* me?"

She looked down at the radio as though she had never seen one before.

"Concorde 02, this is Gabriel 32. Can you hear me? Come in, please."

She fumbled with the volume dials and the microphone but really didn't understand the procedure. She yelled at the console. "Teddy! Teddy! I hear you!" She dropped the microphone in frustration and rushed from the flight deck. She yelled into the darkened cabin filled with nurses and wounded. "They're here! The air force! The air force!" The cabin erupted with noise, and she stood there for a second, transfixed. From behind her she could hear Teddy Laskov's voice as if from a dream. "Concorde 02, this is Gabriel 32. Can you hear me? Can you hear me?" She rushed out onto the wing and shouted. "David! Captain Becker!"

Becker had gone under the craft again to try to talk Kahn into coming up on the flight deck, or failing that, to say a proper good-bye. He had heard the sound of the rocket and the explosion and had known immediately what it was. He was already halfway up the earth ramp when Miriam called him. He pushed past her, tore into the cabin, and fought his way through the crowded aisle into the flight deck.

"Concorde 02, this is Gabriel 32. Concorde 02. Concorde 02. Acknowledge, please."

Becker grabbed the microphone with a trembling hand and squeezed the button as his other hand worked the dials. He squeezed so hard on the talk button that he was afraid the plastic instrument would cave in. "Loud and clear, Gabriel! Loud and clear! Position critical! Critical! Arabs inside perimeter! Can you read me, Gabriel?"

Laskov almost came out of his seat. "Loud and clear! Loud and clear! Understand situation critical, 02. Hold on. Hold on. Charlie-one-three-zero on the way with commandos. Can you hold?"

Becker's voice was quavering. "Yes. No. I don't know. Can you give support?"

"I'm a little far out yet, and I have to pull off speed to come in on you. I'll be on station in . . . four minutes. Can you mark your position with illumination?"

"Yes! I'll turn on my landing lights."

"Roger. How about JP-4?"

"Yes. Yes. We have Molotov cocktails. Will mark boundaries of our positions with fire. Also, look for tracers, Gabriel. Heavy incoming theirs—light outgoing ours."

"Roger that."

Several lightly wounded men and women were jammed into the flight deck behind Becker. Hausner's man, Jaffe, wounded but ambulatory, pushed his way out of the flight deck, through the cabin and out onto the wing. He stood on the wing and yelled out into the storm. "The air force is coming! The air force is coming! Mark our positions with kerosene! Where's Hausner? Where's Burg? Hold on! They're coming!"

Esther Aronson ran past Jaffe and jumped down off the

wing. She stumbled, fell, and rose to her feet again. She raced west across the hilltop to try to stop the Foreign Minister and his group from fleeing down the west slope.

There was a lot of shouting on the hilltop and within a few minutes the Ashbals, as well as the Israelis, knew what was happening.

Rish and Hamadi spurred their remaining troops on. They converged on the Concorde as the Israelis fell back toward it. The last few Molotov cocktails were ignited and thrown. The Israelis began using the last reserves of their ammunition that they had hoarded for the final face-to-face confrontations, and their rate of fire picked up.

The Ashbals, who had suffered so many dead and wounded already, had been moving ahead reluctantly. Each new Ashbal casualty brought general cursing and wailing. They had been caught in an understandable conflict between wanting to go in and finish the job, and lying back and hoping it would resolve itself without their having to become casualties and miss out on the inevitable rape and massacre. Now the arrival of the Israeli Air Force had suddenly altered the situation. They had to capture at least some Israelis alive, and they had to do it fast if they were to have hostages to use as bargaining points.

They fired at the Concorde when the landing lights went on, but Rish did not want a fuel explosion to kill the Israelis, and he ordered the firing on the Concorde to be directed only at the flight deck. In the first illumination of the early dawn light, the outline of the long craft could be discerned whenever the wind dropped.

After the explosion overhead, a few pieces of the Lear had fallen to the ground, and the Ashbals knew they had not much more time. Ironically, the safest place to be when the jets came was as close to the Israelis as possible. Preferably right in the Concorde with them as hostages. It was going to be a close race. A matter of minutes either way would decide it.

The Foreign Minister led his group back to the Concorde. They carried the body of Colonel Thomas Richardson, United States Air Force. They had looked for McClure but could not find him. The Foreign Minister spoke with Rabbi Levin, who reported what had happened in the hut. They both decided that the only proper course of action was to place the remaining men and women from the hut under restraint and the seven unwounded ones, including Leiber, were ordered into the rear baggage compartment.

Uri Rubin's body was carried out of the hut by the two men of the Masada Defense League and placed in a trench that had been dug for that purpose.

Ibrahim Arif carried the body of Abdel Jabari cradled in his arms like a child. He staggered under the weight and wove around with tears blinding his eyes. He refused to let anyone bury the body.

Miriam Bernstein crouched on the wing and saw the body of her friend in Arif's arms. Tears welled up in her eyes. She stood watching as the men argued over the fate of the corpse. "Arif," she shouted.

The big man looked up. "Arif, I loved him as you loved him. But he is dead and he must be put in the ground. Both our religions make that imperative. Please understand. Time is running out. Please do as they say."

Arif looked up and tried to speak but could not get his voice under control. Finally, he took a deep breath and called out. "He loved you—" He turned quickly and ran as best he could under the weight. He reached the slit trench and looked at Uri Rubin lying at the bottom of it. He looked into Jabari's open eyes. Well, good-bye, old friend. He gently lowered his friend atop the body of Uri Rubin and pushed some dirt over them both. Just then, two Israelis with rifles ran up and squeezed into the narrow trench. They felt, then saw the bodies under their feet but did not want to give up the only cover for some distance around because of it. They began firing out into the dust. One of them turned to Arif. "If you don't have a weapon, you'd better fall back. They're closing in."

Arif nodded and turned his steps back toward the Concorde. Life, he reflected, was made up of equal parts of idiocy, fear, irony, and pain. He envied Abdel his cool gardens, flowing wine, and virgins.

Laskov's copilot, Danny Lavon, spotted the kerosene fires first. The small points of light formed a more or less oblong shape around the points of the Concorde's landing lights. Streams of green tracer rounds streaked in from east to west toward the Concorde. A very few tracer rounds moved the opposite way. From time to time, a particularly large billow of dust would obscure the light sources below. From his altitude,

Lavon could see the sun above the peaks of the Zagros Mountains, but the direct rays had not yet touched Babylon. The refracted rays would have brought on first light by now, but the sand and dust looked too thick to be penetrated. He called Laskov on the intercom. "Fires at one o'clock, skipper. At the small bend in the river. We're almost overhead."

"Roger. I see it." Laskov ordered the squadron to make a close dry run at the target.

The twelve F-14's came down in tandem. They swooped out of the sky like the big birds of prey that they were. They came screaming in at low level out of the western desert and banked sharply right. Laskov came in first. He let his computer make the first run to make sure he didn't lead his squadron into an obscured piece of terrain. He cleared the hilltop by less than twenty meters and the Concorde by even less than that. The thunder of the twelve F-14's as they came in, one after the other, was deafening and frightening. The already unsettled dust rose up in huge clouds, and the earth beneath the Concorde shook.

Each fighter came down in the same fashion, its computer and sensing devices following the terrain of the ground, keeping the awesome jets close to the earth. Instinctively, everyone on the hill threw themselves down or ducked as the big fighters blotted out all visual and auditory senses.

After the pass, Laskov ordered half of his squadron south to stand by and be prepared to protect the C-130's and the intended landing strips with fire if necessary. He doubted if there were any Ashbals there, but that was the procedure.

Hausner knelt on one knee and helped Burg up. "They almost took the pipe out of your mouth, Isaac. All right, this is where we part company, my friend. You go back and take charge of the aircraft and the people on it. I'm going to take charge of the delaying action."

"If I thought I had the time to argue with you, I would. Good-bye, Jacob. Good luck." He slapped Hausner on the back and ran off.

Hausner could hear the Ashbals approaching his command post knoll from the east. There were also noises coming from the south as the Ashbal line swung around in an arc. Hausner took a .22 pistol, knelt, and waited.

Out of the dust came Marcus and Alpern. Hausner called out to them, and they ran over to him. "Give me one AK-47 and all of your ammunition. I'll be able to delay them from the cover of this knoll. You get back to the Concorde on the double and help organize a defense there. Use the armor mesh and make the earth ramp and the hut your strongpoints. We should have dug secondary defenses around the craft, but there's no use thinking about that now. All right, you'll take your orders from Burg. No arguing. Do it."

They passed him one rifle and two half-filled magazines. Hausner pulled the bent standard from the ground with the T-shirt that showed the Tel Aviv waterfront and passed it to Alpern. "A souvenir, Sam. Always wear it when you're telling your grandchildren this story. They'll think you're a real moron."

Alpern smiled and took the banner. Both men moved off with only a half wave as a good-bye.

Hausner got himself into position behind the knoll. He fired a few tentative rounds and drew a few rounds of return fire.

Hausner was as happy to see Laskov and his F-14's as he had been to see anything else in his life. But the reality of the situation was that it was too late. Jaffe had reported to him about the C-130's and the commandos on the way, but even if they landed right then, it would be too late. They would have to land on the mud flats, unload, inflate rafts, and cross the Euphrates. If, instead, they landed on the road and their rollout ended where the Concorde had gone off the road, then they would still be almost a kilometer away. And as yet he didn't hear the heavy droning of the four-engine propeller craft.

Paratroopers might have saved them, but that was suicidal in this darkness and dust; the terrain was terrible, and half of them would land in the river. No, it was a good show of force, but it didn't change much. In fact, it made it worse. Before, the Ashbals were intent on massacre, and that at least would have ended the whole affair. Now they would have to take hostages in order to save themselves. After they got hostages, the whole affair would just be beginning. Hausner hoped that Laskov would foresee this and know when they were finished and would not hesitate to napalm the entire hill. If nothing else worthwhile came out of this, at least they would get Rish—and Hamadi, who Hausner thought might be a far more cunning adversary in the future.

In his mind, Hausner made up a long good-bye to Miriam. He was torn between going back to the Concorde to deliver it or staying there, where at least his emotions, if nothing else, were safe.

From his position under the front nose wheel, Peter Kahn had listened to everything that was happening as he worked on the APU. He heard the shouting and the hurried footsteps running toward the aircraft. He saw some people without weapons climbing the earth ramp up to the Concorde's wing. In the distance he could see others kneeling and firing at muzzle flashes. Firing holes had been knocked into the walls of the mud hut. A few men and women took up shooting positions around the earth ramp, and one girl took cover behind his little earth platform. The end was coming one way or the other, but still he continued to labor on the APU.

Suddenly, he rolled off his earth mound under the wheel well, stepped over the prone girl with the rifle, and wiped his hands and face. He walked quickly to the ramp and climbed it, along with a few other fatigued and tattered-looking people. On the wing, Miriam Bernstein took his arm. "Have you seen Jacob Hausner?"

"No, Mrs. Bernstein. I've been under the front wheel. Actually, I'm looking for him myself." He could see that some of the armor mesh that had been on the perimeter was being taken into the aircraft. It was being pressed against the inside of the hull and windows. He liked to see resourcefulness and good thinking right up until the last minute. It was a damned good try if nothing else. "Look, Mrs. Bernstein, you'd better get inside the craft. We're drawing fire here." He disengaged himself from her and walked over to Burg, who was standing at the farthest point of the starboard wing tip. A half-dozen men and women were lying prone on the wing near him and firing out into the darkness.

It had become apparent to Burg and others that the Ashbals did not want to fire at the wings and take a chance on blowing up the aircraft and their potential hostages. The wings had become a relatively safe perch from which to deliver fire.

Kahn tapped Burg on the shoulder. "Excuse me."

Burg spun around. "Oh. Hello, Kahn. Nice try with the APU, son."

"Right, sir. That's what I want to talk to you ... or Mr. Hausner ... about."

"Talk to me, son. Hausner's still out there." He pointed.

"Yes, sir. Well, I think I've fixed it."

"Fixed...?" Burg suddenly burst out with an involuntary laugh. "What? Who gives a damn, son? Get inside the aircraft and keep your head down."

Kahn stood fast. "I don't think you understand, sir. They're not going to reach us in time. We can—"

A loud explosion shook them off their feet. An F-14 streaked by overhead. Another F-14 came in with its 20mm cannon blazing. A third came in off the Euphrates and released air-to-surface rockets over the top of the Concorde. The rockets left a fiery trail overhead and crashed out by the old trenches. Another F-14 released a laser-guided SMART bomb which crashed into the west slope and blew apart the millennia-old crust of earth, sending ancient brick flying into the air and tons of earth careening down the steep glacis, over the bank, and into the river, taking a few Ashbals with it.

The F-14's went through their repertory. The earth shook and quaked, and shock waves filled the air as tons of ordnance detonated on the old citadel that, for over a thousand years, had guarded the northern approaches to Babylon, and for over two thousand years had guarded nothing at all.

The earth split and heaved and threw up sand and clay hundreds of meters into the air. Orange billows burned up the dust and man-made shock waves collided with the ancient *Sherji*. Rockets' red trails slashed across the sky like the shooting stars that had so fascinated the ancient Babylonian astrologers. The F-14's put on a show the likes of which Babylon had never seen. But it was just that. A show. Laskov did not dare deliver any of the ordnance close enough to be effective. Still, it kept heads down and slowed the pace of the ground action. The idea was to buy time. Time for the commandos to arrive. Time.

Burg lay where he had fallen. "What?" he shouted over the explosions. "What?"

"I think we can start the APU and turn over the engines," shouted Kahn.

"So what? What the hell difference does that make? We don't want to run the air conditioning, Kahn."

"We can get the hell out of here! That's so what!"

"Are you crazy?"

A rocket fell short and plowed into the earth near the tail and blew up, sending clods of earth and shrapnel into the Concorde.

Kahn picked up his head. "No, I'm not. We can move this big bird."

"Move it where?"

"Who gives a damn where? Just move it the hell out of *here*. Any place."

Burg looked behind him. He hoped to see Hausner coming up the earth ramp with that by now famous mixture of nonchalance and menace. But only Miriam Bernstein was there, looking out into the fiery night. He wanted to shout to her, but she would not have heard. He turned back to Kahn. "Tell the captain to try to start his engines."

Kahn jumped up before Burg could add any restrictions to his order and dashed for the emergency door. He barreled into the aircraft and fought his way to the flight deck. "David!"

Becker was speaking to Laskov on the radio and waved to Kahn to be quiet.

"David!"

Becker had taken an American Air Force course in calling and adjusting air strikes, and it was proving very profitable at the moment. He could not see much from the flight deck, but he was trying to make himself useful. And, he had to admit, he was having a pret·y good time. "All right, Gabriel. If you have any SMART bombs left, now's the time to bring them in. Make one run along the river bank at the base of the slope in case we missed anyone down there. We may still try to make a run for it that way, and I want the bank cleared. Put another to my right front, about two hundred meters out. I'm going to start blinking my taxi lights now."

"Roger the river, 02, but negative outside your window. Too close."

Kahn was shaking Becker by the shoulder. He was shouting in English, their native tongue. "Didn't you hear me, goddamn it? The fucking APU is fixed." He liked the American idiom and couldn't reproduce it in Hebrew. "Get this big-assed mother-fucking bird fired up and let's haul ass out of this shithole!"

Becker was speechless for only a split second. "Fixed?"

"Fixed. Fixed." Maybe, thought Kahn.

Becker's fingers went to the APU ignition switch. He didn't believe there was enough battery charge left to turn the APU over, but it didn't hurt to try. He hit the switch and looked at the instruments. He tried to listen above the wind and explosions that poured into the cockpit through the shattered plexiglas. The APU was definitely turning over, but it wouldn't ignite. Becker turned off the aircraft lights. Did the batteries have enough remaining power to keep motorizing the APU until the fuel ignited? Without a word between them, Becker and Kahn watched the APU temperature gauge. Their eyes searched for any hint of motion from the needle that would indicate the beginnings of a successful start. The white needle continued to sit rigidly on the bottom mark of the temperature gauge. Becker tried the familiar "Just this once, God. Just this once." But nothing happened.

34

The two huge C-130 cargo craft came in low over the western desert. They had left Israel well before the F-14's, but at a top speed of only 585 kilometers per hour, the flight had taken nearly two hours.

The King of Jordan had quickly given permission to use Jordan's northern air corridor to the Iraq border. It was not until the Baghdad government was presented with the *fait accompli* of the F-14's already in Iraq and the C-130's approaching their border that they reluctantly agreed to let the unarmed cargo craft in. The alternative was to refuse the C-130's entry and to order the F-14's out, which would have necessitated an embarrassing explanation of how they had reached so deep into Iraq in the first place.

After a lot of ominous pronouncements had traveled over the circuitous telephone lines, Baghdad had agreed with Jerusalem that it was a joint operation, and the Israeli Prime Minister and the Iraqi President had prepared a joint news release to that effect. To give credibility to that news release, Baghdad sent a small river unit of the Iraqi Army from Hashimiyah up the Euphrates and ordered the Hillah garrison to stand by, although both governments knew that the unreliable troops were in fact not standing by but standing down. It was felt that many of the troops were in the pay of Ahmed Rish, and their Iraqi officers kept a very close watch over them. Both governments knew that the river unit from Hashimiyah would not make it to Babylon in time to participate in the operation, but the gesture of support was important.

Other Iraqi Army officers from Hillah, plus civil servants and personnel from the small Hillah airstrip, went by motor vehicle north toward Babylon. At a spot somewhat south of where the Concorde had touched down, they secured the Hillah-Baghdad road and set out flares to mark it in the dust-swept dawn. Another contingent crossed the Euphrates by motor launch to mark off a landing strip with flares on the mud flats. Neither action was absolutely necessary to land the C-130's, but it cut down considerably on the risks involved in the procedure.

The Iraqis had made their contribution and the Baghdad government settled back to watch the outcome. An Israeli military disaster wouldn't be viewed as a tragedy in some Iraqi circles, while a successful operation would obviously be the result of the Iraqi participation. Baghdad could not lose. They might come in for a lot of censure from Palestinian groups and perhaps some Arab governments, but the times were such that many Arab governments would officially applaud the move on humanitarian grounds, and Baghdad would reap some goodwill from the West—goodwill that could be turned into something more concrete at a later date. On balance, it seemed the thing to do—especially since Israel had already done so much that was irreversible.

Captain Ishmael Bloch and Lieutenant Ephraim Herzel, piloting the first of the two C-130's, saw the flares along the Hillah road and banked left as they pulled off more power. Three of the F-14's assigned to cover the landings shot past their windshield and dove in along the intended landing approach.

The big cargo craft dropped in very quickly as it was designed to do in a combat situation.

In the cabin, fifty Israeli commandos tightened their straps and braced themselves for the jolt that came with an assault landing. The tie-downs on the two jeeps, one mounted with a 106mm recoilless rifle and the other with a dual .50 caliber machine gun, were checked and tightened.

The doctors and nurses again checked the fastenings on their mobile operating unit and their surgical supplies.

Captain Bloch cut the power again and watched the speed bleed away on his indicator. He turned to Lieutenant Herzel. "When we flipped a coin for the road or the mud flat and I won and picked the road, why didn't you say something?" The giant aircraft seemed to float a few meters above the windswept road. Bloch tried to keep the nearly powerless craft lined up between the flares, but the strong crosswind pushed the plane to the left of the road, and when Bloch tried to slip it back, it yawed badly.

Herzel kept his eyes on the instruments. "I thought you picked the road because you *knew* it was more challenging."

Bloch thought for a moment that he would have to pull up and come around again, but the wind dropped for a few seconds and he lined the craft up over the road and came down hard.

The underinflated tires hit the crumbling blacktop and sent tremendous sections of it flying off at all angles. The wind pushed the high-profile aircraft left, and as Bloch compensated, the craft fishtailed, causing the C-130 literally to eat up the road as it taxied north, leaving a sand trail in the place of what had been a paved road. "My wife is a challenge. My girlfriend is a challenge. Why would I want another challenge?" He reversed the engines and stood on the brakes. The noise of the screaming engines and wheels was deafening, and the men and women inside the cabin covered their ears.

Herzel looked back out of the side window as the aircraft made a small turn to follow the road. He shouted. "Leave some blacktop so we can take off, Izzy."

"Take off, my ass. We're taxiing into Baghdad after this is over."

Outside, by the illumination of their landing lights and the flares, they could see a few Iraqi vehicles sitting off the side of the road at long intervals. A few of the men in them waved as the C-130 lumbered by, and Bloch and Herzel waved back. "Are the natives friendly?" asked Herzel.

"As long as we have fifty commandos back there, they will be very friendly."

The big craft began rolling to a stop at almost the same spot where the Concorde had first touched down. Bloch could see by his landing lights where the Concorde had begun chewing up the road. The C-130 was built for that type of thing. The Concorde was built for wide expanses of smooth runway. He admired the damned fool of a pilot who brought it in. Bloch looked up. He could see the high mounds of Babylon in the distance, silhouetted against the brightening sky. "Babylon."

Herzel looked out the windshield. "Babylon . . . Babylon."

The rear gate was down before the aircraft came to a complete halt, and the commandos began jumping out and deploying on both sides of the road. A group of Iraqi officers and government workers eyed them curiously from a cluster of khaki-painted vehicles on a small hillock. The commandos were jittery, and so were the Iraqis. Both sides spent some time waving and making other friendly gestures.

The two jeeps rolled down the ramp and squeezed by either side of the C-130, keeping to the roadbed as they passed under the huge wings. One squad of commandos formed a perimeter to secure the aircraft. The medical personnel on board began preparing for the casualties.

Three rifle squads, each commanded by a lieutenant, with the overall command under Major Seth Arnon, fanned out on either side of the road, jogging to keep abreast of the jeeps. They headed toward their first objectives—the Ishtar Gate area and the guest house and museum.

Captain Bloch watched them from his high vantage point in the cockpit of the C-130. "It's no fun being an infantryman."

Lieutenant Herzel looked up from his landing checklist. "They slept all the way here, and they'll sleep all the way back. Feel sorry for your copilot for a change."

Captain Bloch looked from the cockpit of the C-130 off to where the Northern Citadel was erupting in orange, yellow, red, and white flames. The sounds of the thunder rolled down from Babylon onto the roadway. "It's those poor bastards up there I feel sorry for. You know, Eph, when they took off Friday afternoon, I said to myself, lucky sons-of-bitches, going to New York all expenses paid for as long as it takes to bring home a scrap of paper that says peace."

Herzel glanced up and looked out the windshield at the light flashes on the far mound. "I guess it's no fun being on a peace mission, either."

Captain Baruch Geis and Lieutenant Yosef Stern could not spot the Iraqis' flares on the wide expanse of mud flats, nor could the three F-14's that were assigned to them. Geis considered waiting for the sun to poke over the distant mountain, but as he monitored David Becker's voice speaking to General Laskov and as he watched the flaming consequences of their conversations, he knew that there was not much time left. In fact they were probably too late already, but he was determined to complete his portion of the mission.

Captain Geis wanted to get as close to the fighting as possible without coming into range of small arms fire from the citadel mound. He gave up looking for the flares and picked an area barely a kilometer south of the fighting—a spot that was marked Ummah on his map. Strange, thought Geis, Arabic was so like Hebrew. Ummah. Community. He radioed to the lead pilot of the three F-14's that were with him. "I want to land so that my rollout will end somewhere near the spot marked Ummah. Can you give me light?"

The fighter pilot, Lieutenant Herman Shafran, radioed back. "Roger. Flare on the way, over."

The F-14 came in on a west-east axis and released a 750,000 candlepower parachute flare. The sky and earth were transformed with a brilliant, eerie glow.

Geis pointed the nose of the aircraft directly into the hard-blowing *Sherji* and began pulling off power. Ahead he saw the outlines of Ummah under the artificial light. He placed the aircraft to the left of the village and put down his flaps. The wind added tremendous lift to the aircraft and it seemed to hover over the mud flats.

Lieutenant Stern looked over his right shoulder out his side window. There appeared to be cooking fires lit among the houses of Ummah. The *Sherji* carried the flare west, and it swung like a pendulum under its sailing parachute, casting distorting shadows across the earth. The flare sailed past the cockpit of the aircraft, and Geis and Stern looked away as it cast a blinding light in the flight deck. The F-14 released another flare over the river, and it too began to float westward toward them.

In the cabin, the fifty commandos listened to the wind blow and the engines whine. In place of the jeeps were a dozen motorized rubber rafts. Everyone in the cabin had a sense of the aircraft hanging, hovering, making no headway at all. Muscles tensed, and as the flare lit up the windows of the cabin, sweat could be seen glistening on brows and upper lips.

The doctors and nurses spoke to each other in whispers. Each

C-130 was prepared to handle twenty-five casualties. But what if there were nearly that many casualties among the peace mission alone? There were bound to be some casualties among the commandos. What if there were wounded prisoners?

Captain Geis was finally able to push the airplane firmly down and hold it down. Thousands of cubic meters of mud flew up and covered the aircraft as it charged through the quagmire and headed toward the village. The parachute flare overhead began to burn out and the land became darker.

A few of the mud houses of Ummah loomed up out of the weak light. Beyond Ummah, Geis could see the Euphrates. He reversed his engines and stood on his brakes. The big craft came to a halt and rocked backwards less than a hundred meters from the nearest hut.

The back gate opened, and three squads of commandos charged out of the aircraft, formed a line, and advanced on the village. A fourth squad fanned out a hundred meters and surrounded the C-130. They immediately began digging foxholes in the mud.

Major Samuel Bartok fired his Uzi into the air, but no one fired back. To the north, across the river, Bartok could hear the sounds of the fight, and he could see flashes of light. He glanced down at his map. If they met no resistance in this village and if they were able to navigate upriver to the hill where the fight was taking place, it would still take them about twenty minutes to get into position to bring effective fire on the Arabs. But even then he couldn't guarantee that he could keep them from advancing on the Concorde if they were to fight a rearguard action against his commandos. How many Palestinians were there? According to the pilot of the Concorde, there were not more than three dozen left out of over a hundred and fifty. That sounded like an incredible feat of arms for a peace mission. Major Bartok smiled grimly. No, that wasn't possible. He'd have to be prepared for any number.

The commandos' line became concave as it bent around the village. To the north, the first Israeli squad reached the Euphrates. The first man actually to stand on the bank of the river, Private Irving Feld, urinated in it.

A few minutes later, the third squad also radioed that they had reached the Euphrates south of the village.

The second squad, with Major Bartok in the lead, advanced up the middle toward the first huts.

BY THE RIVERS OF BABYLON

An old man appeared in the small crooked street and walked slowly toward them. He looked over the heads of the commandos at the high-tailed aircraft on the barren mud flats, its blue Star of David catching the first rays of the sun. He raised his right hand. *"Shalom alekhem."*

"Salaam," answered Major Bartok in Arabic.

"Shalom," said the old man, with emphasis.

Major Bartok was only slighty surprised. He had been told that there might be a Jewish community somewhere near Babylon. If he had had the time, he would have spoken to the old man, but he had not one minute to waste. He waved. *"Alekhem shalom."* By the number of mud huts, he estimated that there couldn't be more than fifty people living in the village. He shouted over his shoulder to the radio operator as he led the squad through the village "Tell Jerusalem we have found a Jewish village." He looked at his map. "Ummah. Ask them if we can take them home. Even if we don't reach the Concorde in time, we can at least accomplish this."

Captain Geis in the C-130 took the message from the radio operator and radioed Jerusalem.

The Prime Minister listened as Captain Geis relayed the message. He nodded slowly to himself. Jews of Babylon. But they were Iraqi citizens. Kidnapping Iraqi citizens was hardly a friendly gesture. And if he authorized it over the radio, Baghdad would hear and the rest of the operation might be jeopardized. Still, the Law of Return provided that any Jew who wished to come to Israel could do so. Sometimes they needed a little help getting there. There were precedents for this. He looked around at the full room. Some of the men and women nodded. Some shook their heads. Many faces revealed the agonizing dilemma they all felt. But it was his decision. There was no time for debate. He spoke into the microphone. "Do you have room?"

Captain Geis smiled. "How could we not have room for them?"

"Well . . . well, if they want to go . . . to come home, then let them come. Out." He settled back into his chair. History in the making. Disaster in the making, perhaps. He had gone so far already that it was easy to ignore the consequences of any further perilous decisions. Once you took that initial plunge, everything else was easier. He asked for another cup of coffee.

35

Laskov watched as the sun spread its first rays over the mountains and the flatlands below. He caught a glimpse of Babylon as he flew by and wondered what it was like down there. He had the same sense of wanting to land as he had had when he flew over the pyramids of Egypt. But his fate was to observe the world from the aerie of his leather seat, with the smell of hydraulic oil in his nostrils. He had spent too much of his life above this teeming earth, and he was looking forward to mixing more with its inhabitants on the ground after this.

He took transmissions from the aircraft protecting the two C-130's. "Roger. Change missions with me now and unload some of your ordnance on the hill. Be careful." He came in low for a last strafing run. The sky was bright, but on the ground the dust storm was still keeping visibility down to a few hundred meters or less.

He pressed a button on his flight column, and the 20mm cannon ripped a path from east to west starting from the outer city wall up to the east slope. He released the button quickly as the rounds passed through the deserted Israeli trenches. There was still not enough visibility to bring effective fire on the advancing Arabs without a risk of hitting his own people.

The Concorde suddenly loomed up in front of him and he pulled back on the stick and cleared it. He saw, in that split second, a woman on the delta wing, and he imagined that it was Miriam. She seemed to be calling for someone.

Laskov wanted very much to ask Becker about Miriam. He ached with the unasked question. But there were hundreds of other people in Israel who wanted to know about their loved ones, also. He'd have to wait and find out along with everyone else.

He banked sharply as he passed over the Euphrates and headed south with his six F-14's to exchange assignments with the other half of his squadron. They would have a chance to lighten up on their load now. He looked as his fuel gauges. The low-level, top-speed flight had burned too much. The combat maneuvers were burning too much. They were cutting it close for the trip home. He hit the intercom button. "Isn't there a gas station down this street?"

"Right," said Danny Lavon. "Turn left here, go a thousand klicks to the light and stop at Lod. All major credit cards accepted."

Laskov smiled. He had alerted Lavon to keep an eye on the gauges without saying, "Keep an eye on the gauges." Why did pilots talk in circumlocution and bad jokes? Even the Red Air Force had practiced that idiocy. The Americans were masters at it. Invented it, probably. It must be universal now.

As he passed over the C-130 on the mud flats he saw the commandos launching their rubber rafts off the quay of a small mud village. He looked at his watch. It had been seven minutes since the C-130 came to a stop. Not bad time. He radioed Captain Geis. "Gabriel 32 overhead now. Nice landing. I still don't see those flares. I'll keep an eye open for foul play."

"Roger, 32. Nice performance in Babylon. How are they doing on the ground?"

"Touch and go. Out."

One of the F-14's peeled off and circled the C-130. Two others took up a pattern around the rafts.

Laskov was on the east bank of the river now. He passed over the C-130 on the Hillah road. Great gusts of wind buffeted the big cargo craft, and Laskov could see that the pilot had left the engines running in order to control it on the ground.

Laskov picked out the guest house and museum and the towers of the Ishtar Gate. His impulse was to put his last SMART bomb into the guest house, but Jerusalem had vetoed that. They had the idea that Dobkin might still be alive in there. Laskov doubted that very much. There was also some speculation based on one of Becker's transmissions, and Dobkin's report, that there might also be a female prisoner alive there. He doubted that, too. But they would find out soon enough. He could see the line of commandos and the jeeps approaching the area. Laskov knew there would be a fight there, and if the commandos were held up for more than ten minutes and couldn't bypass the area, then he had permission to take out the guest house and the museum, if necessary. If there were Israeli prisoners in there, he knew they would understand. He knew he would if the situation were reversed. He wouldn't like it but he would understand. So would Dobkin. Dobkin was a soldier.

David Becker hit the auxiliary power unit switch again. It began to turn over—more slowly this time. The batteries were weakening rapidly—but still no ignition and temperature rise. He looked over at Kahn in the copilot's seat. "Sorry, Peter."

A bullet passed into the flight deck and they both ducked. Becker could smell kerosene and he knew that some of the fuel tanks or the feeder lines had been hit

"Try again," said Kahn. "Try again, David. We've nothing to lose."

Becker shouted over the noise. "Everything to lose. Can't you smell the kerosene?"

"I don't smell anything but hot lead. Hit it!"

"I need the last of the batteries to transmit!"

"For God's sake, try again!"

Becker wasn't used to Kahn being anything but polite and laconic, and he was surprised. He looked down at the APU switch, then up out of the shattered windshield. Three or four Ashbals were moving across the hilltop less than a hundred meters away. Someone, it looked like Marcus, took a single shot at them with his AK-47, and they fell to the ground, scratching for cover and concealment in the flat terrain. The first light was trying to penetrate the sandstorm, and visibility was somewhat better now. Becker could actually see shadowy figures moving in the distance through the grey and dusty dawn. He wondered who they were.

An F-14 came in so low that the Concorde shook, and tremendous clouds of sand pelted the craft and wrapped it in a shroud of dust. Without any conscious thought, Becker hit the APU switch. He looked slowly at Kahn. "Am I hearing things?"

Kahn heard nothing but felt it in the seat of his pants. He shouted above the noise of an exploding rocket. "We have ignition! I fixed the fucking thing with a wrench and a screw driver! I fixed it! Fuck Hausner!"

It flashed through Becker's mind that Kahn didn't care what happened next. He had fixed it, and that was the end of it. It was Becker's show now. He let the APU run for a minute, all the while waiting for it to ignite the thick kerosene fumes and blow them all into next week. But the wind was apparently carrying the fumes away. He relaxed a bit. The emergency power had gone off as the generator charged the batteries, and the primary system took over again. The cabin lights became brighter, and gauges and instrument lights came alive in the flight deck.

Becker wiped his face, then ran his hands over the front of his shirt. He hurried through the starting sequence for the outboard starboard engine. It ignited as easily as if it just come out of the El Al maintenance shop. He glanced over at Kahn, and Kahn gave him a thumbs-up. Becker looked down at the fuel gauges. The indicators weren't even bouncing. They just lay in the red, hard against the zero mark. The single engine was burning tremendous quantities of the nonexistent fuel. Becker couldn't understand it. It had to have something to do with a malfunctioning sensor. Somewhere in this craft, he was certain, one of the thirteen fuel tanks was sloshing with kerosene. He hit the switch for the outboard port engine; it began turning over quickly, hesitating to ignite for only a few seconds. Then, after one puff of white smoke from its exhaust, it began spooling up normally. He hit the inboard starboard switch and the engine balked. He played with it and coaxed it.

Kahn got up and stood in front of the flight engineer's panels where he could be more help. He scanned the gauges and noted the multiple systems malfunctions. Concorde 02 would never fly again, but with any luck it would make its last taxi. "Come on, you old buzzard!"

The inboard starboard engine ignited, but sounded bad. Becker hit the inboard port engine switch. Nothing happened.

He hit it again. Absolutely nothing. Like turning an ignition key in a car without a battery.

Kahn called out. "There's no power going to that engine. The wires must be severed. Forget it."

"Right." Becker locked the brakes and ran up the three functioning engines. The sand that they were ingesting might kill all three of them in a matter of seconds, or they might run out of fuel any moment, but Becker didn't want to release the brakes prematurely—not until he coaxed every last gram of thrust out of them. He shouted to Kahn, "Get everyone inside the aircraft!"

Kahn threw open the door of the flight deck. In the cabin, the wounded lay in the places where the seats had been removed, or sat up if they were able and held sections of the nylon armor mesh against the hull. The people who were caring for them crouched as they moved around the cabin. A few men and women with rifles pointed them through shattered portholes and waited for the expected final Ashbal assault.

Kahn ran out of the emergency door and onto the wing. The huge delta was throbbing with the pulse of the two starboard engines. At least a dozen men and women were kneeling or lying on the huge aluminum surface and firing out into the dust. A few people on the ground were using the desperate infantryman's trick of dry firing their empty rifles and simulating a recoil in order to keep the approaching Ashbals ducking. A few cassette tape recorders were still turning out the sounds of firing, but that and the dry firing were the only ruses still being used. Kahn saw Burg where he had left him on the wing tip and rushed toward him, shouting as he ran. "We're going to move it! Get everyone on the aircraft!"

Burg waved in acknowledgement. He had been trying to keep a tally of everyone. The Foreign Minister's group was accounted for, and the survivors of the group that had tried to commit suicide were safely under guard in the baggage compartment. All the wounded were on board, and he was fairly certain that everyone else was either on the wing, under the craft, or firing from the shepherds' hut. Everyone except Hausner and John McClure, neither of whom had been seen for some time. Burg shouted from the wing but he needn't have bothered. Everyone, including the Ashbals, knew what was happening by now.

The last of the armed men and women on the ground came up the earth ramp. Some climbed over the fuselage and took up positions on the port wing. Others lay prone on the edges of the starboard wing, and two men positioned themselves on top of the fuselage. Alpern came running up the earth ramp carrying the lifeless body of Marcus. The five other men and women of the delaying force followed close behind. Burg looked quickly at his list of names again. It seemed correct. The commandos would exhume the buried dead. They would also find Kaplan's body, he was sure, and perhaps Deborah Gideon and Ben Dobkin as well. Everyone except Hausner and McClure seemed to be accounted for, yet he couldn't be certain. He made a few quick notes in the small book, removed his shoe, stuffed the book into it, and threw the shoe away from the aircraft. If the Concorde burned, at least the commandos would find his notes when they combed the hill, and they would have an idea of how to begin accounting for the dead.

Burg ran over to Alpern who was pulling Marcus's body through the emergency door. "Hausner?"

Alpern shrugged as he drew Marcus inside the craft. "You know he's not coming."

Burg nodded. He caught Miriam Bernstein's eye. She had heard Alpern.

She ran toward the edge of the wing and started to jump. Burg caught her arm and pulled her back. She kicked and flailed her arms out at him, but he held her firm. She shouted at him to let her go, but he dragged her, with the help of another woman, toward the emergency door.

The Ashbals knew that the Israeli commandos were closing in on their rear. They were at the limits of their bravery, and for many the limits had already been exceeded. They were so fatigued that they were numb and barely aware of their surroundings, and every step forward became torturous. Their mouths, nostrils, and ears were clogged with dust, and their eyes were blinded by the sand. They began to think not of the Israelis in front of them but of the Israelis behind them. Each man and woman began plotting an escape route for himself in the event they could not capture hostages before the commandos overtook them.

But still they went on, driven not only by the knowledge that they had to lay hands on the Israelis in order to live, but also by the shouts and threats of Ahmed Rish and Salem Hamadi. And the Ashbals were still a dangerous force, even in their present state. They were like tigers and tigresses—for if nothing else, they were no longer cubs—who, though wounded, must still be respected and given a wide berth.

Rish caught two young girls, sisters, who were moving in the wrong direction. They pleaded that they were confused by the gunfire that was coming from behind them and disoriented by fatigue, dust, and darkness. Rish seized the opportunity to stiffen discipline. He forced the two girls to kneel and shot each in the back of the head with his pistol.

For a moment, Hamadi wondered if that was to be the proverbial straw that would break the camel's back. But the executions had the effect that Rish had anticipated. The small group, not more than two dozen now, moved more quickly toward the thundering Concorde. He marveled at how much tyranny men and women would put up with before they would rebel. There was a lesson there for him if ever again he should be in a position to lead men.

Hausner had been surprised at first to hear the Concorde's engines exploding into life. Then he remembered Kahn's untiring determination, and smiled. He doubted if Becker could produce enough thrust to move the injured aircraft with its long pointed nose buried in the dirt and its main tires flattened. Still, it was a splendid attempt. Even if the commandos moved fast, it could not be nearly fast enough. It might make a big difference if the Concorde could meet them on the east slope. That should surprise everyone, including, Hausner suspected, David Becker. Kahn always knew he would fix it, and he always knew he would taxi out of there.

Hausner knelt, fired, and moved back again and again. Some of the fire from the Concorde had come close to him, but that could not be helped. Now he noticed that the Israeli fire was very erratic, and as he listened it tapered off to almost nothing. Suddenly, the engines whined and he knew Becker was about to release his brakes. He glanced back over his shoulder and saw the red glow of the engines. He turned back, and out of the dust a line of Ashbals came running and stumbling toward him. He could hear Ahmed Rish's voice above the F-14's, above the AK-47's, and above the big engines. "Faster! Faster! This is your last effort! It is now or it is not at all! Come, my tiger cubs, follow me for the kill!"

Hausner understood why men and women followed Rish. The pitch and tone of the voice was familiar, and if the language had been German instead of Arabic he would have had no trouble placing it. Some men were born with command presence, and when their minds were disturbed, the result was deadly.

Hausner fell back to where he knew the burial trench was. He found it and lowered himself into it. He felt the bodies under his feet and wondered who had come to an end in this way. He crouched down and waited for Ahmed Rish in the dark.

Lieutenant Joshua Giddel's commando squad stayed behind at the small museum as the other two squads, with one jeep, bypassed the guest house and moved up the Processional Way.

Giddel's ten men lined up, five on each side of the jeep with the 106mm recoilless rifle mounted on it. They began moving across the flat dust field that separated the museum from the guest house.

With Lieutenant Giddel in the jeep were a driver, a two-man gun crew, and Dr. Al-Thanni, the museum curator. Lieutenant Giddel had discovered him in his office in the small museum. Dr. Al-Thanni had been checking his spring inventory lists as though nothing were amiss outside his window. It reminded Giddel of the story of Archimedes, who was working on a mathematics problem when the besieging Romans entered his city. The Greek inventor had refused to let external events break his train of thought, and an infuriated Roman soldier had killed him. And so, thought Giddel, Archimedes became an instant hero and martyr to intellectuals, and soldiers got another black mark. Giddel had overcome the urge that he knew the Roman soldier had succumbed to and settled for sweeping the inventory lists onto the floor.

Now the curator was in Giddel's jeep, bouncing over the few hundred meters that separated Giddel from his next objective. He spoke to Al-Thanni above the sound of the engine. "How many Ashbals would you estimate are in the guest house?"

Dr. Al-Thanni had a suite in the house, but had taken to sleeping on a cot in the museum. He still took his meals in the guest house and used the sanitary facilities. "They don't confide in me, young man." He straightened his glasses.

Giddel looked at him meaningfully.

"However, I would estimate that there are at least fifty with varying degrees of wounds and about ten or more orderlies with one doctor and a few sentries and duty officers."

"Is there a basement in the building?"

"No."

"All concrete?"

"Yes."

"Any guests in there? Guest house staff?"

"No. The season has not begun."

"Any other civilians or other noncombatants in there?"

"Sometimes a few village girls. You know."

"Is there a radio? Do they speak with the Ashbals in the field?"

"Yes. A radio in the lobby. At the clerk's counter where the duty man sits."

"Do the wounded have their weapons?"

"Yes."

"Any heavy weapons? Machine guns? Rocket launchers? Mortars? Hand grenades?"

"I did not see anything of that sort."

"Where would they keep a prisoner?"

"They had a prisoner—a girl—in the manager's office."

"An Israeli?" Giddel knew of the prisoner from General Dobkin's report to Jerusalem.

"I believe so."

"How about the general?" Giddel had already told him all he knew of General Dobkin, but he could see that Al-Thanni had been very skeptical of this information and probably beleived that the Israelis were playing on his friendship with General Dobkin to use him. "But you did not see the general?"

"I told you, no."

"You heard nothing about the general?"

"I would tell you."

"Where else might they keep a prisoner?"

"I don't know. Not the rooms. They are filled with wounded. Not the kitchen. The dining hall is used for meals. There is a recreation room, but this is also used. I think the manager's office is the most likely. I have not been in the guest house since the time you say you received a call from him, so perhaps he is there."

Giddel glanced up at the guest house. He could make out its outline and saw some lights in the windows. "Where is the manager's office located?"

"To the left of the lobby as you walk in. Immediately to the left of the front doors. The windows face the front."

"Who is the senior man there?"

"A man named Al-Bakr."

"Is he reasonable?"

Dr. Al-Thanni allowed himself a small laugh.

"I mean, do you think he would negotiate rather than have his wounded caught in a firefight?"

"Ask him."

Lieutenant Giddell looked out at the squat building. Incredibly, no one seemed to notice his movement. The jeep maintained a steady 5 KPH, and the commandos jogged along with it. The guest house was more clearly visible now, and Giddel put his starlight field glasses to his eyes. He could see struck tents lying in front of the building. There were a few eucalyptus trees around the house, and they partly blocked the views from the verandas. Some vehicles were parked off to the left of the house. He could see lights in a few of the windows and smoke coming out of the chimneys. Breakfast. A few men sat on the verandas on each floor. No one seemed to see them yet. He turned to Al-Thanni. "But do you think he would listen to *reason*? Do you have any influence with him?"

"Me?" He shook his head. "I am—or was—their prisoner. Make no mistake about that. I am not a part of these people."

Giddel turned his attention back to the guest house.

Dr. Al-Thanni cautiously put his hand on the lieutenant's shoulder. "Young man, if I thought that my friend, General Dobkin, was in there and was alive, I would do anything in my power to get him out of there, but nothing I say can make a difference with these people. I have seen what they did to the other captive. Take my word for it—if General Dobkin was their prisoner, he is dead or he should be shot as a mercy. Don't waste time or men on this thing."

Lieutenant Giddel focused his field glasses. He could see several men looking intently over the railing of the side verandas. They were in white robes, and he could make out bandages on some of them. They were looking toward the Northern Citadel where the sound and light show had attracted their attention. They didn't seem to notice him, but then he saw a few men staring intently in his direction from the top front veranda. He spoke to Dr. Al-Thanni as he watched. "Thank you, Doctor. Please jump off the jeep. Unless you want to come in with us."

"No, thank you. Good luck." He jumped off the side and rolled away from the moving jeep.

Lieutenant Giddel saw several men run into the building. "Increase speed." The jeep moved faster, the commandos went from a jog to a run. "Load a concrete-piercing shell and prepare to fire the gun." The 106mm gun crew loaded and adjusted their aim.

Suddenly, two long streams of green tracer rounds shot out of the guest house and passed overhead.

Lieutenant Giddel gave up any hope of negotiating now.

Another gun joined in, then another. Green tracers arched over the jeep, then dropped lower as the Ashbals began to get the range.

The jeep driver handed Lieutenant Giddel the radiophone. "It's air cover."

Lieutenant Giddel took the phone. "East bank two-six, here."

"Roger. This is Gabriel 32. Can I make that house disappear for you guys?"

"Negative, Gabriel. Possible friendlies inside. We'll do it the hard way."

"Roger. If you change your mind, give us a yell."

"Roger. Thanks." Giddel turned to his gun crew. "Keep away from the left front ground floor. Commence firing."

The gun crew fired a .50 caliber spotter round from the aiming rifle attached to the 106mm barrel. The .50 caliber tracer hit the building on the second story above the front doors, and the crew immediately fired the main round after it. The 106mm round streaked across the open plain and hit the building a meter from the spotter round. There was a deafening explosion, and the concrete shattered. Flames, smoke, and debris erupted from nearby windows. All the lights in the building went out. Lieutenant Giddel told the driver to increase his speed again. The commandos began firing their M-79 grenade launchers, Uzi submachine guns, and M-16 automatic rifles from the hip as they advanced on the run. The 106mm crew reloaded and fired again. The round smashed through the front doors and exploded in the lobby. Two commandos stopped running and set up their M-60 light machine gun. They began raking the building with long bursts of 7.62mm rounds.

The jeep and the commandos were within two hundred meters of the building. The Ashbal firing had stopped immediately after the first 106mm round hit. A third 106mm round entered a shuttered window to the right of the front doors and exploded inside. The right half of the building began to sag.

Flames and smoke poured out of the windows, and the front verandas collapsed on top of each other. Men and women in .white robes began jumping out of the windows and fleeing toward the vehicles. The M-60 machine gun shifted its fires and began pumping incendiary rounds into the vehicles. One after the other exploded and the men and women running toward them fled out into the darkness.

Lieutenant Giddel had little stomach for firing on a place where wounded were kept, but it was also a place, according to Dr. Al-Thanni and General Dobkin, where prisoners were kept, and it was a headquarters as well. In addition, they had been fired at from there. The Ashbals had broken the cardinal rule about mixing medical and military facilities, and now they were paying for it.

At fifty meters the 106mm recoilless rifle fired again through the front door, and again the round exploded in the lobby, this time with a CS tear gas canister.

The façade was a mass of bullet scars, and the wooden louvers were splintered and burning. Smoke billowed from every window, and the smell of cordite was heavy. Screams could he heard from inside the building.

The jeep rolled over the struck tents, up the front steps, over the rubble of the verandas, and into the lobby. The driver turned his headlights on. Each of the commandos picked a window and dove through.

Inside the ruined guest house, dead and dying lay among heaps of rubble and plaster. Part of the floor above the lobby had fallen through, and burning beds and patients lay in a heap in the corner. The Israelis donned gas masks and threw canisters of CS into the doors that came off the lobby. Two commandos fired their grenade launchers with CS rounds up the stairwell and through the hole in the ceiling. Two other commandos ran out the back door onto the terrace in time to see about a dozen men and women in robes and in uniform disappear into the grey dawn. They let them go.

In the lobby, the sounds of screaming and moaning could be heard from overhead. Men and women, in shock, wearing burned and bloodstained night clothes, came marching down the stairs with their hands on their heads, coughing, blinded, and vomiting from the gas.

Lieutenant Giddel burst into the manager's office. It was undamaged expect for the expected cracks in the plaster.

Calcimine dust lay over everything and some of it still sifted down from the ceiling. Giddel spotted the girl first, and as he ran toward her he stumbled over a body on the floor. It was a man lying face down with his hands and legs tied. He recognized General Dobkin from his bulk and height. He turned him over carefully. There was blood smeared over his face and one eye had been gouged out. It was hanging by the optic nerve, resting on his cheek. Lieutenant Giddel had to steady himself and turned away for a second. He took a dep breath and looked back. Apparently his torturer had been in the middle of his work when the first 106mm round hit. He still couldn't tell if the man was alive or not until he saw blood-tinted bubbles forming around his broken nose and puffed lips.

The squad medic ran in and went straight to the girl. "She's alive. In shock." He turned and knelt down beside Dobkin. He examined him quickly. "The General's fading." He looked at his bloody, tattered clothes. "God knows what his injuries are. Let's get them both in the jeep and back to the C-130."

"Right." Giddel called out the window to the jeep driver. "Instruct C-130 to prepare to receive two casualties. Shock and hemorrhaging. Have them radio Jerusalem. We've got our first two Babylonian captives ... alive. ..." He turned to the medic. "But I hope to hell the others are in better shape than this." He looked at the miserable men and women being marched outside. He called to the driver. "And report that we have some Babylonians, too."

36

The two surviving Ashbals at the base of the glacis saw the Israeli force coming upriver in their rubber rafts. There were at least thirty Israelis, but the clear target was irresistable to trained infantrymen. The two Ashbals took cover behind an earth mound and fired on the exposed craft with automatic weapons. Water splashed up all around the rafts. Three rubber rafts were immediately hit and several men wounded. The Israelis quickly returned the fire, but they were in the worst tactical position possible. Major Bartok ordered the craft to beach on the east bank.

The Israeli commandos came ashore and began moving in single file along the flood bank. They were still a half-kilometer from the place where the steep glacis started, and Major Bartok doubted if he could dislodge the Ashbals, who were still firing at them, in less than ten minutes. To save time he would have to cut inland and bypass the Ashbals, then head up the narrow-backed southern approach to the old citadel, traveling atop what was once the river wall. If everything went well, he could be in sight

386

of the Concorde in fifteen minutes. As Bartok ran along with his long file of men, he took the radiophone from his operator. He called Major Arnon. "East Bank 6, this is West Bank 6. How are you making out there, Yoni?"

Major Arnon sounded out of breath, and Bartok could tell he was also running. Arnon spoke in short, choppy sentences. "Passed the outer wall of city—Found one friendly KIA—Mutilated—Thirteen enemy KIA—Apparent ambush—Heading direction of east slope—Half a klick to top—Wait." He paused and stopped running. "I can hear something that sounds like jet engines. Is it possible that they started the Concorde?"

"Wait one." Bartok switched frequencies and monitored Becker and Laskov, speaking on the El Al frequency. He switched back. "Roger. They say the Concorde is started. I don't know what the hell they plan, but keep your head up."

"Roger. Out."

Laskov had been called back on station over the Concorde by one of his pilots. He spoke angrily into his mouthpiece. "What do you think you're doing, 02?"

Becker had put his uniform cap on, and it felt good. He spoke into his microphone. "We're getting the hell out of here!"

"Don't do it! You'll kill everyone!"

"I just asked my marvelous computer about that, and it said, 'Do whatever the hell you want, stupid. Just leave me out of it.' So I'm taking its advice. Sorry, Gabriel."

"You'll kill everyone, damn you!" Laskov almost lost control of himself. He lowered his voice. "David . . . listen—" Becker broke squelch and cut him off. Laskov released his talk button.

Becker's voice came on. "We're all dead anyway. Can't you understand that? You're too late to help us. Too late."

"No. I absolutely—" The squelch cut him off again, and again he released his talk button.

Becker spoke softly. "Sorry, General. You did a marvelous job. Really. Wish us poor sons-of-bitches luck. Out."

"Luck. Out."

David Becker released the brakes and waited. Nothing. He watched the instruments for signs of an engine explosion, but outside of that there was nothing he could do. It was out of his hands. The aircraft seemed to strain forward and it began vibrating ominously. He shot a look at Kahn over his shoulder.

Kahn looked up from the flight engineer's console. "Don't shut it down, David. Just wait."

Becker nodded. One way or the other the aircraft was going to fall apart. Even if they were able to taxi it to the east slope by the sheer thrust of the three remaining engines, the slide down would probably cause it to break up on the way or it would crash when it hit the base of the slope. Even the stationary vibrations now wracking the abused aircraft could cause structural failure before they went even one centimeter. The worst—or maybe the best—that could happen was that the leaking fuel would ignite and blow them all up. In a way he hoped that the fuel would either ignite or run out, and he could not understand why it didn't do either.

With a strange calm, he looked out the windshield. He could actually see men and women firing at the Concorde. Bullets passed into the flight deck and a sharp electrical crackling sound told him that the instrument console was hit.

The Concorde did not move.

Kahn tried to read a message in the flight engineer's instruments, but there was too much damage, and he couldn't tell if it was to the instruments or to the systems.

The two outboard engines were producing near maximum thrust, but the starboard inboard was operating at barely half its capacity. Kahn tried everything he could think of to get more power out of it. If only they could overcome that initial inertia. *Objects at rest tend to stay at rest.* Once the aircraft began to move, it should be all right. *Objects in motion tend to stay in motion.* Come on, you son-of-a-bitch. Kahn suddenly called to Becker. "Pull off power on the outboard port."

Becker understood. If the aircraft wouldn't go forward, then maybe they could swivel it to the left. He pulled back on the port engine throttle. The two starboard engines whined. Slowly, almost imperceptibly at first, the right wing began moving forward.

The Concorde began turning left, its nose moving through the dust in a sweeping motion. The right wing skimmed the top of the shepherds' hut, taking off the roof as it came around. The right main carriage assembly hit the earth ramp. The aircraft nearly came to a halt, but the forward motion continued, and the carriage cleaved through the corner of the ramp.

With the initial inerita overcome, Becker now opened up the left port engine. The aircraft moved forward slightly but continued to slide left as it moved. Instinctively, Becker began operating the rudder pedals and nose wheel to steer the aircraft, but then remembered with some chagrin that he had neither tail nor nose wheel.

Kahn saw him and called out. "Nice trick if you can do it, David."

Becker forced a smile. "I'll have to give it its head and see where it takes us. Listen, if I don't get a chance later let me congratulate you now." He glanced back over his shoulder. "No matter what—" Kahn's body was all the way forward in his chair, his face against the instrument panel in front of him. His white shirt was soaked with blood. "Oh, God!"

Jacob Hausner ran along close behind the slow, lumbering Concorde, firing short bursts all around him as he moved, hidden in the dust blown up by the engines. He had not been able to get to Rish from the latrine trench. Rish was no fool. Rish traveled in the middle of a diamond-shaped formation of seven or eight men, and even if Hausner had let him go by, he would not have been able to come up behind him. He could have taken out Hamadi if he had wanted to, but he didn't want to throw away his life on a second-stringer. He had been forced to retreat to the next place of cover and concealment, the shepherds' hut, but that almost cost him his life when they nearly surrounded it. Now he was running again, covering the Concorde and looking for a place to slip into until he could get close enough to Ahmed Rish to fill his guts with hot, searing lead.

As the Concorde gathered momentum and bounced over the terrain, a dozen men and women fired wildly from the trailing edge of the wings. Alpern clung to the mangled braces of the tail and fired down at the Ashbals through the tremendous billows of dust the aircraft left in its wake.

Several of the people on the wing shouted to Hausner to hurry before the plane picked up speed, but Hausner seemed not to hear. They tied shirts together and hung them over the trailing edge for him to grab, but he did not seem interested.

In the rear baggage compartment, the men and women who had tried to commit suicide were still bunched together, more for convenience than as a punishment. Miriam Bernstein had been placed, nearly hysterical, among them. Beth Abrams was trying to calm her and was holding on to her arm as the tail bounced and shook.

Ibrahim Arif was pressed against the gaping opening of the split pressure bulkhead. As he watched the ground sliding by below the highpitched tail, he saw a man running through the billows of dust behind the aircraft. He yelled to the young interpreter, Ezekiel Rabbath, who was assigned to watch them. Rabbath forced his way to the bulkhead, put his head through, and stuck his AK-47 out and pointed it so that it wouldn't hit any of the aluminum braces. As he was about to fire, he recognized the tattered, shoeless, dust-covered figure. "It's Jacob Hausner!"

Miriam Bernstein pushed her way through the closely packed bodies and squeezed by Arif and Rabbath. With incredible speed, she began crawling through the open bulkhead before anyone could react. Arif caught one ankle and Rabbath the other. She almost kicked free, but Yaakov Leiber got hold of her leg, and between the three of them they began pulling her in. Beth Abrams fell on them from behind and screamed, "Let her go! Let her go if she wants to go!"

There was a great deal of confusion as Beth Abrams was pulled away.

Miriam got hold of two cross braces out in the tail section that had supported the number eleven trim tank and held on to them. She shouted and kicked wildly as they held her legs. They could not pull her in, but neither could she get out.

Miriam shouted herself hoarse, and tears ran down her face. "Jacob! Jacob!"

The Concorde began to gather speed, and it pulled away from Hausner. Hausner fell as he turned to fire at an approaching figure. He lay in the dust and looked back at the blue and white Concorde disappearing through the wind-blown sand. He gave a parting wave to the aircraft. Miriam Bernstein believed that he saw her, and she waved back. "Jacob! Jacob!" She sobbed his name over and over again.

Every time Becker tried to control the aircraft by pulling off power on one engine or another, the aircraft slowed threateningly, and he had to open the throttles again. The result was that the Concorde half-spun and half-sideslipped to the left. Becker wondered if the main carriage wheel would snap off, moving like that. Every few seconds, he would glance over his shoulder at Kahn and look for some sign of life, but he saw none.

Occasionally he could see an Arab appear briefly out of the dust, then disappear again from his view as the aircraft spun slowly while it moved generally westward away from the slope that he wanted to reach.

Becker knew that a few more people had been hit in the cabin. He had the feeling that by the time the aircraft came to rest, it might be full of corpses. He had a mental picture of blood running from holes in the aluminum skin. Then, for some reason, he had a picture of everyone staggering down an earth ramp from the main boarding door. Everyone was covered with blood and their eyes were black and hollow. They were . . . brain-damaged. He felt the sweat run down his collar, and his hands shook. He had to get the damned thing over the edge someplace. Dying at the bottom of the mound was better than this.

He saw the edge of the west slope through his left windshield. What would happen, he wondered, if he went down that steep slope into the river? Would the aircraft break up in the fall? Would it sink quickly in the river and drown everyone? There was only one sure way of finding out. He took a chance and chopped the power off the port engine. The starboard wing swung around quickly; then he gave the port engine full power and at the same time chopped the power off the damaged inboard starboard. Both wings had equal thrust now, and the maneuver had pointed the Concorde directly toward the edge of the slope. The craft's momentum carried it forward. Both running engines sounded as though they had all the sand they could digest and they began making sickening, rattling noises.

The Concorde approached the edge of the glacis a few meters from where McClure and Richardson had dug their position. Becker prayed that a wheel strut wouldn't get stuck in a foxhole as the Concorde moved over the old positions. To his right he saw the small mound that was Moses Hess's resting place. The place that he had chosen for him, overlooking the Euphrates. Becker shouted back into the cabin. "Everybody inside! Crash positions! Pillows! On the floor! Heads down!"

The men and women on the wings had already begun moving inside the craft. In the cabin everyone faced rearward and sat or lay on the floor. Pillows and blankets were stuffed against the hull and bulkheads. Everyone tried to hold the wounded as best they could.

The long, damaged nose of the Concorde poked over the edge of the glacis. Becker imagined the aircraft must have looked like some creature from a fantasy—or nightmare—kneeling at the edge of a precipice, its wings—or cape—spread out, ready to spring up and jump into the sky.

Becker opened up the malfunctioning engine for an extra measure of thrust. The Concorde seemed to hang as though it were unable to make the decision—and perhaps reflected the ambivalence of its pilot. Becker looked out over the nose and watched the wide Euphrates below. The grey dawn light brought out highlights on the river's restless, wind-driven ripples.

Becker looked down at his console. His instruments showed the outboard starboard engine spooling down, and, in fact, he heard it dying. Whether it was out of fuel or filled with sand was irrelevant—it was dying. Then the outboard port flamed out suddenly and the inboard starboard, never operating at more than half power, began to cough black smoke. The Concorde hung halfway out into space.

Spurred on by the half-crazed shouts of Ahmed Rish, the remaining Ashbals doggedly continued their pursuit of the aircraft as it thrashed across the ground like a great wounded bird. There was only some light fire from the aircraft, coming from one or two portholes. There was, however, a man braced in the mangled tail section. He had not gone inside with everyone else and he was delivering accurate fire from his perch. Rish ordered all guns turned on him, and tracer rounds streaked through the half-light, up toward the high-raised tail. The man seemed to have taken many hits, but he continued to fire.

The Ashbals called on their last reserves of energy, and in a burst of speed, led by Salem Hamadi, they closed in on the tottering aircraft. Ahmed Rish ran behind them, alternately firing his rifle into the dust at their feet and using the butt to strike their backs and buttocks. Led by a near madman and pursued by a certified one, fewer than twenty wretched young men and women ran, stumbled, and crawled forward.

To anyone who was familiar with the myth, it must have looked like the scene of Charon, the ferryman of Hell, beating the damned souls with an oar as he took them across the River Styx. And it had all started so well, too. A proud fighting unit of over one hundred fifty men and women, reduced now to fewer than two dozen terrified, humiliated, and miserable human beings who looked and sounded more like jackals than tiger cubs.

Rish shot a man who fell and could not get up fast enough. Behind him, as he pursued the Concorde, he heard the firing of the approaching Israeli commandos as they pursued *him*.

• • •

Laskov watched from overhead. He wanted to try to take out the Ashbals who were intermittently visible now, but they were clinging too close to the Concorde and he was unable to get an accurate fix on the approaching commandos. The stall speed of the F-14 was too high to make it very effective for close-in support. It was because of their speed and range that the F-14's had been chosen for this mission. To try to put a bomb or rocket accurately on the racetrack-sized hilltop, in the dawn light, with high buffeting winds and obscuring dust, traveling at a minimum speed of 195 kilometers per hour, was out of the question with so many friendlies in the area. He considered asking the commandos to pull back, but in the final analysis, it was they who had to effect the rescue. Again, he settled for buzzing the area at low levels and setting up strafing patterns that would not come near the Concorde on the west side of the hill or the commandos approaching from the south and east. He led his six Tomcats in on a last strafing run that exhausted the remainder of their 200mm cannon rounds.

Hausner lay in a shallow depression, covered with dust, and listened to the small cannon rounds exploding around him. The Ashbals had not seen him fall in the dust and had run past him.

As he took cover he heard the whining down of the Concorde's engines as they died one by one. He looked up cautiously. The Concorde hung precariously at the edge of the slope. In the weak light of dawn he could see the fire dying in its huge engines. The Ashbals were closing in on the aircraft. From the east he could hear the random firing of the commandos as they worked their way up the slope. He got up on one knee and checked the mechanism on his AK-47. As he reloaded, he looked around him and realized that he was kneeling in the same hole where he and Miriam had made love. He ran his hand through the warm dust that had been their bed.

He looked up again at the Concorde as he finished reloading. His plan had been to kill Rish although he knew he himself would die whether he succeeded or not. But now it appeared that he would survive and that everyone else would die, because even if Rish did not reach them and massacre them or take them hostage, then this foolhardy attempt to slide into the river would surely kill them. All Hausner had to do now was to wait until the commandos reached him and he could go home. But he couldn't do that and he knew it. He rose to his feet and made off in the direction of the Concorde.

Becker couldn't decide if he wanted to go over the side or not. The longer he looked at the river, the farther away it seemed. But what were his options?

Burg had come into the flight deck and was strapping Kahn into the flight engineer's seat. Kahn was breathing, but a sucking chest wound was making that increasingly more difficult. Burg looked around, found a map, and stuffed it into the foaming hole. The sucking sounds quieted.

Becker watched for a second, then yelled to Burg. "Get a dozen people in the forward galley!"

Burg nodded and ran out the cockpit door and barked an order.

A dozen unwounded and ambulatory wounded got up quickly and crowded into the small forward galley. The Concorde tipped further and slid forward. Burg ran into the flight deck and strapped himself into the copilot's chair.

Salem Hamadi, well in the lead of the straggling Ashbals, ran at an angle alongside the leading edge of the upturned starboard wing until he reached the point where it came within two meters of the edge of the glacis. A second before he would have run off the side, Hamadi slung his rifle over his shoulder and leaped into the air.

Hamadi landed flat on the wing with his arms and legs spread out. At that moment, the ground that the underside of the flight deck was resting on gave way. The Concorde pitched further down and slid a few meters forward. Hamadi scrambled upward and tried to find some purchase on the sleek supersonic wing. His foot found a tear that had been made by a burst of bullets, and he vaulted toward the open emergency door and grabbed the door frame. No one seemed to be looking out the windows or the door. He pulled himself toward the opening.

More ground gave way under the aircraft, and the Concorde seemed to spring over the crumbling edge. It careened down the steep gracis toward the Euphrates. It looked very graceful to the fighter pilots in the air.

Salem Hamadi saw through the open door that everyone was in the crash position with their heads between their legs and pillows and blankets in front of their faces. He dropped into the dark cabin and let go of the door frame. The steeply pitched aircraft propelled him toward the flight deck door and he smashed into it. He put his back to the steel door and waited for the crash. Hamadi could not imagine what kind of fate awaited him—drowning, shooting, capture, maiming—but he knew he did not want to be around Ahmed Rish when the end came.

Becker saw the line of burnt castor oil bushes come up very fast. He saw two badly wounded Ashbals running off in opposite directions along the river bank. He felt the main wheel assembly collapse, and the Concorde slid faster on its belly. The nose cleaved through the high bank and the belly slid over it, lifting the aircraft slightly like a sled going over a bump. The Concorde belly-dived into the Euphrates, and Becker heard the thump of the impact at the same time he felt it hit. He saw the river come up to his windshield and pour through, sending shards of glass and sheets of water over him and Burg. Then everything went black.

Great billows of steam rose as the hot Olympus engines vaporized thousands of liters of the Euphrates. There was a rushing sound inside the aircraft as the belly filled with water and it settled into the river, then a stillness as it reached a level at which it could float. The passengers began to look up.

Salem Hamadi slid quickly through the door into the half-lit flight deck. He saw first a crewman strapped into the flight engineer's seat. He was bleeding and his blood colored the water sloshing on the deck. There was also a crewman sitting in the pilot's seat, slumped over the control column. Next to him in the copilot's seat was a man in civilian clothes who also seemed to be unconscious. There was sparkling plexiglas lying over everything. As he watched, the instrument lights began to fade, then the overhead lights went out. Hamadi pulled out his long knife. He knew instinctively that the man in civilian clothes was important and went for him first.

37

Jacob Hausner stopped short of the line of Ashbals. He watched them as they began firing down into the river at the Concorde as it began floating slowly downstream. He raised his rifle and tried to pick out Rish among them, but they all looked the same with their layer of whitish dust.

Overhead, Laskov's F-14 circled lazily over the mud flats, then suddenly came streaking in toward the crest of the hill, directly at the Ashbals. Laskov had instructed Major Arnon's force to stop their advance and take cover until further notice. Major Bartok's force had changed direction and was heading at top speed back down the ridge line toward their rafts in an attempt to intercept the Concorde.

The sky was brightening noticeably and the wind was dropping. The Ashbals, who had traveled clothed in the dust and the darkness for so long, suddenly realized that they were naked. The F-14 released his last four rockets and pulled up sharply. The line of Ashbals on the crest disappeared in an inferno of orange flame and shrapnel.

The concussion knocked Hausner down, and when he looked

up, he saw Ahmed Rish standing by himself well back of the crest where the dismembered bodies of his last soldiers lay smoldering. A smell of burning hair and flesh hung around the crest until the wind blew it away.

Hausner rose and looked around him. He and Rish were the only men left standing on the hill as far as he could see. Rish appeared to be contemplating the safest line of retreat. He had his back to Hausner as Hausner walked casually over to him. "Hello, Ahmed."

Rish did not turn. "Hello, Jacob Hausner."

"We won, Rish."

Rish shook his head. "Not completely. Hamadi is on that aircraft. Also, it may sink yet. And I'm sure the Peace Conference is finished. And please don't forget all your dead and wounded. Shall we call it a draw?"

Hausner tightened his grip on the AK-47. "Drop the rifle and your pistol. Turn slowly around, you son-of-a-bitch. Hands on your head."

Rish did as he was told. He smiled at Hausner. "You look terrible. Would you like a drink?" He inclined his head toward a canteen on his web belt.

"Shut your goddamn mouth." Hausner's hands were shaking, and the muzzle of the rifle moved with short, quick movements. He couldn't seem to make up his mind what to do next.

Rish smiled at Hausner. "This was all your fault, you know. None of this would have been possible without your incompetence. You don't know how many nights over the past year I've awakened in a sweat dreaming that Jacob Hausner would think of making a complete nose-to-tail search of his Concordes. Jacob Hausner. Legendary genius of El Al Security. Jacob Hausner. You don't know how we worried about the overrated Jacob Hausner." He laughed. "No one told us that Jacob Hausner was just a creation of Israeli public relations. The real Jacob Hausner has no more brains than a camel." He spit on the ground. "You may live and I may die, but I wouldn't change places with you." He laughed.

Hausner wiped the dust from his mouth and eyes. He knew Rish was trying to goad him into pulling the trigger. "Are you through?"

"Yes. I have said what I wanted to say to you. Now kill me quickly."

"I'm afraid that's not what I had in mind." He thought he could see Rish turn pale under his layer of dust. "Did you capture General Dobkin? How about the girl that was on the outpost? Do you have them? Come on, Rish. Answer me truthfully, and I'll put a bullet into your head, clean and quick. Otherwise..."

Rish shrugged. "Yes, we captured both of them. They were both alive the last I saw them. However, I received a radio transmission from the guest house where they were kept saying that your soldiers were blowing it up and machine-gunning the wounded." He shrugged again. "So, who can say if they are still alive?"

"Hospitals and headquarters don't mix, Rish, so don't give me that shit." He coughed and spit up some dust.

"Some water?"

"Shut up." Rish would be the intelligence prize of the decade. Rationally, he should take him alive. Rish would answer a lot of questions that had been bothering Israeli Intelligence for some time. Hausner wanted to know a few things himself. "Who passed on the flight information to you?"

"Colonel Richardson."

Hausner nodded. He asked suddenly, "Miriam Bernstein's husband? The others? What of them?"

Rish smiled.

"Answer me, you son-of-a-bitch."

"I think I'll take that information with me to the grave."

Hausner's finger tensed on the trigger. If he took Rish alive, he would spend the rest of his life staring through the barbed wire at Ramla. Life imprisonment was harsher justice than a bullet in the head and oblivion. But on a more primitive level Hausner wanted an eye for an eye. He was filled with all the primal passions and hate of mankind and wanted to see Rish's blood run. Rish was an unspeakable evil, and even barbed wire was no guarantee that his malevolence would be contained. While he lived and breathed, he was as dangerous and threatening as a contagion. "We killed your lover, didn't we? And it was a double blow to you because she was your sister, wasn't she?" The psychological profile had been vague on that point, but he knew now that it was so.

Rish did not answer, but his lips drew back in a feral grin that sent a shiver up Hausner's spine. Standing there in the dawn wind with his hands spread out, his face and clothes the color of the dead earth, and the rising sun showing a malignant gleam in his eyes, Hausner saw Pazuzu, the East Wind, harbinger of plague and death. Hausner's whole body began to shake with exhaustion and emotion. He lowered the barrel of the rifle and fired.

Rish's kneecap shattered and he fell in the dust. He howled with pain. "A quick bullet! You promised!"

Hausner was inexplicably relieved to see blood coming from Rish, to see the shattered bone splinters and marrow, and to hear the howling. Irrationally, he had thought there would be no blood and no pain.

"You promised!"

"When have we ever kept promises to each other?" He fired again and blew off the other kneecap.

Rish howled like an animal. He pounded his fists into the dust and bit his tongue and lips so hard they gushed blood. "For the love of Allah! For the love of God, Hausner!"

"Were your ancestors Babylonian, Rish? Were mine a part of the Captivity? Is that why we're here in the dust all these centuries later? Was that your purpose?" He fired twice and splintered Rish's right wrist and right elbow.

Rish collapsed with his face in the dust and sobbed "Mercy! Mercy. Please."

"Mercy? We Semites have never shown mercy to each other. Did you show mercy to Moshe Kaplan? Did he show mercy to you, for that matter? Our people have slaughtered each other without mercy since the Flood receded and probably before. The land between the Tigris and the Mediterranean is the biggest graveyard on this earth, and we made it that way. If the dead rise up on Judgment Day, there won't be room to stand." He fired a full burst and the rounds caught Rish on his left forearm and partially severed it.

Rish fainted, and Hausner walked up to him, reloaded a fresh magazine, and fired a bullet into the base of his head.

Hausner gave the lifeless body a violent kick. It rolled over the crest, slid down the steep glacis, and dropped into the Euphrates.

As he watched the body sinking, he noticed that there were still two Ashbals at the base of the glacis. They were firing at the floating Concorde, and by the look of their tracers they were scoring hits. Hausner aimed his rifle down at them and moved the selector switch back to automatic fire. Out of the corner of his eye, he saw the F-14 diving straight down at him out of the brightening sky. He thought that if he dropped his rifle and waved his arms, the pilot might not fire at him. He hesitated, then fired down at the two Ashbals with a long, unrelenting burst.

Teddy Laskov held back for a split second, then hit the switch for his last rocket.

Hausner's rifle clicked empty. There was no more movement as the base of the glacis, and there were no more tracer rounds following the Concorde. He heard the rocket coming at him over his shoulder, then saw the F-14 as it pulled up over the Euphrates. He knew that all his actions, not only over the past days, but over the past years, had been self-destructive. God—the Perverse One, not the Benevolent One—had only waited until Hausner imagined that he had something to live for before he pulled the rug from under him. Hausner knew it would happen that way and was neither bitter nor sorry. If he felt any sorrow at all, it was for Miriam.

The last thing Hausner saw was Laskov's tail number. Gabriel 32. A blinding light enveloped him, then he was suffused with a golden warmth, and an image of Miriam, looking very serene and eating dinner in a sunlit room, passed through his consciousness.

Laskov looked back and saw the top of the western crest erupt in orange flame.

Salem Hamadi moved forward quickly. The high-backed bucket seats did not show much target, and he wondered for a moment about the best way to proceed. He came up behind Burg and grabbed his thin white hair, pulled his head back, and exposed his throat. He looked down at the man and recognized the chief of the hated Mivtzan Elohim. His hands shook. It was like having Satan himself at the mercy of his long knife. His blade came across and cut into the side of Burg's neck. He was about to draw the knife across the jugular and windpipe when he saw a movement to his left. He looked at Becker, who had regained consciousness and was staring at him. All he could see in Becker's eyes was contempt and disgust. Not one bit of fear. Hamadi's hands began to shake and his eyes and lips twitched. He looked down at Burg. It occurred to him that killing this man was not going to make any real difference in the outcome of events. Not killing him might make a difference at least in regard to his own life. It would be the first time he had not killed an enemy when he had the chance. He wondered if he could do that. He took the knife away from Burg's neck.

Becker pointed to the shattered windshield.

Hamadi nodded. He spoke in slow Hebrew. "Tell them in Israel that Salem Hamadi spared a life. Tell Isaac Burg that he is in my debt for one favor." Perhaps he could collect on that someday. You never knew. Most agents on both sides carried these favors around with them as life insurance. "Salem Hamadi. One favor." He slid between Becker and Burg, over the instrument panels and squeezed through the shattered windshield and onto the nose cone. He rolled off and disappeared into the water.

Becker was fully awake now. He knew it wasn't a dream because he could see the gash on Burg's neck. It was too strange to dwell on. A strange incident in a strange land. Hamadi. Salem Hamadi. He'd report that, if he ever saw Jerusalem again.

Becker shouted over his shoulder into the cabin. He looked at Kahn and called to him. "Peter!" There was no answer. He could not see the foaming at the chest, which meant that either the hole was sealed or he was dead.

The Concorde was floating mostly as a result of the tremendous surface area of its wings, but Becker knew that the wings wouldn't keep them afloat much longer. Even as he looked back out of his side window, small waves broke over the big deltas. The water in the compartments below deck was pulling the craft down, and the heavy engines were causing the broken tail to sit low in the water. Becker felt the nose beginning to rise as the tail sat deeper in the water.

The door from the cabin was thrown open. Yaakov Leiber rushed in. "Captain, the rear baggage—" He saw Kahn and Burg slumped in their seats.

Becker noticed that Leiber seemed to be in full control of his faculties now that he was needed in his professional capacity again. "Go on, Steward. Make your report."

"Yes, sir. The rear baggage compartment and galley are swamped, and I've evacuated the—the potential suicides, and I can see water through the floor in the compartments below. Also, we can't account for Alpern. I think he was on the tail when we went over."

Becker nodded. "All right. Please get Beth Abrams and someone else in here to take care of Mr. Kahn and Mr. Burg. Then instruct everyone to put on the life jackets that are still available, if they haven't done so already. And get a more complete damage report for me."

"Right, sir." Leiber ran into the cabin. The passengers had

come through the fall with barely an injury, but they were all anxiously eyeing the six-potential exits and beginning to cluster around them. Leiber found Beth Abrams sitting against the galley bulkhead with Miriam Bernstein. He whispered in her ear, then moved off and spoke to Esther Aronson and the Foreign Minister.

Beth Abrams, Esther Aronson, and Ariel Weizman moved quickly up to the flight deck. The two women immediately unstrapped Kahn and Burg. They began carrying the men, one at a time, back into the cabin.

The Foreign Minister leaned over Becker's shoulder and spoke quietly. "Are we sinking?"

Becker waited until the two women were out of the door with Burg. "Yes. We are. If we sink suddenly, we will all be drowned. You may want to order an evacuation now."

"But the wounded—"

"Put life jackets on them, sir. They can't stay here."

"Can't we get to land?"

Becker looked out the side windows. To his left he saw the mounds of Babylon slide by. He looked back at the citadel mound where he had thought he was going to meet his end. He could see a few commandos on the top of the glacis and a few on the bank waving to him. Some of the commandos had lowered rubber rafts in the river and were pursuing the Concorde. Ahead on the west bank, he could see an earth quay in the distance and a small village. There appeared to be commandos there as well. Help was all around them, but it might as well be in Jerusalem. The Euphrates had him caught in midstream, and he didn't see how he was going to beach the aircraft. No one could say that he should have thought of that when he took it over the side. He had thought of it, but it seemed like a totally inconsequential question ten minutes before. He looked out the right window. The aircraft might beach itself if it could float on for some distance. But it couldn't. "We've come so far," he said.

"And we're so close," said Ariel Weizman. "And we did *not* come this far to drown like rats in this cursed river of our sorrow." He looked out at the muddy water encircling them.

"Did Hausner ever get aboard?" asked Becker.

"No. He stayed."

Becker nodded. "How's Miriam—Mrs. Bernstein?"

Weisman shot a glance at Becker. "She'll be fine, Captain," he said formally.

Becker turned as the two women carried Peter Kahn out into the cabin. He looked at the bloody water on the floor running back into the cabin as the aircraft tilted upwards. He turned back in his chair. "Salem Hamadi was in here."

"What's that?"

"Nothing, sir. Just thinking out loud." He watched the two banks slide by. The aircraft was moving more slowly now as they took on more water. Someone—the commandos, the fighter pilots, or he himself—would have to think of something very quickly.

Becker settled back in his chair. He had finally become accustomed to sitting in a downward-pitched flight deck, and now it was pitched upward. Strange how these minor irritations loomed so large during a crisis. He tried the radio just to satisfy the requirement that it be tried, but it was as dead as everything else that was electrical. He spoke to the Foreign Minister, who had sat down in the copilot's chair. "I'm the Captain and I could order the evacuation if you'd prefer not to, sir."

Ariel Weizman kept his head and eyes straight ahead. "Will we have *any* warning if it is going to sink?"

Becker turned and faced the Foreign Minister. "It's sinking *now*, sir. It's only a question of the *rate* at which it is sinking. If it continues to sink slowly, we can ride it a while longer. If it suddenly slips into the river, then that's it."

The Foreign Minister looked at the earth quay in the distance, then back out the side window at the rubber rafts gaining on them. "We'll wait," he said hesitantly.

"Fine." Becker settled back and stared out the window at the new day. They had done some remarkable things with Concorde 02, but now the innovations and cleverness had come to an end. Great seabird that she seemed, she couldn't float worth a damn.

Miriam Bernstein stared out the porthole at the Euphrates. She looked up and watched the desolate east bank slide by. Her vision was blurred by her tears and the shattered glass distorted her view of the terrain, but she knew she was still looking at Babylon. A mud village appeared and people moved on the bank. A great assembly of them lined the shore and stared. The prismatic effect of the shattered glass gave the black *gellebiahs* and dun-colored huts a rainbow hue. Like Babylon of the colored brick. She thought she could feel, sense, almost see the Jews of the Captivity as they labored on the banks of the river,

their harps hanging on the ghostly willows. She sighed and
pressed her forehead to the glass and tears ran down her face.
She knew he was dead. He had a preordained rendezvous with
Ahmed Rish—or someone like him. She only hoped that he had
found some peace at the end.

Danny Lavon spoke into his intercom. "Fuel, General."
Laskov looked at his fuel gauges. The aerial combat
maneuvers had burned more than he had figured on. "Roger.
Send everyone home. We're going to have to hang around a little
longer."
"Roger." Lavon radioed the squadron.
The squadron went into a V-formation and flew by Laskov.
They came in low over the river and dipped their wings in
unison, then turned west and headed home.
Laskov looked out of his cockpit as they disappeared, then
turned away. The sun sat on the highest peak in Iran, and its rays
came down into Mesopotamia and turned the the grey land
golden. The wind had dropped, and he could see only an
occasional line of dust clouds racing across the flat alluvial
plains. He looked down at the two C-130's, the smoking guest
house, the ruins of Babylon and the village of Arabs sitting in the
middle of them. He stared down at the village of Jews on the
opposite shore, and the huge, white, delta-winged Concorde
floating toward it. "Incredible," he said into the intercom.
"Incredible," agreed Danny Lavon.
Laskov wondered if she were on the Concorde. He could see
that the wings looked blurry now, which meant that they were
awash. He didn't give the aircraft another two minutes. He tried
the El Al frequency again. "Concorde 02, this is Gabriel 32. Bail
out, damn it! Bail out! Can you hear me?" There was no answer.
Laskov could see five rubber rafts closing in on the Concorde
from the rear. He wondered if Becker knew they were there.
They weren't much, but at least some of the wounded could get
on them. The rest would have to swim or float if they had life
jackets. Why the hell didn't they get out? Laskov spoke to the
two ground commandos and the two C-130 captains. Everyone
had ideas, but no one really knew quite what to do. There were
contingency plans for just about every situation, but no one, not
even the think-tank boys in Tel Aviv, had foreseen this. Major
Bartok in the rafts seemed to have the closest shot at rescuing

them. The squad of commandos in Ummah had recruited the villagers and many of them took to the water in *gufas* and tried to pole upriver to meet the approaching Concorde.

The Foreign Minister nodded. "We'll lose some, but what can we do? Let's evacuate."

"Wait one minute." Becker watched Laskov bank sharply to stay with them over the river. Bank sharply. Bank right. He looked down at his dead instruments. He moved his hands over to the emergency power switch. He turned it on. Dead. He already knew that. But he needed power. Power. The engines were dead and so the generator was dead. The batteries were under water. The nitrogen bottle was back in Babylon, and the primary hydraulic pumps were submerged or damaged. Still, there was a source of power left, and he didn't know why he hadn't thought of it sooner. He quickly reached down under his seat and pulled a manual handle that he never imagined he would use and never wanted to have to use in the air. A nonelectric hydraulic pump activated itself, and the trap door beneath the Concorde opened and the small generator propeller dropped out.

Instantly, Becker saw a few gauges come alive as the propeller turned under water and activated a generator. The propeller also worked an emergency hydraulic pump, and he saw that he had pressure again in some of the systems. The Concorde was being powered by a water wheel. Desperate—but *très pratique*. If Kahn were sitting at the flight engineer's console, he would say that everything was looking good.

Becker knew that he had only a few seconds before the water caused this emergency system to fail also. Already the electrical and electronic components were flickering on the instrument panel. The hydraulic pressure, however, was holding. Becker turned his wheel, and the big starboard aileron went down as the portside aileron went up. The right wing dragged in the water and the left wing began to come around.

The Foreign Minister shook his shoulder. "David! I said—"

"Wait!" The Concorde began moving—banking—to the right. It partly changed direction and partly sideslipped toward the west bank. Ahead, Becker could see the earth quay of Ummah sticking into the river. Becker wanted to hit that quay and nestle the aircraft between its protective arm and the river bank. If he hit the bank downstream of the quay, the aircraft might not beach itself but only slide and spin along the shore and come apart.

The Concorde was going down as fast as it was turning now. The change of direction had jolted it out of its lethargic sinking and speeded up the rate at which it was taking water. Becker gripped the wheel so hard his knuckles turned white. As he alternately watched the gauges and the ailerons, he could see that the hydraulic as well as the electrical power was failing. The gauges flickered and the ailerons began to straighten out. Now they were both horizontal again, trailing loosely in the water. Becker swore in English.

Still, the Concorde had begun its turn, and as with an aircraft in its proper element, thought Becker, inertia should carry the motion through.

But a flowing river was not exactly like the thin air, as Becker was rapidly learning. The Concorde again assumed the position of least resistance, with its nose and tail lined up in the direction of the current. But at least they were now closer to the shore, and the water moved faster here, giving the Concorde an almost imperceptible quantum of added buoyancy. Becker thought they might just hit the quay.

Suddenly, Becker heard cheers and yelling coming from the cabin, and he looked over his shoulder. Yaakov Leiber appeared at the door and ran into the flight deck. "The commandos are alongside in their rubber rafts!"

The Foreign Minister looked back out the side window. "Perhaps I should try to evacuate the wounded."

"Nobody moves," said Becker. "And I mean that literally. No moving around back there. We're about five degrees from sliding ass backwards into the Euphrates."

Leiber walked more gingerly into the cabin and passed on Becker's orders.

Becker saw a rubber raft come alongside the flight deck on his side. The officer in it, Major Bartok, shouted something about evacuating. Becker shook his head and made a motion with his hand to indicate that both the situation and the aircraft were very shaky.

Major Bartok nodded in understanding. He gave a thumbs-up and shouted something about Becker being not a bad pilot.

Becker turned his face away from the side window and

looked downriver. The quay was about 150 meters away now—about twice the length of the Concorde. The *gufas* were sliding past him on both sides, and he could see the strange-looking Jews in their primitive boats. He looked back to his front. It did not appear to Becker that the Concorde could intersect the quay. Yet he knew that somehow it would. He suddenly felt that their trials were over and that there would be no more tests and no more tribulations. An easy calm came over him for the first time in a very long time, and he relaxed as he stared through the broken windshield, a breeze blowing on his face. As he watched, the Concorde seemed to slide right. Or was it a visual distortion caused by the light on the rippling water? Were they headed for the quay ever since he'd gotten the Concorde to turn? He'd have to ask General Laskov later.

His right wing suddenly skimmed the shore and rode over the top of it, cleaving through mud huts as it went. The drag caused the Concorde to turn more sharply to the right, and as the shore got higher, the right wing rode higher and pushed the opposite wing deeper into the water.

The quay came up fast. The commandos and the villagers moved back and to the sides but stayed on it. The downward-pointed nose of the Concorde hit it first, just below the water line, like a Roman warship with an iron ramming prow. The quay trembled and split as the nose buried itself in the ancient mud brick and slime. Becker found himself staring at someone's boots outside his windshield less than a meter away. The Concorde sank perceptibly, and Becker could feel its main undercarriage, or what was left of it after the slide, settling onto the bottom. People were all over the aircraft now—commandos, villagers, and survivors. He heard them on the roof of the fuselage, and he heard them wading over the left wing and coming in through the aircraft's doors. He was vaguely aware of people shouting, weeping, and embracing. The next thing he was aware of was standing on the quay, saluting the Concorde. Someone led him away.

38

Miriam Bernstein and Ariel Weizman found Major Bartok in the confusion of the quay. The Foreign Minister indentified himself and asked quickly, "The Peace Conference?"

The Major smiled and nodded. "They are still waiting for Israel in New York."

At the C-130, a crewman asked David Becker if they weren't short of water during their ordeal.

Becker replied. "Yes, of course. Can't you see everyone is very thirsty?"

"I see that," said the crewman. "But I wondered why all the men are clean-shaven."

"Shaven?" Becker ran his hand over his face. "Oh. He made us shave."

Rabbi Levin had cornered Major Bartok at the edge of the quay and was demanding that he be taken by raft to Major Arnon, who was now on the hill, so that he could supervise the locating and exhuming of the bodies. Major Bartok assured the rabbi that there was no need for him to go back, but Rabbi Levin proceeded to tell Major Bartok why he was wrong.

The village of Ummah had never seen anything quite like the procession marching through its one crooked street and was not likely to see anything like it again. The villagers helped carry stretchers and passed food and wine to those who wanted it. There was a mixture of crying and shouting and impromptu songs and dances. Flutes appeared, and their haunting notes lay over the quay and village as the people of the Concorde moved slowly toward the huge, towering C-130. An old man gave Miriam Bernstein a stringed instrument. A harp.

Everything was happening too fast for the survivors, and very little of it was registering consciously. Everyone had questions to ask, and the more questions the commandos asked, the more questions the people of the Concorde asked.

Major Bartok picked up his radiophone and called Captain Geis, whom he could see sitting up in the big flight deck of the C-130. "Tell Jerusalem.... Tell Jerusalem they have freed themselves from their Captivity. We will carry them home. Casualties and after-action report to follow."

"Roger," said Geis, and relayed the radio message.

The Prime Minister sat back and wiped his eyes as the radio message came over the loudspeaker. He thought of how they had been unsure of themselves and how they had doubted. But in the end they had said *Zanek*—"Go"—and that was what was important. He wondered who had lived and who had died. Was the Foreign Minister alive? The delegates? Bernstein? Tekoah? Tamir? Sapir? Jabari? Arif? How about Burg? And how about Dobkin? Would he live? And Hausner. The great enigma and troublemaker. How long had the Deputy Minister of Transportation—Miriam Bernstein—kept the Minister of Transportation from firing him? He had a lot of questions to answer if he were alive. The Prime Minister opened his eyes and looked around the room. "Heroes, martyrs, fools, and cowards. We're going to need at least a month to sort out who is who."

Captain Ishmael Bloch taxied his C-130 up the Hillah road. On board were all Major Arnon's commandos, fifteen exhumed or unburied bodies from the hill, including Alpern's, plus a mutilated corpse from the base of the hill. The commandos had found Burg's shoe with his daybook stuffed inside, and this enabled them to move quickly to complete their unpleasant assignment.

There was also a body so badly torn by the shrapnel that it was almost left behind as an Arab, but a sharp-eyed soldier had noticed the Hebrew letters חיי hanging from a heavy chain around the neck. Also on board were thirty-five wounded Ashbals along with half a dozen Arab dead who were identified as possible wanted terrorists. Ahmed Rish and Salem Hamadi were not believed to be among them.

On the operating tables were General Dobkin and Deborah Gideon. The two surgeons were waiting for the aircraft to lift off before they could go back to work.

Rabbi Levin, who had gotten his way about being returned to the hill, came over to the operating tables and looked up at the surgeons. The man operating on Deborah Gideon looked up and nodded quickly. The woman who was operating on General Dobkin pulled down her surgical mask. "I have never seen such brutality." She paused. "But he'll live. You're not needed here, Rabbi." She smiled and pulled her mask back in place.

Rabbi Levin turned and walked to the rear of the aircraft to find Lieutenant Giddel so that he could continue their argument on the necessity of serving only kosher foods during field operations.

The C-130 was taking a long time to lift, and Captain Bloch was becoming impatient. "I told you we'd roll to Baghdad."

"I hope this isn't a toll road, Izzy."

The big aircraft finally lifted off, and Bloch banked it sharply to the left over the Euphrates. He looked down at the Concorde, almost directly below him. "You know, Eph, I'd like to meet the crazy bastard who flew that thing in here and sailed it out."

"Becker. I've flown with him on reserve training. He's pretty good."

Bloch smiled. "Hey, this was one hell of an operation, wasn't it?"

Major Bartok watched the old man on the donkey as he made his way at his own speed across the mud flats. The C-130 was nearly loaded and its engines were turning, but that didn't seem to impress the old man in the least. Bartok stood patiently on the huge tailgate and waited.

Shear-jashub seemed to have no fear of the monstrous machine, and neither did his donkey. The old man rode the beast up onto the ramp and stopped when he came abreast of the Major. He did not dismount but asked abruptly, "What has become of *Aluf* Dobkin?"

"He is in that aircraft, Rabbi." He pointed overhead. "He is well."

The old man nodded. "You will give him a message for me?"

"Of course."

"It is also the answer to your question." Shear-jashub straightened himself on the donkey. "We of Ummah thank you for your kind offer, but we cannot go to Israel with you."

The major shook his head in frustration. "Why not? There is no future for you here."

"We are not concerned with the future here," said Shear-jashub, stressing the last word.

"Come home to Jerusalem, Rabbi. We have room. March everyone into this airplane right now. There is nothing to be frightened of. Go. Gather your people. Bring your goods and your animals, if you wish. Ummah will fit nicely in the belly of this big bird. Go and gather them up, Shear-jashub. The Captivity is over. Come away from Babylon."

The old man peered into the cavernous craft. Strange lights and noises came out of it. He could see those other Jews in there—the Israelites—walking, sitting, weeping, laughing. He had not understand all that had happened, but he understood enough to know that they came from a powerful nation and that Ummah could join that nation and the sons and daughters of Ummah could grow up in this nation. "We have many friends and kin in Hillah and Baghdad. What will they think when they come to Ummah and find that we are gone? We cannot go like that."

Bartok made a gesture of impatience. "I can't believe you would want to *stay* here. This is a terrible place."

"It is *our* place. Let me tell you that which I told the *Aluf*. There must always be a remnant left behind. In every nation there must always be we of the Diaspora. Nevermore can they lay hands on us all by taking Jerusalem. Do you understand that?"

Major Bartok looked out over the mud flats, then back at the old man. "Yes, I understand that. But this land is different. There is something evil about this place. You who are in this

land came here as slaves, and you are still thought of as slaves."
He saw that he was getting nowhere and he sighed. The last of
the wounded were taken aboard, and he knew he could not wait.
His first obligation was to them. He forced a smile. "Rabbi,
remember this—if this Brit Shalom that everyone is speaking of
goes well, then all the Jews of this land will be able to come to
Israel if they wish. Tell them in Hillah and in Baghdad that we
are waiting for them. And we are waiting for Ummah . . . and for
Shear-jashub."

"I will remember."

Major Bartok nodded. "I wish I had the words to convince
you. Perhaps if the *Aluf* were here . . . Well, good-bye Shear-
jashub. We must go . . . to Jerusalem."

The old man smiled at the name of the city. "It is a strong and
powerful city now."

"Yes."

"Good-bye." He reined the donkey around and rode down
the ramp.

Major Bartok watched him for a few seconds, then turned
and signaled the crew chief. The gate began to rise and the major
walked along it into the big cabin. He turned to the crew chief.
"Tell the pilots, please, that we are ready to go home."

In the cabin, he could hear a group reading from
Jeremiah: . . . *a great company shall return thither. They shall
come with weeping. . . .*

EPILOGUE

For thus saith the Lord; Sing with gladness for Jacob,
   and shout among the chief of the nations:
publish ye, praise ye,
   and say, O Lord, save thy people,
   the remnant of Israel.
Behold, I will bring them from the north country,
   and gather them from the coasts of the earth,
   and with them the blind and the lame,
   the woman with child and her that travaileth with child together:
   a great company shall return thither.
They shall come with weeping,
   and with supplications will I lead them:
I will cause them to walk by the rivers of waters
   in a straight way, wherein they shall not stumble:....

Hear the word of the Lord, O ye nations,
   and declare it in the isles afar off, and say,
He that scattered Israel will gather him,
   and keep him, as a shephered doth his flock.
For the Lord hath redeemed Jacob,
   and ransomed him from the hand of him that was stronger than he.
      Jeremiah 31:17–11

The two C-130's flew west, in formation, over the Iraqi desert.

Isaac Burg sat on a canvas chair and spoke quietly with Major Bartok, who was filling out his after-action report. Burg's arms and bare torso were splotched with iodine, and he had a white pressure bandage on his neck, which he kept touching questioningly.

Bartok kept shaking his head in disbelief at Burg's answers to his questions. Bartok, the soldier, was trying very hard to understand how the peace mission had decimated a full rifle company of trained soldiers. Out of professional inquisitiveness and personal curiosity, he was trying to discover the element or elements that had made that military miracle possible. "Perhaps we could use a few battalions of peace-delegates in the army," he said.

Burg smiled. "It was just that they believed so much in peace, I think, that when someone tried to spoil that peace, they were so angry that they reacted like a lioness defending her cubs. It is a paradox, I know, but it is the best I can offer you."

"Sounds good," said Major Bartok. "But I'll just write that it was a combination of good leadership, good defensible terrain, and innovative defenders."

"Sounds good," said Burg.

Burg accepted another cup of coffee from a flight steward and settled back. It was a short flight, but it was the longest flight of his life.

The major began reading back what he euphemistically called his Line Ones, Line Twos, and Line Threes. Killed in Action. Wounded in Action. Missing in Action.

Burg looked around the big cabin. There were so many absent. So many who deserved to be there instead of in green body bags on the other aircraft.

"Your security people took a hell of a beating," said Bartok.

Burg nodded. An incredible five out of the six security men were dead. Brin, Kaplan, Rubin, Alpern, and Marcus. Only Jaffe remained, and he was wounded. Hausner's palace guard. His instrument to effect his *coup d'état*. They were loyal to him and he was loyal to them. What more could men ask of one another? They were professionals, and professionals always suffered disproportionate casualties, but that was the way it should be.

And the El Al crew. They were professionals as well, and they had suffered disproportionately, too. It was their aircraft, and whether it was in Lod or in Babylon, they had felt a responsibility for the passengers. Daniel Jacoby and Rachel Baum were both wounded very badly, but Burg could see that they were still on the operating tables, and that was better than being under the green tarpaulin that was lying on the tailgate. Peter Kahn was serious, also, but stable. He was off the table now. The surgeon had shown Burg the bloody map that Burg had stuffed in Kahn's wound. "It saved his life," said the surgeon. "He owes you one when he gets out of the hospital." He crumpled it up and threw it into his surgical waste pail.

There were the dead among the secretaries, interpreters, and aides. There were the four slaughtered men and women of the outpost, and there were those who would die before the plane touched down in Jerusalem. But Burg did not know them all, and he was glad that the did not because there was no more room in his heart for sorrow just then.

And then there were the missing. That was the cruelest statistic of all. Did you mourn for their death or hope they were lying somewhere, suffering but alive? Did you pray that they were interned in some Arab hellhole? Miriam Bernstein could answer that better than anyone. Now she had two to wonder about.

Naomi Haber was missing. Burg thought he had accounted for everyone, but apparently he had not. No one had any idea what had become of her. Someone had suggested that she might have slipped off downslope and actually gotten close enough to put a bullet into Moshe Kaplan. Everyone had heard that bullet fired and it made no sense that Kaplan's tormentors had suddenly shown mercy and shot him. But where was she? The commandos had not found her.

And then there was John McClure. The shadowy man had disappeared. Burg understood McClure's world because it was his own. Anything was possible in their world, but disappearing from one's rescuers was a little odd even by their standards. Did he kill Richardson? Burg suspected that he had, and he knew why. The doctors on the other C-130 had reported that the bullet that killed Richardson was not recovered. It had been fired at close range and had gone through him.

But where was McClure now? Probably at the American Embassy in Baghdad by now, or perhaps at the home of a CIA contact in Hillah. He'd turn up someday posing as an archivist in the United States Information Service Library in Beirut. They always turned up like that.

Major Bartok wanted to know if Burg knew Jacob Hausner well. "Was he the actual leader?"

"Very much so." Hausner. Where was Jacob Hausner? Dead, probably. Would they ever know?

The man was so complex that his death—or disappearance—left one with complex feelings. His staying wasn't simply a matter of his wanting personal revenge against Ahmed Rish, although that was certainly part of it. It was more involved than that. He had wanted to die, but he had also wanted to live. You couldn't lose on a deal like that. And Hausner *was* a winner up to and including the end. Returning to Jerusalem would have exposed him to questions that any excessively proud man would not care to answer. So he had stayed.

Miriam Bernstein sat on the deck with her back against a bulkhead. Her legs were drawn up and her cheek rested on her knees. The quiet drone of the engines lulled her numb body. The

Foreign Minister sat next to her on a canvas bench pulled down from the wall. The euphoria had passed. Around her some people were drifting off to sleep. A few were still manic and talked incessantly to people who were barely conscious. Even the soldiers seemed not to want to listen or to speak and had moved off and segregated themselves toward the tail. The whole cabin smelled of bodies, anesthetic, and medicine.

She looked at David Becker sitting on the deck a short distance from her with his back against the hull. He was awake, but he seemed far away. There were many heros, thought Miriam, but if there was any single hero, it was surely David Becker. He had accepted the professional praise of Captain Geis and Lieutenant Stern with self-effacement and almost boyish charm. He was a good-looking aviator. The perfect hero material. They would treat him royally in Jerusalem. The American background would help. She found herself staring at him. He seemed alone.

Becker's mind came back to the present as he found he was staring at Miriam Bernstein. He tried a smile, but he knew it came out wrong. He cleared his throat and spoke softly. "We lost our logbook."

She smiled. "And my chronicle was probably blown up by a bomb."

"We are not very good scribes."

"It was the thought."

"Yes." He smiled and closed his eyes.

Miriam saw that he was sleeping and felt like doing the same. She closed her eyes.

The Foreign Minister leaned over and tapped her on the shoulder. "We will have to prepare a single statement for when we land. Above all, we must separate what happened here from the Peace Conference. We must rebuild and recapture the spirit that existed before this . . ." he waved his hand, ". . . before this happened."

Miriam Burnstein looked up at him. "I won't be going to New York with you."

The Foreign Minister looked startled. "Why not?"

"I don't believe in it."

"Nonsense."

She shrugged. What would Jacob Hausner have advised? He had always been cynical of the peace mission, but maybe he'd advise her to go and make them know that she was going to be one hell of a tough negotiator. If the Arabs had counted on her as the weakest link in the Israeli mission, then they had better think again.

"You'll feel differently in a day or two, Miriam."

"Perhaps I will." She didn't feel like arguing. She heard the voice of Esther Aronson coming from somewhere in the mid-section of the cavernous compartment. She was reading from Jeremiah: . . . *for, lo, I will save thee from afar, and thy seed from the land of their captivity; and Jacob shall return.* . . . Seed? His seed? His seed out of Babylon? Maybe. Unconsciously, her hand moved to her abdomen.

The Foreign Minister reached over and tapped her again. "I said, that was a truly selfless and altruistic act . . . for him, I mean . . . staying behind and keeping the Ashbals at bay."

Miriam forced a smile. "Altruistic? Jacob Hausner didn't know the meaning of the word. No, it was purely selfish, I can assure you. He didn't want to face an inquiry—not only concerning the bombs, but also concerning his leadership—his usurpation of leadership and all those killed while he was in command. He'd rather die, I think, than stand in a dock." She tried to smile again, but tears rolled down her cheeks.

Ariel Weizman was uncomfortable. He patted her arm. "Well now, maybe he's not dead."

She thought of her husband. That's what they kept telling her about him. And there were still Jews in Europe pinning pathetic notes on public bulletin boards, looking for their husbands and wives and sons and daughters after all these years. She looked at Ariel Weizman and her face became harder than he ever remembered seeing it. She spoke through clenched teeth. "He's dead, damn it. Dead. And damn him for throwing away his life." She buried her face in her arms and wept.

They were both dead, and there was no place where she could go to visit their graves any more than she could visit the graves of her parents, her sister, or her stepfather. There was nothing palpable about her past, nothing she could reach out and touch. It was as if these people had never existed. And so many of the places associated with them were outside her world. Europe. Babylon. She was engulfed by a sense of loss, a sense of overpowering sadness. Jacob said scream and shout and carry on and let the world know how you suffer, but she couldn't and wouldn't do that. And even if she did, it would not stop the pain. If only he hadn't told her that he loved her. Then it would have been so much easier for her to pass it off as passion or insecurity or something other than what it was.

Someone tapped her on the shoulder and she looked up. A young crewman was staring down at her, smiling. He handed her a scrap of folded paper. "Radio message."

She stared at it for a few seconds, then opened it and read the scribbled pencil lines to herself. *I love you. Teddy.*

"Any answer?"

She wiped her eyes with both hands. She hesitated, then shook her head. "No. Thank you."

The surprised crewman turned and walked off.

Miriam looked down at the note again, then slipped it into her pocket. Her fingers touched the silver star Jacob had given her. She drew her hand out of her pocket. She'd have to see about Jacob's seed before she knew about Teddy Laskov.

Teddy Laskov made a final pass over Babylon. Nothing seemed to move on the ground except the wind and the sand and a solitary man riding a donkey westward across the mud flats, looking up into the sky. The big blue and white Concorde lay submerged at the quay of Ummah. It should have looked more out of place than it did, reflected Laskov. The village and the aircraft were the culmination of twenty-five hundred years of separate development, yet there was a common thread there.

Laskov banked sharply and streaked west, away from the Cradle of Civilization, away from the land of Captivity, out over the Shamiyah Desert, west toward Jerusalem. The swing-wings on his jet, which had been spread out for combat, now folded back like a cape as he soared upward.

In a few minutes he came abreast of the two C-130's.

Miriam had not responded to his public announcement of his love, and he felt a bit of a fool—still he knew that he should show the colors to the people on board. It was good for morale. He shot between the two aircraft and tilted his wings. He banked around, pulled off speed, and extended the wings so that he could fly more slowly. He passed by again and waved from his cockpit bubble.

From every porthole on the C-130's people waved back as he circled the big craft.

Miriam Bernstein rose hesitantly and stood along with the others who were looking out of the portholes. She gave a belated half wave to the fighter as it passed by again, then turned away from the porthole, sunk to the floor, and fell asleep before she was completely stretched out. David Becker laid a blanket over her.

Laskov had had enough of the acrobatics and did not bank around again, but climbed west out of sight of the transports. He put the aircraft on a heading toward Jerusalem and passed through the sound barrier. He would be on the ground to meet them—showered and back in civilian clothes—when they arrived with the dust of Babylon still clinging to them. Situations changed with incredible speed in the modern world. There seemed to be no fixed point, like Polaris, that you could navigate by. He wondered if Miriam had changed much in Babylon. No. Not Miriam. She was steady, almost indifferent. There would be that initial strangeness and coolness that sometimes comes when two lovers meet after a separation, but it would pass.

Laskov soared up into the stratosphere for no reason other than that he wanted to see the curve of the earth below and the perpetual stars in their black heavens above. One's perspective changed up here. Babylon. Jerusalem. God. Miriam Bernstein. Teddy Laskov. They all began to sort themselves out in this cold, airless void. He would figure it all out before he saw the domes and spires of Jerusalem.

It was ten P.M. in New York. The Arab and Israeli delegations had assembled in the Conference Building of the United Nations. Status reports out of Baghdad and Jerusalem had been circulated every fifteen minutes. The most recent teletype reports had finally brought encouraging news to the assembled delegates.

Someone broke out a bottle of arak and it was passed around. There wasn't much talking in the meeting room, but as the tension eased, a feeling of confidence, even friendship, was developing between the two groups gathered there. An Arab delegate made a toast. Soon everyone was proposing toasts, and the arak and sweet wine flowed.

Saul Ezer, a permanent delegate of the Israeli Mission to the UN, reflected that this was probably the most congenial group of advance personnel he had ever seen at a conference. The arriving delegates from Israel and the Arab countries would land on very fertile ground. He got up quietly and went to a telephone in an adjoining office. He dialed a midtown hotel and rebooked the Israeli peace delegation.

Shear-jashub lost sight of the aircraft and turned his donkey east, across the mud flats, back toward Ummah. It had been a strange interlude in the timeless, changeless life of the Euphrates.

A remnant had again returned from Babylon, and a remnant had again chosen to stay behind. Shear-jashub imagined there would be great feasting in Jerusalem, but for Ummah there would be uncertainty. If Ummah did not survive, however, the communities in Baghdad and Hillah would. And if they did not, Jerusalem, or some other place, would. One day, God would cease His testing of His children, and then all the scattered remnants could return to the Promised Land, safe in the knowledge that they of the Diaspora were not needed outside of Zion to insure that their blood would survive.

In the distance, the sun came over the mounds of Babylon. Shear-jashub lifted his head and sang out in a clear voice that carried across the desolate plains and rolled across the Euphrates and into the ruins of Babylon: "And I will gather the remnant of my flock out of all countries whither I have driven them, and will bring them again to their folds; and they shall be fruitful and increase. And I will set up shepherds over them which shall feed them: and they shall fear no more, nor be dismayed, neither shall they be lacking, saith the Lord."